Meredith Webber lives on the sunny Gold Coast in Queensland, Australia, but takes regular trips west into the Outback, fossicking for gold or opal. These breaks in the beautiful and sometimes cruel red earth country provide her with an escape from the writing desk and a chance for her mind to roam free—not to mention getting some much needed exercise. They also supply the kernels of so many stories that it's hard for her to stop writing!

Born and raised on the Wirral Peninsula in England, **Charlotte Hawkes** is mum to two intrepid boys who love her to play building block games with them and who object loudly to the amount of time she spends on the computer. When she isn't writing—or building with blocks—she is company director for a small Anglo/French construction firm. Charlotte loves to hear from readers, and you can contact her at her website: charlotte-hawkes.com.

THE DOCTORS' CHRISTMAS REUNION

MEREDITH WEBBER

UNWRAPPING THE NEUROSURGEON'S HEART

CHARLOTTE HAWKES

MILLS & BOON

First Published in Great Britain 2019
by Mills & Boon, an imprint of HarperCollins*Publishers*
1 London Bridge Street, London, SE1 9GF

The Doctors' Christmas Reunion © 2019 by Meredith Webber

Unwrapping the Neurosurgeon's Heart © 2019 by Charlotte Hawkes

ISBN: 978-0-263-26995-6

MIX
Paper from
responsible sources
FSC™ C007454

This book is produced from independently certified FSC™ paper
to ensure responsible forest management.
For more information visit www.harpercollins.co.uk/green.

Printed and bound in Spain
by CPI, Barcelona

THE DOCTORS' CHRISTMAS REUNION

MEREDITH WEBBER

MILLS & BOON

CHAPTER ONE

Ellie Fraser studied her husband across the breakfast table.

Rather stern profile, with a straight nose and high forehead—until he smiled, of course, when the crinkly lines fanning out from his eyes made you want to smile back at him.

Brown, those eyes were, and she knew them both warm and soft as a cuddly blanket *and* hard as stones.

Dark hair, cut stubble-short—a number one, but due for a cut, so nearly a number two at the moment. It would feel like the fuzz on her old teddy if she ran her hand across it, but it had been a while since that had happened.

And that funny little whorl of hair, just on the hairline above his left eyebrow. A whorl she'd touched so often, twirled around her fingers, back when his hair was longer...

Her heart ached, just from looking at him.

She'd loved Andy. She knew that with the deep certainty that had been with her from the day he'd asked her to marry him.

She loved him still—she knew that, too—but she had somehow lost him, and along with him the oneness of them as a couple that had seemed so normal for so long.

Ellie and Andy. Andy and Ellie. All through university; through the almost soul-destroying work schedules of their internship; through their volunteer work in Africa—where they'd seen the worst that human beings could do to each other—their oneness had remained. Their goals, dreams and futures had been inextricably entwined in a way she'd thought would never fray, let alone be pulled apart.

And yet right now they couldn't have been further apart, for all that Andy had asked her up to his flat in the top section of the old house to discuss some idea he had about a soccer team that he was setting up, which seemed to be of far more interest to him than the split in their relationship.

Or was it a useful diversion from it?

She'd thrown herself into work, but still had far too much time to think of the past and what might have been...

Andy had even cooked her breakfast, though she could have done without the pain that the pretend intimacy of eating together brought with it.

'So I thought I'd have a barbecue here on Saturday—about lunchtime, before the game. Until we get a proper clubroom there's nowhere else. I'll ask some of the older team members to organise the food—just sausages and onions and bread, or bread rolls.' He looked up at her and grinned. 'And, yes, I'll make sure the boys do some of the shopping, not just send the girls.'

Heaven help me! We've barely spoken for months, apart from work stuff, and still that grin makes my stomach churn...

Ellie swallowed a sigh along with the last of her toast, left the dirty dishes on the table—after all he *had* invited her as a guest—and made her way downstairs to her own flat, with its well-set-up medical surgery, enclosed under the old timbered home.

Ellie and Andy had moved to Maytown six months ago—she pregnant at last and Andy excited to be back in his home town, doing the job he'd always dreamed of doing: providing medical care for people in the often harsh Outback.

Maytown, a small town in the mid-west, had been established when settlers had brought sheep to the area, although now it was mainly cattle country. A large coal mine, opened twenty kilometres north of the town, had brought in extra business in recent years, with some of the mining families settling in the town while other workers lived in the on-site camp, flying in and flying out from places on the coast, working shifts of two weeks on duty then one week off.

Ellie had become as keen as he was on the town, both from Andy's talk of growing up there and her visits to his family, so they'd leapt on Andy's parents' suggestion they buy the old house and practice. Andy's parents had both been doctors, his mother running the practice, his father working at the hospital. The senior Frasers had wanted to move closer to the coast, cutting back on their workloads as they prepared for retirement.

To Andy and Ellie, it had seemed a magical coincidence—a little bit of serendipity—because they'd both wanted to bring up their longed-for child in the country. And it had been an ideal situation, with Ellie working from the surgery downstairs, knowing when she had the baby she'd get help but would still always be on hand, while Andy took over his father's post at the hospital.

They'd moved in late July, and Ellie had practically danced through the old house, imagining it festooned with Christmas decorations. With the baby due in November, their first Christmas in their new home would be spent celebrating his or her—they hadn't wanted to know the sex—first Christmas, too.

Just the three of them this year, a family...

It should have been perfect.

Until, at twenty-three weeks, when they'd settled in, and everything seemed to be going so well, she'd lost the baby and somehow, in the ensuing pain and anguish, lost Andy, too.

They'd turned to each other for comfort and support in those first hard weeks, and had also discovered that they were part of a very caring community. The local people had helped them through their grief with comforting words and little acts of kindness, flowers left on the front steps, a picture drawn by a kindergarten child, and more food than they could ever eat.

And, slowly, they'd made their way back to a different kind of peace, each wrapped in their private sorrow, but together still.

Until, six weeks after the loss…

Ellie sighed again.

Had she been wrong?

Pushed too hard?

She didn't know.

But when she'd talked to Andy about one last attempt at IVF—not immediately, of course, but when her body was ready—Andy's response had staggered her.

He had been adamant—enraged, really. His answer had been an adamant *no*.

Their two—well, three now—failed IVF attempts had already cost them too much, both financially and emotionally, and no amount of arguing was going to change his mind. He was done.

Completely done.

And if she thought they needed a baby to make their marriage complete then it couldn't be much of a marriage.

Stunned by his pronouncement, Ellie's immediate reaction had been to pack her bags and head back to the city, but she'd grown far too fond of the town and its people to just walk out and leave them without a GP.

Early on, she and Andy had tried to talk—one or other of them calling a truce—but the talk had soon become a row and now too many bitter, hurtful words hung in the air between them. Although Ellie could concede in her head that they would never have a child, she found it so much harder to accept it in her heart.

Even harder to accept that Andy wouldn't consider trying…

So she'd opted to stay, but *had* packed her bags, moving into the flat downstairs, built to house the locums his parents had hired to replace Andy's mother during her own maternity leave.

Did the townspeople know?

Was there gossip?

Ellie assumed they did and that the gossip existed as it did in all country towns, but few attempted to discuss their situation, although she often felt the warmth of their compassion.

The separate living and work situation had turned out for the best, Ellie thought glumly as she made her way through to the surgery and nodded a good morning to Maureen, her receptionist-cum-nurse, who was busy hanging tinsel along the front of her desk.

Dismissing the idea that it could possibly be that close to Christmas when she herself felt so bleak, her thoughts tracked back to Andy… But how were they going to cope with Christmas?

Didn't the very word conjure up togetherness?

Joy and laughter and sharing…

Happiness, and hope for the future…

Could they carry on with Christmas celebrations as if nothing had ever happened? Sit at one of their tables—

just the two of them—with silly paper hats on their heads, reading even sillier jokes?

The ache in Ellie's heart deepened, but suddenly she knew.

She couldn't do Christmas, not here, not with Andy—she couldn't go on with things the way they were. If she advertised now, she might find a young doctor, fresh out of GP training, who'd like the challenge of working in the bush. Or a skilled, well-qualified migrant, happy to spend three years working in the country before applying for permanent citizenship.

She was sure there'd be someone.

She wouldn't actually get a new appointee until January, when staff changes were generally made, but if she stayed until just before Christmas, then Andy could manage any emergencies for a week or two.

She'd go—

Where would she go?

Where the hell would she go?

Back to the city?

To what?

Ellie shook her head. That idea had zero appeal to her.

And she'd grown to love this town and its people so maybe she should go to another country town—one without Andy in it!

Ellie could feel her heart weeping at the thought, but she had to accept they couldn't go on as they were.

'What's Andy up to with this soccer club idea of his?'

Maureen interrupted her gloomy thoughts as she pushed the final tack into place on the tinsel and fetched Ellie the mail.

Ellie shook her head, clearing Christmas—and leaving—from her mind.

Why *had* Andy started the soccer club? Had he told

her while she was busy checking out all the familiar bits of the man she knew so well?

Loved, even?

'I know he's having a barbecue for them on Saturday; our side veranda seems to have become the unofficial club-house. And some of the kids I've seen coming and going are far from athletic types, so I guess he's doing it to raise their fitness levels.'

'My Josie's joined,' Maureen said, 'and you know the worry I have with her weight. I would have thought she'd be the last person picked for any team, so maybe fitness is behind it.'

Ellie thought of the motley lot she'd seen on the side veranda from time to time, and for the first time wondered just what Andy *was* up to with this soccer club he'd started. The ones she'd noticed were a very mixed bunch.

There were a couple of gangly Sudanese lads from the group of refugee families who'd been re-settled in the country town, a young teenage girl who was often in trouble with the police, two girls from a remote aboriginal settlement who boarded in town for schooling, and a rather chubby lad she suspected was bullied at school...

Ellie took the mail through to her consulting room, aware yet again of the painful arguments that had split their oneness, and the gulf that had widened between them. Once Andy would have shared his interest in the team, and she'd have shared his enthusiasm...

This was no good, she needed to focus on work.

Ellie scanned the patient list, surprised to see Madeleine Courtney back again. Madeleine was a puzzle—one she would have shared with Andy had things been different.

But they weren't, she reminded herself sharply, stamping down on the little kernel of unhappiness inside her before it could open, overwhelming her with memories and grief…

Only one other name stood out—Chelsea Smith. She frowned, trying to remember a patient of that name, then rubbed at her forehead because she knew she'd be frowning and it wouldn't be long before she had permanent frown lines, and became known as Grumpy Doc Fraser.

'Who's this Chelsea Smith?' she called to Maureen.

'She's a new patient. She phoned earlier so I put her in that space you leave every morning for emergencies.'

Thanks a bunch, Ellie thought, but she didn't say it. New patients always took longer to treat as Ellie had to gather as much information as possible from them.

But Maureen had done the right thing, they made a point of never turning anyone away.

Shrugging off her rambling thoughts, she sorted through the mail, setting bills aside and tossing advertising bumf into the bin.

Andy sat in the tiny space that was his hospital 'office', scanning the internet for videos of soccer coaching, although images of Ellie as she'd sat in the kitchen again kept intruding. The hospital was quiet—too quiet— leaving him far too much time to think of Ellie and the mess their marriage was in.

Shouldn't losing a child have brought them closer together, not thrown up a wall between them?

It was because thinking of Ellie caused him physical pain that he had thrown himself into establishing a May-town soccer team, allowing soccer to block out all but his most insistent thoughts.

Would their son have played soccer?

The wave of pain that accompanied *that* thought sent Andy back to the videos.

How could he not have known how much it would hurt—losing the baby, losing his son?

He took a deep breath and went back to the videos. He needed to do something constructive and worthwhile.

The call to the emergency room—hardly big enough to deserve the name 'department'—sent him in search of work, which was an even better diversion than the soccer team.

Although the ghost of Ellie always worked beside him, for this had been their dream: to work together in the country, bringing much-needed medical services to people who'd so often had to go without.

The patient was a child, a young boy—maybe twelve—bravely biting his lip to stem the tears while he clutched at his injured side.

'Bloody fence strainers broke,' a man Andy assumed was the father said. 'The barbed wire whipped around him like a serpent. I'm Tim Roberts, and this here's Jonah.'

Andy shook hands with the pair, then leant over to examine the wound. A red weal showed where the wire had hit the boy, but the serious wound was just above his right groin.

'Bit of a barb got in there, but the wife pulled it out with tweezers and put some cream on it last night, but you can see how it is now.'

The area was red, swollen, and obviously infected.

'I'll need to open it up,' he said. 'We'll just give Jonah light sedation and clean out the wound.'

There was no need to mention there could be damage to the bowel, but Andy would have to look carefully, which was why he'd chosen to give an anaesthetic over a local pain injection.

His mind ran through the roster of staff on duty. Tony was a good theatre nurse but Andrea—who was the only nurse trained to give anaesthetic—was off duty. He'd have to phone Ellie to come in and do it.

And the stupid flip of his heart when he even thought her name reminded him that the love he felt for his wife had never gone away.

Yes, they'd parted—pushed apart by the pain of loss— but the love he felt for her was as strong as ever.

Or was it longing more than love…?

'I won't be able to operate until later,' he told Tim. 'If you've other things to do in town, Jonah will be quite safe here. In fact, he'll probably be thoroughly spoilt by the nurses.

Ellie was about to tackle her first patient of the day when her cellphone rang.

Her heart leapt when she saw it was Andy.

'Sorry, El, love, but could you grab a half-hour later in the day to do a mild anaesthetic for me? Kid with infection just above the right groin. X-ray shows foreign object in there. He's had breakfast so I'm happy to wait a few hours. How's your day looking?'

Ellie switched back to her patient list.

'I could do eleven-thirty,' she said. 'That would run into my lunch break so there'd be no rush.'

'Grand!'

And he was gone, so suddenly that Ellie found herself peering at her cellphone as if *it*, rather than Andy, had caused the abrupt farewell.

Grand?

How could their love have grown so cold that 'grand' had become 'goodbye'?

She was being silly, of course. It had been months since a telephone conversation had finished with 'love you'.

Although he *had* called her 'love', the way he always had done…

That was just habit, she told herself firmly and hauled her mind back to work.

For all their separate lives at home, their professional lives had barely changed, their work lives remaining stable as they followed their usual routine, assisting each other when needed, discussing patients they shared.

They were even enjoying the togetherness of that side of things—well, Ellie did and she thought Andy seemed to…

Although that would stop—and soon—if she went ahead and moved.

Even thinking about it caused her pain.

Putting the mail aside for later, she powered up her computer, checked test results that had come in, then switched to her appointments list.

Back in work mode, she speed-read down the appointments, putting asterisks against the patients who'd be coming in for test results so she could be sure she'd re-read the results before the patient arrived.

Busy with the list, she barely heard the outer door open, but Maureen was greeting the first arrival, no doubt handing her the patient information forms to fill in.

She pressed the buzzer, and heard Maureen tell Chelsea to go on through.

It was a pregnant young woman who came in. A *very* young, not *very* pregnant woman, slight and blonde, who seemed strangely familiar.

'Don't I know you?' she asked, smiling at the obviously nervous young woman.

A nod in response.

Ellie smiled again as she asked, 'Do I have to guess how, or will you tell me?'

Another nod, then Chelsea drew in a deep breath.

'I thought Andy might be here,' she said, 'although Aunty Meg always worked here and Uncle Doug at the hospital.'

Aunty Meg, Uncle Doug: Andy's parents?

Light dawned.

'Of course I know you! You're Chelsea Fraser. I'm so sorry I didn't recognise you, but you've kind of grown since you were flower-girl at our wedding. Did you come here to see Andy?'

Chelsea frowned.

'Well, I came to see both of you really. I'm pregnant, you see, and I wondered whether I could stay with you until I have the baby, because you probably heard Mum and Dad split up and Mum's gone off to find herself, whatever that means. She's in India, or maybe Nepal, and Dad's gone to Antarctica again, and Harry—you remember my older brother Harry?—well, he's supposed to be looking after me but he's at uni most of the time or out partying so he's never there.'

'You're all on your own?' Ellie asked.

'Well, Alex—that's my boyfriend—he comes over...'

Tears began to stream down Chelsea's face, and Ellie left her chair to walk around and wrap her arms around the unhappy, lonely child. Ellie held her tightly and let her cry out her tension, handing her the box of tissues when the sobs became hiccups as the tears dried up.

'I didn't mean for this to happen,' Chelsea whispered, patting the bump. 'But I was so lonely and Alex loves me, and I was on the Pill but must have forgotten to take it or something and then I wasn't sure, you see... But of course I *was* pregnant and Alex wanted to tell his parents and have me come and live with them, but then they might think Mum and Dad are really awful parents, and they're not, you know, they've just kind of lost their way.'

Tell me about it! Ellie thought, but didn't say, although she did think Chelsea's mother could have waited a little longer to find herself. She shook the thought away and pressed Maureen's buzzer twice to warn her the next appointment would be late.

'They brought us up to be independent,' Chelsea explained, 'and to think for ourselves, but I didn't want everyone at school to know about this, or the cousins and all, so I thought if you and Andy let me stay here until the baby's born, then I can go back to school and no one would know.'

Except there'd be a baby somewhere, Ellie thought, but didn't say.

'No one back home knows because it's been cold and I've been able to wear baggy jumpers back at home. I told my friends my uncle needed me out at his place in the bush and here I am.'

She'd so obviously practised what she was going to say that it came out in a slightly garbled rush, and Ellie had to be careful not to smile.

'Does anyone know where you are?'

Chelsea nodded.

'I told Harry and he thought it was a good idea. He said there wasn't anything Mum or Dad could do to help at the moment and at least I'd be safe with you and Andy.'

'Of course you will be,' Ellie assured her, then, after a niggle of doubt, added, 'I'll have to talk to Andy, but I'm sure he'd be happy to have you. It's not as if there aren't plenty of bedrooms in the old house.'

'And there's the little flat downstairs. We often stayed in it when we came for Christmas.'

My little flat.

And with Chelsea here how long would it take for word to travel along the family grapevine and Andy's parents to realise things had gone wrong between her and Andy? They'd kept it from them while Meg had been going through chemo for breast cancer and they hadn't wanted to heap more worries on her head.

Meg had become more of a friend than a mother-in-law for Ellie, who'd known from the first time she'd met Andy's family that she'd love to be one of their warm, happy household. Her own father was dead, and her mother drifted from one country to another, one man to another, much as Chelsea's mother appeared to be doing. Family had been a big gap in Ellie's life.

So upsetting Meg with the story of their split had never even been a consideration.

And now here was Chelsea, and there was no getting away from it, despite the current circumstances, the Frasers were Ellie's family now, so Chelsea was her responsibility as well as Andy's.

'I should be examining you, not chatting,' she said. 'Do you want to hop up on the couch? Nothing invasive, I just need to feel what's going on then we'll take some blood for tests, and check your blood pressure and pulse, and Maureen will make an appointment for you to come in for a scan later in the week.

'Relax!' she told Chelsea as her patient lay rigid on the couch. 'Do you know how pregnant you might be?'

A quick shake of the head was the only answer.

'No worries!' Ellie told her gently. 'We can do a measure of what we call the fundal height and that will give us an approximate time. It's not entirely accurate, and is a better guide after twenty weeks, but let's see.'

The measurement of fourteen centimetres gave her a gestation period of twelve to sixteen weeks.

'Does that seem about right to you? Can you remember when you had your last period?'

Chelsea shook her head.

'I was so sad and lonely when Mum went away, and then Dad did, too. Alex has been my boyfriend for ages, and he comforted me and stayed over a few times and it just happened.'

Of course it did, Ellie thought, but didn't say. Poor kid must have been totally lost, with her parents not only breaking up but taking off. Mum heaven knew where, and Dad—who Ellie remembered now was a climatologist—heading off to the ice and snow at the very bottom of the world.

I need to talk to Andy.

This thought had passed through Ellie's head earlier, but now it became insistent.

'Well, you seem totally fit to me,' she told Chelsea, 'and as you know there's plenty of room for you. How did you get here? Did you bring clothes?'

'Train, and not much, to answer both your questions. The train got in this morning, and as far as clothes, I knew it would be hot, and I didn't really know what to get.'

Of course, the train had come in this morning; it was the big weekly event in the town, for it not only brought people but fresh fruit and vegetables.

'Well, how about you go upstairs and choose a room along the back veranda—Andy uses the side one for his soccer club and people come and go along the front one. Have a shower and then, if you're up to it, you could walk uptown—it's only two blocks—and check out the limited array of clothes in the general store. I'll phone them and tell them to put anything you want on our account.'

'Oh, no, I've got my own credit card,' Chelsea protested. 'But I'd like to get a few things.'

'Great! And when you get back you can help yourself to anything in the kitchen. There's bread and ham and cheese for sandwiches, and plenty of salad things. I might be late back for lunch as I have to help Andy with an op, but just look after yourself. And come and see Maureen down here if you need to ask anything. I know that doesn't sound very hospitable, but I've got patients all morning. Will you be okay?'

To Ellie's surprise, Chelsea flung her arms around her neck and hugged her hard, tears in her voice as she said, 'You've been so kind. I know I don't deserve it, but I'm really grateful!'

'Of course you deserve it,' Ellie said, a little choked up herself. 'You're family!'

How best to help her?

What would Andy advise?

CHAPTER TWO

SHE SET ALL thoughts of Chelsea—*and* Andy—aside as she went through her list of morning patients, pleased with some, concerned about others, mostly elderly men who seemed more aimless and depressed than ill. In other places, they could have a community garden or an allotment to work on, but out here, where water was a very scarce commodity, such a thing would be a luxury.

But her thoughts returned to Chelsea as she walked briskly to the hospital, sighing as she went in through the side entrance, where more Christmas decorations were already in place.

But Christmas cheer was the last thing on her mind as she considered the discussion she'd have to have with Andy.

Not right now, when there'd be other people around, but later on they would definitely need to talk.

Chelsea's arrival had thrown their arrangement into disarray. It had seemed sensible to live separately within the house, mainly to avoid gossip and speculation, but Chelsea would pick up on it immediately, and word would spread around the family, and Ellie knew it would cause distress to Meg.

She pushed into the theatre changing room and found Andy already waiting for her.

'Sorry, I was held up on my first patient and I've been late all morning,' she explained.

His beautiful Ellie looked so tired and stressed that Andy wanted nothing more than to take her in his arms and hold her—to find their way back to where they'd been. But pain and grief and too many harsh words had opened up a gulf between them, and as yet, he could find no way of bridging it.

And did he even want to?

He shook his head. That was a stupid question when there was a patient waiting.

Of course he wanted to! The thought of living without Ellie was…well, inconceivable.

'The patient is a young lad who got hit by a strand of barbed wire when he was helping his father repair a fence. Apparently, the fence strainers snapped, the wire flicked back, and a piece flew into his lower abdomen. They got it out, and cleaned and dressed the wound, but there's a bit still in there—one of the barbs, I'd say—and it's badly infected. I need to go in and clean it out before it develops into sepsis. He's on IV antibiotics, and I'll leave a drain in place for a few days if it looks at all dubious.'

Andy watched as Ellie greeted Tony, a nurse who loved theatre work, then checked the drugs and instruments he'd laid out for her.

Once upon a time, in what seemed like another life—in another country, for that matter—they'd worked together like this. The lack of specialist doctors in some of the African countries where they'd lived meant you had to do whatever was required of you, and often it was surgery—he cutting while Ellie did the anaesthetic—basic though it had been.

He held back a snort, disgusted that he could be distracted by such trivial thoughts. All that was so far in the past it was history now.

Yet how could he not watch as she spoke quietly to the boy, explaining how he'd be getting sleepy, checking the cannula already attached to the back of one small hand and smiling gently. She was so good with children—the children they would never have…

Satisfied that all was well, Ellie took up the prepared anaesthetic, and with a nod to Andy injected it, waiting until the boy dozed off before securing the oxygen mask over his mouth and nose.

How many times—?

Enough!

The past belonged in the past. Here and now, he needed one hundred percent concentration on Jonah. Electrodes already attached to his patient's body told the monitor everything was stable, and Ellie would keep an eye on it while he cut carefully into the pale skin on the lower abdomen, Tony beside him to mop the blood and cauterise any small bleeders.

Andy glanced across the table, and by chance met Ellie's eyes above her mask. She winked at him—something she'd done a thousand times before—a 'going well' kind of wink, but the sight of such a silly, insignificant facial tic brought an arrow of pain into his innermost being. One he tried to ignore…

The infection was obvious, the culprit a small piece of metal—a tiny scrap had broken free from a barb on the wire. No wonder the boy had been complaining of pain.

Andy irrigated the wound and searched for any secondary sites of infection, but everything was clean and clear.

'I won't leave a drain,' he said, as much to himself as to the staff around the table. 'In that position it could be easily dislodged, especially considering he's an adventurous young boy.'

He closed the wound, and nodded to Ellie to reverse the anaesthetic, then stood back while Tony did the dressing.

He should go and change. This team knew what they were doing. The boy would be transferred to a bed and wheeled through to the small recovery room. Ellie was in charge of him now and would be watching over him until he was fully conscious and aware of his surroundings.

But sometimes Andy needed to watch his wife—to watch and wonder what had happened to them to end up on either side of what was now an abyss.

Was it his fault?

Those final, hurtful words about the state of their marriage had certainly marked the end of life as they'd known it, but what had brought them to that?

Did he still feel a lingering resentment about the money the IVF had cost?

But it had been he who'd first suggested IVF, so it couldn't be that that burned inside him.

Yet *something* did.

He'd been keen to have a family—as keen as Ellie was—but that had been back before he'd known about the pain of loss; how much each failure would hurt, although that was nothing compared to the terrible piercing pain of losing the baby.

But worst of all had been watching Ellie's pain and being unable to take it away from her. *That* was the part he'd found so bloody impossible…

It wasn't that she'd pushed him away at the time, more that she'd wrapped herself inside it—made a cocoon of her pain—and had no longer been part of him, no, of *them*, cutting their oneness…

Now Andy watched Ellie sadly as she followed the trolley out of the theatre, before heading for the shower. There was nothing like water to wash away pointless suppositions and what-ifs that were too late…

Ellie waited as the youngster came around, checked he was sufficiently conscious to be given a few sips of water, and tell her who and where he was, then she departed, hurrying now, as she'd been due to see a patient at one-thirty and it was already close to two.

But her thoughts remained firmly stuck on Andy.

His skill as a surgeon was undeniable, and while still at university he'd even considered making a career of it, but during their time in Africa he'd realised that his skill lay with people; with helping them, comforting them and, yes, healing them when it was humanly possible.

And it had fired his determination to return to the isolated regions of Australia—areas always crying out for doctors—where his patients would be people he would get to know and care about, not simply a person needing an appendectomy or a new knee.

Ellie caught up as she worked through the afternoon's patients, so had seen the last one out when Chelsea returned, laden with bags and filled with excitement.

'You should rest,' she told the young woman as she locked the surgery door then walked up the front steps and along the veranda to the room Chelsea had chosen.

It had belonged to one of Andy's sisters, and although Ellie had put fresh sheets on the bed in case of unexpected visitors, she'd done little in the way of redecorating, so it still had posters of old rock bands on the walls and a bookcase full of science-fiction books that the whole Fraser family had loved to read.

Ellie half-smiled, remembering how she'd felt an utter

alien herself among people who knew a genre she'd never read as well as the Frasers knew sci-fi.

After depositing Chelsea's few possessions, Ellie showed her the nearest bathroom, then led her into the kitchen.

'You'll probably remember that the kitchen is the centre of the house, it's where we mainly live,' she said, adding rather ruefully, 'That's when we're actually at home.'

And living together... She *had* to talk to Andy!

She'd barely finished the thought when her cellphone buzzed in her pocket.

'Can you come back up, Ellie? Jonah's temperature has shot up, and his heart rate is ninety-five. I'm afraid I must have missed something and he could be heading into sepsis.'

'I'll be right there.'

She looked at Chelsea, new in town, still uncertain of her welcome, and crossed the room to give her a hug.

'I hate having to leave you like this on your first day here but I have to go up to the hospital, and from what Andy said I could be a while,' she said. 'There's food in the fridge, or you could walk up the road and get a burger and chips. The TV in the sitting room only has a couple of channels, but feel free to use it, and there are plenty of books around the place. Do you think you'll be okay?'

'Don't worry about me,' Chelsea assured her. 'I sat up all night on the train and I'm exhausted. If it's all right with you, I'll just get a drink of milk and a sandwich and go straight to bed.'

'Bless you,' Ellie said. 'But I'll leave both my and Andy's numbers and if you're at all worried about anything, please phone one of us.'

'I'll be fine,' Chelsea assured her. 'I *have* stayed here

before and I know my aunt and uncle were often called out at night. You go and do your work.'

But as Ellie walked swiftly up the road to the hospital, she couldn't help thinking of the young woman alone in the big house, and wonder just what she was thinking, not to mention what Andy was going to make of it all…

She arrived to find Andrea, a senior nurse who had specialist anaesthetic training, already in Theatre.

'I'll need you to assist,' Andy said, as Ellie walked in. 'There's gear set out in the ante-room, and Tony will help you scrub.'

Ellie took a deep breath. It wasn't that she hadn't assisted in operations before. It was part of their medical training, and they'd done a lot in Africa, but surgery had always made her feel anxious, as if she had no business having her hands in someone else's body. It was impersonal, yet at the same time deeply moving.

Shaking away the thoughts, she changed, scrubbed her hands and arms and held them up for Tony to slide on the gloves. He tied an extra apron around her waist, and she was ready.

'Will you enlarge the wound you made earlier?' she asked Andy as she took her place beside him.

A quick headshake.

'It was big enough, but I must have missed something.'

The tightness of his voice told her how stressed he was—stressed because he felt he'd somehow failed the boy.

'There was nothing obvious,' she reminded him, 'and you didn't want to interfere with his bowel by poking around under it.'

She paused then added, in a deep, terrifying voice, 'Never touch the bowel.'

Andy laughed. Her mimicry of a lecturer they'd had in

third year had always been good, and the words took him back to when, as students, they and their friends had used the words in more earthy ways.

It broke his tension and he opened the wound, holding it for her to clamp so he had a clear view.

'Think about the barb,' he muttered, and although she knew he was talking to himself, she understood what he was getting at. The barb could have pierced a muscle, tendon or even the bowel, and infection had developed in the second site.

But there was nothing obvious. Lecturer or not, he was going to have to touch the bowel.

He gently lifted the nearest coil of the large intestine, checking all around it for damage.

Nothing.

They irrigated the wound again, and closed it up, then all stood frowning at the monitor, which had no good news for them.

'Hang on,' Ellie said. 'Didn't someone say he was fixing a barbed-wire fence? Imagine what happened. The fence strainers broke, the loose wire would have flicked back, one barb would have pierced his skin. How far apart are the barbs on barbed wire?

'Roughly a hand span.' It was Andy who answered, catching on quickly to Ellie's train of thought.

So some things hadn't changed...

'That means the next barb would be here,' he said, measuring across the boy's abdomen with his hand.

They all peered at the spot but there was no sign of damage to the skin, or any indication of infection.

'Imagine him with clothes on,' Ellie said. 'Jeans, most likely, and low slung how the kids wear them these days. That barb would have hit the double layer of the pocket, possibly even a stud, so the next barb would be here...' She used her hand to measure the distance, brushing Andy's hand then glancing up, meeting his eyes above his mask—a flash of something as sudden and powerful as lightning flashing between them. 'If the wire wrapped around him.'

They found the wound beneath their patient's left hip, a tiny pinprick of a mark, surrounded by swollen, angry redness.

While Tony went for the portable X-ray machine, Ellie and Andy propped the boy on his side, careful not to touch each other after whatever it was that had flashed between them earlier.

'From the size of it, it's just an infection rather than another foreign object,' Ellie said, and Andy nodded, although she could tell he was furious with himself for not checking more carefully earlier.

She opened her mouth to say, 'You weren't to know,' but Andrea beat her to it.

Not that Andy would have found any comfort in the assurance. He prided himself on his physical examination of all patients, although earlier this morning the pinprick of a mark could have been all but invisible.

The X-ray showed no foreign matter in the wound, but Andy opened it up anyway. Clearing out the infection already there would lead to a quicker recovery for the boy.

'Do you still hate it?' Andy asked Ellie as they left the hospital an hour later. It was only when she didn't reply that he looked around to find she'd halted, twenty or so paces behind him, and was gazing up at the night sky.

'Still gets to you, huh?' he teased as he walked back to join her, resting his hand on the small of her back as he had so often in the past. Often just a touch in passing, often a prelude—but he wouldn't go there.

She smiled at him.

'I just cannot believe how many stars there are. I know they are there, in the city and we just don't see them for the other lights, but out here...'

She waved her arms around as if to encompass the beauty she couldn't put into words.

'And all yours,' Andy said, wondering if she remembered his promise to give her the moon and the stars...

And looking at her, her clear skin luminous in the starlight, her golden-brown hair framing a face he'd always thought perfection, he wanted to take her in his arms again, take her back to that time, make her really his once more.

'Did you ask me something?'

Her question broke the moment, although he knew the moment he'd felt had never been possible.

Thought back to his question.

'Oh, I just wondered if you still hated surgery?'

She'd started forward but now paused again, turned back to him.

'I've never really *hated* it so much as felt very uncomfortable. It seems so intrusive to be fumbling around inside someone else's body.'

Ellie sighed, and shook her head as if to chase the thoughts away.

'And speaking of bodies, I really need to talk to you about something that came up today. Shall we get a pizza and sit in the park to eat it?'

'You've hidden a dead body somewhere, and need my help to bury it?' Andy said, hoping the teasing words hid a sudden panic inside him.

Was she tired of their pretend marriage?

Was she leaving him completely?

Did she want a divorce?

Nonsense! he told himself. She'd mentioned bodies. It was something from work she wanted to discuss.

But the tension she'd aroused remained with him as he ordered their pizza, half with anchovies and half without, took extra paper napkins as they'd be eating in the park, and waited while Ellie chatted with the young girl behind the counter, blithely unaware of the torment her words had caused him.

Their marriage as a marriage might be virtually over, but could he live without the woman he loved?

The woman, he was fairly certain, who still loved him?

And could their marriage really be over?

He thought of the times when they'd tried to talk about it, as two intelligent people working out their differences. But the problem with loving someone was that you knew their sore and vulnerable spots—knew the words that would stab them in those places…

Worse still, you used those words as weapons.

So not talking had seemed easier, although Ellie deciding to make the move downstairs had left him feeling hollowed out inside. He was aware it could be a prelude to her leaving altogether for all she'd said they both needed their own space for a while.

Andy carried the pizza up to the park, which was deserted at this time of night, and set it down on a table, aware as he always was of Ellie's warmth by his side.

But worry about this 'talk' now nibbled at his mind so, as he placed a piece of pizza—from the anchovies' side—on a napkin, and passed it to his wife, he said, 'Okay, talk. What's up?'

Ellie turned, questions in her night-dark eyes, and he realised he'd spoken too abruptly.

'Right!' she began, apparently reading his anxiety in his face. 'Chelsea arrived this morning—your cousin Chelsea—and she's pregnant and wanted to get away from home and people who know her until after the baby's born. Apparently both her parents are off somewhere and Harry's been looking after her—'

'Not very well, if she's pregnant!' Andy muttered. 'Does he know she's here?'

'Apparently so,' Ellie said, 'although I will phone him when we get home to tell him she's arrived safely. I tried earlier but his phone was switched off.'

'But where's her mother, for heaven's sake? I know her father's probably off saving whales somewhere, but her mum? And Harry's what? All of nineteen, I imagine, and far more involved in his own life at university than caring for his sister. Of all the irresponsible—'

He realised he was yelling now and it really wasn't Ellie he should be yelling at, but she simply smiled at him and said, 'She's off finding herself, apparently.'

'Mad, they're both mad, they always have been. How Dad and Ken can possibly be brothers beats me. And as for Jill, why isn't she at home, looking after a kid who's barely out of childhood? I would have thought teenage years were when young girls, in particular, needed their mothers around.'

'She's sixteen,' Ellie told him, 'and twelve to sixteen weeks gestation. A bit hard to be precise at that stage and she has a very slight build.'

She paused, and Andy wondered what worried her about the situation. Apart from it being Chelsea. Teenage pregnancy was far from uncommon these days.

Was she thinking of their arrival here in town—of the coincidence of her being sixteen weeks pregnant when they'd first begun their move to Maytown?

Andy watched as Ellie ate her slice of pizza, chewing and swallowing it before she smiled at him, then shrugged as if uncertain where to begin.

'I can understand her turning to a boyfriend for comfort, with her parents gone, and that the pregnancy was an accident, but I didn't want to push her to talk too much about the future.'

He saw the worry in the little crease between her eyebrows, and read it in her voice.

'The thing is, Andy, we'll take her in, I was sure you'd agree with that, but I wondered if she—if we…'

It was so unlike Ellie to be this hesitant over something that he reached out and took her hand, feeling her fingers curl into his, warm and sticky from the pizza but accepting his support.

'I wouldn't like your mum to find out about our marriage right now and be upset, which she will if I'm downstairs and you're upstairs while Chelsea's with us. I mean, it's a bit like shouting it to the world.'

Her head lifted so she could watch his face as he considered it.

'Easily fixed,' Andy said, barely suppressing his delight because the top part of the house was desperately empty without Ellie in it. A cool, contained and even frosty Ellie was better than no Ellie at all.

If only he'd realised that before she'd made the move downstairs. He should have talked to her about feeling shut out; about his own pain, and how much it had frightened him; about feeling cast adrift after she left —

'You'll move back up? I'm still sleeping in Dad's old room, so you can go back into Mum's.'

She half smiled and he guessed that life in the downstairs flat hadn't been entirely joyous either.

'I didn't take all that much,' she said, 'but, yes, I think that would be best.'

'And Chelsea? Has she planned anything beyond escaping to Maytown for the period of her pregnancy?'

Ellie shrugged.

'We barely talked, and right now she's confused, and lost, and really needs to know she's safe and loved and cared for. I do wonder about Jill going off like that when Chelsea is still so young. Do you think because her husband is always off somewhere, she felt it was her turn?'

Andy grinned at her.

'Who knows what goes on in other people's relationships?' he said, and she responded with a small smile, turning her fingers so she could squeeze *his* hand.

'Too true. Look at ours!' she said with a smile.

The smile and something in her tone of voice suggested there was more hope than defeat in the words but before he could pursue it, Ellie was talking again.

'Well, all we can do is be there for her. I can only help her with her pregnancy at the moment, and perhaps you and I can both talk with her about the future. About the baby, maybe—'

'No!'

The word seemed to echo around the park, far too loud, far too strong, far too emotionally charged…

Andy breathed deeply, counted to ten then another five, and regained a semblance of control over the dark fear that had seized him.

'I know she's family and I'm happy to take her in, but just what is going to happen to the baby when it arrives? Will you want to keep it, too? Is this your way of getting back at me for refusing more IVF? How long before you start thinking of it as your baby?'

Obviously, the counting hadn't helped because he was shouting now. Ellie's face looked white and strained in the gloom.

The silence that fell between them was somehow louder than his words, broken only when Ellie stood up and said quietly, 'I was only thinking we might help her. Yes, take her in, she's family. It's up to her to decide about the baby but while she's with us we might both be able to help her find a path ahead—at least begin to plan for her future.'

She stepped backwards away from the bench she'd been sitting on, and turned away, pausing only to say, 'And it was *our* baby I wanted, Andy, not someone else's.'

CHAPTER THREE

How HAD THEY gone from hand-holding to being back at war? From what had felt almost like old times to cold apartness?

Andy caught up with her as she stormed away, his long strides easily covering the ground he'd lost.

But getting past his careless words wouldn't be as easy. There'd been no mistaking the raw pain in her voice, even months after they'd lost their baby.

'I'm sorry,' he began, wondering why the words sounded less meaningful than they would have if his arms had been around her, holding her as he whispered them into her ear.

But he did touch her shoulder, draw her closer, so he could look into her eyes.

'Of course we'll help Chelsea decide what she wants to do.' He ploughed on, realising this wasn't such a great idea as Ellie's lips were right there in front of him, and so damn kissable.

He needed to take a deep breath and walk on.

He needed to walk and talk, not stop and kiss...

'I imagine she'll be at school during the day, and hopefully she can make some friends before the end of term.'

But Ellie, he realised, was no longer by his side. This time she'd stopped several paces back and was muttering to herself.

'You okay?' he asked.

'Yes!' Ellie caught up with him. 'I just hadn't thought about school. Chelsea's only sixteen so of course she should still be at school.'

She hesitated again.

'Although maybe sixteen is an acceptable age to leave school—I'll have to find out. And will going to school, being pregnant in a place full of strangers, be frightening for her?'

Andy imagined a pregnant Chelsea having to brave it up in front of a room full of teenage strangers. Guilt at his earlier reaction ate into him. Wasn't their profession meant to be a caring one?

Then he smiled as the answer came to him.

'Well, if she's with us for the weekend, she can join in the soccer barbecue. Most of the team are at the high school. They're all good kids, they'll look after her.'

'Oh, Andy! That's a wonderful idea,' the woman he loved replied, with such enthusiasm that she threw her arms around him and gave him a hug.

It was just a quick hug, and maybe it was the shock of it that stopped him returning it, or the thought of it turning it into something longer, more intimate. There was that kiss idea again...

The mere thought of kissing Ellie made his head spin.

But it was not to be. Although it did seem to Andy that maybe they could make their way back to being friends—something that had seemed impossible when the emotion-driven arguments had sent her off to sleep downstairs two long months ago.

Back then, he hadn't realised just how broken things had become between them, possibly because his mother had often sought refuge from her loud and boisterous family by escaping to the downstairs flat. Even when they had both been upstairs, his parents, in his memory, had never shared a bedroom, his mother being a light sleeper and his father often being called out in the middle of the night.

After a while he'd accepted it was easier this way—easier to have Ellie in a separate space even if he lay awake at night wondering if she, too, was awake.

Wondering if she, too, was thinking of their first night together, of their wedding night...

Sharing a bed and not sharing love, *that* would have been impossible...

'You're really okay about having Chelsea to stay?' Ellie asked, linking her arm through Andy's as they walked through their gate, down the path, and stopped at the bottom of the steps that led up to the veranda.

'Of course I am. Though we should do something about one of the girls' rooms to make it comfortable for her.'

'Or let her do it up how she wants it. It will give her something to do over the holidays and I think she'd probably enjoy it.'

'You're a good woman, Ellie Fraser,' Andy said, his voice curling into her ears, the deep tone finding its way into her heart.

'You're not so bad yourself, for a bloke!' she parried, afraid, because what was happening inside her felt a little bit like falling in love, or the tentative, fragile, beginning part of falling in love, *again*.

She'd worked out, back when their world had crashed, that it was okay to still love Andy—that would never change—but it would be better not to be 'in love' with him, because that would make the gulf between them too hard to bear.

'You might want to check on Chelsea, while I move

my things back into your mother's room,' Ellie said. 'She was going to grab something to eat and go to bed, but if she's awake I know she'd like to see you and know you're happy to have her here.'

And being downstairs, packing what few things she'd actually moved, would give Ellie time to think about her feelings for Andy, something that was easier to do when he wasn't around, his body sending messages to hers, reminding her of what they'd had.

She had to think, too, about the decision she'd made so recently—the one to give up and go back to the city.

She could hardly do that with Chelsea here, and become yet another person leaving her in the lurch!

She watched Andy take the steps two at a time and turn along the veranda, peering into rooms to find their guest.

She'd shower downstairs then gather up her things. Upstairs, they'd share the en suite bathroom, as they had when he'd shifted into his father's room.

Back then, in the beginning of the separation, any physical contact between them had actually seemed uncomfortable—dangerous even—but these days, close proximity, particularly in a hug of all things, was reminding her body of the passion they'd shared, and sending little flares of desire skittering along her nerves.

Had he felt it, too?

He certainly hadn't hugged her back, or swung her around the way he used to...

He'd smelled like Andy when she'd hugged him, the faintest lingering scent of his aftershave reminding her—

The thoughts followed her to bed, where she lay wondering about love and loving and sex and Chelsea until, in the middle of a totally unconnected thought about her mother's recipe for Christmas pudding, she fell asleep.

* * *

Having found his young cousin fast asleep in one of his sister's rooms, Andy headed for the kitchen and made a cup of tea. He momentarily considered calling to Ellie to see if she wanted one, then remembered the way his body had reacted when she'd hugged him.

It was far better to concentrate on soccer, and focus his mind on doing his best for the makeshift team he was building…

He closed his eyes and cleared his mind, then sat down at the kitchen table with a large notebook in which he was devising soccer practice strategies for his team. With the help of numerous internet videos, he felt he was getting closer to being able to call himself a coach.

At least Andy had help from Madeleine Courtney, one of the high-school teachers, who claimed to have learned soccer coaching. But as her system seemed to consist of dividing the participants into two teams and letting them go at it, he had his doubts about its effectiveness.

His soccer club had started as something he could get his teeth into to stop himself thinking about Ellie and the mess their life was in.

For the first few weeks he hadn't bothered too much about skills or techniques, concentrating on getting the participants interested enough to keep coming. Which had simply meant playing.

But now he wanted more of them than that. There was an inter-town competition beginning in the New Year, with a trial game this weekend, and he wanted them competitive, keen to win, but able to lose gracefully.

Some of these kids had had very little discipline at home, and too much time on their hands. The local police sergeant had introduced him to five of them, so in reality they were doing time for misdemeanours. If he, Andy, could get them fit and interested in the game, who knew where it could lead?

Three others, two girls and a boy, had been brought to Outpatients by their parents because his father had started a weight-loss group and he, Andy, had been prepared to continue it.

But in his opinion, playing sport would not only help their weight loss and build healthy muscle, it would improve their self-esteem as well.

It was win-win, all the way...

But it was up to Andy to get it right. And for that he needed practice strategies for dribbling and passing, things he could easily demonstrate to the kids so they could practise them in their correct positions. And, of course, he needed to teach them the rules. It was one of the reasons he'd arranged the barbecue—so they could have a sit-down session on the veranda going over the rules, and the importance of them in the game, before they ate.

And played.

Should pregnant women—girls—play soccer? Another player would even up his numbers. Even if Chelsea only stood in goal, she'd be handy.

He'd have to check.

Or maybe he could ask Ellie...

He was an idiot. He was only plunging himself into this challenge so he didn't have to think about Ellie.

Or the mess he'd made of things between them...

It would be impossible to have her on the team.

He should think about soccer, not Ellie.

It had become a kind of mantra to keep him sane.

Andy divided up his players into two teams and marked out their positions—four defenders, four midfielders and two forwards, plus a goalie for each team, or for one team if he couldn't persuade their new housemate to play.

He wrote out a programme for warming up, some aerobic exercise, and then the drills he wanted them to do. If they worked this way two days a week, they could then have a game after warm-up on Friday. This would be a practice game—a rehearsal for Saturday afternoon—when more and more parents and other spectators were turning up to watch the newly minted Maytown Soccer Team.

In fact, they could do some of the drills on the old tennis court area here at home, which would mean they'd be less likely to skive off into an impromptu game.

And he'd appoint Rangi, one of the Sudanese lads, as his offsider to run the programmes on afternoons he couldn't make it or was running late.

Satisfied that he had, at last, brought a little structure to the group, Andy put away his notebook and headed for bed, wondering if Ellie might get interested in the team even if she wasn't playing. Pictured them together on the sidelines, as one again…

He sighed as he went to bed—alone—and shut his mind against all the questions that were too dangerous to consider: all the *what if I'd done this or said that*, all the useless, totally impossible, ever-haunting *what-ifs*…

Although knowing Ellie was back in the bed they'd shared helped chase the dark thoughts away.

He had nearly kissed her, and he could practically hear her breathing…

Ellie woke early, showered, and dressed for work, then went to check on their new lodger.

Chelsea was up and dressed, sitting on the bed as if uncertain what to do next.

'Come on,' Ellie said to her. 'You'll have to learn to treat this house as your home, and to a certain extent look after yourself because Andy and I are often called out and you'll starve if you can't manage.'

She opened the pantry and pointed to a range of cereal, tea-bags, coffee, even drinking chocolate.

'And there are always eggs and bacon in the fridge if you like a cooked breakfast, but it will be a case of help yourself because we tend to get up, eat, then go to work.'

Chelsea settled on cereal, while Ellie made toast for herself and a pot of tea that she set on the table, along with mugs, milk, and sugar.

'Will you be okay here on your own while we're at work?' she asked, and Chelsea smiled at her.

'I'm just so happy to have a home. Ours was so lonely without Mum and Dad. Harry was hardly ever there. I'll sort out my things then sit on the veranda and read a book. From what I've seen, the Fraser passion for sci-fi is alive and well in this house.'

Ellie shuddered.

'It was totally foreign to me when I first met Andy, and I've never got caught up in it, although I have read some of it.'

At lunchtime, when she and her new boarder sat together in the kitchen, Chelsea explained she was old enough to leave school but she really hadn't wanted to. She'd always wanted to be a scientist so she desperately wanted to finish her schooling, and if possible get into a university.

'How much school have you missed now?' Ellie asked her.

The girl frowned as she worked out her answer.

'About three—maybe five—weeks,' she said. 'I just sat around wishing it would all go away.'

'And if you went back to school here, could you make that up?'

'You mean now, this year, before the end of term—with this?'

She patted her bump.

'Why not?' Ellie said. 'Even if you go back long enough to get some work to do over the Christmas holidays that will catch you up, then you can go back full time next year.'

'And when the baby comes?'

Ellie sighed.

'That's going to depend on what you want to do about the baby. You don't have to make any decisions right now, but there are really only two choices.'

'Keeping it or adoption?'

Tears filled the girl's eyes.

'We've plenty of time to sort that out,' Ellie told her. 'We'll talk about it, you and me, and Andy. Your boyfriend, Alex, too. Talk to him. He should have some say. Between the lot of us we'll work out what's best for both of you.'

Ellie pushed back her chair as she stood up, needing to get back to work and not yet ready for tearful discussions about the baby's future.

Any baby's future…

'If you wouldn't mind clearing away our plates, then you could have a good look at your room, maybe take down the old posters. You'd better roll them up and put them away somewhere in case they turn out to be precious to their former owner. We can get some paint to freshen up the walls and some new bed linen for you.'

The tears Ellie had been hoping to avoid arrived in full flood, along with mutterings of 'too good to me,' and 'you're too kind'.

But Ellie was already heading down the steps.

'Have a shower and a lie down. You'll feel a lot better after you've had a rest.'

The afternoon was blessedly free of any drama, and she

even had one cancellation, which gave her a few minutes to think about her concern for the elderly men in town. Her grandmother had regularly attended a sewing, knitting, and craft group once a week in the hall at a local church, going along for a chat more than the knitting or sewing. The Country Women's Association—an institution in Australia—provided for the women as well, but finding something for the men might prove more difficult.

Many of the local farmers retired to houses in the town, leaving their sons to run the property, and things like indoor bowls or card games might be too tame for them.

A Men's Shed, that was what she needed, but one with a purpose. She'd talk to Andy about it tonight.

And the ease with which that thought came out startled her enough to spend the rest of the afternoon with her mind focussed fully on work.

Which was just as well, as her next patient presented with a racing pulse and a pallor that would make cream look suntanned. Bill Stevens had a history of atrial fibrillation which was usually controlled by his medication. He'd sensibly bought an app for his phone that could tell him when he was in AF, so he could take three more tablets, upping his medication from one hundred to a total of four hundred mgs.

'It usually works for me,' he told Ellie plaintively.

'Well, maybe it still will,' she told him, 'but I'd prefer it if you were in hospital. If it doesn't settle down, they can give you the drug intravenously, and keep you on a monitor so they know what's happening. How did you get here?'

'My wife drove me. She's doing some shopping while she's in town.'

The 'while she's in town' reminded Ellie that many of her patients came from properties up to eighty miles away, and although she knew Bill was closer than that, she certainly didn't want him out there with his heart still playing up, risking a stroke unless they stabilised it. She pressed the buzzer that would bring Maureen into the room.

'Would you please phone an ambulance for Bill, then keep an eye out for his wife. She'll be back when she finishes shopping and we need to let her know he's gone to hospital.'

'Will I phone and let them know he's coming?' Maureen asked.

'No, I'll do it. Andy can access Bill's file there but I'd like to fill him in on today's situation.'

'And if we don't get it back in rhythm with medication?' Andy asked, when Ellie had explained that Bill was on his way.

'Are you up for a cardioversion or will you fly him out?'

Andy peered at the phone for a moment. Was Ellie really asking him that?

Okay so he'd trained in the use of the defibrillator—hadn't they all? He'd even used one to re-start a patient's heart. But the difference with cardioversion was that it had to be synchronised to a particular point in the heart's rhythm, and although the machine itself did that job quite efficiently, as long as you pressed the sync button before shocking, he felt uneasy about it.

If something were to go wrong—if Bill had a seizure when they shocked him—what back-up did he have? One anaesthetic-trained nurse and Ellie at a pinch. No cardiologist for hundreds of miles.

'Send him to the coast,' he heard Ellie's voice say, coming from afar as he still had the phone in his hand in front of him, not up to his ear. 'Presumably he's had lunch, which means you can't anaesthetise him for a few hours, so far better to have a specialist do it. He should be at your hospital by now, I'll send his wife on there. She can either fly out with him or drive to wherever they're taking him. Maybe do neither. If all goes well, they'll send him back tomorrow or the next day, whenever they have an ambulance car coming this way.'

Andy was grinning as he hung up. Ellie was so far ahead of him in some ways, you'd think it was she who'd grown up in the bush with its limited facilities, not him. But everything she said made sense. The state-funded ambulance system had several helicopters used for ferrying patients from outlying districts to specialist hospitals.

He went to meet Bill and explain what was going to happen, asking Andrea, who was on duty in the small ED, to phone for the air ambulance.

'It'll fix itself, it always does,' Bill argued as Andy removed the ambulance leads, replacing them with hospital ones and attaching them to the monitor. Bill's heart rate was still spiking around the one hundred to one hundred and twenty mark, the line occasionally dropping down to ninety-five at the lowest.

'When did you take the extra dose?' he asked Bill, who looked mutinous for a moment, then finally admitted it had been first thing in the morning. That he'd woken with his heart bouncing around in his chest.

'Well, that's what it always feels like,' he added, and Andy nodded, imagining how frightening it must feel even to people who'd experienced it before.

He saw Bill safely away, returning home much later to find Chelsea in the kitchen.

Oh, Andy,' she said, spinning around with a half-peeled potato in her hand and enveloping him in a tight hug. 'Thank you so much for having me. Ellie's been so kind, and I'll try not to be a nuisance, see...'

She held out the potato.

'I'm fixing the veggies for dinner!'

He eased out of her embrace and smiled at her.

'You don't have to earn your keep here,' he said gently. 'After all, we're family.'

Laughter greeted his pronouncement.

'I know but I love cooking, so if you and Ellie don't mind, I might do some now and then.'

'I'm sure neither of us will mind, we're often so tired it's a choice between Thai or Chinese takeaway.'

'It's bad for your health, too much takeaway,' his young cousin said sternly.

Andy laughed.

'You're right, but apart from cooking to keep us healthy, I'm hoping you might be a help to me in another way. Do you know anything about soccer?'

'I was in a team back home, and I played at school,' she said. 'Do you think it would hurt the baby if I played?'

'I'll check that out. I imagine the baby wouldn't be too happy being hit with a soccer ball. But you could be goalie. None of them are good enough to score many goals yet, but you could yell advice to them if they got close. And if a ball actually comes near you, you could always hide behind the post.'

'Not that I'll fit behind a post for much longer,' Chelsea said, and returned to peeling potatoes.

He watched her for a moment, then said, 'When you've finished those, would you mind sitting down with me to look at the drills I've been working out? I only know the game from school, where it didn't seem to matter what you did, but I've watched about a thousand internet videos on coaching it.'

She put down the peeled potato and came towards him, wiping her hands on an old apron of Ellie's she'd put on.

'Let's see what you've got.'

She stood over his shoulder and read what he'd set out, with stick-figure illustrations, and smiled.

'For someone who only played the game at school, that's excellent. You could probably give your forwards more goal-kicking practice. Your two forwards should be the best strikers and they really need to practise a lot so it comes more easily to them in a game.'

There was a slight pause, before she said, 'I used to be a striker.'

'You were?' Andy asked in delight. 'That's just perfect. Even if you can't play, you can take the striking practice, try to help them understand different tactics.'

He paused, then said, 'They're all misfits, Chelsea, my soccer players. A few of them are kids who badly need to lose weight and somehow getting them into something that would interest them seemed a better way than nagging them to diet. There are a couple of migrants and it's helping to settle them into the community, and two of the girls are recovering drug addicts so they're a bit tetchy at times.'

She smiled at him.

'Then a pregnant teenager should fit right in,' she said, and went back to the sink, to peel carrots this time.

As he, Ellie, and Chelsea sat down to a meal of lamb cutlets with mashed potatoes, peas and carrots a couple of hours later, he realised just how big an asset Chelsea could be. Not only by helping to prepare meals, but her cheerful chatter broke through the tension that usually reigned when he and Ellie were together.

Tonight they'd even laughed, teasing each other, remembering silly things, something that had become so rare it made his heart ache for what had been.

'You prepared the dinner, Chelsea, so I'll clear the table and stack the dishwasher,' Ellie announced.

'And I'll do the pots and pans,' Andy volunteered. 'Have

you got something to do, something to read?' he asked Chelsea. 'Or feel free to use the television in the sitting room. Ellie might have explained there are only two channels but you might find something you'd like.'

'I'd rather read and there are plenty of books in the bedroom.'

She paused.

'Whose room was it?'

Andy thought for a moment.

'The three girls were always swapping rooms, but I think it was Eliza who ended up in that one. They were definitely her posters on the walls.'

Chelsea disappeared, but as he washed the few pots and pans, Ellie by his side, stacking the dishwasher, life felt almost normal—like the *old* normal…

He waited until she straightened then slid an arm around her shoulders.

'It might be good for us, having Chelsea here,' he said, then he couldn't resist drawing her closer and pressing a kiss, not on her lips but on her temple. He felt her tremble in response, then ease herself away.

But the dreamy little smile on her face told him she hadn't minded…

Ellie woke suddenly, startled by something she couldn't immediately place.

It had been a phone ringing. It must have been Andy's mobile because she could hear his voice now.

Had he changed his ring-tone that she hadn't immediately recognised it?

But why?

Maybe she was just confused.

She lay awake, aware a phone call to a doctor in the middle of the night wasn't a good thing.

The talking stopped, then she saw his shadowy figure appear in the doorway.

'Did it wake you?' he asked quietly.

'Habit,' she said. 'Do you need me?'

'Only every day!'

The words were barely there, nothing more than a jumble of sounds, and probably she'd imagined it for now he was talking again. Asking about someone, a patient apparently…

'Yes, Madeleine's one of my patients,' she said, catching up with the conversation although the 'only every day' words still hovered in her head.

And heart…

'Has something happened to her?'

'Accident out on the Wyndham Road,' Andy said, pulling on the clothes he must have carried as far as the doorway. 'I don't suppose—'

'You need me to come? Why didn't you say so?'

Ellie was out of bed and pulling on the clean clothes she'd left out on a chair for the morning.

More mumbling from Andy—what was wrong with the man?

But her own guilt was more urgent now than whatever was worrying Andy. For weeks she'd been seeing Madeleine for what had seemed like minor and confusing symptoms—aches and pains, tiredness, night cramps.

Ellie had seen her so often without pinning down a diagnosis that thoughts of Munchausen's syndrome had flashed across her mind, but the symptoms had never seemed serious enough. Not that she knew much about the syndrome.

'She *has* been complaining of dizzy spells lately. Where is she?'

'Apparently, she ran into a tree. Someone saw the accident and phoned the ambulance so she should be at the hospital by now.'

'I'll come with you,' Ellie said, and was startled when Andy gave her a hug as he thanked her.

Although after that kiss, mild though it had been…

She followed him out to the car—rarely used as the hospital was only three blocks away—wondering what was going on. Could Andy also feel that they could make their way back together as they'd first begun their courtship?

With touches, shared glances, even a little kiss…

But if Andy was happy to have her company, Madeleine seemed less so.

'You didn't have to come,' she told Ellie as Andy completed the handover from the ambulance personnel.

'You're my patient,' Ellie said, hoping she sounded more sympathetic than she felt. 'I was worried about you.'

'Well, I told you I was having dizzy spells and what did you do?'

Quite a few investigations, Ellie would have liked to remind her, but this was hardly the time.

Though Madeleine seemed only a little the worse for wear. A graze on her forehead was the only visible injury.

'Did your airbag deploy?' Ellie asked.

'No, it didn't!' her patient snapped. 'The ambulance people insisted on bringing me here and calling Andy,' she said, 'although I'm really perfectly okay.'

'Best we keep you under observation for the night,' Andy said. 'I'll do a scan of your head to make sure there's no internal damage, and nurses will check you every two hours. You won't get much sleep as they have to wake you, as well as check your blood pressure and temperature.'

'You'll be here, won't you?' Madeleine asked. 'Just in case anything goes wrong?'

'I *could* stay,' Andy said, and Ellie raised her eyebrows. The woman was playing him—surely he could see that!

She stomped out of the cubicle, then heard Andy leave behind her.

'There's no way you need to be up here all night just to hold that woman's hand,' Ellie told him.

He looked slightly startled.

'I'll do an X-ray and a scan first and take it from there,' he said.

'It's a graze!' Ellie reminded him. 'She didn't hit the tree hard enough for the airbag to deploy.'

'But there could have been whiplash,' he said.

'Believe me, there will be!' Ellie muttered. 'That woman comes to see me at least three times a week and I swear she's the healthiest patient I've ever seen.'

Andy looked puzzled.

'But if you don't like her, why did you come up to the hospital with me?'

She looked into the dark eyes she knew so well.

'I don't dislike her, and anyway, you asked me to,' she reminded him, which seemed to make him even more puzzled.

'I'll walk home,' she said, desperate to get away from the hospital and Madeleine Courtney, but most desperately needing distance between herself and Andy—distance so she could think...

CHAPTER FOUR

'I MIGHT JUST as well have stayed with you at the hospital for all the sleep I got,' Ellie grumbled as she bumped into Andy in the en suite bathroom next morning.

A freshly showered and shaved Andy. The scent of his familiar aftershave filling her with a sense of longing.

'I slept like a log in a spare room at the hospital,' he said cheerfully. 'The nurses knew to wake me if Madeleine's condition showed any signs of deterioration, but there was really nothing wrong with her. I saw from her file she'd been seeing you quite often—is there something specific, do you think?'

'Not that I and a battery of tests can find,' Ellie muttered, so distracted by her husband's proximity she could barely think straight.

Had Andy picked up on a terseness in her voice that he said, 'Well, she's been very helpful to me with the soccer teams.'

Ellie bit back the comment, *I'm sure she has*, which she'd have liked to utter, and backed out of the room. Maybe if she took a few deep breaths, the room would be vacant by the time she returned.

And had Andy always worn aftershave to work?

She didn't think so, given the variety of allergies doctors were likely to encounter in their patients.

Was that jealousy coiled like a serpent in her stomach? And, if it was, did she have any right to be jealous? Whatever she and Andy had, it was hardly a marriage in the real sense of the word.

Not now. Not any more...

But I love him, a voice whispered in her heart, which she instantly dismissed as nonsense.

She was tired. She needed to have a shower, a quick breakfast, and get back to work. She must remember to phone the high school about Chelsea getting in there, probably starting next week as there were only a couple of weeks left in the term...

And she should give their guest some money for paint. The previous night, after some prodding and prompting, Chelsea had admitted she'd like pale green walls, and both Andy and Ellie were happy to go along with that idea.

Ellie would need to buy brushes and rollers, a tin for the rollers, and some plastic spreadsheets.

By the time Ellie was showered and dressed the list she'd been using as a distraction had grown so long she knew it would be easier to take Chelsea to the hardware store in her lunch hour with the car, so they could bring everything back home.

The gods had decided to be kind to her. She reached the kitchen to grab some breakfast, to find it was Andy-free.

'He only came home for a shower and some fresh clothes,' Chelsea explained to Ellie. 'He said he'd had a patient in a road crash last night so I suppose he was up all night.'

There was no point in disabusing Chelsea of that notion, no reason why she should be caught up in their marital stalemate...

Much better to concentrate on pale green walls.

'I should be home by twelve-thirty,' she told Chelsea.

'If you grab something to eat before then, we'll go down town and get what you need for decorating your room. Have you done any painting?'

Chelsea beamed at her.

'Dad taught me. He said girls should be useful around the house, so when I turned ten I got to choose what colour I wanted my room, and he showed me how to paint it.'

Not a totally absent father, then, Ellie thought.

Ellie's morning passed smoothly, although again, as she listened to some of her elderly male patients, she wondered what could be done to occupy their time.

Chelsea picked up on it when they were in the hardware store, where several older men were poking around, fiddling with bolts and nuts, lifting things and putting them back, looking, more than shopping.

'Don't they have anything to do?' she asked.

'Not a lot,' Ellie told her honestly.

'They need a Men's Shed,' Chelsea said, echoing what had only been a nebulous thought in Ellie's mind.

'What do you know about Men's Sheds?' she asked, and Chelsea smiled.

'My gramps—Mum's dad—belongs to one. They get old bicycles and old plastic chairs, sometimes from hotels, and turn them into wheelchairs that they send off to Africa and the Pacific Islands—anywhere people can't afford fancy wheelchairs.'

'Does your gramps still do it?' Ellie asked, excited by the idea.

'Sure.'

'And would he send you instructions on how to do it?'

'I'm sure he would.

'Well, let's phone and ask him—you can use our phone.'

'I'll write to him,' Chelsea replied, 'because I'll have

to explain why I'm here and not at home. He'll probably assume Mum arranged it before she went away.'

They collected all they needed, Chelsea insisting on paying with her credit card, and headed home, seeing more elderly men sitting on a bench outside the supermarket.

The Men's Shed idea was growing, but how many old bicycles and plastic chairs could they source in Maytown?

'Plenty!' Andy said, when they were discussing the idea over dinner. 'I bet you've never had a good look in our garden shed. I'd say there'd be half a dozen in there. We all had bikes as kids, and when we outgrew the small ones, we got bigger ones, or for the girls just fancier ones. The old ones always ended up in the shed—just in case we might need them later, or could give them to a friend or a cousin.'

'And I suppose the garden shed might also house any number of old plastic chairs?' Ellie said, with only a slight edge of sarcasm.

'Well, if you mean those white ones that stack easily, then yes, there'd be some. We always needed extra chairs when relatives came for Christmas, and Mum and Dad never threw anything away. You never know when it might come in handy, that's Mum's favourite saying.'

Ellie could only shake her head, but Chelsea was all for going down to explore the garden shed immediately.

'Not at night, my girl,' Andy said firmly. 'The place hasn't been opened for months and who knows what snake might have made his home in there. I'll go down in the morning and open the doors and bang the sides a bit so any nasties lurking in there will have time to get out before we explore.'

'Oh, well,' Chelsea said, 'I have to email Gramps anyway, so I'll do that now.'

'Just as soon as we've cleaned up after dinner,' Ellie

reminded her, and Chelsea leapt to her feet and began to clear the table, Andy deciding that with two people already cleaning up, he could get on the internet and investigate wheelchairs made from old bicycles. The idea intrigued him, although how they did it, he couldn't imagine.

He paused in the doorway, looking back at Ellie, who was stacking the dishwasher.

'This Men's Shed is a good idea,' he said. 'I'll phone Ray at the pub about old plastic chairs.'

Ellie smiled at him, feeling that this was as close to normal as they'd been for many, many months.

Could working together on a project like this heal the breach between them?

Or was it simply because they had a third person around—someone with her own problems—that the tension between herself and Andy seemed to have eased somewhat?

Andy had barely left the room when his phone rang.

It was Madeleine Courtney, who was feeling faint and dizzy, and wondering if it could be delayed concussion.

'Are you at the hospital?' he asked.

'No, I didn't like to drive,' came the weak and plaintive reply.

'Then I'll let Ellie know and she'll come to you,' Andy said. 'She's your GP.'

He could hear Madeleine suggesting he'd be better, but he stopped the conversation, returning to the kitchen where Ellie was on her own, doing the last of the wiping down of the benches.

'It's Madeleine Courtney,' he said, aware that the name had come out as a growl. 'She thinks she might have delayed concussion.'

'She's at home?' Ellie asked, and he nodded.

'I'll go,' Ellie told him. 'But if there's any doubt at all she should be in hospital, shouldn't she?'

The frown on her face told him more than the words.

'*Is* there something wrong with her?' he asked.

'Apart from a maybe concussion that had her phoning you rather than me?' Ellie muttered. 'I'm beginning to think she feels I've failed her. There's nothing I can find—or have found so far—but you know full well that we do miss things.'

She sighed, then gave a little shrug.

'I'll go and see her and if I'm worried I'll drive her to the hospital myself and ask the staff to do hourly obs. And maybe if she's in hospital you can run more tests on her to see if I've missed something. Her symptoms are so vague, and change from pains in the abdomen to pains in her shoulders, to general tiredness, fuzzy concentration and, really, there's something new each visit. I've done tests for a thyroid condition—both hyper and hypo—but nothing's come back positive.'

'Could it be some kind of lupus, do you think?'

'I really don't know. None of the blood tests showed indications it could be that, and her urine analysis was clear, but I'll keep looking.'

She sighed.

'Sometimes I wonder if she's just homesick, but she always talks quite happily about the school and all she's doing.'

Ellie sounded so depressed by the thought Andy wanted to hug her.

Damn it all, why shouldn't he?

He gathered her in his arms, holding her close.

'We'll work it out, I promise,' he said, then bent and kissed her, a feather brush, nothing more, on the lips.

Startled blue eyes looked into his as Ellie shuffled back, turning towards the door, already on her way...

Escaping?

'I'll get her to the hospital. Should I ask for half-hourly obs? Quarter-hourly?'

She paused, looking up at him, doubt clouding her eyes.

Andy shrugged, then he remembered the light-hearted dinner they'd shared, the hug, the almost-not-there kiss, and swore softly.

'No, damn it all! Why should either of us be running all over town after her? I'll phone the ambulance to pick her up, and ask someone to call me as soon as she's settled, then I'll pop up and see her there. If there's any doubt, I can repeat the X-rays and scans we've already done, just in case there's something we've missed.'

'Are you sure? I'm happy to go.'

'No, let's get her to hospital, then tomorrow, when we've both had a good night's sleep, we can sit down with your notes and have a think about what the symptoms could indicate.'

'You've got soccer tomorrow,' she reminded him, and he was surprised she'd remembered.

'We'll do it after soccer.'

Andy phoned the ambulance and then the hospital, assuring them he'd be up to have a look at Madeleine, and ordering the X-rays of her head and neck.

He was about to leave when he thought of something, tapping on Ellie's door before going in. She'd had a shower and was wrapped in a towel, her wet hair hanging straight down by her face.

How could he not remember times he'd have ripped off that towel and tumbled them both onto the bed? His voice was croaky when he said, 'If we can't find anything maybe we should send her to the city. They have the facilities—not to mention the budget—to run tests we couldn't attempt.'

Ellie smiled at him, exacerbating all the reactions going on in his body.

'You'd have to hope they find something—some of those tests cost a mint—and maybe it *is* nothing more than hypochondria.'

Andy didn't respond but Ellie knew he would be grumbling and growling under his breath.

Could it be hypochondria? Ellie wondered when Andy left, fixing her mind on her patient to try to still the excitement Andy's kiss earlier had left in its wake.

Unfortunately, there was a strong possibility there *was* something wrong with Madeleine, in which case both she and Andy would regret it if they didn't do all they could for her.

Andy wandered off, probably to walk up to the hospital so he could meet the ambulance when it arrived.

Ellie shed her towel and pulled on pyjamas, glancing with a little regret at the pretty lingerie that occupied the other end of the drawer.

She laughed at her own stupidity. As if seducing her husband in sexy night attire could mend a marriage that harsh and hurtful words had ripped apart.

Ripped…

It was the strange word—describing well the seismic shift between them—that made her look through the more attractive negligees, down to the bottom of the pile where a dark blue, lacy, thigh-length piece of apparel still showed clearly that *it* had been ripped apart.

By passion, excitement, and a fiery need that could not be delayed…

And for a moment, holding it, she closed her eyes and remembered, awakening memories in her body as well, so she ached for Andy in a way she hadn't since they'd split apart...

Could they heal the rift—cross the abyss between them?

Had she been so wrapped up in her own pain she'd not considered his?

If so, wasn't it up to her to at least try to sort things out?

But where to start?

Determinedly putting aside such thoughts, she went in search of Chelsea. The teenager appeared to be coping well—talking enthusiastically about school and soccer—but the future of the child she would produce had hardly been mentioned.

Might she want to talk more about it?

And if so, should Ellie bring it up?

Doing so now, it would be as a friend. Or would it be better to do it at an appointment, as a doctor?

'Come and see,' Chelsea called to her as she dithered on the veranda, and Ellie entered the room, the soft green walls making it seem bigger somehow.

'Do you like it?' Chelsea asked, her face alight with so much joy Ellie could hardly find fault.

Not that she did.

'It looks great,' she said. 'But you don't want to sleep with the paint fumes tonight, so take one of the other rooms, then, in the morning, Andy will give us a hand to move the furniture back in. Unless...'

She hesitated.

'You might like to paint the furniture as well. I'd say the bed and desk and dressing table were painted white years ago, but they might look shabby in here now. There's probably white paint in the shed. What do you think?'

Chelsea settled on the bottom rung of the ladder she'd been using for the top of the high walls. She studied Ellie for a while before she spoke.

'Are you this kind to all the strays who land on your doorstep?' she asked softly, her eyes now bright with tears.

'Not *all* of them,' Ellie said gently. 'Only ones who know how to paint, and can help Andy with his soccer team, and bring a lot of pleasure to our house with your smile and enthusiasm—especially your smile!'

She went to squat beside Chelsea as the tears that had shone in her eyes now trickled down her cheeks.

'Besides,' she said, hugging the girl, 'you're family and if there's one thing Andy and I feel very strongly about, it's family.'

Her heart felt heavy as she said the words, but in spite of all that had happened, she knew family *was* important to them both.

'We'll do whatever we can to keep you safe and comfortable,' she said, 'and you can talk to either one of us about anything at all, but in the end everyone has to take responsibility for his or her own life, and that includes their own happiness.'

'And my baby?' The words came out as a quavery whisper. 'What should I do about that?'

Ellie hugged her.

'Let's wait and see,' she said. 'There's plenty of time to think about what you want both for yourself and for the baby. Have you thought much about it?'

She felt Chelsea nod against her chest.

'Only every day!' the girl whispered. 'It's my responsibility, isn't it, but what kind of life can I give a baby?'

She raised her head to look directly at Ellie, and added, 'But can I just give it away? As if it were an old bicycle I don't need any more? I'm not sure I could do that. Then I think that plenty of adopted babies grow up happy and contented and they bring joy to their new parents, so would I be selfish not letting it be adopted? Not giving the joy of a baby to someone who can't have one?'

The words cut into Ellie's heart. How easy would it be—
No! She mustn't think that.

Thrusting the thought away, Ellie drew Chelsea into
her arms again, dropping a kiss on the top of her head.

'There's a lot to think about but nothing has to be decided right now. Any time you want to talk about it, Andy
and I are here to listen. But right now you've had a busy
and probably exhausting day, so why don't you have a
shower and go to bed? Remember you're helping Andy
with his soccer team tomorrow.'

Andy had arrived at the hospital as the ambulance pulled
in. He greeted Madeleine and walked beside her as the
ambulance men wheeled her into the observation room in
the hospital's small Emergency Department. Her health
records were already up on the screen and he checked the
tests Ellie had previously ordered, and read the results.

As she had said, there was nothing to indicate any un-
derlying cause for Madeleine's various symptoms, but
there was still the possibility of delayed concussion from
the accident.

He watched as the nurse on duty hooked Madeleine
up to the monitor and wrapped a blood-pressure cuff on
her arm.

'This will drive you nuts,' the nurse said cheerfully. 'It
inflates every hour to record your BP, and it's usually just
as you're dropping off to sleep. But we have to know what
your body's doing, and if there's any major change then
bells and whistles will let us know you need attention.'

'Bells and whistles?' Madeleine said faintly, perhaps
regretting her decision to phone a doctor.

'More like a loud beeping noise,' Andy told her, as the
nurse dashed off to answer a loud beeping noise elsewhere.
'Are you in any pain?'

'Well, my neck and shoulders ache, but they often ache, and I took some paracetamol for my headache about an hour ago, but the pain's not so bad. I'm used to it. It's the dizzy feeling I've got that worried me.'

Andy felt her head, his fingers seeking any lump he might have missed earlier, but the only sign that there'd been an accident was a slight graze and a tiny bit of swelling on her forehead.

He checked Madeleine's eyes but both pupils reacted evenly to the light, and asked her some basic questions to test for confusion, but nothing obvious showed up.

'Try to get some sleep,' he said, and went back to the desk to go through Madeleine's file again.

Ellie arrived as he was checking the X-rays they'd done earlier.

'You'll be busy tomorrow and I thought we could go through her history together,' she said.

He smelt the bath soap she'd used, and felt her freshness against his shoulder, her head so close to his that a single turn of his head and he could kiss her again…

But he wouldn't. They were at work.

'I'm checking the X-rays—' as if she couldn't tell '—wondering if I've missed a hairline fracture anywhere.'

'There's nothing I can see. Are there scans as well?' Ellie asked.

But the scans showed Andy hadn't missed a bleed at the back of the brain from a contra coup injury. Ellie used a light beam to search every section of the brain.

Finding nothing, Andy shook his head, sorry Ellie had straightened up as he'd enjoyed her closeness.

'Well, all that's left is to go back through her medical history.'

Thanks to a government initiative, more than seven million people now had their health records available to doctors and hospitals all over Australia. Would Madeleine's be online?

It was, and this time Ellie squeezed onto the chair beside him. It was uncomfortable but, oh, so, comforting!

'As you can see,' Ellie said, 'she rarely visited her GP back in Sydney. She's had the usual flu vaccinations, scripts for oral contraceptives and apart from a bad case of laryngitis she suffered two years back, she's had no real health issues.'

'Until she came to Maytown,' Andy pointed out.

Ellie leaned over his shoulder again, resting her hands on the desk beside the keyboard.

She was so close he could feel the contours of her body against his back and was reminded of how they'd slept, spooned together.

'You can see everything seems trivial,' Ellie said, using the mouse to scroll down the visit list. 'Sore hip, bad neck, not sleeping, feeling of exhaustion even when she did sleep…'

But when Andy saw the battery of tests Ellie had run, he knew she was taking Madeleine seriously. He read on through the file, Ellie pulling up a chair and sitting beside him now.

Some months ago she had prescribed Madeleine a mild anti-depressant, which was good thinking when nothing could be pinned down clinically, but apparently the tablets had made Madeleine feel nauseous and hadn't improved her aches and pains.

An anti-anxiety tablet had had much the same effect, with no positive outcome.

Frustrated by the lack of clinical evidence, Andy went back to see his patient, who was now sleeping even as the blood-pressure cuff inflated on her arm.

If the symptoms had only begun when she'd come to

the high school here in Maytown, maybe Ellie was right about her problem being psychological.

'Was she unhappy about the transfer?' Andy asked his wife, as she, too, peered down at the sleeping patient. 'Could she just be miserable?'

He could practically hear Ellie thinking.

'We *have* talked about it,' she said at last. 'It was easy to bring up because I'm a newcomer to Maytown myself, but she's always responded enthusiastically: about the town, the school, everything...'

'You're starting to sound uncertain,' he said, and saw the little frown line between Ellie's grey-blue eyes—a line she tried to rub away whenever she was aware of it.

Like now...

'She might have been too positive about it all,' she eventually admitted. 'But, honestly, Andy, I think whatever she has is real. I've been thinking fibromyalgia but that's such a hard thing to pin down and I've never known a patient with it, so I've no comparison I can make.'

'It's a good thought, though. That or some other auto-immune problem,' Andy told her. 'And having something like that, which *is* difficult to diagnose, could make her more anxious about possible concussion.'

'Because she knows there's something wrong with her but if the doctors can't find what it is, could they also miss something else?'

Andy put his arm around Ellie's shoulders, thinking of the times when they'd been studying or working together, and their minds had been so aligned they could finish each other's thoughts.

How could something that had been so strong—so right in every way—break down the way their marriage had? How had grief pushed them apart when it should have drawn them closer together? Had he been wrong, not sharing his feelings at the time, not wanting to burden her with more angst?

He pushed the thoughts away, and focussed on his patient. His go-to strategy since the break-up…

'I think we should leave it for another day,' he said. 'I'll stay a while in case she wakes with more confusion, but I'll let you go.'

Andy suggested it because it had been a long day and he knew Ellie would be tired, but thoughts prompted by the words 'I'll let you go' kept running through his head.

He walked back into the ward where Madeleine was still sleeping.

He *had* let Ellie go—quite literally—when the pain of the loss of their baby had been so overwhelming, so all-encompassing for him, he'd felt he hadn't been able to help her with *her* grief and despair.

Or done enough to get through the layers of protection she'd wrapped around her own grief.

So guilt had been added to his certain knowledge that he could never go through that anguish again—never face the hope and elation, the despair and pain…

'No, no, no!' he'd shouted when she'd suggested one last round of IVF. 'No more, not now, not ever.'

Then he'd killed any chance of redemption with his bitter, caustic words: 'If this marriage needs a baby to make it complete, then it can't be much of a marriage.'

CHAPTER FIVE

SATURDAY DAWNED AND Madeleine insisted she was feeling much better, so she was the first person Ellie saw when the soccer players started gathering on the side veranda. Madeleine looked fit enough, although she appeared to be limping. Had she bumped one of her legs in the car accident, mild though it had been?

Ellie introduced Chelsea to those players she'd met as patients, and, after leaving an ice-box full of cold drinks in a shady part of their 'clubhouse', she departed.

But with plenty of open doors leading out that way, she was able to observe what was going on without actually spying.

Her thoughts inevitably led to her and Andy. Though things were better between them, they were still living apart. Perhaps she and Andy should formalise their separation—people could be separated and continue living in the same house.

It wasn't that she wanted to be with anyone else, but Andy might… Despite the kiss, he'd made no further moves, so maybe he didn't want to be with her.

But that thought, and the one that followed it—separation usually led to divorce—made her feel cold all over.

Could she live without Andy?

It was impossible even to envisage such a thing. Just

imagining it filled her with a deep, primeval pain. Losing Andy would be like losing part of herself...

But *if* he wanted his freedom, surely she should—

No!

A future without Andy was like looking into a bottomless pit or a black hole. It was emptiness, nothingness, a space she didn't want to inhabit...

It was better to think about other things, like the Men's Shed. They'd need a shed, of course, but from what she'd seen, sheds were common in this country town, and there was an old School of Arts building—very dilapidated, but perhaps their first project could be renovating it.

For which they'd need money.

Maybe they could ask one of the service clubs in town to help them raise funds. Ellie had already volunteered to bake cupcakes on the last Friday of each month for a stall raising money for soccer uniforms.

But the Men's Shed would need more money than a monthly cake stall could provide.

Who among her patients might belong to a service club?

Madeleine's arrival in the kitchen stopped further thought.

'I didn't think I hurt anything in the accident,' she said, with no hint of apology for disturbing Ellie at the weekend. 'But it's my knee. It was fine yesterday but this morning, after I left the hospital it felt a bit swollen and sore, and now it's getting worse, and I feel really unwell.'

She did look ill, so Ellie led her into one of the spare bedrooms and asked her to lie down.

The knee was red and inflamed but there was no hint of a scratch or graze that could have led to infection.

Was it because none of the other areas of pain Madeleine had complained of—the neck and shoulders—had been likely to swell, that Ellie had leaned more towards fibromyalgia than lupus? Joint pain and swelling definitely pointed to lupus.

'I know it's painful, but it might mean that we can pin down what's wrong with you and give you a proper diagnosis that fits all your symptoms,' Ellie told her. 'There's a strong possibility that it could be lupus.'

'Is it curable?' Madeleine asked.

'Unfortunately not,' Ellie told her. 'But a short course of corticosteroids will ease the pain and the inflammation in your knee. If it *is* lupus, your immune system is attacking you. All your joints have small fluid sacs, bursae, in them to protect the bones and their attached muscles and tendons as you move. Your immune system is attacking that fluid in your knee. The tablets will help you now, but we'll have to look at a longer-term solution to keep you as symptom free as possible.'

Madeleine frowned at her.

'So it's not going to go away like measles or something else contagious?'

Ellie shook her head.

'Are you going back to the city for the Christmas holidays?' she asked Madeleine.

'Yes, I'm going down to stay with my parents in Sydney.'

'Then I'd like you to see a specialist in clinical immunology while you're down there. I can make the appointment for you, because you're more likely to get in to see someone at short notice if a doctor asks. I can do most of the tests so he or she will have all the results before your visit.'

'But if you do the tests and have the results, why can't you treat me?'

Ellie sighed.

'I could, but a specialist will be able to do more for

you, and make more appropriate suggestions about your treatment long term. Then I can follow up on it. There are drugs that can help when you have a flare-up like your knee, some drugs that can suppress your immune system, which might provide a little protection, and drugs like anti-malaria drugs that affect the immune system, but all these drugs have side-effects. If we have a specialist giving an overview of your treatment, we'll be getting advice about new treatments and suggestions when things don't seem to be working.'

'Will it kill me?'

Ellie shook her head.

'It shouldn't, but it can affect your kidneys and your liver, neither of which you want to damage. A specialist will advise on the best way to protect and watch over them.'

She was silent for a moment, dredging up all she knew about the disease.

'A lot of people go for long periods with no problems, beyond an occasional flare-up like your knee. They take non-steroidal anti-inflammatories when they have aches and pains, and cortisone when there's a painful attack like you're having now. I've some tablets in the surgery I'll give you to take now as any steroids are best taken in the morning—'

'So I'm not totally hyper at bedtime,' Madeleine said, and Ellie smiled.

'Exactly,' she said. 'I'll give you a script for more, but they are things you can't stay on long term because of side effects, but you also can't come off them suddenly. You should take one full tablet for four days, then a half for four days, then, believe it or not, a quarter for four days, then stop until you get another bad attack. You rest here while I slip down to the surgery.'

And to her surprise, Madeleine reached out and touched her on the arm.

'Thank you,' she said. 'I know I've been a nuisance, but I've always been so healthy and all the aches and pains took me unawares.'

Ellie grinned at her.

'Me, too,' she said. 'And I'm sorry we didn't get it worked out sooner, but I think we're onto it now.'

She hurried down the stairs, mentally listing all the tests she'd want to repeat and the new ones she'd have to order before Madeleine saw the specialist.

Andy had noticed Madeleine limp away from the group on the veranda, but he was far too busy trying to get his squad in order for some warm-up drills to wonder what was wrong with her now.

It didn't seem to matter how far and how fast modern medicine progressed, something new was always appearing, although the more he'd thought about Madeleine's file, the more he'd wondered about lupus.

Ellie had written 'query lupus' early in her contact with Madeleine, but the normal tests like a full blood count, erythrocyte sedimentation rate, and urinalysis hadn't shown anything abnormal. There were more tests, but all testing was expensive, so both hospital doctors and GPs tried to keep to the budgetary restraints imposed on them.

Practice over—the old tennis court had proved its worth—he set the older boys to tend the barbecue and left Chelsea to organise slicing onions and buttering bread. Sausage and onions in a slice of bread was standard fare for lunch before a game, while the icebox contained various kinds of water—plain and lightly fruit flavoured, carbonated and still.

'This is a far better idea than a barbecue in the park,'

Madeleine said, joining them on the veranda, her right knee bandaged. 'You can keep them all in one place, not drifting anywhere they fancy. Do we walk down to the field?'

Andy grinned at her.

'When we've got the school bus to take us? No, we'll conserve all our energy for the game. Woonunga has two teams but as it's just a trial before the start of the season in the New Year, we'll just play one game, swapping the players at half-time. We haven't got two full teams so some kids will have to play a bit longer but we'll sort it out.'

Chelsea appeared at Ellie's side as she sat at the kitchen table, writing lists of people she wanted to contact about the Men's Shed, either for advice, donations, or help.

'It's their first real game against opposition, and Andy's got the school bus to take us down.'

Ellie looked at her young boarder, in shorts, a loose shirt and, incongruously, football boots.

'Someone had a spare pair. And I won't join the game because Andy checked and I can't play after the first trimester. I just wanted to feel I was part of it,' Chelsea explained. Then she looked up at Ellie.

'Do come,' she said, and Ellie knew she couldn't resist.

She started on the sideline, standing next to Andy, feeling the tension in his body as his team took to the field for their first game against an opposition.

She slipped her hand into his and squeezed his fingers.

'They'll be fine,' she said. 'And when all's said and done, it's just a game.'

He gave her a horrified look,

'Just a game?' he echoed, then grinned and returned the pressure of her fingers.

But as soon as the game began, he was racing up and

down the sideline, yelling orders. Other people joined her, people she knew as patients, or had met around the village.

'It's a damn good thing for the kids that Andy's started this,' the butcher told her, and the warmth of pride spread through her body.

To Ellie's surprise, the Maytown team seemed to be doing well. The young person in charge of the score was a bit erratic, but Ellie knew they'd definitely scored two goals to Woonunga's one.

But what really surprised her was the support—not only from the parents of participants yelling encouragement from the sidelines but half the town seemed to be there.

'If we go over there to play them when the season begins in earnest in the New Year, I reckon I can get a bus-load of supporters,' the butcher said.

The game finally finished, a three-all draw, and one of the local service clubs put on a barbecue for the players and supporters.

It was an opportunity for Ellie to mention the Men's Shed idea to one of the women there.

'Oh, bless you for the wheelchair idea,' the woman said. 'A group of us have been discussing getting something started but they need a goal, something to focus on. They don't want to be learning wood-turning or polishing stones—they need a project they'll really believe in. You leave it with me now, I'll get my husband onto it.'

Ellie felt an arm slide around her waist, and Andy was there.

'Are you lobbying these people for support for your Men's Shed?' he asked, smiling at the group who'd now gathered around Ellie.

'Just talking,' Ellie replied, through lips that were suddenly dry, while her knees were definitely wobbly.

But the women were all talking to Andy now, congratulating him on setting up the soccer team, explaining how so many of the kids had too much time on their hands in summer when their normal Rugby League football season was over.

There were offers of help with fundraising for uniforms and maybe setting up a regular canteen at matches.

'With coffee,' another woman said. 'I could have murdered a cup of coffee at half-time.'

Realising this was Andy's show, Ellie was about to step away, but Andy's hand in the small of her back stopped her moving.

Stay, that touch seemed to say. Stay and share the talk with me.

Excitement built within her. They'd been studying together when their first romance had begun, and now they were kind of working together, occasionally at the hospital *and* on projects like the soccer teams and Men's Shed. Andy might like to get involved with that, too, while she could do more to help with the soccer team.

They walked home, just the two of them, Chelsea having gone to look at old bicycles one member of the soccer team knew of, and Madeleine having left early to go home and rest her knee.

Ellie could feel Andy's closeness through every nerve ending in her skin, could feel the warmth of his body next to hers.

Should she take his hand?

'If I change Joe—he's the rather overweight boy with ginger hair,' Andy announced, shocking Ellie from her wayward thoughts, 'from that back position to the forwards, then—'

No, she wouldn't take his hand.

She'd tune back into Andy's conversation instead, show an interest.

But their shoulders were touching, and his hand was right there, by hers.

'Then Rangi can go—'

Ellie gave up. There'd be other times they could hold hands and, really, wasn't being interested in what he was doing more important?

But did she have to be interested in the technical stuff? Wasn't organising cake stalls and raising money for uniforms just as important?

'Then Chelsea can give them some goal practice—'

'Only practice,' she reminded him as they turned in at their front gate. 'You'll work it out.'

Maybe they could sit down and have a drink together.

'Not if I don't write it all down. I can already see how it would make a difference.'

Frustrated that her imaginary scenario wasn't going to play out—at least not tonight—Ellie was about to say, *It's not the World Cup*, but she caught herself just in time.

That was the kind of sniping thing they'd said to each other too often in the past months. If she wanted to fix things—and she knew that she did—all that had to stop.

She must have sighed as she climbed the steps, for Andy turned to her, concern on his face.

'Are you okay? You probably shouldn't have stayed for the whole game—it was hot out there in the sun. Come inside and I'll get you a cold drink.'

And he put his arm around her shoulders just as he would have in the old days, and led her into the kitchen, pulling out a chair for her then finding an open bottle of white wine and pouring her a glass.

'There,' he said. 'And let's not bother with dinner. I'll run up the road later and get a takeaway.'

After which he went to the far end of the long table where

all his soccer papers were and began writing furiously, crossing out and shifting names as if his life depended on it.

How long since he'd touched Ellie—even for something as simple as an arm around her shoulders?

Yet that touch had stirred so much back to life, Andy knew they had to try again—to give it one last go to find a way back to each other, to the love they'd shared.

For a moment the flood of memories blanked everything from his mind. The pair of them as students, and the overwhelming joy of first love. Africa, where passionate, sweaty sex had helped them block out the horrors they'd seen during the day; where they'd kept going *because* they'd had each other. More recently their joyous arrival in Maytown, where they had hoped to grow from couple to family, sharing the delight of their new home, and their joy in their new baby.

There was far too much to throw away...

And if they did sort it out?

What next?

Was he willing to concede to one last attempt at IVF?

A huge black cloud immediately descended over his brain and pain tightened his chest.

How could he *not* have known how much losing a child—even an unborn one—would hurt? Yes, he'd been upset when the IVF attempts had failed, but more for Ellie's sake as he knew she'd somehow felt responsible.

But then it *had* worked, and he'd been talking to the bump in her stomach every day, often sharing silly things that had happened at work, sometimes just talking about the weather, the shining sun or sparkling stars.

They'd opted not to know the sex of their child, and somehow, when they'd lost it, finding out that it had been a boy had worsened his pain...

He forced himself to focus on the names on the paper in front of him, trying to remember all the changes he'd thought of for the soccer team as they had walked home.

Walking home with Ellie had felt so normal—so right—that he'd tried to keep his mind on soccer to stop himself from taking her hand.

If only he could get over the loss of the baby they *had* finally conceived.

Surely the pain should have grown less by now? Perhaps he should see a psychologist—take some time off and go down to the city. Better yet, find one on-line, someone he could talk to on a regular basis without it affecting his work...

Should they both have done that after the loss?

He tried to concentrate on soccer again.

If he shifted Joe—

But his mind had moved beyond football.

'I'll get the takeaway,' he said, standing up and closing his folder of soccer papers. 'Thai or Chinese?'

'Thai,' Ellie said, setting down her half-empty glass and standing up as well. 'I'll pop this in the fridge and come with you.'

He watched her walk to the fridge. Gold-blonde hair tangled by the breeze, slim waist and rounded hips as she bent to settle the wine. Then as she straightened and turned his heart leapt at the sight of his Ellie—her nose and cheeks pink from the sun, her grey-blue eyes smiling at him, her beautifully shaped lips echoing the smile...

His heart began behaving badly in his chest.

Could it be possible that she felt the same way—that *she* felt an easing of the tension between them?

'Well, are we going?' she said, and Andy realised he was standing by his chair, immobilised by the thoughts skittering around in his head, and the emotions churning in his body.

Hope—that was the main one. After all those weeks and weeks of nothingness, he'd felt the tug of a slender thread of hope...

Chelsea came home with news of bicycles, and talk about the Men's Shed dominated their meal.

'I'll leave you two to clean up,' Ellie said, when they'd finished. 'I need to do some research.'

She turned to Andy.

'With Madeleine's knee flaring up the way it did today, I'm back to thinking lupus so I'll do all the tests I can, and see if I can get her an appointment with a specialist when she's in Sydney for the holidays. Speaking of which...' she turned to Chelsea '...do you know when the school holidays begin?'

'Two weeks,' was Chelsea's prompt reply. 'Everyone in the team has been talking about them, where they're going, what they're going to do. Some of them have jobs lined up.'

'Then I'd better find a specialist soon, before everything stops for Christmas.'

Ellie left the room, left also an awareness of Andy's presence that she hadn't felt for months. They'd walked together, talked together, in a comfortable way—he'd even put his arm around her shoulders, drawn her close to his side. And whether it was Chelsea's presence in the house, or some force beyond her understanding, for whatever reason suddenly she could feel the knots of hard, hot resentment she'd felt towards him crumbling inside her.

Yet what she felt was more than hope.

Just as they'd fallen in love the first time, surely they could do it again? Could make their way back to each other, to togetherness, slowly and tentatively maybe—but eventually...

She grabbed the keys for the surgery and made her way down the stairs. Madeleine's file would have her Sydney address, and Ellie wanted to find her a specialist within reach of her parents' home, not in some far distant part of the sprawling city.

But when she unlocked and opened the door, she stepped back in dismay. While half the town had been at the football game, someone from the other half had broken into her surgery.

Broken glass that lay scattered across Maureen's desk in front of a window told her how they'd got in, but what had they taken?

Patient paper files were in locked cabinets, her work computer and Maureen's, and all the drugs, even non-dangerous ones, were locked in the safe.

She yelled up the stairs for Andy, although she could tell from the stillness that whoever had done this was long gone. But her knees were shaking, and she wasn't sure whether she should go in and check the safe or wait for the police.

'Oh, Ellie!' Andy whispered as he arrived by her side. Then he wrapped his arms around her and held her close.

'I think we phone Chris,' he said, speaking of the sergeant in charge of the local police station. 'Then wait and go in when he tells us it's okay.'

He held her steady with one hand so he could pull out his cellphone and speed-dialled the police station.

'He'll be here in ten minutes,' he told Ellie. 'Do you want to wait here or go up and lie down for a while?'

'I could get you a cup of tea,' Chelsea suggested from halfway down the stairs where she'd followed Andy.

Ellie shook her head.

'I'm okay. It was just the shock.'

She paused, her brain racing.

'Would they have gone upstairs? Should we check there? They wouldn't need to break in, there's always one of the doors open.'

'Best go and check,' Andy said. 'Chelsea can go with you, though I can't imagine anyone being so bold. Down here, with the garden all around, someone passing in the street wouldn't have noticed a stranger in the yard, but upstairs—even going up the steps—someone would have been sure to see them.'

Ellie knew he was talking to reassure her, but he was probably right. She joined Chelsea and they both went slowly through the house, checking easy-to-steal things like laptops, cellphones and other electronic paraphernalia.

But nothing appeared to be missing, although checking the drawers in Chelsea's room revealed just how little clothing the teenager had brought with her.

'This reminds me,' Ellie said to her as she slid the drawer shut, 'we should really go down to Croxton and get you some more clothes. It's the nearest decent-sized town and it's only about an hour's drive. What you managed to fit into your backpack won't last you through summer.'

'I don't want you having to fuss over me and drive me places,' Chelsea protested. 'I'm already so grateful to you both for taking me into your home. I can't let you do more.'

'Of course you can!' Ellie told her. 'But if it will make you feel any better, I love an excuse to go down to Croxton and poke around the shops there.'

Chelsea chuckled, but the sound of a vehicle pulling up had them both heading out onto the veranda.

'That's Chris—he's in charge, and the lad with him is—'

'Zeke!' Chelsea finished for her. 'He looked after me on the train and made sure no one bothered me. He's new in town, too, and he's staying in a hotel while he waits for a flat that will be empty when the school year ends. One of the teachers is leaving and Zeke's made arrangements to take it over.'

'You know more about what's going on in this town than I do,' Ellie told her. 'Shall we go down to hear what they say?'

There'd been a touch of hero-worship in Chelsea's tone as she'd spoken of Zeke, so it wouldn't do her any harm to meet up with him again.

And Ellie would check him out as well. He'd be nineteen or twenty if he was fresh out of the academy, and Chelsea wasn't always going to be pregnant, although she might always be in love with the boyfriend, Alex…

Ellie closed her eyes for a moment, thinking of the word 'always' and how she'd automatically attached it to love.

Because for her that's how it had seemed…

Chris greeted her with a smile and introduced Zeke, who immediately introduced Chelsea to his boss.

'It *has* happened before, in your parents' time, Andy,' Chris said. 'You'd think they'd learn there's nothing here to steal, although maybe someone in every generation has to have a go.'

He paused, then shrugged his shoulders.

'Come and see,' he said. 'There's plenty of glass. Are you both wearing something on your feet?'

Ellie looked down at her own and Chelsea's sandals and nodded.

They checked the window first. It was easy to see what had happened. It had been broken by a brick or rock, then a big enough hole bashed in it for the culprit to put his arm through and unlock the other side.

Smears of blood on the broken glass still in the window suggested whoever had done it hadn't left unscathed.

As Chris led the way to the back storeroom, where things like paper towels and first-aid supplies were stored, Ellie stayed by the window, seeing where quite a lot of blood had pooled.

Anxious now, she followed the men and the blood spots on the floor, arriving in time to see Chris studying the big old safe in the corner of the room. Sooty black marks were all over the door.

'Kids, I reckon,' Chris said. 'Saw a movie where safe-crackers used a blowtorch to open an old safe and they've bought one of those little burners that some people use in the kitchen, or to solder maybe a broken link of a chain. All it had the power to do was make a mess, but it does point to it being someone quite young. I think even teenagers would know better.'

'Do you take fingerprints?' Ellie asked, although she was still thinking about the blood. 'Of young kids, I mean? Are you allowed to?'

Chris smiled at her. 'Young Zeke here, who's not long out of college, can probably quote the entire passage from the rule book on this, but, yes, we can take a child's finger-prints if we take him or her into custody and have both the child and the responsible adult's consent. There are rules about how long fingerprints, particularly of minors, are allowed to be kept, so we don't have file-drawers or even many digital records full of young offenders' fingerprints.'

'So, will you take fingerprints here?' Ellie asked, di-verted from the blood by the working of the law.

'We will, and then we'll round up half a dozen young hooligans and give them a scare.'

'You might not need fingerprints to find our offender,' Ellie said. 'There was blood on the glass and it led into the storeroom, and look…'

She bent to pull a roll of blood-soaked cotton wool out from behind a cupboard.

'I'd say he's cut himself quite seriously. Wrapped the wound in his T-shirt so there's not much blood at the scene, but there's the occasional drip and now this.'

Andy reached her first, and felt the squelch of blood in the wool.

'He's bleeding badly,' he said. 'We need to find him.'

Chris reacted first to the urgency in Andy's voice.

'Zeke, get on to the local radio station and ask if they can put out a call for someone who suffered an injury that caused a lot of bleeding today. Tell them to get up to the hospital to be checked out. Ask parents to check their children to make sure they're not hiding an injury. Then get on to regional TV and see if they can do a similar flash notice across the bottom of their screens.'

As Zeke hurried away, Chris sighed.

'Short of door-knocking the entire town, I don't see what else we can do.'

He thought for a few minutes, then added, 'Mind you, there are a few places I *can* door-knock.'

'You know the young rascals in town, then?' Ellie asked, and Chris nodded.

'In fact,' he said, 'I've been meaning to talk to Andy about them. Can you take a few younger ones into your soccer teams?'

'As many as you like,' Andy assured him. 'It would be good to have a team at every age level.'

'Then I'll give you five for free,' Chris joked. 'When should they turn up for practice?'

Andy thought for a moment.

'Tuesday afternoon. They can meet the older group and learn from them. Eventually we'll have separate sessions for the younger ones, but we can only do that if Ellie and I can work out a good job-sharing system.'

'Oh, you'll manage that, no problem,' Chris assured him. 'The way you two work so there's always someone on call for the hospital has impressed everyone in town. Not that your parents didn't do a good job, Andy, but the hospital had more staff then, and always two doctors.'

'Cloning one or other of us might help,' Ellie whispered, but Andy knew Chris was right. They *would* work it out. Even when their relationship had been at its worst, they'd managed their job-sharing efficiently and well, as if, in their work life, nothing had changed.

And thinking of work… 'I should get up to the hospital to wait for whoever was bleeding to come in. If it's a child, the parents might have bandaged the wound tightly enough to slow the blood flow, and not realised it's probably serious.'

'Or not reported it in case the child ended up in trouble,' Chris grumbled.

'I'll clean up here, then join you in case I'm needed,' Ellie offered.

Chelsea stepped forward.

'No, you go with Andy, I'll clean up here.'

'And I'll stay to help, if you can spare me, boss,' Zeke offered.

'Go for it,' Chris said, 'but both of you wear thick gloves—you can grab a couple of pairs from the car, Zeke—and get some more clothes and be very careful. That glass is old and extremely sharp. I don't want either of you joining the injured list.'

Ellie touched Andy lightly on the arm.

'I'll have a quick shower and then head to the hospital,' she said. 'I want to change my shoes because there's sure to be little bits of glass in the soles and I don't want to spread them wherever I walk.'

'Good thinking,' Andy said, smiling down at the practical, sensible woman he couldn't help loving in spite of all that lay between them. 'I'll change mine, too, then when I've got time I'll attack them with a wire brush. Yours and Chelsea's, too. Best to leave them on the veranda.'

His chest tightened, and inwardly he cursed himself that all he'd managed by way of conversation was safe glass removal from the soles of shoes.

There was so much he'd wanted to say, especially when she'd been holding his arm and looking up at him with a slight smile hovering around her lips.

Kissing her, which was what he *really* wanted to do, was impossible with everyone around, but even that desire had been absent for so long it had startled him.

'I'll see you upstairs,' he said, hoping his hurried exit didn't look as desperate as it felt.

She followed him up—had his thoughts drawn her to follow him?—and he held her arm to steady her as she slipped off her sandals.

And as she leaned into him, what else could he do but hold her, *and* kiss her, just as he'd envisaged it down in her surgery.

'Well, that was unexpected,' she said, her eyes dancing as she stepped, barefoot, away from her sandals. 'Something to do with the young love downstairs?'

'Young love downstairs?'

Had the kiss addled his brain?

'Didn't you see the way Chelsea blushed when Zeke got out of the car? There's a little bit of hero-worship going on there.'

'Nonsense, she only met him on the train.'

Ellie smiled.

'And you'd only met me that day in the refectory when you inveigled me into that corridor near the fire doors and kissed me almost senseless.'

'But I'd been looking at you all day in lectures.'

'As if that was an excuse,' Ellie teased, and for all the pain and anguish in between, the memory was enough to make him kiss her again, moving within seconds from a slow, exploratory kiss towards passion.

'You should be going,' Ellie whispered, but she didn't move out of his arms. In fact, this time it was she who kissed him.

'I've missed this so much,' she murmured against his lips. 'How could we have let it all happen? Was my mentioning another IVF a kind of last straw for you?'

He held her closer, trying desperately to find the words he needed, but none seemed right, so he kissed her again.

That seemed right…

Until Chelsea appeared with a dustpan and brush, and wolf-whistled as she passed them.

'Cheeky brat!' Andy muttered, while Ellie laughed, but Andy's mind as he strode the couple of blocks through town was on Ellie more than the patient, who might or might not turn up.

He took a deep breath and refocussed on the patient.

What if he wasn't a local?

Could it be someone who'd come to the soccer but slipped away from his family or mates?

Could he have had a mate with him?

Might there be two patients?

An ambulance screaming into the hospital entrance ahead of Andy, suggested a lot of his questions had been answered.

'He's suffering from shock from a massive haemorrhage from an arm wound. The babysitter bandaged it and didn't realise it was still bleeding until the kid passed out.'

The ambo who'd leapt out on Andy's side filled him in as he hurried to the back doors, where his partner was already wheeling out the patient.

The lad lying on the stretcher couldn't have been more than ten, and looked more like a ghost than a living being.

Andy didn't hesitate, hauling off his shoes as he walked through the doors and dropping them in a bin, grabbing the first nurse he encountered.

'Get on to my wife and tell her we need her ASAP,' he said. 'You'll find the number on the list above the triage desk.'

The stretcher was now through the door, and he helped steer it towards one of two resus rooms.

The ambulance monitor showed him the child's blood pressure was dangerously low, while his pulse was racing as his heart tried desperately to keep what little blood there *was* in his body pumping around the major organs.

'We put in a fluid line and have been giving him FFP, but we don't carry full blood,' the senior ambo told Andy.

'Neither do we—it just doesn't keep well—but we do have an O Group donor. And hopefully she's on her way here.'

Ellie walked in at that moment.

'Blood?' she guessed, and he nodded.

'I have to find the wound and do what I can to stem the flow,' he explained, 'so could you find one of the nurses with training to take yours? Just one bag to start off with, and stay lying down when it's filled. No heroics, understand?'

Ellie grinned at him, and walked out.

Andy released the tourniquet the ambulance men had put on the lad's upper right arm, and sighed when he saw the gash about five centimetres above the thumb and the spurt of blood when he released the pressure. The cut had gone deep enough to catch the radial artery.

He put a new pressure pad on it and wrapped it tightly, retightening the tourniquet while he found what he'd need for the repair.

In a child, the blood vessels were tiny, and in the city the repair would be a job for a micro-surgeon, but out here you did what you could. Particularly when there was no time to wait for the flying ambulance or even the flying doctor service.

Not that they'd have a micro-surgeon on board...

But in truth he liked the challenge to his skills that working in a fairly remote country hospital provided.

By the time he returned, the boy had been cleaned up and dressed in a hospital gown, ready to be transferred to their small operating theatre. In there, Andy had already set up the instruments he'd need, including the extremely expensive magnifying glasses most small hospitals didn't carry.

They'd been a present from Ellie when they'd moved up here.

Just in case, she'd said, and he'd had to use them several times, repairing delicate tissue.

And far from resting for a few minutes after donating her blood, it was Ellie who met him in Theatre, carrying the bag of blood she'd just had drained from her.

Back in the city, blood of the same type was mixed so recipients and donors rarely knew each other, but out here where fresh blood could take four hours to reach a patient if it had to be flown from the nearest city, having an O group donor—the universal group that mixed with all other blood—on hand was priceless and often could be life-saving.

Best of all, the blood had been collected in an approved blood collection bag, which held the appropriate amount of anti-coagulation chemicals, so it was safe to use immediately.

'Did you also bring a filter line?' he asked, unable to help grinning at her.

'Of course,' she said. 'And if you're doing a repair on a tricky little blood vessel you'll need help, so there's no point in my lying around resting.'

'We might need more blood,' he said, serious now.

'Well, I've got plenty more,' she assured him. 'Let's get this show on the road!'

CHAPTER SIX

THE WOUND TO the radial artery was more a nick than a slice, and the uneven nature made it harder to repair as one wrong stitch could close off the artery completely.

Ellie watched as Andy used the finest gauge needles, and thread as fine as a spider's web, to delicately join the torn edges. He was so careful, so precise with his microscopic stitches that she wondered why he'd never considered a career in surgery.

But it would have meant a different life—mainly a city life—and Andy would have had to steer his registrar jobs in that direction almost as soon as they had become fully qualified.

But Africa had called to them. Films they'd seen of the colour and the vibrancy of the people had attracted them, and the knowledge that doctors were badly needed in many parts of the big continent had sent them in that direction.

They'd always seen their work in war-torn African countries as a kind of gap year—an adventure as well as a chance to hone their skills in often impossible situations.

It had been good training, too, for work in remote areas back home—their ultimate aim—where you couldn't just phone a specialist already in the hospital to pop down to the ED to see a patient.

But when she had failed to get pregnant, they'd stayed

on in the city, Andy keen to try IVF, more keen than she'd been in the beginning.

Deep down she knew he'd always had this dream of reliving his happy childhood by living and working in a country town, bringing up a horde of kids in a place where life was not too hectic.

They'd known the facts and figures about success rates with IVF, but like most hopeful couples had been sure theirs would be a lucky, first-time success. And when it hadn't been, trying again had seemed the natural thing to do, and so it had gone on...

Ellie pushed the thoughts away and concentrated on her job.

Acting as Andy's assistant, she had to keep the small wound clear of blood so he could see the artery at all times. When he'd tied his last knot, she held her breath, praying the stitches would hold when the tourniquet was released.

'Done!'

Andy gave a fist pump in triumph when no leakage appeared, then bent his head to piece together the wound itself.

'I'll need to repair the tendon,' he muttered under his breath, and seeing how the pale sinewy strand had shrunk back into itself, Ellie knew it would be nearly as difficult as fixing the artery.

Now her job was to ease one end of the cut tendon out from the mass of bone and muscle into which it had retreated, straining it towards the end Andy was pulling from the other side.

Using forceps, she finally held both sides together, while, working slowly and meticulously, Andy joined the two ends, then finally cleaned and closed the wound.

'BP's still low,' Andrea told them as she began to reverse the anaesthetic.

Ellie glanced at the bag of blood that hung by the boy's side.

Nearly empty.

'Do you want more or will you use FFP?' she asked Andy, aware that the hospital had a store of fresh frozen plasma.

'He's only small so FFP should do it,' Andy replied.

'Which means you get to keep your blood,' Andrea said, and Ellie smiled at her, aware they were all feeling relief that the operation was over, although the risk of infection would still be alive in everyone's mind.

'Do we know who he is?' Ellie asked, having missed the introductions while she was giving blood.

'Kid called Logan Grant,' Andrea explained. 'Dad's a miner. Mum hated the country—she lasted about a month after he took the job out here. The family had barely settled in before his wife headed back to the city.'

'Leaving Logan behind?'

'He's not the only one. There are three kids in his family and I know of at least one other family where it's happened, although in that one the wife went off with another miner, so it broke up two families. It's becoming the way we live these days, especially out here in the bush.'

It's not the way I live, Ellie was about to say, when she realised her situation wasn't so different. Okay, so she and Andy didn't have children to consider, but if they didn't have the tie of the house and the responsibilities of the positions they'd taken, would they both have stayed?

Would *she* have stayed?

More to the point, *could* she have left Andy?

Andrea was taking Logan through to the small recovery room, and Ellie and her thoughts followed Andy into the changing room.

'Would you have taken off back to the city if it wasn't

for the house and job?' Andy asked, shocking her with the
words that were echoes of her own thoughts.

'No!' she said, and only just stopped herself saying, *I
love you*, because at the moment she wasn't sure how he'd
take such a declaration.

Even after the kiss—kisses—they'd shared…

'Me neither,' he said, stripping off to reveal more of his
strong, lean body than she'd seen for ages, before disap-
pearing into the shower.

Ellie stripped off her theatre gear and used the second
shower. They might have showered together many times at
home, but never at the hospital—any hospital—although
she did remember Andy suggesting it once when they'd
been courting…

Were they courting now? Could starting over be called
courting?

Wasn't that what she was…not exactly planning but
working towards?

And was it in Andy's head as well? After all, not only
had his arm been around her shoulders earlier, he had definitely kissed her on the veranda!

She could still feel the thrumming in her veins the second, harder kiss had caused…

If Chelsea hadn't suddenly appeared—

But she had, not that it stopped Ellie thinking of the
kisses now, or hoping there'd be more before too long.

Andy was gone by the time she left the shower—the
hospital had its own bore for water, so she sometimes
sneaked a little extra shower time when she was there.

Would Andy still be at the hospital?

In with Logan perhaps…

Ellie made her way to the recovery room. There was
no sign of Andy but Logan was just waking up, while his
devastated teenage babysitter sat beside him.

'I need to get back to the girls,' she said. 'I left them with a neighbour but they'll play up with her and they'll be worried about Logan, but his father's not off shift.'

Ellie held up her hand to stop the flow of words.

'I'll stay with Logan,' she said, taking the child's hand in hers and giving it a little squeeze.

'That okay, Logan?' she asked, and the lad smiled.

The babysitter left and Ellie asked Logan about his family and school, pleased he was becoming more coherent as he answered.

'Am I in trouble?' It was his turn to ask a question.

'Maybe a little,' she said.

'Poor Dad,' he said. 'He'll think it's his fault, what with Mum going and all of that.'

'Why did you do it?' Ellie asked, sensing Logan was ready to talk.

'I'd seen the safe there when I had to get a tetanus shot last year and I thought there'd be money in it, and if I got some money then Mum might come back in time for Christmas.'

He made it sound so simple it made Ellie's heart ache.

'Love doesn't always work that way,' she said, gently stroking the boy's cheek. 'But it was a nice idea. And if you want to earn some money, I've got a garden that's getting far too overgrown for me to cope with. You could come over after school a couple of afternoons a week to pull out weeds and I'd be happy to pay you.'

Logan grinned at her.

'I'd like that,' he said, then slipped into sleep.

Would he remember this plan in the morning?

It didn't matter, Ellie could contact him.

But as her husband came in to check on his latest patient, she was wondering how love *did* work.

'Logan seems to be doing well,' Andy said, his hand

dropping to rest on Ellie's shoulder, sending messages—of love?—shooting along her nerves. 'His blood pressure is back to normal, and his heart rate down.'

'He was lucky the babysitter realised it was serious.'

'The main thing is we got him in time,' Andy reminded her. 'He's going to a ward now, so I'll walk you home.'

As they left the hospital, his hand brushed hers, and as the electricity from that casual touch shot through her body, she realised it hadn't been so casual a touch because now his fingers were tangled with hers.

They were hand in hand.

'Is it better if we don't talk?' he asked quietly. 'I think talking hurt us both too much.

'I've been thinking the same thing,' she whispered back, and his fingers tightened on hers—just briefly—signalling agreement, and something else; the beginning of a thaw...

Although hope seemed brittle—fragile—something one wrong word could break, the warmth of Andy's hand in hers, or hers in his, was sending so many messages leaping along Ellie's nerves that her brain was sizzling with visions of the future they had dreamed of.

Forget leaving Maytown at Christmas. *This* was where she belonged—with Andy by her side...

Childless, but still with a future where they stood together, loved and loving.

'Could get Rangi to take the younger boys and be their coach. He knows more about soccer than I do and if Chelsea would be willing to help him, we'd have a new, younger team in no time.'

So much for sizzling visions!

Andy had probably taken her hand out of habit and didn't fully realise he was holding it.

Well, she had agreed it was better not to talk about their problems...

They'd reached the bottom of their stairs and Andy dropped her hand and peeled away.

'I want to open up the shed and bang around a bit so anything that's crawled in there to live might decide to leave.'

And with that he was gone.

Ellie was in bed by the time he returned, and when Andy slipped through the shared bathroom to look down at her, there was enough moonlight coming through the French doors to see she was deeply asleep.

It had been the nearly full moon that had made him think about kissing her earlier—not the first kisses but the later ones—when they'd walked home from the hospital together. He'd even picked out a spot, tucked against the old camellia at the bottom of the front steps.

The idea was so overwhelming he was sure Ellie could feel his emotion through his fingers, feel his body trembling slightly at the thought of it.

Then, like the idiot he was, he'd started worrying about pushing things too fast, about maybe her not wanting to be kissed. She'd only shifted back upstairs so news of their separation didn't reach his mother while she wasn't well after all. Maybe he'd imagined her wanting those kisses.

So he'd started burbling on about the soccer team, and her hand had slid from his before they'd reached the front gate—let alone the camellia bush!

But as she lay there, beautiful in the moonlight, he knew they had to patch things up.

He wouldn't think about the baby side of things, instead he would work out the best way for them to be together, slowly and tentatively, a bit like when they had first gone out. Even though what he really wanted was to climb into bed beside her and ravish her right now.

Ravish her?

Where *had* that word come from?

Yet when he considered it, it was apt because surely the word covered kisses, and touches, and all the joys of foreplay. It covered kissing as much of her skin as he could manage, running his fingers through her hair, nibbling at the little erogenous zones he knew so well—all that and more—far beyond what might be described as sex…

Ravishment?

He padded slowly back to his own room—the room he'd sought refuge in when he'd walked away from her—unable to stay lest they tear each other to pieces even more and end up too wounded to ever recover what they'd had…

Ellie slept well but rose earlier than usual, anxious to see just how much mess remained in the surgery. But when she made her way downstairs after a swift breakfast of tea and toast, she was amazed at what Zeke and Chelsea had accomplished.

True, there was a piece of chipboard where the window should be, but when she opened it, it was barely noticeable and she'd get someone in to repair it during the day.

But the broken glass was gone, all signs of blood mopped up and, in fact, the floors were sparkling clean.

And in the storeroom, where young Logan had obviously rummaged desperately for something to staunch his blood, the first-aid equipment was once more neatly arrayed, the shelves as tidy as Maureen had left them.

Even the black soot from around the safe had been wiped away.

She'd have to thank them both.

'I came in early because I heard you'd had a break-in and wanted to clean up but you've already done it,' Maureen said, looking around in amazement. 'You must have been up at crack of dawn.'

'Not me,' Ellie told her. 'Zeke, the young policeman, and Chelsea did it all last night while Andy and I were at the hospital with our young burglar.'

'I believe it was Logan Grant.' Maureen said with distinct disapproval. 'He really shouldn't be left on his own when his dad's at work, but although Mr Grant's had any number of women in to keep an eye on him, he outwits them all, and sneaks out to do who knows what mischief.'

'Well, we know where he was making mischief yesterday but maybe now he's learned his lesson,' Ellie said, deciding not to reveal the child's reason for the break-in. 'And if we get him to join the soccer team, he'll have less time for mischief.'

Maureen checked that all was well, then settled down to run through the patient list and send it to Ellie's computer, but Ellie was already out of the door.

'It's Chelsea's first day at school,' she said over her shoulder. 'I want to see that she's okay and has everything she needs.'

Upstairs Chelsea was not only ready—in a uniform someone had found for her—but three of the soccer team, including Rangi, were waiting to take her to school.

'Looks like I'll have my own bodyguard,' she joked. But Ellie could see how pleased she was to have someone with her on that nervous first day.

'I've spoken to Mr Grayson, the head teacher, and as soon as you know who your home-room teacher will be, I'll come up and have a talk to him or her as well.'

'I'll be fine,' Chelsea assured her, coming across the kitchen to give Ellie a big hug. Then she stepped back and studied the woman who'd taken her in. 'I think you're more nervous than I am.'

'Probably,' Ellie admitted, wiping her slightly damp hands surreptitiously against her jeans.

But as she stood on the veranda, waving to them as they trooped away, she wondered just how shaken up she'd have been if it was her own child—hers and Andy's—going off to a new school for the first time.

Given how bad she felt, watching Chelsea leave, she had to admit she'd have been a complete mess, and been one of those mothers who stood outside the school gate, sobbing piteously...

Though these days children were introduced to school early. Most would go to kindergarten or preschool first and from there visit whatever school they'd be attending next.

Good grief! Was she really leaning on the veranda railing, mooning over a child that would never be—worrying about him or her going to school even...

Ellie headed back down to work, where Maureen tutted because she was all of three minutes late for her first appointment.

The morning passed swiftly, allowing her a little time at the end of her appointments to do some necessary paperwork, then phone Madeleine, who would be on lunch, to check on her knee and general health.

'I've made an appointment with Maureen to come in on Wednesday for the other tests you wanted to run,' Madeleine explained. 'I have a half-day off because there's a Year Nine school excursion to the mine, and the boss doesn't want me walking around too much.'

'Are you the Year Nine home-room teacher?' Ellie asked, thinking that's where Chelsea would probably fit.

'Yes, I saw Chelsea this morning, and had her for a maths lesson. I think with some extra work over the summer holidays she can skip straight through to Year Eleven in some of her subjects. She's a bright student, very advanced for her age.'

She paused, then added, 'At least that's what I'm hearing from teachers who've already had her in their classes.'

Andy checked on the few hospitalised patients, and the elderly people who lived in the annexe, as the town was too small for a separate retirement village or nursing home.

He had appointments in Outpatients from ten-thirty, but until then he had far too much time on his hands. Too much time to think about Ellie, and whether they *could* get back together again.

Remembering the kisses they'd shared on the veranda, he guessed she was as desperate as he was to sort something out.

Yet he'd shied away from the kiss he'd planned for the camellia bush.

Afraid he might be pushing things too fast?

Afraid—

What *was* he afraid of?

He couldn't answer that thought, although he realised that, somewhere in his head, he'd written off their marriage—had decided it was over.

He'd hurt the woman he loved with his cruel words, could still hurt her if their conversation in the park was anything to go by.

For a long time it seemed that every word he'd spoken had been a brick in the wall he'd—they'd?—built between them, and he had no idea how to break it down.

Had he stopped loving her?

Andy shook his head as much to clear it as by way of an answer.

Because he knew the answer, and had probably known it all along.

A resounding *no!*

Ellie was in his blood, and bones, as much a part of him as a limb…

He loved her with every fibre of his being, yet somehow they'd pummelled each other with words until they'd had to part before the damage to both of them became more severe.

But now?

He banged his hand on the desk, causing the piles of paperwork to flutter into an untidy mess. The bang had been one of frustration at not being able to see a clear path ahead for the two of them, but the fluttering had reminded him of what he *should* be doing, which was some of the never-ending paperwork that came with the job.

A call from Becky, on duty in the ED, saved him from both useless thoughts and paperwork. There had been a traffic accident at a crossing ten kilometres out of town, and the ambulance was already on its way.

Aware they'd send a status report as soon as they'd summed up the situation, Andy went through to the ED to ensure they were prepared for a number of casualties.

He'd barely walked in when the information came clearly from their radio.

Two vehicles, a sedan and a ute, with three injured and a second ambulance on its way. The police were in attendance.

'This is Ted Buckley, the ute driver,' the ambo said, when Andy met the ambulance to help wheel the patient in. 'He was conscious when we reached him, and he's fretting about his dog. Chris has the dog safe in the police car if he asks again.'

Something in the man's voice made Andy ask, 'And *is* the dog safe?'

'It might have a broken leg. I gave him something to keep him comfortable.'

They'd moved Ted into the ED and onto an examination bed as they'd talked, Andy aware the ambulance would be needed back at the scene.

'Where's Rudi?' Ted demanded, opening his eyes as Andy ran his fingers over the old man's bald head.

'Rudi?' Becky echoed, although Andy guessed he was the dog.

'Me dog!'

'Rudi's fine. Chris is looking after him in the police car.'

'Well, don't let anyone take Rudi,' Ted said. 'Some of the neighbours have been after him for years. Best dog in the area. One of them gets hold of him I'll never get him back.'

The old man lapsed into silence again.

'We'll X-ray his skull just to be sure, but I can't feel any damage. He'd been wearing his seatbelt because there's just the beginning of bruising diagonally across his chest.'

'*And* driving at about ten kilometres an hour, knowing Ted,' Becky said. 'If anyone's badly injured, the other car must have been speeding.'

And if anyone was badly injured he'd probably need to get Ellie back in again.

An image of her as she'd lain in bed the previous night flashed into Andy's head, and remembering the thoughts he'd had then spread warmth through his body. He had to win Ellie back and somehow make their marriage work—no, more than that, make them one again.

They'd have to talk, but this time openly, honestly and carefully so as not to make things worse. If he could explain about the baby, how he felt...

Andy had already spoken to a counselling service and was hoping to find someone he could speak to regularly.

He had to sort himself out before he could really sort out his marriage...

The other accident victims arrived, thankfully having sustained little injury.

The driver had a high ankle injury, probably to the syndesmosis tendon, a tear that would require him walking around in a moon boot for a month but not needing plaster, while the passenger beside him had escaped with nothing more than cuts and bruises. Andy decided to keep them both in hospital under observation in case there was anything more serious.

But there was another victim that had everyone excited, the female nurses particularly. A fine baby girl, maybe five or six months old, kept safe by her state-of-the-art car seat, was looking around the ED with huge blue eyes, apparently up for any adventure that came her way.

'Well, she's the last thing you'd expect those two larrikins to be travelling with,' Becky said. 'I doubt she belongs to either of them.'

'The car seat is top of the range, and her clothing looks expensive, too. Do any of you know the two lads?'

There were head shakes all round, though Becky, who'd lifted the baby from her car seat and was giving her a cuddle, said, 'I agree about the young men's scruffy clothes.'

They all stared at the baby girl, who smiled obligingly at them all, reaching out to grasp some tinsel that hung from the reception desk and drag it towards her mouth before Becky removed it firmly from her grasp.

'She's gorgeous, isn't she?' Andy said, aware that the small mortal was already winning a way into hearts normally hardened by the stresses and sights of the ED.

'She needs changing. There are boxes of nappies in the storeroom at the back of the building,' Becky said, and one of the aides hurried off to find them.

But Andy was transfixed by the child.

She's been in an accident, you should be examining her, a voice in his head was insisting, and although he knew the voice was right, he just knew that she was fine.

Although as Becky began to change her nappy, he finally stepped forward.

'We'd better take a look at her,' he said, and helped Becky peel off the jumpsuit she was wearing.

But the little body was unmarked, no sign of the accident at all.

But as Becky started to dress her again, something struck Andy.

'I know baby skin needs protection but isn't that jumpsuit too hot for her to be wearing on a summer's day? It's more like something she might wear on a cool night.'

Becky stared at their young charge, lying on the now discarded piece of clothing.

'You're right,' she said. 'It *was* cool last night, even out here. Maybe the mother's ill and those lads are taking her to stay with relatives?'

She sounded so doubtful Andy knew she didn't believe that particular scenario for one instant.

'See if you can find a light top for her—even a singlet—then turn on the local radio, see if there's a report about a missing baby,' Andy suggested. 'I'll go and speak to the lads.'

But he had the same reaction from both of them.

'What baby? We don't know anything about a baby! It must have been the old fellow's.'

Realising it was pointless pushing them further, he phoned Chris, who confirmed the baby had come out of the lads' car and it had puzzled him as well.

'They're denying she was in their car, let alone had

anything to do with them,' Andy told him, and heard Chris sigh.

'Well, someone called Lydia Francks is the registered owner of the car, but we can't contact her at the address she gave for her licence. I'll send someone up to question the lads, not that they'd get far out of town without a vehicle. Don't let them go until someone gets there.'

Andy smiled.

'I doubt they'll want to go,' he said. 'We stripped off their clothes to examine them properly and they're both wearing very fetching hospital nightgowns.'

He heard Chris's answering laugh.

'I do hope they're the ones that are open all down the back.'

But as Andy made his way back to the two newest admissions to check their clothing had been removed from their rooms, his mind was on the baby.

Someone *had* to be missing her.

And she must have been in a car somewhere, given that she was still in her car seat...

Surely she couldn't have been left in a car park? At this time of the year, even a short time in a locked car could kill a young child, the summer heat baking the interior to over fifty degrees centigrade.

She was happy so she was presumably not hungry. Had they fed her something or had she been fed just before they had taken her?

He checked the young men's clothes had been bagged and passed to the ward secretary, not back to the owners. And much as he'd have liked to question the two himself, he knew that Chris or one of his men would have far more expertise in that area than he had, even though questions were a huge part of his job.

He had appointments in Outpatients, yet was drawn

back to the ED, where Becky was now cuddling the baby as she fed her a bottle.

'Good thing we keep baby formula in stock,' she said, as the baby broke off her noisy guzzling to bestow a milky smile on Andy.

It made his heart hurt and he hurried away.

No more. Never again.

The words were like a mantra as he strode through the hospital on his way to the people waiting for him.

CHAPTER SEVEN

ZEKE BROUGHT THE dog to Ellie's surgery during what would normally be her lunch hour.

'They're busy at the hospital with the three accident victims and the baby, so I thought you might be able to take a look at Rudi. Ted just adores this dog, and he'd hate anything to happen to him.'

He was carrying the mildly sedated dog gently in his arms, and while Maureen scolded about hygiene and being a doctor's surgery, not a vet's, Ellie ran her fingers over the dog. With no vet in town, she'd known she might come up against injured pets, but this dog was her first. She'd grown up with dogs, so had a fair knowledge of broken limbs and battered heads, but Rudi, as far as she could see and feel, was fine.

Until she pressed his left rear foot, and he snatched it away with a yelp. Lifting it more gently this time, she examined the pad for a tear or a foreign object lodged in it, but could find no damage. Was it the joint?

Tentatively, she moved the foot, and this time Rudi had recovered enough to growl at her.

'I think I'll just bind it reasonably tightly and we'll see if he can put weight on it. Can you hold him while I do it?'

She was pleased when Zeke nodded, because she really

didn't fancy putting Rudi on her examination couch, no matter how many sheets of paper she'd spread beneath him.

'Tell me about the baby,' she said to Zeke, as she worked to stabilise the ankle.

Zeke shrugged his shoulders.

'She was in the back of the sedan that ran into Ted. Two young lads—the driver and a passenger—both denying any knowledge of a baby in a very smart safety seat in their vehicle. They're lying, of course. From the baby stuff we found in the car—bottles and formula—at least one of them had enough gumption to realise she'd need to be fed.'

'A car theft and they didn't realise the baby was there until it was too late?' Ellie guessed. 'But someone must be missing her.'

Ellie led the way outside so they could try Rudi on his legs.

'You'd think so,' Zeke told her, as he gently put Rudi on the ground, keeping a firm hold on his collar in case he took off.

Rudi moved cautiously, but within minutes was using all four feet.

'Now, what do we do with him?' Zeke asked.

'Well, we don't have a proper fence here so maybe he could go in one of your nice cells, just until his master is sorted at the hospital.'

Zeke smiled at her, and bent to gather the dog into his arms again, carrying him over to the police car and strapping him into the back seat.

'Thanks!' he said, then seemed to hover by the car, eventually coming out with what was bothering him.

'Does Andy want any older players on his soccer team, or perhaps someone to help with things?'

Ellie beamed at him.

'I'm sure he'd be delighted to have you. As far as I can see, it's a kind of "the more the merrier" situation.'

Ellie stood there as he drove away. Was his interest in soccer or Chelsea?

Not that it mattered, but she'd keep an eye on things.

She was turning to go into the house when a council truck pulled up across the street, men and ladders tumbling out of it.

'It can't be that close to Christmas!' she wailed as she watched the men begin their decorating.

But looking further down the street, she saw that Christmas decorations were already up, all the way to town—and hadn't she seen some at the hospital?

Christmas had sneaked up on her without her realising it. One year ago, they had spent the day with her family, a boisterous reunion of siblings, aunts, uncles and her one remaining grandparent.

She had been due to start IVF in the New Year, and was imagining another Christmas—the next one—perhaps with them as a family of three...

She had to stop thinking about it, and the memories that caused so much pain. Yet weren't the memories what kept Andy and her together? Weren't they the reason she knew she wanted to put things right between them again?

Logan had thought money might bring his mother home for Christmas, but wasn't it love that cemented a marriage and kept it strong?

And she knew she still loved Andy and was almost certain he loved her, so how could they bridge the gap between them?

At least they were getting closer, holding hands, kissing even...

And as memories of that last kiss they'd shared sent

shivers down her spine she knew that, come what may, they *had* to heal the rift.

She knew she'd started the argument that had led to the final straw for Andy with the suggestion of one last go at IVF, but why had it escalated?

Had she been too stubborn about it?

Was she still aching to hold her own child in her arms?

Ellie tried to push the thought away but a spark of it must have remained that she finally walked up the stairs and into the house, rubbing at the frown line she knew was on her forehead.

But if she wanted Andy—and she knew now just how much she *did* want him—then she had to accept that it would never be.

She had to kill that spark of hope that still nestled deep inside her, and get on with her life.

She'd reached the veranda before she realised she was supposed to be at work, so back down the stairs she went, dead-heating at the door with Andy, who was holding a beautiful baby in his arms.

Was this the baby Zeke had mentioned?

'I've admitted two cases of measles to the hospital this morning so she can't stay there,' Andy was saying as he handed her the baby. 'Do you think that you and Maureen could keep an eye on her? Chris's wife went down to Croxton for last-minute Christmas shopping and there's really no one else even semi-official. I'll just get her car seat.'

The baby girl was sound asleep, as angelic as only sleeping children could be.

'But—' Ellie began, and realised she was speaking to space as Andy had dropped the car seat and a bag containing nappies, bottles, and formula on the floor and was already gone.

'*Can* we cope?' she said to Maureen, the weight and

warmth of the infant feeling so right, Ellie knew that killing that spark of hope she'd been thinking about only minutes earlier might prove impossible.

'While she sleeps, I suppose we can,' Maureen replied a trifle tautly.

'Well, Chelsea will be home from school before long, so I guess we can manage until then.'

Andy drove back to the hospital in the police car he'd borrowed to deliver the baby. His chest felt tight and his stomach knotted. The sight of Ellie with the baby in her arms had awoken all the stuff he'd been desperately trying to put behind him.

She'd looked so right, and natural.

He tamped down the panic that thought brought with it, and the pain that he'd thought he'd conquered. He closed his eyes and tried to see ahead to their future, his and Ellie's, when they were back together again.

He remembered the kisses they'd shared. The passion they'd known was still there, he knew that much, he just had to—

What?

Tell her how he'd felt? How much it had hurt? Still hurt?

Did he blame her for not knowing—not seeing it for herself?

Hardly, when she'd been so grief-stricken and racked with blame that hadn't been hers at all...

But now things were easing between them, maybe they could talk about that time without the emotion that had ripped them apart.

If only they could talk, and touch, and ease their way back into the love he knew was still there between them...

Chris's voice came through the vehicle's radio. There

was still no lost baby alert, and no idea as to who she could be.

But the baby wasn't Andy's problem. Chris could deal with that. His focus, apart from work, had to be on Ellie, and their future.

He'd just pulled into the hospital car park when his phone rang. It was Ellie.

Chris brought the news that the baby had been identified. Her nanny had been found and had admitted she'd put the baby in the car to drive her around for a while to get her to sleep, then stopped at a corner store for cigarettes, leaving not only the baby but the keys in the car.

The temptation had been too great for the two lads. They'd got a lift down to the coast with a friend, and right in front of them was a car, keys inside, just waiting for them.

Although they'd gone a fair distance before they'd realised they'd had a passenger, and then only when she'd cried.

One of them now admitted having younger siblings and knew enough to assume the baby was hungry so they'd stopped in Croxton, gone to a chemist and bought a bottle and some baby formula, fed the baby and, for lack of any other idea, driven on.

Undaunted by this lack of a plan, they'd told themselves they were doing the baby a favour as she shouldn't have been left in the car in the first place—everyone knew that children could die in hot cars...

From that point on their stories varied. They were taking the baby to the nearest police station when they had the accident, or were turning to go back and leave the car where they'd found it. Either way, the baby remained safe.

'But what happened to the nanny?' Ellie demanded, as

Chris was explaining all of this to her, Andy and Chelsea, who was now back from school and delighted by the baby.

'Well, she was too frightened to admit that she'd lost her charge so she ran off to a friend's house. It was the friend who convinced her to contact the police and the parents.'

'She'd have panicked, that's only natural,' Ellie said. 'But at least she did the right thing in the end.'

'Anyway, the parents are on their way. They should be here in a couple of hours,' Chris told them. 'Are you okay to keep her here?'

Andy smiled at him.

'I think you'd be hard pushed to get her away,' he said, nodding to where Chelsea now rocked the baby in her arms.

But when Chris left to get back to work, Andy suggested they put the baby into her car seat to sleep.

'Babies can get very heavy when you're holding them for a long time,' he added, smiling at Chelsea, who nodded but let go reluctantly, watching to see Andy carefully secure the little one in her seat, talking quietly to her as he did it, although she was asleep.

And with the job finished, he stayed there, squatting in front of her and reaching out to run a finger down her cheek, and touch her tiny hand.

'I've got homework,' Chelsea announced, when they were all happy that the baby had slept through the move.

'And I could do with a cup of coffee,' Andy said, straightening up and walking swiftly away from the distraction. 'I have to go back to the hospital, but it's been such a weird day I feel a need a break to catch up with myself.'

'Sit down and I'll get it,' Ellie told him, and as she pottered around the kitchen, turning the machine on, getting out mugs, she felt more at ease with Andy than she had for months.

'So, what was *your* impression of Chelsea and the baby?' Andy asked, the question so unexpected she needed a moment to process it.

'Well,' she began cautiously, 'it could just be normal teenage girl reaction to a baby. With all the hormonal stuff going on inside them, I think that's only natural.'

'You don't sound too sure,' Andy said, smiling at her teasingly, because he knew she was usually definite in her opinions.

'I'm not,' she admitted, 'and neither, I imagine, is Chelsea. It's probably created all kinds of emotions inside her, and raised so many doubts and issues in me, so I hope her homework is very difficult, and absolutely has to be done for tomorrow.'

She sighed.

'We might talk about it over dinner,' she suggested, and Andy nodded, finished his coffee, and stood up.

'Lacking any very difficult homework, I'd better get back to work.'

And just like that he left, Ellie staring after him, puzzling over his words.

Could he really be saying he'd felt something in his heart as he'd held the baby, secured her safely in her seat and knelt in front of her for those extra minutes…?

A longing?

Or just sadness?

Ellie knew she was frowning.

Ellie went down to the surgery to check on the next day's patients and finish off some paperwork. She really had to get Chelsea in for an ultrasound sometime soon, and suspected she was putting it off as it was going to make the baby more real to both of them.

And for all she told herself that Chelsea was just a patient like any other, she couldn't help but feel connected to the new life growing inside their guest.

Was she jealous?

She didn't think so.

Just uneasy, somehow...

'Forget it!' Ellie muttered to herself, checking the appointments book on the computer and putting Chelsea down for a scan after school the following Monday. 'Think about Andy instead!'

And this second order made her smile, although there was definitely a little flutter in the region of her heart.

She was saved further speculation by the sounds of arrivals, as at least two vehicles pulled up outside.

She slipped out of the surgery, locking the door behind her, in time to hear a man saying in a determined voice, 'And just where are these so-called lads? I'll need their details. I'm going to sue them, you know. Get them for the pain and torment they've caused Melissa and I.'

'Melissa and me,' Ellie corrected beneath her breath, already disliking this pompous man who, as far as she was concerned, definitely didn't deserve such a beautiful daughter.

'The law will take care of the lads,' Chris said firmly. 'It's the baby you'll both be wanting to see.'

'She's just upstairs,' Ellie said. 'I was going to give her a quick sponge over before you came. It's been a hot, dusty day.'

Andy arrived from the hospital at that stage, full of his usual good cheer.

'I'll do that,' he said. 'Now, come on up, you'll be anxious to see her.'

The newcomers followed, and even when they arrived in the living room and saw their daughter safe and sound—

in her car seat—the only reaction from the mother was, 'Why is she wearing that old singlet?' although she did go and kneel by the chair and kiss the forehead of her sleeping child.

'It was all we had at the hospital that was cool,' Andy said.

'Did you bring clothes for her?' Ellie asked.

Both shook their heads.

She paused, and Andy, only half-aware of what she might be about to say, held his breath.

'I've got some clothes you can have for her. In fact, if Zeke wouldn't mind going back to the hospital for more formula, you could bath her and change her here, then feed her and she should sleep on the trip back.'

'Leave the bath to me,' Andy said, aware that the offer of clothes must have caused Ellie enough pain and wanting to distract any attention from her.

'Well, I suppose as a doctor you can do this kind of thing,' the father said, and Andy had to close his lips on the retort that most men could do it.

'Actually, I'm happy to do it,' he growled. 'Babies are great.'

Zeke had disappeared on his errand and Ellie had also left the room, but he knew where she'd be, and knew what clothes she'd find for the baby.

He followed her into the small room off the side of the room Ellie used. Thank heavens they had been too busy settling in to decorate it in preparation for *their* baby. It was bad enough that it still had a small chest of drawers, filled with baby clothes and gifts from friends and relations when they'd left the city…

Ellie had the second drawer open and was running her fingertips over the contents.

'It's a good thing we've got intelligent friends so we

were given clothes in every size from preemie to two years old.'

He could hear the battle she was having to keep her anguish out of her voice.

Andy came fully into the small room and wrapped his arms around her, holding her tightly, feeling the tension drain from her body as tears she'd tried to hold back slid down her cheeks.

'It will be all right,' he whispered against her hair. 'We'll work things out. You know I love you—I always have and always will—the rest's just been a distraction.'

She looked up into his eyes, her own pinkened by her tears.

'You really believe that?'

He tightened his grip on her, and kissed her lips, the softness of them startling his nerves and tightening his body.

'You know I do,' he said against them, and felt her mouth open, her tongue touch his, electrifying every cell in his body.

'We should get going,' she whispered to him, when it seemed they'd stood like that for an age.

'We probably should,' he said, but he continued to hold her, just a little longer, while all the memories of the passion they'd shared welled up in their bodies until the effort of breaking apart was one of extreme willpower.

'Later!' he murmured in her ear, then he wiped the tears from her cheeks and took the tiny garments from her as she lifted them carefully from the drawer.

'I'll get some warm water to sponge her down,' she said, her voice shaky but determined. 'And a couple of towels.

Glad to have something to do, Ellie hurried to get what Andy would need, depositing the towels and water on the coffee table, spreading one towel so Andy could put the baby on it.

Aware that her eyes would be red and tears not far away, she then retreated, going into the kitchen and staring unseeingly into the fridge because she was fairly sure she should be doing something about dinner.

But the feel of Andy's arms around her, the hardness of his body as he'd held her close, stayed with her, stirring her senses and tightening her body.

She was still staring at the meagre contents of the fridge when Chelsea breezed into the kitchen.

'Is it okay if Zeke takes me to the Thai place for dinner? A few of the soccer team are going. Someone's birthday, I think.'

'As long as you're home by ten,' Ellie said, glad to be distracted from the tumult of her body. 'It's a school night, remember.'

'Yes, Mum,' Chelsea teased, and she slipped away, pausing as she passed the living room to call out, 'Goodbye, baby!'

Ellie closed the fridge and sat down at the kitchen table, resting her elbows on it, with her head in her hands. She heard the sound of movement and knew the unwanted guests were departing, but she felt no obligation to speak to them again, so she was still sitting there when Andy returned to announce that everyone was gone.

He slumped into a chair opposite her.

'I can't believe that was so hard,' he said, staring up at the ceiling.

'The baby?'

He nodded, then turned to her, reaching out to take her hand.

'And I can only imagine what you felt, taking that little outfit out of the drawer and handing it over. Your baby's clothes—*our* baby's clothes. Oh, Ellie, darling, it's been one shit of a year, hasn't it?'

He stood up now, and walked around the table to pull her to her feet, take her in his arms, hold her tightly.

'I thought my heart would break back then.'

The words startled Ellie so much she couldn't speak, only hold him as close as he was holding her.

'I didn't know,' she whispered. 'I didn't know how you felt. I was too wrapped up in my own misery to even think about the man I loved.'

'Well, at least you knew you still loved him—me,' he whispered, 'at times I even wondered about that.'

'Oh, Andy, what a mess we've made of things—I've made of things. I was so exhausted, so lost, but I should have made time for you.'

'No, you were right the first time—*we* made the mess—and it's understandable when you think about how traumatic it was for us at the time.'

She raised her head and looked at him, at the face she knew so well, the dark eyes smiling quizzically at her, the love he felt for her there, shining in them.

'Take me to bed, Andy?' she said quietly, and he turned with his arm around her shoulder and slowly and silently they walked through to the bedroom.

By which time Ellie was shaking so badly she wasn't sure she'd manage to take off her clothes, but Andy, who seemed to have similar tremors, somehow managed to get them both naked. In a matter of moments they stood, running their hands over each other's bodies, learning them again through touch, then taste as their lips met, desperately seeking each other, teeth clashing, tongues twining, lips moving over skin now—

'Bed?'

Andy breathed the word into her ear, and within minutes their hunger for each other had them joined in a frantic coupling, murmurs of love and pleasure providing a soundtrack to their passion.

They lay spent, their bodies still entwined, remembering the feel of skin on skin, the cries of their release; remembering how things used to be…

And could be again?

Ellie smiled, knowing it not only could but would.

'Hungry?' Andy asked, and when she nodded sleepily against him, he eased away and she heard him rattling around in the kitchen. She was half-asleep when he returned, bearing a tray with two small but perfect omelettes on it, cutlery for two, two wine glasses, and a bottle tucked under his arm.

It was if the last few months had never been—as if it was only yesterday Andy had cooked an omelette for her, and brought it to her in bed.

They talked of the weird day they'd had, of Ted Buckley, and Rudi the dog, about everything but the baby and the clothes she had worn as she'd left the house.

Then sleep overtook them both, but it was deep and dreamless, their bodies still curled together, once again…

But as the dawn chorus of the magpies and butcher birds woke them, to a pink sky announcing the coming dawn, they turned to each other, and slowly, languorously made love again.

Taking their time to learn each other again, prolonging the passion that built between them until it consumed them in a fiery blaze of lust and left them sated, exhausted on the sweat-drenched sheets, with no words for this reunion—this miracle of love returned…

CHAPTER EIGHT

COULD IT REALLY have been so simple? Ellie wondered a week later. Could she and Andy have slipped back into their old passionate relationship so easily?

Even thinking about what happened in bed excited her, sending warmth flooding through her body and desire tautening her nerves.

At work, she had to concentrate to put thoughts of Andy right away, but not as far away as they had been…

She took the tests Madeleine would need for the specialist in Sydney, arranging for her to get copies of the results. She scanned Chelsea's bump but didn't reveal the sex of the baby, something Chelsea had decided she didn't want to know.

Work was less busy as people prepared for Christmas. The stores along the main road were bright with lights, each trying to outdo each other with their Christmas decorations.

But the phone call from the local newspaper was totally unexpected.

Would she please judge the decorated houses? They had prizes for the best house and the best street, where neighbours got together to light up the skies with Christmas cheer.

'I'm not sure I'd be up to that,' she told the young man who'd phoned her.

'It's simple,' he said. 'The other Mrs Dr Fraser always did it. The judging is tomorrow night. I can pick you up at seven if that's okay?'

Tomorrow night?

Andy came home as she was frowning over this latest assignment.

'I've got to judge the best decorated house,' she told him, and he laughed.

'It's easy, Mum always did it. She reckoned the winner always stood out.'

'Oh, yeah? Well, I think I'd better have a practice run tonight. Will you come with me?'

'If you really think it's necessary.'

Andy was hardly enthusiastic, although when they finally set out, Chelsea having joined them, it turned into a riotous affair, with all of them choosing different houses, then changing their minds about it when they saw the next one.

The decorations were unbelievable. Santa rode his light-festooned sleigh across one rooftop, and was clambering down a chimney on another. In some gardens he'd be surrounded by his elves, all animated so they seemed to be making toys, while others were more a light and sound show with Christmas carols playing against lights that changed and seemed to dance with the music.

Even the mine was decorated. Although some kilometres out of town, the tall structure that operated the lift was ablaze with coloured lights.

'You're both hopeless and no help at all,' Ellie told them, when they'd completed the circuit of decorated houses for the second time.

But the following night she was glad she'd checked them

out, because it became easier to see who'd put the most work into the colourful spectacles, and she settled on the house with Santa's sleigh on the roof. The sheer effort of getting it and a rotund Santa up there deserved a reward.

But seeing how much effort people put into their decorations made Ellie realise she and Andy had done nothing to decorate their own house. So finally she found the courage to investigate the shed where she knew Andy's parents had left their Christmas decorations, claiming there were far too many for the small apartment they'd moved to at the coast.

Maureen had already decorated the surgery with tinsel and baubles and a small tree, which had all been stored away to be used year after year.

So it was left to Ellie and Chelsea—and Logan, who'd turned up to do some gardening—to decorate the house. Andy was still too involved in shifting people about in his soccer team, or teams as it was now, to be much help. They began on the veranda, stringing lights along the railing and hanging twinkling stars from the posts that supported the roof.

And the air in the house was lighter somehow, warm with love and laughter, the excitement of Christmas an added bonus.

'Chelsea and I are going down to Croxton this afternoon,' Ellie announced at breakfast, on the second last day of the school term. 'It's late-night shopping and she needs some clothes.'

Andy looked across the table at her and smiled.

'And you don't? How long since you've been to that boutique you love down there? Buy yourself something special for Christmas—something from me.'

Far too much in love to be offended by this male attitude to gift-giving, Ellie simply smiled. She'd already done most of her Christmas shopping online, and had even found the perfect gift for Andy—an elaborate watch that could time the practice drills he did with his team and about a hundred other things she didn't understand but knew he would.

Christmas fever was spreading through the town. People were already wearing T-shirts with reindeer heads or snowmen on them, and white pom-pommed Santa hats as they shopped in forty-degree Celsius heat.

And this Saturday would be the town's Christmas parade, which acted as a celebration of the end of the school year as well as being less than a week to go before the big day. The soccer team would be marching in it, most of them now in uniform, although some of the younger newcomers, like Logan and his mates, might have to make do with yellow T-shirts.

Chelsea had made a bright yellow flag and appointed herself to carry it at the head of their group. The 'Maytown Soccer Club' emblazoned across it would be held proud for all to see.

When they were in town Ellie did visit the boutique in Croxton, finding there a lovely, slinky, satin nightdress in a soft oyster colour that felt so sexy on that she blushed in the changing room.

But as she slipped into it that night, she wondered if she should have kept it for Christmas night, and made *it* the gift from Andy.

But the glow of physical love and satisfaction had her in its thrall. Everything was going so well—they were Andy and Ellie again, at one with each other, their love as strong as ever.

Maybe even stronger?

So she wanted to feel the tempting garment on her—for him to see it on her—to have him take it off…

'Is this my Christmas present to you?' he asked, smiling as she twirled in front of him later that night, the soft material clinging to every curve of her figure.

'No,' she whispered, 'it's mine to you.'

She put her arms around him, kissed his lips, then said, 'Stand still.'

And slowly, teasingly, she removed his clothes, pressing kisses against skin as it was bared, trailing her fingers over the body she knew so well.

They made love slowly, hands and lips exploring, until a single touch from Andy's finger sent Ellie spiralling into space, her body still tingling as Andy entered her, and teased her into another climax, matching it to his own.

And afterwards, lying on their sides, facing each other, Ellie traced his profile with her finger, traced his lips, his ears, the little whorl in his hair above his left eyebrow…

This was how life was meant to be—hers and Andy's. Surely now they could go on as they had begun, not only in love but in tune with each other. They could share their work and their interests—well, she'd go to *some* of the soccer games—but working together they could offer so much to the community, while their own lives would be enriched by their participation in it.

And just perhaps…

She was so filled with happiness, so in love with this man, that it seemed only natural to speak about a thought that had occurred to her earlier today.

'Do you know?' she began in a drowsy, satisfied voice. 'I hadn't realised until today but this week has probably been a very fertile time for me. Though I can't be sure— you know how irregular I am. Do you think, after all these years and the IVF and everything, we could be lucky enough for it to happen just like that?'

But Andy was out of bed before she'd finished her

question, grabbing at his shorts, hauling them on, his face ablaze with anger.

'You seduced me! You tricked me! Take me to bed, Andy, you said, when all along you knew how I felt about another baby—all along you knew I couldn't go through that again.'

He snatched his pillow from the bed and marched away, through the en suite bathroom and back to the other bedroom—the bliss and happiness of the last week dissolving in front of her, his harsh words of blame cutting her heart into pieces…

She didn't cry—couldn't. Perhaps she'd already used up her life's allotment of tears.

Or perhaps the shock and pain was too deep for tears…

She closed her eyes and tried to work out why he had reacted as he had. Yes, he'd said no to more IVF but surely…?

What did he feel about it all that she should know?

Andy had been upset, yes, they both had…

But had she crawled into herself with her misery, wrapping it around her like a cocoon? Had she not shared it, not talked enough with Andy about how he might have been feeling?

Back then Ellie had assumed his 'no more IVF' had meant he just didn't want to go through the whole process again, and, in truth, neither had she. Not really. The drugs had made her feel ill at times, and at other moments the process had seemed so clinical she'd wondered if she could care for a baby conceived this way as much as one she'd carried from day one in her womb.

And while their love-making had left her languid, that feeling had turned to one of devastation.

How could she not have known Andy's feelings about another baby? How could she have simply assumed he was over the IVF process and it was her suggestion of that which had shattered their happiness?

What *did* Andy feel?

And worst of all, how did she not know?

Morning brought no answers. Andy had already gone by the time she reached the kitchen. In fact, Chelsea was ready to leave as well, a watermelon for the final-day festivities tucked under one arm.

'Have fun!' Ellie said to Chelsea, and hoped the words hadn't sounded as hollow as they felt.

But as she worked through the day she knew she couldn't go back to the way things had been recently. She wanted a real marriage or none at all.

She had to talk to Andy.

But Andy was conspicuous by his absence. He was off organising something with the soccer team, Chelsea told her as they ate their dinner.

'There are no games tomorrow because of the parade, but he wanted to sort out how they'd march so they looked professional rather than a rabble.'

'And you're not there?' Ellie asked.

Chelsea smiled at her.

'You know I'm the flag bearer. I know where I've got to go.'

'*And* there are more uniforms,' Chelsea continued. 'The butcher has decided to sponsor us and he donated them— well, him and his customers—he's got a box on his counter collecting money for us.'

'Good for him,' Ellie said, and felt the warmth she kept finding in this small community, the sense of everyone pitching in to help, no matter what.

Could she move away?

She'd talk to Andy, first time she had a chance, and convince him she'd been feeling so happy the words had just come out. She'd apologise for upsetting him and try to get him to talk about whatever he was feeling…

But he was gone again the next morning.

'He's organising off-duty hospital staff to be posted along the parade route,' Chelsea informed her. 'In case anyone faints.'

'Humph!'

Ellie hadn't realised she'd actually let her disbelief out until Chelsea raised her eyebrows at her.

'You'll see him at the parade,' Chelsea reminded her, but a fat lot of good that would do. She could hardly yell an apology at him as he marched past with his soccer team.

Chelsea headed off, and Ellie cleaned up the breakfast things, swept the kitchen, and had a cool shower. It was already hot, and unless she could find some shady spot on the parade route, she was going to get even hotter.

In shorts and a tank top, sandals on her feet, she slapped a wide-brimmed hat on her head and set off, all the anticipation she'd felt earlier for this annual event draining from her.

Ellie wouldn't come, Andy decided as he lined his players up behind the rugby boys and girls. She'd been so excited and he'd virtually slapped her down, killed that happiness he'd seen in her eyes. Damn it all, how could he not explain, not tell her how he'd felt? But remembered pain had torn through his body, piercing his heart and opening up old wounds and the deep black hole and before he'd known it, the words had come tumbling out.

He tried to concentrate on the parade—on what he was supposed to be doing—but in his head he could see the colour leaving Ellie's face, the light dying in her eyes, as he'd rounded on her…

He tried to shut out the memories and think about the parade. Cubs and Scouts, Guides and Brownies led the way, then the rugby lot, his soccer team, a band from the school, and a series of floats and special attractions, including stiltwalkers and dancing girls in parade order all the way down the main street and into the park.

He walked with his team, but his mind wasn't on it, his eyes sweeping the crowd that lined the street.

Ellie still might come…

And even if she didn't, did that mean anything?

She could have had an emergency…

Or he might have ruined things between them for ever.

His gut twisted.

He could hear the yells of delight from the crowd so the fire engine, resplendent in tinsel and balloons, with Father Christmas sitting on his throne on the tank at the back, must have come into view. The yells of delight were probably the fact that he was throwing wrapped sweets into the crowd.

He could hear the cries of the children, and see the smiling faces. It was Christmas, a time of joy, and here he was wondering if he'd ever feel such an emotion again.

Although his heart *did* do its customary flip when he saw Ellie—picked her out fifty metres away—squashed in beside a couple of women he recognised as soccer mums. At least she'd come…

He'd escaped the house early this morning, on the pretext of having to check in at the hospital before heading over to the marshalling ground for the parade.

Deep down he knew he should have stayed and talked and tried to explain to her just how much the loss of their unborn child had hurt him. His counsellor had told him that was the place to start. But how to explain something he couldn't explain even to himself. It was a black hole in his head, with its own black cloud that hovered above him when he remembered that time.

He'd turned his attention back to the team when he saw two figures fly out of the crowd, a man and a woman, the woman middle-aged, the man younger.

He was at the back of the group to hurry along the stragglers so he couldn't see their faces but as they'd now reached Chelsea and had practically strangled her with hugs, he wondered if it could be her family—her mother, who had just been found—and her brother, Harry.

To their credit, his squad barely faltered in their steps, and somehow Chelsea had sorted out the newcomers, who were now marching with her, one each side, beaming at the crowd and giving little waves.

He caught sight of Ellie in the crowd again, waving with all the onlookers.

Was it possible that she'd pulled this latest stunt on him because she really hadn't known what he'd been through when their unborn baby had died?

Andy thought back to that terrible time, to their shock and pain—shared at first, then as the reality had sunk in, Ellie, though exhausted by her grief, had gone back to work, determined not to let her patients and the town down.

Work had become her escape from thinking, as it had for him much earlier.

And, if Andy was honest, how could Ellie have known when he'd found it impossible to talk about—to even think about most of the time…

He couldn't go back to living as they had been, before they'd ended up in the same bed again. They had to talk—just talk this time—without the pain and hurt and harshness that had followed their loss…

* * *

Ellie searched for Andy at the showground, where the parade had ended. A fair had been set up for the children, hot dog stalls, and baked potatoes with a dozen different fillings.

A search of the beer tent, which was only slightly more crowded than the local women's group tent supplying tea, with scones and jam and cream, failed to produce her husband, so Ellie settled for the latter, gratefully accepting the tepid-looking tea as she'd finished the water from the bottle she carried by the time the parade had only been halfway through.

She still wanted to find Andy, to talk to him, but now she'd had her tea and settled down, she realised that somewhere a little less public than these festivities would be more appropriate.

Chelsea had found him first, so when Ellie saw them under a big eucalypt, talking to a young man and a vaguely familiar-looking woman, she wondered if she should interfere.

But Chelsea beckoned her over, her face bright with happiness.

'You'll never guess who came,' she said, almost glowing with pride. 'My mum and Harry. Here they are.'

Ellie looked at them, remembering now how pretty Chelsea's mother was, although it had been years since she'd seen her. And Harry was now a handsome young man.

Jill was effusive in her thanks for them looking after Chelsea, trying to explain what had led her to taking off and leaving her two children behind.

'It was stupid,' she said. 'I've known since before I married Ken that he'd always be off somewhere, worrying about the planet, but this last time, when he left, I felt let down, useless and unnecessary to requirements. The kids were practically grown up and before long they'd be gone, and I began to worry about who I really was if I wasn't a mother or a wife—which is all I'd been for a long time.'

Ellie nodded. Her mother had been much the same when she, Ellie, had left home—cast adrift somehow, until she'd decided to go back to school.

'I do understand,' she said to Jill. 'But at least you're here now, and Chelsea knows you'll be with her through the months ahead.'

'Me, too,' said Harry as Jill hugged her daughter, apologising for all that had happened and promising they'd work things out together.

But Jill was still trying to explain.

'I should never have left! I love my family, I really do, and what made me think I needed more than that—needed something special—I don't know.'

'Probably Dad spending half his life away from us,' Harry said, putting his arms around his mother and giving her a hug.

'Yes, but you both know that when we are together, we more than make up for it.'

Ellie thought of the nights she'd shared with Andy recently and couldn't have agreed more.

Until she'd accidentally spoiled it.

Or had she?

Ellie looked at Andy and read the anguish in his eyes. She touched his arms just lightly, and was pleased when he didn't pull away but actually smiled at her.

'They've driven up from Sydney, so I've asked them to stay, at least for one night, before they drive back,' he said.

And Ellie echoed the invitation, insisting they come to the house now to have a shower and cool off from the heat.

'I'll show them the way,' Chelsea said, linking her arms through theirs, so she had family on both sides.

'I've got to stay a while,' Andy said. 'I don't like leaving the younger ones without a responsible adult with them.'

'I don't blame you for that,' Ellie said as she spied Logan climbing into one of the cars on the octopus ride. 'But, Andy, I do want to say something.'

He met her eyes, but his were cautious. There was none of the warmth and love she'd read in them recently.

'I didn't take you to bed deliberately. I had no idea how you felt about the baby. I just needed you so badly that night, needed your love and your loving. It was only later that I realised, and mentioned it because I thought you'd be happy.'

He stared at her for a moment, then shook his head.

'You have no idea how it made me feel, losing our baby. How much it hurt, the things it killed inside me,' he said, and turned away.

Ellie watched him go.

Was that it?

Was it over?

Did the week they'd just shared mean nothing to him?

The years they'd shared less than nothing…?

That was not happening, she decided. And now at least she had a clue. She'd had no idea how he'd felt—that's what he'd said.

Looking back, she'd known he'd been as upset about losing the baby as she had been, and they'd grieved together.

But had it been more than that to Andy?

Some deeper, more visceral pain that had made him adamant he couldn't go through it again.

And instead of talking properly, instead of listening to

him, learning how he felt, she'd wrapped her own unhappiness around her like a shroud, ignoring him...

And later, she remembered only the cruel words he'd thrown at her and how she'd hit back at him, until they'd had to stop before they'd destroyed each other.

But now?

Why hadn't Andy spoken to her about it during the last week? They'd talked and talked in bed, but about the present, not the past.

About love—not bitterness...

She walked home slowly, uncertain where her husband, or their guests, might be, wanting only to be alone to think, although by now her mind was running around in circles like a demented mouse in an experimental maze.

Every thought led to a dead end.

And how could she possibly work out just what was bothering Andy about the whole baby business if she didn't know what he was thinking?

Didn't know how he had felt, for that matter...

She had a shower, which cooled her off for about ten seconds, then wandered into the kitchen to make dinner for their guests.

She had a leg of lamb in the fridge but the thought of turning on the oven in the already oven-like temperature made her shake her head.

Maybe they should have a takeaway?

She knew her thoughts about what to feed people were irrelevant but thinking about Andy was tying knots in her head so it was infinitely preferable to thinking about him.

Feeling the pain thinking about him caused.

With a huge sigh, she opened the fridge, where she found the stack of T-bone steaks the butcher had pressed on her yesterday. She decided to make a salad, brimful of lettuce and spinach and tomatoes, some avocado and a tin of chickpeas for extra protein.

And later maybe she and Andy could talk…

She could go to *his* room this time.

Excitement that had risen at the thought hit a wall.

What if he rejected her?

Sent her away?

She was letting her imagination run away with her, coming up with all manner of stupid scenarios.

She heard the sound of cars pulling up outside.

She splashed water on her face, aware her last imagined scenario had brought tears to her eyes, and went out to greet their guests.

Apparently, Chelsea had ducked home earlier and put clean sheets on the beds in the rooms on either side of hers, and it was there she led Jill and Harry, with Ellie trailing along behind.

'You'll probably need a shower after your travelling and the heat out here,' she said. 'There are bathrooms off your bedrooms, so feel free. And if you'd like a rest before dinner, that's fine, or you could sit on the veranda outside your room. It will be cooler there and you'll get to see a spectacular sunset.'

'That's true, Mum,' Chelsea said. 'It was like I'd never seen a sunset before until I came here.'

Ellie left them with Chelsea to settle in, covered the big salad with cling film, and set it in the fridge.

She was cleaning up the mess she'd made in the kitchen when she heard a siren, and her heart stood still.

It came from the mine outside town. Her first thought was that it was a practice drill—she'd heard it a few times before—but Ellie really knew it was too late in the afternoon to be a practice drill.

She hurried around the veranda.

'Chels, will you look after your family? Get them drinks and anything else they need. I've got to pop out for a bit. There's a salad in the fridge, and steaks for the barbecue. Can you manage dinner if I'm late?'

She hoped they wouldn't ask about the noise that was still wailing over the small town.

She escaped before they could.

Mine safety was a priority these days, the miners might be trapped, but surely they'd be all right?

Ellie went to the hospital first, which was the rallying point for all medical staff, but one of the ambos saw her and offered her a lift to the mine.

'They say it's bad. Andy's there already and they might need you as well, Doc.'

Ellie climbed into the vehicle, telling herself there were safe places along all the tunnels in the old coal mine— places protected from rock falls, with supplies of water, biscuits, torches and even phone lines to the surface.

Any miners in a tunnel or a shaft could seek shelter there. They would all be safe.

As long as they hadn't been directly under the fall…

The first person she saw was Andy, talking to the shift engineer near the head of the main shaft.

'You don't need to be here.' he said, and she grinned at him.

'Oh, no? And you do?'

'We don't know who we'll need,' the engineer said. 'But it was good of both of you to come. The ambos are busy talking to the relatives of the men who are on shift.'

'Logan Grant's father?' Ellie asked, thinking of the little boy they'd got to know after his father had brought him around to apologise to her, and had since become a nearly constant presence around the house, digging weeds from her garden and teasing Chelsea to distraction but really loved by all of them.

The thought that he might lose his father, as well as his mother, was unbearable…

'We'll go over to the main office,' the engineer said. 'Word will come through to there first.'

But even as they left a cheer went up, and Ellie looked back to see the elevator rising up the shaft, a group of blackened men packed inside it.

Cries and questions rang out, but the on-duty manager herded them all into the washrooms, determined to keep to routine, even at a difficult time.

'Are they all up?' Ellie asked the engineer, who had also stopped to watch the spectacle.

He shook his head.

'We always knew this lot was safe. The fall was further down number five. There were another dozen men working down there.'

Ellie closed her eyes, an unconscious prayer for their safety forming in her mind.

'Have you heard from them?' Andy asked, and the engineer shook his head.

'But that doesn't mean much as the fall could have cut the phone lines and, of course, mobiles won't work that far down.'

He paused then added, 'But remember we have one of the best mine rescue teams in the world and they are already down there, using all manner of equipment to work out the depth of the fall, and setting up listening devices to pick up any voices.'

'How do you know they're the best in the world?' Andy asked, and Ellie had to smile. It was such an Andy kind of question, wanting proof of things people told him.

'Interstate comps, then world competitions, believe it

or not,' the engineer said. 'Our team won the international title three years in a row.'

'Of course,' he added, 'underground mining is fast being phased out. It's nearly all open cut now, and not much of that going on as the power companies have begun experimenting with cheaper, renewable energy options.'

He led them into the office and showed them, on a map on the wall, just where the miners were trapped.

'There's an air shaft just here,' he said, pointing to a windmill-shaped symbol, 'so they should be getting air.'

If they'd made it to the safety bay, Ellie thought, but didn't say, aware everyone was probably thinking the same thing.

Another man approached them, carrying overalls and safety helmets. He helped them into the heavy, fire-retardant overalls, and showed them how to switch on the lamps on their helmets.

Swamped by the overalls, Ellie was bent over, rolling up the legs, when Andy touched her shoulder.

'Let me,' he said, and squatted down, doing a far neater job than she'd been doing.

'Now your arms. Hold them out.'

He rolled up the sleeves, then patted the pocket where she knew from drills the heavy gloves were kept.

'Remember they're there if you need them,' he said sternly, and even though she didn't think she'd be digging through coal and actually require them, she smiled as she thanked him. It was nice having Andy fussing over her...

Once dressed for action, she and Andy stood, a little apart from the professionals, who all appeared to know exactly what they were doing.

So it was a rise in the level of the excitement of the men in the room—the managerial *and* engineering staff—that told them there must be some news.

After some discussion, one of the engineers crossed to speak to them.

'We've found five at the near end of the fall,' he said quietly. 'The men are still digging them out but—'

'We're happy to go down and treat them before they're moved. They'll need to be stabilised at the very least,' Ellie told him, before Andy had time to suggest he go alone.

'If you're sure,' the man said, and although Andy shook his head at her, Ellie nodded.

'This way!'

He led them briskly out of the office towards the elevator that would take them down the shaft. Two of the ambulance crew were already there, carrying their bulging backpacks of emergency equipment and drugs.

The elevator was well lit but even so, what light escaped the cage-like structure was absorbed by the inky blackness outside so it was only when they reached the bottom and walked out into a well-lit, cavernous area that Ellie was able to get an idea of the scale of the operation.

'You should have stayed up top,' Andy murmured to his stubborn wife, as a coal-blackened miner gave orders to the rescuers. 'There's the rescue team, probably all paramedic trained, *and* the ambos—'

'*You* came,' she pointed out, stabbing him in the chest with a forefinger, 'yet you expect me not to!'

He *had* to smile.

'Not *expect* exactly, I just would have preferred, wished, in fact. I hate to think you might be in danger, Ellie, you must know that, for all that's been going on between us.'

He rested his hand lightly on her arm, wanting suddenly to be holding her; for all his anger to be gone, and the two of them be one again.

But he could hardly give her a cuddle in front of this

audience, and after the way he'd reacted to her happy announcement, she'd probably slap him.

But his heart ached for her, whilst his body was tense with concern.

She really shouldn't be here...

Not that he'd win that argument if he raised it. As if his Ellie would have held back when medical assistance might be needed.

His Ellie?

Well, she was and as soon as this business was over he was going to sort it out.

'They're over here,' a voice was saying. 'We've propped the area so it's safe to work there.'

The man who'd spoken led them further into the mine, coming eventually to an area lit now by bright LED floodlights. Five coal-darkened figures lay on the ground. A paramedic was kneeling by one, a miner by another, while one of the ambos took another.

'One each,' Andy said, and reached out to grab Ellie's hand and give it a good squeeze.

He watched as Ellie took the closest man, and moved on to a big fellow whose legs appeared to be still trapped by the fallen rocks. Setting down his medical bag, he pulled on blue nitrile gloves.

'I'm Andy,' he said. 'Can you hear me? What's your name?'

The man nodded to the first question and offered up his name as Jason.

Andy slipped his fingers around Jason's wrist to feel his pulse.

Fast but not too fast.

'I'm going to check you over but, first, are you feeling pain anywhere?'

'Everywhere, mate,' the man said. 'Except my legs. Can't feel them at all. Shoulder's bad, and m'head. Stupid hard hat came off.'

Aware that being able to speak in sentences meant the man's airways must be working, Andy started a search for blood. He probed all around his patient's head, checking his hands for any sign that there was bleeding.

Nothing.

No sign of swelling, and no grating noises suggesting a skull fracture.

He moved on to the shoulder, stripping open the man's overalls to see his skin. Dark with coal but not with blood. But when he lifted Jason's right arm to test his shoulder, a yowl of pain stopped him short.'

'Bloody roof came down on me there,' Jason told him. 'That's when m'hard hat came off.'

Suspecting a dislocation, Andy rested his patient's arm across his chest, and pulled out what was now known as the magic green whistle, an inhaler of methoxyflurane, which would help the pain now and especially when they moved him onto a stretcher to get him out of the cramped tunnel, already filled with too many people.

'Just suck on it. A few sucks will help the pain now and you can use it again when they move you,' he said, aware the device gave metered doses and Jason couldn't hit himself with it all at once.

He continued his examination by feeling down the man's back and onto his thighs.

Here, two miners were carefully lifting lumps of rock from Jason's legs, working with great care in case one wrong move brought more rocks down.

'We should have him out in a few minutes,' they said, 'but we reckon his legs'll be okay because these rocks slid from the main fall, not directly from the roof, so he'll have cuts and bruises, but with luck nothing broken.'

And no major vessel bleeding freely, Andy hoped.

He pulled a pad from his bag and wrote: 'Conscious, query dislocated shoulder, no obvious bleeding.'

He stopped there, because the rescue team was about to remove the last rocks from Jason's feet.

'Can you move your feet?' he asked Jason, who carefully lifted first one foot and then the other.'

'You bloody beauty,' he said to his rescuers, raising his good hand for a high five with each of them.

'Stretcher needed,' Andy called, and two ambos came hurrying over.

Andy added 'Given self-administered methoxflurane' to his note, wished Jason well, and moved over to check the next patient.

'See to the chap who's with your wife,' the paramedic told him. 'This bloke's under control.'

Andy knelt beside Ellie, who had the man's chest bare and was counting down his ribs, a large-gauge needle in her hand.

'Haemothorax,' she said briefly, stabbing the needle into a cleaned patch on the man's chest, then watching as blood and air escaped.

Andy found a catheter and handed it to her so she could slip it in over the needle as she withdrew it. He watched as she taped the little tube securely in place, attached a water seal to stop air entering the tube, and covered it with a light dressing.

'Other injuries?' he asked, as she squatted back on her heels.

'He might have a dislocated knee. He fell very awkwardly. I gave him light sedation before I stuck a needle in his chest so he's not feeling pain at the moment.'

'Are you happy for him to go?' Andy asked, and Ellie nodded, then, as he called for a stretcher, she caught his arm.

'It's no good sending people to the hospital if you're not there,' she said. 'You go back, and at least triage them so you know who will need to be sent to the hospital at Croxton, and who might need to be airlifted out for specialist treatment.'

'But you'd be useful at the hospital, too,' Andy argued.

'Not as useful as I am here,' she said, in a voice he knew would withstand any argument.

CHAPTER NINE

IT WAS CLOSE to midnight before the five safe men had been sent off to hospital, and Ellie wondered what she should do. Those badly injured would be sent out to bigger hospitals, so Andy wouldn't need her help.

Should she go home and feed the visitors, although she guessed Chelsea would probably have done that already. Who'd wait until midnight for their dinner?

And if they'd heard about the mine accident they were likely to be in the crowd she'd heard were clustered around the fence outside the mine.

People with more knowledge than she had would be keeping them updated, so…

'Can you stick around?' a burly miner asked her.

'Of course,' she said. 'What can I do?'

She saw white teeth flash as he smiled at her.

'Right now, not a lot. There's a camp bed through here…' He led the way back towards the lift, to an open, high-ceilinged area with tunnels branching off it.

'This is the nerve centre of the rescue operation now,' he said. 'Grab some sleep while you can. The rescue men are clearing from the top, but they have to drill supports into the roof as they go so it doesn't collapse again. This means it could be some time until we clear the blockage. But the engineers are drilling a smaller hole through the lower part so they can thread a wire through and regain contact with the men on the other side.'

Ellie was pleased to hear he was positive there *were* men safe on the other side.

'Once we've got contact with them,' her informant explained, 'we can find out about injuries. You'd be very useful telling them how to treat their injured, or even just talking to them. A woman's voice, you know…'

His voice trailed away lamely, worrying Ellie because he no longer sounded quite as positive.

'How long have you been down here?' she asked him.

'Eleven hours. I was just coming off shift when it all came down.'

'Then my first advice for treatment is that you go up top, get some food and a hot drink and if you absolutely refuse to go home, at least lie down for a while to rest your body for an hour or two. We don't need any more casualties.'

To her surprise, the man headed off towards the lift. He must have been exhausted.

Although he did turn back halfway.

'And you have a rest, too, lassie. It's going to be a very long night.'

Ellie took his advice, and was surprised to find she had fallen asleep on the camp bed and, in fact, she'd slept quite deeply.

Had it been the rattle of cups and the clunk of huge teapots, the sound of things being unwrapped, and the smell of muffins that had woken her?

Whatever the case, she'd woken in time for breakfast.

Ellie took a short break in the bathroom near the lifts, washing her face and running her fingers through her tangled hair.

'We're nearly through with the communication cable,'

one of the engineers said to her, 'and we'll soon find out how the guys are.'

It still seemed to take for ever for the small hole to be drilled through the fall, but eventually the engineers were able to speak to the survivors on the other side.

'Two injured,' the man on Ellie's end of that fragile wire said. 'One badly.'

'I'm putting the doctor on the line,' she heard him say, then took the old black receiver and held it to her ear, introducing herself as Ellie in response to Dave at the other end.

'It's Eddie,' he said. 'He's lost his hard hat and there's blood all over his face, and he's mumbling at us.'

'It may be less serious than it seems,' she told Dave. 'Head wounds bleed a lot, even from small injuries.'

'Okay!'

'Is he breathing?'

'Yes, and he's got a pulse. We checked that first.'

'Are you in a safety area and if so, what first-aid things have you got?'

'There's a big red box with lots of wrapping type stuff,' Dave told her.

'Something you can use to clean him up? There'll be sterile water in little clear plastic packs. Just rip the tops off them, and wet the cloth and try to clear all the blood from around the wound. Go gently so you don't worsen the injury.'

There was silence for a while, although she could vaguely hear conversation in the background, presumably Dave giving orders to the other men.

'Doing that,' he said. 'It seems the wound is on his head at the hairline above his right eye.'

'Have someone keep pressure on it with a pad of cotton while you feel gently around it. See if there's a lump from the bump.'

'Not much of one.'

'Okay!' Ellie was thinking fast.

'Now run your fingers all over his head, gently but firmly. You're feeling for any movement in his skull or swelling anywhere else.'

Silence as the man felt his mate's head, but Ellie had thought of something that should help.

She turned to one of the men clustered near her.

'Do you have one of the big red first-aid boxes somewhere here?' she asked, and watched as someone ducked away, returning with the box and setting it at her feet.

She opened it up and was surprised at the amount of first-aid equipment in it, the contents listed by number on a sheet of paper inside the lid.

She was checking the contents when a voice said, 'He seems all right.'

'Okay! Now I have a box with me. Do you see the green gauze pads labelled twelve and a rolled bandage labelled twenty-four?'

'Got 'em both,' her new friend at the other end of the line said cheerfully.

'Then use the gauze to cover the wound and keep it there by wrapping the bandage around his head. The bandage is self-adhesive so when you've done a few firm turns just cut it off and it will stick to itself and stay there.'

She waited while Dave gave instructions for the bandage, then said, 'I need you to take his pulse again. Can you time it? Does one of you have a watch with a second hand.'

They must all be able to hear her voice for several voices offered the use of theirs.

'Then count the beats. You need only do it for half a minute then double it to get beats per minute.'

'It's very hard to feel, it's kind of weak.'

'Try the carotid artery just below the angle of his jaw. If you feel around there, you should get it.'

'Tom's got it! He's the fit one of us, he goes to the gym and takes his own pulse all the time to make sure he's alive. He says it's ninety.'

'Not too bad,' Ellie said, trying desperately to picture the situation at the other end of the line.

'Has he any other injuries that you can see or feel?'

'No, we checked that first of all. Just all the blood on his head.'

'Okay, now, is he conscious? Can you ask him his name?'

'He just mumbles. He must hear our questions because we asked him earlier where he hurt and those kinds of things, and made him move his feet and hands, but anything he says isn't making sense.'

Ellie thought she heard a mumbled protest at this stage, but it seemed he'd been lucky, and escaped with nothing more than concussion.

'I want you to keep talking to him, keep him responding even if it's only mumbles. It's probably just concussion from the knock on the head, but don't move him anyway.'

She was about to pass the phone back to the man who'd given it to her when she remembered someone had said there were two injured behind the fall.

'Who's the other injury?' she asked.

'Oh, that's Pete, but he's nearly always injured.'

The men's laughter came clearly through the phone.

'In what way?' Ellie asked.

'Ankle this time! His boot got stuck in the fall and we had to dig him out. We've taken off the boot and bound his ankle up. There's instructions in the first-aid box about bandages and things, and we just did what it said and told him to sit down and shut up his whining while we looked after Eddie.'

'There are painkillers in the box inside a blue plastic box. The ones labelled eight are paracetamol. You could give him two of them, and another two after four hours, but no more than eight in twenty-four hours.

'Yep, I can see them, but he says they're no better than spit and he needs something stronger.'

'You could give him a couple of those to begin with,' Ellie said firmly. 'And if you really believe he needs more pain relief, the tablets labelled ten are codeine and paracetamol, but you're still looking at no more than eight in twenty-four hours, and that's counting the first two.'

'He's grumbling that there should be something stronger. He's saying there should be morphine.'

'There probably is,' Ellie told him, having already found some in her red box. 'But we don't know how he'd react to it, so it's best administered by a doctor.'

'I reckon you're right. We'll keep an eye on him and if he starts to look bad, we'll talk to you about it.'

'Sounds good,' she said, then hesitated for a moment.

'Is Logan Grant's dad with you?' she asked.

'That's me,' a new voice said. 'You're Dr Ellie, aren't you?'

'I am, and I'm very pleased to hear your voice. I'll get on to your babysitter. If she can't manage the kids, they can come to my place. I've got some adults staying there who should be able to handle them.'

'Handle young Logan, you've got to be kidding!' someone said, and Ellie smiled.

'One of my visitors is a six-foot-tall rugby player. Logan might just have met his match.'

'Thank you!' Logan's father said. 'I've been worried to death about them. Our young babysitter is good, but overnight is hard, and Logan runs rings around her even in the daytime. As you know.'

'Well, rest assured they'll be well looked after.'

She checked on the welfare of the rest of the men, then phoned Andy.

'Will you tell Jill to expect the kids? Chris is here somewhere. I'll get him or Zeke to help them pack a few things and take them over to our place. Just warn Harry that Logan needs careful watching.'

'They'll all be okay,' Andy told her. 'I've got some old video games Logan might like to play, and Jill's already getting grandmotherly about Chelsea's baby so they'll be good practice for her.'

There was silence for a moment, before Andy continued, 'Are you all right? Are you still in the safe assembly area?'

Ellie had just assured him she was when a noise like thunder rolled along the tunnels, and she quickly hung up lest Andy hear it and start to worry.

She waited, wondering what had happened, but no one around her seemed particularly alarmed, until someone snapped, 'Hey, watch what you're doing!'

The voice came from one of the men stabilising the tunnel ceiling and it wasn't so much the words as an ominous creaking that had everyone move forward.

'Keep back!'

The sharp command had Ellie backing as quickly as she could, though she could still hear the man in charge, only this time he was speaking on the phone.

'You guys back there—you're all in a safety pod, aren't you? Right in it?'

Affirmative noises came through, and Ellie wondered just what was happening to make everything much more urgent.

The creaking noise had stopped, but somehow the silence seemed much louder.

'What's happening?' she murmured to the man clos-est to her.

'Something's moving and we don't know whether it's this end or the other.'

'Or in another tunnel altogether,' someone offered.

As all but the trapped men were out of the mine, Ellie realised the danger must be to those trapped, hence the questions about where they were.

The rescue team working on securing the top of the tun-nel had retreated towards the group at the lifts, then an-other roaring noise filled the air with dust, which finally settled to reveal a further fall.

The men in charge began discussing what this meant, and as far as Ellie could make out, the prediction was that they would have to work more slowly and it could be an-other two days before they freed the men.

And their fragile telephone link to the men was no lon-ger working.

'We should get you back up to the top,' someone said, realising Ellie was still in their midst. 'Although…'

He paused.

'Although?' Ellie prompted.

'I was thinking of the air shaft.'

'You can't ask a woman to go down that,' one said.

'And a small worker could do it just as easily,' another added.

'But there are injured men in there,' Ellie reminded them, 'and we've only got reports that they're okay. I'm happy to go in that way. After all, it's only two days until they're free, you say. I'll be home for Christmas!'

The group of men moved a little away from her as a furious, whispered argument took place but in her heart she knew she should be the one to go.

Even Andy called her a skinny little runt at times. This was a time when size *did* matter.

'I'll go,' she told them. 'Just tell me what I need to do.'

The whole group was now looking at her.

She smiled at them.

'I'm happy to do it.'

'You'll need a canister of air and a mask over your face. The air vent will be lined with coal dust that'll be everywhere once you disturb it,' one of the engineers told her. 'I'll send a team up to clear the machinery at the top of it. And we'll have you double roped, with one rope attached to a safety harness and another you can stand on as you go down.'

He seemed excited, but worry was creeping into his voice again as he discussed the practical side of things.

'Are you *quite* sure?'

'I am,' she assured them all. 'But I'll need a few things lowered down as well. My medical bag, and perhaps a container of water, and some chocolate as treats for the men. I could go first and you could lower other stuff down to me.'

And although he'd been the one to send the order about removing the machinery from the top of the shaft, the engineer still seemed doubtful.

'What if it's blocked?' he said.

'Then you can pull me up,' she told him, 'but you know it isn't blocked. The men have told us the air is fresh.'

'You're a champ,' someone said, while another man patted her shoulder.

Then everyone was moving, some taking Ellie back to the surface in the lift, and as they did so were discussing the mechanics of what lay ahead.

It was probably best if she didn't listen to that part.

Again, she considered phoning Andy, but she knew he'd forbid it, and then be furious with her for doing it anyway.

Besides, he'd worry…

* * *

Andy heard the news from Chris when he delivered Logan and his sisters to the house.

'She's going down an air shaft? Whoever thought of such a crazy idea? Nobody knows if they'll get those men out of there. She could be trapped. There could be another fall!'

Chris's reassurances that all would be well and that the mine engineers had it all under control fell on deaf ears as panic spread through Andy's body.

His imagination was only too willing to supply him with plenty of 'worst' scenarios: Ellie trapped in the air shaft; another rockfall; the trapped men... He couldn't—or wouldn't—think of any scenarios including them...

His heart was stuttering in his chest, and for all he knew there were things he should be doing, like calling Maureen to cancel the morning's patients, but his mind couldn't move past the image of his wife trapped a mile or so beneath the ground.

And suddenly all they'd been through seemed so trivial he could have cried. The time they'd wasted, the pain they'd caused each other. What if something happened and he couldn't hold her again, tell her he loved her, explain his panic about having another baby?

Moving like an automaton, Andy did what had to be done: he saw to the guests; phoned Maureen; and finally went back to work. Not that he could stay there, not when his wife was—

No, he wasn't going to start that again, but at least if he waited at the mine, he'd hear all the latest news, maybe even get a message to her. Would they send a message saying 'I love you'?

And would that be enough when there was so much more he needed to say?

He told Andrea to contact him if he was needed, and headed back out to the mine.

Offering to be lowered down a long, dark ventilation shaft was one thing. Doing it, Ellie soon realised, was entirely different. For a start, it wasn't a darkness she'd ever experienced before. It was as if the blackness was physical so it seemed to press against her.

And the shaft seemed to grow narrower as she went down, although she knew this was her imagination.

Then light appeared and before she knew it, eager hands were helping her stand on firm earth again, undoing her harness and generally welcoming her presence.

She stepped away from them and stripped off the filthy overalls she'd worn down the shaft, which were now black with coal dust.

'We'd better stand clear, there's more coming,' she said, and smiled when the men looked puzzled.

'Extra water because I thought Pete's ankle might need an open cast.'

She waited until the bundle arrived before mentioning chocolate, which had the desired effect of lifting the men's spirits, especially as it came in the form of little chocolate Santas.

Her rescuers clustered around her and the only one she recognised, Logan's dad, gave her a hug.

'Hey, I'm the patient here,' someone complained, and Ellie guessed it was Pete, lying on the floor with his ankle bandaged.

'I'll just check Eddie then come back to you,' Ellie promised.

Eddie was still and quiet, but as far as Ellie could tell the injury hadn't been severe, and the pupils in both eyes reacted equally to light.

'Just sit by him in case there's any change,' Ellie told the man nearest to her. 'You can talk to him if you like, or not. He'll have a crashing headache and might not feel like responding. But stay near him, check his pulse every ten minutes or so, and let me know if anything changes.'

She looked at the few men clustered around her.

'You can do that? Take turns?' she asked, and was assured they'd stay close to him, one of them settling beside Eddie to begin telling him a long story about when they were kids, asking Eddie questions to which he sometimes mumbled an answer—or what might have been an answer.

Ellie went to kneel beside Pete, handing him a green whistle to suck while she unwrapped the bandage.

She suspected he could have broken the ends of his tibia and fibula when the rocks had landed on him, which meant he had reason to complain. She'd checked the big red box before she'd come down the air shaft, and knew there was treated cloth in it. She could fashion it into an open cast for his ankle and lower leg, and hold it in place with the bandages.

It would allow for swelling and its rigidity would prevent further displacement of the bones.

It took all her concentration to get it right, but around her she could hear the jokes and quips of the men and was pleased at how high their spirits seemed to be, although, to a certain extent what was to her a grim, dark, rather frightening tunnel was a second home to them.

With both patients checked, Ellie turned her attention to the other men. Kane Grant in particular was showing evidence of stress.

'My family will take good care of your children,' she told him, but it didn't ease his concern. His main lament was that he should have got a different job so he could be at home more often with his children.

'But any job will take you away from them for part of the day,' Ellie reminded him, 'and mining's been your life.'

'But Logan's going to be in trouble wherever he goes,' Kane lamented. 'I should have done better with him.'

Ellie knew she had to listen but other men had worries as well.

'When did you last sleep?' she asked Kane, who shook his head.

'I've no idea! I've been sleeping badly even at home and haven't slept down here since the cave-in.'

Ellie opened her own bag and found an anti-anxiety drug to give him. Even if it didn't make him sleep it would calm his nerves.

Kane accepted the tablet and the water Ellie offered him, then took her advice and went over to one of the hammocks the men had rigged up out of their overalls, climbed in, swung back and forth a bit, then fell deeply asleep, unaware of the men setting up a game of poker practically underneath him.

And life underground settled into a strange kind of normality, with everyone taking turns to sleep in the two rigged hammocks, Ellie listening to stories of other hair-raising events in the miners' lives, playing cards, telling jokes. Kane Grant, his anxiety abated, revealed a wonderful supply of limericks and short poems, some of which, Ellie was sure, he cleaned up for her benefit.

The breakthrough came earlier than they'd expected, and once one man came through others followed, helping the trapped man over the still-existing mound of rubble, and out to waiting health professionals on the other side.

Ellie waited until they'd all been taken up, then one of the engineers insisted she go topside herself.

As she rode up for what seemed like for ever, the tiredness she'd managed to keep at bay crept over her, and though she obediently trudged through the shower rooms and out through the clean room, she wondered how she'd have the strength to get home.

Until familiar arms folded about her, and Andy drew her close, his body shaking with emotion as he held her, whispering her name like a prayer.

'Oh, Andy, thank you for coming,' she said, as she disentangled herself.

'You don't have to thank me for anything,' he said gruffly. 'I've been going out of my mind with worry about you, about something happening to you before I could talk to you and make things right between us. I came because I needed to see you, and hold you, and say I'm sorry I've been such an idiot and caused you so much pain.'

He paused before adding, 'Not that you haven't caused me the torment of the damned these last few days. I *do* understand you felt you had to go, but the agony of not knowing what was happening down there... Perhaps I deserved it for being an ass.'

He was leading her towards the outer fence where he'd obviously parked the car, and although his conversation was confusing she was so grateful for his supporting arms, she didn't try to make sense of it.

It was enormously comforting and that was enough.

'It was the baby—our baby!' he said, as he settled her into the car and then got into the driver's side himself and continued without losing a beat.

'I was devastated. I'd never felt pain like it, but I knew I had to be strong for you, so I just kept going. I know now— I've been talking to people on help-lines—that I should have dealt with it instead of just shoving it aside until it became such a big thing in my subconscious mind. The very thought of another baby—another possible loss—brought back all that stuff so strongly…'

'You couldn't bear the thought of it happening again?' Ellie said softly.

'Exactly! I thought I couldn't handle it or look after you when I knew it would paralyse me.'

She reached out a hand and held it against the strong column of his neck.

'And it took me being down in a big hole with a lot of very dirty miners for you to figure it out?'

He turned with a slightly shamefaced grin.

'I did worry about you being down there, but I'd been on to the helplines before that. I contacted them when I had that stupid reaction to something you'd said with so much love and happiness, about a miracle chance of a pregnancy. I went to pieces and knew I needed help, so I went looking for it.'

'And got it?'

He smiled and nodded.

'I'll keep having counselling sessions with the person they've found for me—there's a lot of ugly stuff to get through, but never doubt my love for you, my Ellie.'

He'd drawn over to the side of the road and halted the car, sliding the gear stick into Park so he could take her in his arms again and kiss her, gently at first, then with increasing passion.

'I should have known how you were feeling,' she said quietly, but he shook his head against her neck.

'*I* should have shared,' he said. 'Stupid macho posturing, that's all it was, and it caused us both so much pain and wasted so many months of our lives together.'

Ellie held him tightly, feeling the tension drain from his body as he talked.

But how could she *not* have known?

Whatever, it must never happen again, and now he'd spoken of the depths of his grief and despair when they'd lost the baby, she could understand him never wanting to go through something like that again.

Could she understand and accept?

In her head, she shrugged.

Of course she'd accept. She loved Andy more than life itself and to know she'd caused him pain…

'We'd better get home,' he said, slowly disentangling himself from her arms and the bits of car that had been sticking into him. 'You've no idea what a circus we've got there, but Jill and Harry have been wonderful. They not only fed me, but they've been sending boxes of sandwiches up to the mine for people waiting for news. Is this it now—everyone out?'

Ellie smiled at him. Her body was still tight with emotions she'd have to sort out one day, but ordinary chat was just what she needed right now.

'Everyone, and only two a bit the worse for wear. Logan's dad, Kane Grant, is emotionally fragile. I've asked him to bring the kids and come to us for Christmas dinner.'

Andy nodded, and Ellie continued, 'And I thought I'd ask Jill and Harry to stay on for Christmas, rather than driving back to Sydney in all the Christmas holiday traffic. It'd be a two-day drive for them, so why not stay and we can all celebrate together?'

Andy laughed.

'I daren't even begin to count how many that will give us. It will be Jill and Harry and Chelsea. But after Christmas Jill wants Chelsea home, and will home-school her if Chels decides she can't face school.'

'That's not so bad, just add the four Grants and us—
that's nine, which is a great number for a real family kind
of Christmas.'

CHAPTER TEN

Expecting chaos, Ellie was pleasantly surprised to arrive home to a quiet house that welcomed her not only because it was home but because someone—Jill most probably—had arranged fresh flowers from the garden in every room in the house.

And everyone was out.

A note on the kitchen table explained that.

Thought you might like the house to yourself, so we've all gone off to the Thai and then to a movie. Join us if you like, but I'm thinking you'll be tired.

I'm sorry my family seems to have taken over your life, but we can pack up and go to a motel if you would prefer.

Love, Chelsea

Bless the girl! Ellie thought, walking around the spotless house, smelling the faint fragrance of the flowers, and wondering why it was taking Andy so long to put the car away.

She heard him coming before she saw him, huffing and puffing up the back steps.

'What is Christmas without a tree?' he gasped, plonking a decent-sized cypress pine down on the floor of the veranda.

'Oh, Andy, it's beautiful. I had no idea we could get a live tree out here.'

'I'll have you know that they grow out here, my girl,' he said. 'One of the porters at the hospital has a small stand of them on his property and he brought it in for me—well, for us!'

'Let's decorate it now!' Ellie said, and Andy groaned.

'They must have been feeding you down in that hole in the ground, but I'm starving and unless I was mistaken, Jill was going to leave a casserole in the fridge. We need only bung it in the microwave and perhaps have a glass of something while we wait for it to heat.'

'But—' she began, but Andy cut her off.

'But nothing. Come and sit on the veranda with me while it heats. I've a very nice bottle of bubbly in the cooler out there.'

They ate on the veranda, but although the food was delicious, Ellie couldn't manage much, the stress of her underground days catching up with her.

Andy cleaned up after their dinner, while Ellie showered again, this time in her own bathroom, with her own soap and shampoo, then she slipped into bed, a little uncertain.

Would Andy join her there?

Were the problems of the past really behind them?

She still felt bad that she hadn't known how much he'd struggled with their baby's death, and wondered if he'd blamed her for not knowing.

But he did join her in bed, and as his hands slid over her body, each touch a silent word of love, she discovered she wasn't as tired as she'd thought she was. They made love slowly, teasing each other with kisses, until they joined in a cataclysmic release that wiped away all the pain, and doubts, and remembered loneliness, reaffirming the love they'd always known existed but had somehow lost its way in sorrow, and taken time to find again.

Bright and early next morning, Ellie made her way to the kitchen to find all their guests in occupation, and a vast array of freshly baked rolls, tubs of yoghurt, and bowls of fresh fruit set out on the table.

'You must think we're terrible,' Jill said. 'Taking over your home while you've been helping the miners. Please take whatever you like for breakfast.'

Ellie helped herself to yoghurt and cut mango, talking as she grabbed a couple of rolls to sustain her through the morning.

'I'm just glad you're here,' she said. 'You've kept Andy's mind off what was happening in the mine, done a huge amount of shopping so we can all eat, and put flowers everywhere. Thank you so much. The roses are always so lovely in summer but I never seem to get time to do anything with them.'

'You've such a lovely garden and the roses are so beautiful I couldn't resist.'

Ellie thanked her again, adding, 'I really should get back to work. Heaven only knows how all my patients have been managing.'

'If you're going to be busy you don't want all of us staying here,' Jill said in a no-nonsense voice.

'Of course we do. Andy told me he'd invited you for Christmas and I'm really looking forward to having a crowd. It would have been very lonely for just Andy and me when we've always had family Christmases.'

And especially when she'd have kept thinking of the baby who wasn't with them. She closed her eyes, remembering that terrible time when it had seemed as if their world had crashed to pieces around them, and how Andy hadn't been able to share his grief.

'But what we do need to do, Jill, is count heads and work out food. I've asked Kane Grant and his three kids.'

'And I thought we might ask Zeke.'

This from Chelsea, turning a little pink as she mentioned the young policeman's name.

'So add it all up,' Ellie told her. 'I make it ten so we need to see the butcher and ask if he can get us a large turkey and ham at this late stage. I'd prefer a turkey buffe—you know, the ones that are just the breasts—but we might need the whole thing to feed us.'

'We'll sort that out,' Jill assured her, as Ellie checked her watch and knew she should have been gone ten minutes earlier.

Maureen greeted her with a big hug.

'I don't know how you did it,' she said. 'My husband's a miner and I went down once, but never again. Talk about claustrophobia.'

'But it's as big as a cathedral down there where the lift ends,' Ellie protested. 'There were trucks down there.'

She didn't mention the shaft or the fact that it had given her many uneasy moments, or the cramped safety bunker they'd all crowded into.

'It's still under the ground and unnatural for anyone but a rabbit or wombat,' Maureen said, before handing over messages and sending a list of patients through to Ellie's computer.

One of the messages was from Madeleine Courtney, thanking Ellie for the referral to the specialist, who had given her so much information she knew she'd be able to handle her lupus much better now.

Ellie was thrilled, that was one problem solved, and she didn't need to worry about Madeleine any more.

The day began...

Andy walked around his small domain, assuring himself that there really wasn't anything he could do here.

With only two days to Christmas most patients had made sure they were well enough to go home, and even most of the elderly had gone to relatives.

And if he went home he could decorate the tree and house and surprise Ellie.

Ellie.

How close had he come to losing her?

He didn't know the answer to that question, but just the thought that it might have happened made him feel ill.

He told the hospital manager where he'd be and walked home, the morning sun just warming up for another very hot day.

His tree wasn't looking too perky, having been abandoned on the veranda floor all night, but once he'd managed to pack it, upright, into a bucket of wet dirt, it looked a lot better.

The box of the family's old decorations was still on the veranda, so he dragged it closer to the tree then realised that this had always been a job his sisters had done. How the hell did you decorate a Christmas tree?

Can't be that hard, he decided, and began to strew the contents of the box around it on the floor, seeking something like a length of tinsel or maybe fairy lights to wind around it for a start.

There was nothing.

Had his mother decided to throw away anything that looked too tattered?

He could go up town and get some lights and tinsel, but

he'd really wanted to do this as a surprise for Ellie when she finished her morning's work.

There were heaps of baubles.

Should he do a colour theme—all red or all silver, or maybe red and gold, or silver and blue? All those colours were there and he had vague recollections that the tree had always looked beautiful but not always the same.

He didn't really have time to think it through, so he set to work, hanging baubles on the tree, cursing the ones that had broken tops and wouldn't hang, moving up and down the tree so there was an even spread.

Except he was fast running out of baubles and he had the back half of the tree still to do.

Maybe Ellie wouldn't notice that, because he really wanted to get some gold angels, which he'd just discovered in a smaller box, attached here and there, and he'd found the angel for the top in another box.

With the fairy lights.

And underneath them, another package, wrapped in faded brown paper. He opened it carefully and stared in disbelief at the contents—one red and white Santa suit, complete with cap and beard and glasses.

He had to smile, remembering his father, when he'd been younger and slimmer, clambering into it each Christmas, and doing the rounds of the hospital and the older people's annexe, giving out chocolates.

Could he bring back the idea and make a Santa call at the hospital?

Tree first, he reminded himself, and began to wind the lights around his tree.

But trying to wind them around the tree *and* the baubles was far harder then he'd realised. With three sisters, tree decoration had always been their domain, and since he and Ellie had been together, because they'd usually spent

Christmas at one of their families' homes, Ellie had kept only a small tree at home. Sometimes just some twisted bits of willow, sprayed gold and decorated with odds and ends they'd picked up in their travels.

So he was standing in a tangle of wire and bulbs and baubles when he heard Ellie coming up the steps.

He stepped forward, hoping to head her off, and the tree followed him, just tilting at first, then crashing to the floor.

'I was doing it as a surprise for you,' he muttered, as she stood and laughed at the chaos.

'Well, it's certainly that!' she said, trying to stifle the giggles that kept coming.

But she came towards him and knelt beside him, all tangled in wires, on the floor. She put her arms around him, lights, baubles, tree and all, and gave him a big hug.

'Just stay still so I can untangle you,' she said, when she was done with her hugs and kisses. 'It was a lovely idea and I'm sure we can fix it up, but first let's get the lights sorted.'

She sat beside him, lifting the loops of wire over his head.

'Have you tried the lights? Tightened all the little bulbs? Found any dead ones?'

He looked blankly at her.

'You do that first,' she said, 'before you put them on the tree because, especially on older strings of light, if you've got one dead or loose bulb the whole lot doesn't work.'

Andy shook his head, then smiled and kissed her.

'Isn't it nice to be us again?'

And the simple question struck deep into her heart, forcing a lump too big to swallow into her throat, so all she could do by way of agreement was kiss him back.

Hold him and kiss him, and let all her love flow into him, while she felt his flow into her.

'Well, that must have been some kiss to have brought the whole tree down.'

The voice, coming so unexpectedly, had them moving hurriedly apart, Ellie to frown in confusion at Chelsea, who'd appeared as if from nowhere.

But Andy handled it better.

'Don't be cheeky, young lady,' he said with mock severity, 'or I'll make you clean up the mess.'

Chelsea laughed and came forward to begin the job, carefully rescuing any unbroken baubles and brushing dirt off them, setting them on the table until they could get the tree upright again.

Ellie left them to it. She wanted to have a quick snack then go back to work, making up missed appointments, so she could be home in time to have dinner with her visitors for the first time.

'Where is everyone?' she asked Chelsea, who came into the kitchen for a dustpan and brush.

'Mum's on the scrounge for Christmas stuff, and Harry's decided he wouldn't mind being a policeman so is tagging around with Chris and Zeke for the day.'

She was heading out the door when she turned.

'Do you really not mind us all being here?' she said. 'I feel dreadful. If it wasn't for my own stupidity, none of this would have happened, and you wouldn't be lumped with all the family for Christmas.'

Ellie smiled at the young woman she'd grown so fond of.

'Christmas is for families,' she reminded Chelsea. 'Andy and I would probably have been quite miserable on our own, or wouldn't have bothered much with a celebration and just treated it as an extra day off.'

She paused, thinking of the decision she'd nearly made to leave Maytown before Christmas, back before Chelsea had somehow brought happiness back into the house.

'So really you're doing us a huge favour,' Ellie said, and meant it for she knew now, as well as she knew her own name, that she and Andy were as one again.

And always would be.

Chelsea grinned and headed back to the mess on the veranda, Andy demanding to know what had taken her so long.

'Girl talk,' Ellie heard Chelsea say. 'Just girl talk!'

CHAPTER ELEVEN

By lunchtime Ellie had caught up on all her appointments, so she sent Maureen home and went up into the house.

She needed to find Jill and discuss the food situation.

She discovered Jill at the butcher's, discussing sausage meat and giblets for the stuffing, totally unfazed by the numbers.

'I've done Christmas for two dozen,' she said. 'I'm one of six so Christmases were enormous.'

Jill took the parcel from the butcher, refused to let Ellie pay, and led the way out the door.

'It's a good thing you've got the barbecue with a lid because we can use that as an oven to cook the ham. Now, let me look at my list.'

She produced a piece of foolscap-size paper.

'That's not a list, it's an inventory!' Ellie said, and Jill smiled.

'You just go away and do something for yourself, or have a little rest. Leave this to me.'

Having a little rest sounded like a very good idea, but she knew there'd be presents for her and Andy already under the tree from the visitors, so she needed some small gifts to give them, and something for the children, so she went shopping instead…

* * *

Christmas Eve was a day of celebration for the entire town. The rescued miners were ferried down the streets on gaily decorated utilities, each in an armchair on the tray back. Even the two injured men took part, while what seemed like the entire town turned out to cheer them.

'Whose idea was it to release the red balloons?' Andy asked Ellie when he caught up with her outside the hospital.

'Chelsea's, of course. She's had all the soccer team and half the high school population filling balloons with helium she conned out of the two-dollar shop. They've handed them out to people up and down the main road with orders to release them as the men went past.'

So the hot, dry air was filled with red balloons floating lazily above the parade, some of the miners catching hold of strings and making a bunch of them.

'You should be up on one of those chairs,' Andy told her, an arm around her shoulders.'

'More like the whole rescue team,' she reminded him. 'But I think it's nice to see them celebrated, even though it's so close to Christmas. Things tend to get back to normal so quickly and in another week or so it will be forgotten.'

'Except by the engineers and managers who'll be trying to work out why it happened,' Andy said. 'Are you heading home now?

Andy watched her walk away. She was special, his Ellie, and for about the thousandth time since they'd made up he wished he had a special gift for her.

He'd bought her favourite perfume, a couple of books

by authors he knew she enjoyed, and an eternity ring because now their marriage *was* going to be for ever.

But the 'something special' he felt sure was out there had eluded him.

He headed back into the hospital, not that there was much to do, except the endless paperwork that he tended to put off until the last possible moment.

Which was today, if he wanted to take a few days off over Christmas. Not that he'd be off duty, just on call from home, although he'd do morning and evening rounds as usual.

He smiled to himself as he thought of the tree they'd finally managed to decorate, its lights shining brightly on the veranda. Not to mention the tinsel that seemed to adorn every room, and the golden bells that hung in every doorway, the fairy lights strung around the veranda railing, and the little nativity scene Jill had brought with her as a gift for him and Ellie.

Christmas was going to be special, very special!

If only he could think what to get Ellie…

The sun eventually rose on the great day—a huge red orb in the eastern sky, promising a fiery heat for foolish people sticking to the traditional roast turkey and ham of their European forebears when the temperature was in the forties.

Ellie woke early, moving quietly through the sleeping household. Chelsea's family had been to the midnight church service so she was certain they'd sleep in, while she wanted to grab a cup of tea and sit outside and think of all that had happened in the tumultuous twelve months since last Christmas.

True, she and Andy had been through sadness, and the unbelievably hard consequences of losing the baby, but wasn't their marriage all the stronger for that suffering?

Hadn't they found a whole new level of happiness, a new depth of love, in the last few weeks?

She smiled, pushing aside memories of that time when she'd thought their marriage wouldn't survive, pushing aside remembered pain and anguish.

Today was Christmas Day, a day of celebration...

'Join you?'

Andy settled beside her on the top step, set down his cup of tea, and put his arm around her shoulder.

'It's been a tough year, hasn't it, my darling, but we made it.'

She turned and kissed him.

'Indeed we did.'

She shifted so she could see him—look at him.

'You all right?' she asked, and he smiled at her.

'More than all right,' he told her, and the strength in the words told her they were true. 'And while we're on our own, there's one thing I want to do.'

Intrigued, Ellie let him pull her off the step and lead her to the tree, where he produced a parcel wrapped in gold tissue paper.

He handed it to her and for some reason her fingers shook as she unwrapped it, so it took a while to reveal the contents—an angel dressed in white, with gossamer golden wings and a golden crown.

'For our tree?' she whispered, and Andy held her and kissed her lips.

'For our tree and our baby,' he said, his voice hoarse with emotion. 'Angels were all male, you know, so shall we go and put him up, right at the top where he belongs, so we can share every Christmas with him?'

Ellie wiped the tears from her face and led the way to the tree, carefully removing the old and rather battered angel and replacing it with the new one—*their* angel.

Andy hugged her.

'*Now* we're ready for Christmas,' he said. 'It will be like old times for me, family, and whatever strays Dad or Mum picked up, all together in the dining room.'

'So maybe next year we could ask them and my family if they'd like to come out and join us. After the crowd this year, just the two of us would seem odd.'

A tiny dart of pain pierced Andy's heart. Ellie's assumption that there'd be 'just the two of us' this time next year told him she'd accepted there'd be no baby.

Had it been his confessing how hard the loss had hit him that had drawn a line under the baby idea for ever, as far as Ellie was concerned?

He didn't know, but as he could hear people stirring behind them in the house, it was hardly the time to be telling Ellie he'd quite like to try again...

Breakfast was a riotous affair, Harry telling stories of university pranks, Chelsea happily enlarging on his tales and topping them with stories of the soccer team.

And once the breakfast things were cleared away, they adjourned to sit around the tree where piles of gifts were stacked. Andy played Santa, even donning a red cap, reading out the names on the greetings tags and passing over the gifts.

It soon became apparent that Jill, as well as a gift for cookery, was a seamstress and embroiderer. For Ellie, there were half a dozen linen handkerchiefs, embroidered with a flowery E and tucked into a satin bag. Andy's gift was similar, big manly handkerchiefs with a no-nonsense A embroidered on them, but also a small, smooth, wooden box, felt lined, for cuff links or tie pins or whatever manly jewellery he might have.

'Not much,' he joked as he thanked Harry for the beautifully crafted box. 'At least now I won't lose what I do have.'

'Well, I've brought you something to start off with,' Chelsea said, producing a small box with an opal set into a tie pin.

'I've noticed at the hospital on days when you're wearing a tie, you tuck it between the buttons of your shirt so it doesn't dangle on the patients.'

Andy laughed.

'I *do* do that,' he admitted. 'I always wear a tie if there's to be a board meeting, or someone from the Health Department visiting to check we're not using too many pens and pencils.'

'More likely ear swabs and hypodermic needles,' Kane said.

And so it went, Ellie and Andy's gifts to everyone small jars of spicy nuts and pretzels that were about the only special culinary talent Ellie had.

Lunch followed, Jill, Harry and Chelsea dishing up, Logan and his sisters ferrying the overflowing plates to the table.

And once they were all settled, party hats on heads, and feeble jokes read out, they all gave thanks for the day, and the meal before them, and began to eat.

And eat...

'It's far too delicious to leave any but I really can't manage any more,' Ellie declared, having eaten a large serving of the main course, and three-quarters of her Christmas pudding and custard.

'In fact,' she added, 'if I didn't have the clearing up to do, I'd be staggering to my bed.'

'We'll clear up,' Jill said, but Ellie raised her hand.

'*You* will do nothing,' she declared, 'except put your feet up and catch up with Chelsea. I know you want to get away early in the morning so, later in the afternoon, when it's cooler, Chelsea and Harry can help pack the car. And for now Zeke and Logan can help me and Andy in the kitchen while the girls tidy up the discarded wrapping paper around the tree.'

'She's right, you've done a marvellous job, Jill,' Andy said, 'so please go and rest. The little general here will sort out the mess.'

'Little general indeed,' Ellie said, as she and Andy finally finished in the kitchen and retired to their bedroom, collapsing onto the bed.

'You can give me orders anytime,' Andy teased, turning onto his side so he could pull her close and kiss her.

'Mmm…nice!' Ellie said. 'And did I thank you for the lovely gifts? You didn't get that perfume at the local chemist.'

'No, and while I do try to shop locally whenever possible, the internet is a wonderful thing.'

They lay, content to be together, exchanging a kiss now and then, until Andy moved a little apart, reaching out to the bedside table on his side of the bed and producing another little parcel, wrapped in Christmas paper and tied with ribbon.

'I do have one last gift,' he said, and passed it to her. 'Well, two actually, but I'll give you this one first.'

He passed it to her.

It was a small, square box that shrieked ring, and her fingers trembled as she opened it, then tears slid down her cheeks when she saw the tiny circlet of gold and diamonds—an eternity ring!

'Because we know now our marriage is for ever,' Andy said, his voice husky and his hand shaking as he put the ring on her finger.

'I love you, Ellie, always have and always will,' he said.

'And even when we'd lost our way and started hurting each other, I knew the love was still there if we could just get past the pain.'

He put his arms around her and held her close.

'I was an idiot for not talking to you, but I felt you had so much of your own emotion to deal with that adding mine to it might sink you completely!'

'And I was stupid not to realise how much you were hurting. I was wrong to wrap myself in grief and not consider you,' Ellie whispered against his neck.'

She eased away and kissed his lips.

'Never again,' she said, and as he kissed her he echoed the words, then reached for the second gift he had for her.

'Well, you're not going to top this ring, whatever it is,' Ellie told him, over the tears of shock and waving the ring delightedly in the air so sunbeams could catch the diamonds and make them wink at her.

'No,' Andy said, and sounded serious, 'but I hope you'll think it's worth just as much—perhaps more. I hope you'll understand what it's saying to you, what *I'm* saying to you!'

He handed her the second box, and once again she felt the tremors that were going through his body.

Whatever it was, it meant a lot to Andy…

It was light in weight, a smallish rectangular box of some kind, and as she tore the paper off it and saw what it was, she sat up in bed and looked at him in wonder.

'You're giving me a pregnancy test?' she said, disbelief vying with happiness.

'You know I'm probably not,' she added.

'Or you could be,' he said. 'If not now, sometime in the future.'

Ellie knelt on the bed and took his face between the palms of her hands so she could study the man she loved to distraction.

'And you'd really be okay with it? You'd be okay, even knowing we haven't had a lot of luck so far?'

He leaned across and used his hands to draw her close and kiss her lips.

'More than okay. I'd be delighted. And, yes, things can go wrong, but I can handle that now.'

He looked deep into her eyes.

'I can handle anything. With you beside me and your love giving me strength, I can take on the world.'

He grinned at her.

'But for now, don't you need a pee?'

Ellie's hands were shaking so much as she tried to open the protective box, Andy took it from her and handed her the simple test strip.

She slid off the bed, heading for the bathroom, knowing not to expect too much, not to get excited about it. There'd been too many times…

But as she sat on the loo and stared at the strip, watching the blue line spread across its width, she could only shake her head.

She should tell Andy, call him in, but her mind was blank, her tongue and lips not working.

But he came anyway, and together they stared at the strip.

'We'll need other tests. They're not always accurate—anything could happen…'

She'd gone from speechless to babbling!

How could this be? After all the tests had said it wouldn't happen? After all the years of trying had failed?

Ellie just couldn't get her head around it! The tests weren't one hundred percent accurate…

She swiped tears from her cheeks and stared at the blue line, shaking her head and hugging her body to stop herself getting too excited over it.

Until Andy knelt beside her and put his arm around her.

'And just maybe it's right and we're going to have a baby. How's that for an unbeatable Christmas present?'

He helped her up and held her in his arms, certain that this time all would be well.

'I love you, Ellie Fraser,' he said quietly, his lips moving against the hair on the top of her head.

'And I love you, Andy Fraser,' she whispered back, the air from her words warming his chest.

EPILOGUE

WHY HAD SHE thought asking both sets of families to come for Christmas a good idea? Ellie wondered for about the fourteenth time as she settled her just-fed son James into his cot in the downstairs flat.

She smiled at James's sleeping face, touching her fingers to the spot where the little whorl of hair—just like Andy's—was beginning to show above his left eyebrow...

Even with Andy's mother running around with lists and ticking things off, Ellie still felt there was something she'd forgotten.

Vegetables—tick. Christmas pudding—tick. Bonbons and sweets and little gifts for everyone—tick...

No, it was something different—something special—and she knew she'd forgotten it.

Baby brain.

Maybe it would come to her. Andy should be home soon. He was up at the hospital doing his Santa thing again and having his photo taken with children on his knee.

She'd already taken a photo of him as Santa, holding James, and knew it was something they would do each year until James was old enough to rebel against such things.

No, whatever it was—the bright idea she'd had in the middle of the night a week ago—still eluded her, and with a heavy sigh she gave up thinking about it.

After all she'd updated the watch she'd given him last year with the computerised one, and found some opal cufflinks to match the tiepin Chelsea had given him last year, and a few silly odds and ends.

More than enough.

Besides, it was Christmas Eve and the shops would be shut soon.

All the shops!

Racing up the steps, she found her mother-in-law, asked her to keep an eye on James, slapped a hat on her head and headed for town.

Christmas Day dawned with a promise of some relief from the heat for the sky was covered with thick cloud, and rain from a cyclone that had crossed the coast far to the west was coming their way.

Rain was the best Christmas present of all for the surrounding farmers, and it would freshen up the town and replenish the dams, so it was a win-win all around.

'We should get up and see to our visitors,' Ellie said, as she snuggled closer to her husband.

Andy turned over and kissed her.

'From the snuffling coming from the other room, I'd say I'd better get up and look after our visitors while you feed that ever-ravenous child we produced. How does he get so hungry when all he ever does is smile and wave his arms and legs about?'

'He's growing his brains,' Ellie replied, easing herself out of the comfort of her husband's arms. 'I'll feed him then come and join you in the kitchen.'

But once there, James already handed over to a willing grandmother, she realised breakfast was already sorted, cereal, yoghurts, fruit and toast already laid out along the veranda table for everyone to help themselves.

Breakfast done, they adjourned to the living room where the beautifully decorated tree—grandmother again responsible—was stacked around with presents.

And for someone so small, James seemed to have attracted most of them, although he was sleeping blissfully on a rug on the floor while Ellie and Andy unwrapped his treasure-trove of gifts.

'That's far too much,' Ellie protested, as more stuffed animals appeared.

'We'll find homes for all of them,' Andy whispered to her. 'In fact, some of the toys at the hospital are getting very threadbare.'

So, gifts given and admired, there was barely time for a short walk through the decorated streets, calling Christmas wishes to neighbours and friends, before returning to eat a gargantuan meal.

The day ended with a scratch supper of whatever leftovers anyone fancied, then people wandered off to their rooms or to the veranda to watch the first drops of the promised rain arrived.

Ellie fed her son for the last time—hopefully until morning although she wasn't counting on it—had a shower, then climbed into bed beside her husband.

'I've got you something else,' she said, and felt under the bed where she'd tucked a shoebox-size parcel.

She had to laugh as Andy ripped off layer after layer of wrapping, finally arriving at a small, rectangular parcel that seemed somehow familiar.

Slowly he unwrapped it then stared in disbelief at another pregnancy test.

'So much for the contraceptive effects of breastfeeding,' Ellie said to him as he continued to stare at it in disbelief.

'Do you really think?' he said. 'After all the problems we had, could we possibly have—?'

'Another?' Ellie said quietly. 'Hand it over and we'll see.'

* * * * *

UNWRAPPING THE NEUROSURGEON'S HEART

CHARLOTTE HAWKES

MILLS & BOON

To my very first hero, who introduced me
to mountains, maths and Marmite—love you, Dad xx

CHAPTER ONE

'ANOUK?' THE RESUS WARD'S sister poked her head around the Resus bay curtain. 'Are you running the seven-year-old casualty who fell off a climbing frame?'

'I am.' Anouk spun quickly around. 'Is she in?'

'Yes, the HEMS team are on the roof now.'

'Thanks.' Nodding grimly, Anouk turned back to her team for a final check. 'Everyone happy? Got your gear?'

The only thing she was missing was the neurosurgeon. The department had been paged ten minutes ago but they must be swamped up there. Still, she needed a neurosurgeon for the young kid. Sucking in a steadying breath, she ducked out of the bay, and slammed straight into Moorlands General's hottest commodity.

Solomon Gunn.

Six feet three of solid muscle, more suited to a Hollywood kickboxing stunt guy than the average neurosurgeon, didn't even shift under her flexing palms as the faintest hint of a woody, citrusy scent filled her nostrils.

Her skin prickled instantly. *How could it not?* It was all Anouk could do to snatch her arms down to her sides and take a step back, telling herself that the alien sensation currently rolling through her was nothing more than a basic physiological reaction.

Instinct. Nothing more.

She couldn't possibly be so unlucky as to have the Smoking Gun as the neurosurgeon on her case, could she? And, for the record, she didn't think much of the idiot who had bestowed that moniker on him. Not that it would be unlucky for the poor girl who had fallen, of course. As he was one of the up-and-coming stars of the region, the girl couldn't be in better hands than Sol's.

If only the guy weren't so devastating when it came to women who weren't in his care.

He practically revelled in his reputation as a demigod neurosurgeon and out-of-hours playboy. And still it seemed that almost every woman in the hospital wanted him.

Including, to Anouk's absolute shame, herself.

Not that she would ever, *ever* let another living soul know that fact. Solomon Gunn was the antithesis of absolutely everything she should want in a man.

Yet, caught in the rich, swirling, cognac-hued depth of his gaze, something inside her shifted and rolled deliciously, nonetheless.

She'd only been at Moorlands General for a couple of months and been in Resus when Sol had, but so far they'd never worked together on the same casualty. A traitorous part of her almost hoped that tonight was different.

'Dr Anouk Hart, I believe.'

'Yes. Are you here for my case?' Self-condemnation made her tone sharper than she might otherwise have intended.

'I don't know.' He grinned, as though he could see right through her. 'Which is your case?'

'Seven-year-old girl; climbing frame,' she bulletpointed.

'Then I'd say you're in luck. I'm here for you.'

Her heart kicked. Anouk told herself it was frustration, nothing more.

'Lucky me,' she managed, rolling her eyes.

'Lucky both of us.'

He flicked his eyes up and down her in frank appraisal. On another man it would have appeared arrogant, maybe even lewd. But Sol wasn't *another man*; he pulled the act off in such a way that it left her body practically sizzling. An ache spearing its way right down through her until she felt it right *there*. Right between her legs.

What was the matter with her?

The man was damned near lethal.

'You might be accustomed to women throwing themselves at you.' She jerked her head over his shoulder to where a group of her colleagues was shamelessly clustered around the central desk and shooting him flirty smiles and applauding gestures. 'However, I certainly don't intend to be one of them.'

'Oh, they're just enjoying the home-made mince pies I brought in.'

'Sorry, what?'

'It *is* Christmas, Anouk.' His grin ramped up and she almost imagined she could feel those straight, white teeth against her skin. 'No need to be a Grinch.'

He couldn't have any idea quite how direct a hit his words were. She hated Christmas. It held no happy memories for her. It never had. Not that she was about to let Sol know that.

'Home-made? By whom? Your housekeeper?'

'My own fair hands.' He waggled them in her face and she tried not to notice how utterly masculine they looked. Not exactly the delicate hands people usually associated with a surgeon.

Those hands had worked magic on hundreds of patients. But it wasn't quite the same kind of magic she was imagining now.

Anouk blinked hard and tried to drag her mind back to the present.

'That's as may be, but I don't think it's your mince pies they're interested in.'

'Oh, I don't know. They're pretty good, if I do say so myself.'

'So modest.' She snorted. 'Well, if you've stopped playing *Great British Bake-Off* with your home-made mince pies…'

'"Playing *Great British Bake-Off*"?' He flashed a wolfish smile, which made her skin positively goosebump. 'I would ask if you're passive aggressive with everyone, or if it's just me, but, given the reputation you've already garnered amongst your colleagues in the few months you've been here, I fear I already know the answer.'

She shouldn't take the bait. She *mustn't*.

'And what reputation would that be?' she demanded, regretting it instantly.

His eyes gleamed mischievously. She half expected him not to answer her.

'Focussed, dedicated, a good doctor.'

'Oh.' She bit her lip. 'Well…then…thanks.'

'Even if you do walk around like you've got a stick up your behind.'

'I beg your pardon?' Heat flooded her cheeks. She could feel it.

'Sorry.' He held his hands up as though appeasing her. 'Their words, not mine. But you have to admit, you are a little bit uptight. A little *prim and proper*.'

She opened her mouth to reply, then snapped it closed again.

If she was honest, she'd heard worse about herself. At best, she was considered to be a good—even great—

doctor to her patients, but cold and unapproachable to her colleagues. A bit aloof.

The only person who knew different was Saskia; her best friend since their Hollywood A-list mothers had declared each other their nemesis, over twenty-five years ago.

'Of course, *I* don't think that,' Sol continued, clearly enjoying himself. Not that she blamed him—he couldn't have any idea of her inner turmoil. 'But then, most women have a way of…melting around me.'

'How do you get away with that?' She shook her head. 'Do you actually enjoy living up to all the worst stereotypes of your own Lothario reputation?'

'Let me guess, in your book that's wrong?'

'Oh, you're incorrigible,' Anouk snapped. 'Though I assume you'll take that as a compliment.'

'You mean it wasn't?' He clasped his hand over his heart, laughing. 'I'm cut to the quick.'

A deep, rich, sinful sound, which had no right to flood through her the way it did. She hated how her body reacted to him, despite every order from her brain to do the opposite. Tipping her head back, she jutted her chin out a fraction and ignored him.

'All we know so far is that we have a seven-year-old on her way having fallen approximately nine feet off a climbing frame in a park…'

'She landed on her head and suffered loss of consciousness for a minute or so,' he concluded. 'The heli-med team are on the roof now and our response team has gone to meet them.'

'Right.' She didn't do a very good job of covering her surprise. 'So, if you could just stop making eyes at the female contingent of our team long enough to concentrate on the casualty, that would be great.'

The amusement disappeared from his face in a split second. His tone was more than a little cool.

'I *always* put my patients ahead of anything else.'

She actually felt chastened.

'Yes… I…I know that.' Anouk flicked out a tongue to moisten her lips. 'I apologise, and I take it back. Your professional reputation is faultless.'

Better than faultless. He was an esteemed neurosurgeon, rapidly heading to the top of his field.

'It's just my personal reputation that languishes in muddier waters?' he asked, apparently reading her thoughts.

But at least the smile was back, his previous disapproval seemingly forgotten. Still, Anouk was grateful when the doors at the far end of the trauma area pulled open with a hiss and the helicopter team brought their patient in.

In an instant, Anouk was across the room and in the Resus bay, vaguely aware that Sol had fallen in quickly beside her.

'This is Isobel, she's seven years old and normally fit and well. No allergies or medications, and up to date with her jabs. Around one hour ago she was climbing on a rope basket climbing frame and was approximately nine feet up when she had an altercation with another child and fell, landing on her face or head with a loss of consciousness of perhaps one minute. She has a laceration above her left eyebrow and she has also lost two of her teeth.'

'Okay.' Anouk nodded, stepping forward. 'Thanks.'

'This is Isobel's sister, Katie.' The doctor turned to where another young girl was standing, and Anouk didn't know when Sol had moved but he was next to her. 'Katie was with her sister when she fell, and has accompanied her whilst Mum is on her way.'

Strangely, Katie lifted her head to Sol and offered a tiny,

almost imperceptible shake of her head, but Anouk didn't have time to dwell on that; she needed to help her patient.

'Hi, Isobel, I'm Anouk, the doctor who is going to be looking after you. Do you remember what happened, sweetheart?' She turned to her team, who had already stepped into action. 'Two drips in, guys?'

Isobel muttered something incoherent.

'Can you open your eyes for me, Isobel?' Anouk asked, checking her young patient's pupils. 'Good, that's a good girl. Now, can you take a really big, deep breath and hold it for me?'

She palpitated the girl's chest and stomach.

'You're doing really well, sweetheart. Can you talk to me? Have you got any pain in your tummy?'

'No,' Isobel managed tearfully. 'Katie?'

'Your sister is right here, my love. We just need to check you over to see if you hurt yourself when you fell, and then she'll be able to come and talk to you.'

'Yep, got blood,' one of her team confirmed.

'Great. Okay, and let's give her two point five milligrams of morphine.' She looked back at the child. 'That will help with the pain, all right, sweetheart? Good girl.'

Quickly and efficiently Anouk and her team continued to deal with their patient, settling the girl, doing their observations, and making her as comfortable as they could. Finally, Anouk had a chance to update the girl's mum, but it was still only the sister, who couldn't have been more than ten or eleven herself, who was waiting outside the bay. Anouk remembered how Isobel had asked for Katie, and not her mum.

'Katie, isn't it?' Anouk asked softly, going over to the worried little girl and sitting on the plastic seat next to her.

The girl nodded.

'Mum isn't here yet?'

'No.' Katie shook her head before fixing Anouk with a direct gaze, her voice holding a level of maturity that set warning bells off in Anouk's head. 'But you can talk to me. I'm eleven and I can answer any questions you need me to about my sister. I'm responsible for her.'

An image of Sol and Katie exchanging a concerned look crossed her mind.

Was the girls' mum at work? Uninterested? She knew those feelings all too well. Still, she had her own protocol to follow now.

'I understand that, and you seem like a very good sister,' Anouk confirmed, standing back up. 'But I think it's better if I talk to your mum when she gets here.'

'No, wait.' Katie stood up quickly, glancing at her and then across to the team.

It took a moment for Anouk to realise that she wasn't looking at her sister so much as looking at Sol.

'You know each other?'

'I need to speak to him.' Katie nodded.

'He's just looking after your sister right now.'

'I know, he's a neurosurgeon.' The young girl clucked her tongue impatiently as though she thought Anouk was treating her like a baby. 'And you're probably going to be taking Izzy to scan her head and see if there is any damage from her fall.'

Anouk tried not to show her surprise.

'We will be.'

'Well, when he is free, Sol will come and talk to me,' Katie said confidently, but Anouk didn't miss the fear that flashed briefly in the girl's eyes.

As if sensing the moment, Sol lifted his head and looked straight at them. Then, with a quick word to one of the senior nurses in the team, he made his way over.

'You doing okay, Katie?'

Quiet, professional, compassionate. It had been one thing to see Sol working from across a ward, to know of his reputation as a good doctor, a good neurosurgeon, but it was another actually to witness it first-hand.

Her mother had always ranted about the beauty of a brilliant actor playing a different role from the one the world was used to them adopting. That moment when the audience suddenly realised that it had forgotten who the actor was and got lost in the character.

Watching Sol at work made it almost impossible to remember his reputation as a womaniser.

And it certainly wasn't helping to smother her inconvenient crush on him.

'The doctor won't tell me anything,' Katie replied flatly.

'I'd rather explain to Mum.' Anouk bit back her irritation as Katie and Sol exchanged a glance, hating the feeling that she was missing a vital piece of information.

'Bad day?' he asked Katie simply.

She bit her lip. 'She can't even get up today. But she was resting so I thought Izzy and I could have an hour at the park before we went back and started our chores. There's no way she will be able to get here on her own.'

'I'm on call so I can't leave.' He rubbed his face thoughtfully. 'But I could call Malachi. He can help if she'd be happy about that?'

'Yes.' Katie's relief was evident. 'Please call him. I'll text Mum.'

Shifting her weight from one foot to the other, Anouk tried to control her heart, which had decided to pick up its pace as she listened to the conversation. It was aggravating feeling as though she wasn't entirely following, but the tone of it seemed all too painfully familiar. Or was she just reading too much into it?

Still, she had nowhere else to be for the moment; a nurse

was with Isobel and they were waiting on a few results before they could move her to CT.

'In the meantime,' Sol's voice dragged her back to the moment, 'let me try to explain to Dr Anouk here why she can speak to you.'

Katie narrowed her eyes uncertainly.

'You're going to have to trust her,' Sol cajoled. 'I do.'

They were just words to ease the concerns of a kid, Anouk knew that, and yet she was helpless to stop a burst of...*something* from going off inside her chest.

'The more I understand, Katie, the more I can help.' She fixed her gaze on the young girl, whose penetrating stare was unsettling.

'Okay,' Katie conceded at last, before turning back to Sol. 'But you'll call Malachi?'

'Right now,' Sol confirmed.

For a moment it looked as though her face was about to crumple, the pressure of the decisions clearly getting to her. But then she pulled herself together, sinking down onto her chair and fishing out a mobile phone to begin texting. As if there wasn't time for self-indulgent emotions.

As if she was a lot older than her years with far too much adult responsibility.

Anouk fought back the wave of grief that swelled inside her. All too familiar. All too unwelcome. Coming out of nowhere.

'Anouk.'

She snapped her head up to find that Sol was beckoning her, his eyes on Katie to ensure she was preoccupied as he moved across the room.

Wordlessly, Anouk followed, letting him lead her around the curtain and into the central area, keeping his voice low.

'Katie and Isobel are young carers. They look after their

mum, who suffers from multiple sclerosis. Some days are good, some not so good. Today, unfortunately, is a bad day, which means Michelle can't even get out of bed without their help.'

'I see.' Anouk breathed in as deeply and as unobtrusively as she could and tried to fight back the sense of nausea that rushed her. Her own situation had been vastly different from the girls', but the similarities were there. 'Dad?'

'Died in an RTA two years ago. He'd just popped out to get cough mixture.'

She exhaled sharply, the injustice of it scraping at her. 'Who's Malachi?'

'My brother. He'll go round and help Michelle. See if there's anything he can do to get her here. Otherwise you keep me informed throughout and we'll agree as much as we can tell Katie. She's mature, but she's still only eleven and she has enough to deal with.'

'Isn't there anyone else?' She already knew the answer, but she still had to ask. 'Any other family member?'

'No. Let me see what I can do but there are a few people I could call as a last resort. They're from the centre and they can at least sit with Katie so that she isn't alone until my shift finishes or I can get someone to cover for me.'

'Why would you do that?' She folded her arms across her chest as though the action could somehow contain the churn of…*feelings* that were swirling inside her, so close to the surface that she was afraid they might spill out.

She wanted to pretend that it was just empathy for Katie, the familiarity of a young girl who had far too much responsibility for her tender age. But she had a feeling it was also to do with Sol. His obvious concern and care for the young girl and her sister and mother was irritatingly touching.

She was ashamed to admit that she'd been attracted enough to the man when she'd thought he was just a decent doctor but also a gargantuan playboy. Seeing this softer side to him was only making the attraction that much stronger.

'Why not do it?' He shrugged and the fact that he was clearly hiding something only made Anouk want to get to know him that much more.

It was galling, really.

Checking on little Isobel and consulting with her team was the opportunity Anouk needed to regroup, and as she worked she let the questions about Sol fall from her head, even as he worked alongside her. Her patient was her priority, as always. Soon enough it was time to take the girl to CT to scan her head and neck.

'Can I go with her and hold her hand?' asked Katie, the concern etched over her face jabbing into Anouk's heart.

She usually let parents go in to be with their child, but unnecessarily exposing an eleven-year-old to ionising radiation, however short a burst, was different.

'How about if I go in?' Sol announced over her shoulder. 'You can wait outside but I'll hold Izzy's hand for you?'

Katie eyed him slowly for a moment.

'Okay, thank you,' she conceded at length.

'Great, you walk with Anouk here and your sister. Okay?'

Something jolted in Anouk's chest at the weight of Sol's gaze on her.

'Fine with me. You're going to get leaded?'

'I thought I might. They probably won't let me in the room otherwise.'

He made it out to be a light-hearted joke, but Anouk knew better. Usually only parents were allowed to accompany their younger children into the room when the imaging was in progress.

'You don't have any patients up on Neurology?'

'I'll sort it. The only one I'm worried about right now is a Mrs Bowman, but I'll deal with that.'

The fact that Sol was putting himself into that position in lieu of the girls' mother said a lot more about him than Anouk expected.

She couldn't shake the impression that it was also more than he would normally like a colleague to know about him. Why did she feel compelled to suddenly test him?

'Boost your reputation around here to compassionate hero as well as playboy, huh?' she murmured discreetly, so only Sol heard.

He glanced at her sharply, then formed his mouth into something that most people might take to be a smile. She knew better.

'Something like that,' he agreed with deliberate cheerfulness that instantly revealed to Anouk that this was the last stunt he wanted to be pulling.

He didn't fool her. She couldn't have said how she knew it, but Sol was doing this for Isobel and for Katie, *despite* the fact that it was going to make him all the more eligible within the hospital's pool of bachelors, and not *because* of it. Which suggested there was more to Sol Gunn than she had realised.

Anouk wished fervently that the concept weren't such an appealing one.

'Right.' Shoving the knowledge from her head, she smiled brightly at Katie and then at her patient. 'Let's get you to CT, shall we, Izzy? Don't worry, your sister will be right beside you until you go in, and then again the moment you come back out.'

And that sharp jab behind her eyes as Katie slipped

past her to walk next to the gurney and take her sister's hand in her own wasn't tears, Anouk told herself fiercely.

Just as she wasn't softening in her opinion of the Smoking Gun. She couldn't afford to soften, because that would surely render him more perilous than ever.

CHAPTER TWO

'WHAT'S THE STORY, *BRATIK*?'

Lost in his own thoughts, a plastic cup of cold, less than stellar vending-machine coffee cupped in his hands, Sol took a moment to regroup from the out-of-the-blue question from his big brother.

Then another to act as though he didn't know what Malachi was getting at.

'The scan revealed no evidence of any bleed on the brain and Izzy hadn't damaged her neck or broken her jaw in the fall, which we'd suspected, hence why she's been transferred to Paediatric Intensive Care. Maxillofacial are on their way to deal with the teeth in Izzy's mouth that are still loose. We have the two that came out in a plastic lunchbox someone gave to Izzy, but I think they're baby teeth so that shouldn't be too much of an issue. We won't know for sure until some of the swelling goes down.'

They had left Izzy with her mother and sister for some privacy, but, without having to exchange a word, both brothers had chosen to remain on hand. The girls' mother was going to need help, if nothing else.

'I know all that,' Malachi cut in gruffly, as though it pained him to ask. 'The paediatric doctor told me. I was asking what the story was with you, numb-nuts.'

An image of Anouk popped, unbidden, into Sol's head, but he shoved it aside.

'Don't know what you're talking about.'

It was only a partial lie.

He knew what his brother was getting at, which was surprising since they didn't *do* that *feelings* stuff, but he didn't know the answer to the question himself.

'You know exactly what I mean.' Malachi snorted. 'You forget I've practically raised you since we were kids. You can't fool me.'

Sol opened his mouth to jibe back, as he normally would. But tonight, for some inexplicable reason, the retort wouldn't come. He told himself it was the situation with Izzy. Or perhaps the fact that sitting on hard, plastic chairs, in a low-lit, deserted hospital corridor in the middle of the night, played with the mind.

He had a feeling it was more like the five-foot-seven blonde doctor who was resurrecting ghosts he'd thought long since buried. He had no idea what it was about her that so enthralled him, but she had been doing so ever since the first moment he'd met her.

It had been an evening in a nightclub where Saskia, already a doctor at Moorlands General, had brought Anouk along so that she could meet her new colleagues. The night before, he'd seen Anouk as a focussed, driven, dedicated doctor. And she'd been so uncomfortable that it had been clear that clubs definitely weren't her thing.

He'd seen her from across the room. She'd looked up and met his gaze and something unfamiliar and inexplicable had punched through him. Like a fist right to his chest. Or his gut.

If it had been any other woman he would have gone over, bought her a drink, probably spent the night with her. Uncomplicated, mutually satisfying sex between adults.

What could be better? But as much as his body might have greedily wanted the pretty blonde across the room, possibly more than he'd wanted any woman, something had sounded a warning bell in his head, holding him back.

And then someone had spiked her drink—they must have done because he'd seen her go from responsible to disorientated in the space of half a drink—and he'd found himself swooping in to play some kind of knight in shining armour, before any of her colleagues could see her.

Sol couldn't have said how he knew that would have mattered to her more than almost anything else. There was no plausible explanation for the...*connection* he'd felt with her.

So he'd alerted the manager to the situation before pushing his way across the room, grabbing the dazed Anouk's bag and coat and putting his arm around her before anyone else could see her, and leading her out of the nightclub.

Only one person had challenged him on the way out, a belligerent, narrow-eyed, spotty kid he hadn't known, who he suspected had been the one to spike Anouk's drink. It hadn't taken more than a scowl from Sol to send the kid slinking back to the shadows.

He'd got Anouk home and made sure she was settled and safely asleep in bed before he'd left her. The way he knew Saskia would have been doing if she hadn't snuck away by that point. Along with his brother. Sol had seen them leave. Together. So wrapped up in each other that they hadn't even noticed anyone else.

He'd headed back to the club to advise them of the situation, before calling it a night; there had been a handful of women all more than willing to persuade him to stay. None of them had enticed him that night.

Or since. If he was being honest.

Not that Malachi knew that he knew any of it, of course,

and he wasn't about to mention it to his big brother. Not here, anyway. Not now. Not when it included Saskia. If the pair of them had wanted him to know they'd ever got together then they wouldn't have pretended they didn't know each other back when Malachi had brought Izzy's mum up to the ward and Saskia had explained to her what was going on with the little girl.

He'd tackle Malachi about it some other time, when he could wind him up a little more about it. The way the two of them usually did.

Sol glowered into his coffee rather than meet Malachi's characteristically sharp gaze.

'I haven't forgotten anything.' He spoke quietly. 'I remember everything you went through to raise us, Mal. I know you sold your soul to the devil just to get enough money to buy food for our bellies.'

For a moment, he could feel his brother's eyes boring into him, but still Sol couldn't bring himself to look up.

'Bit melodramatic, aren't you, *bratik*?' Malachi gritted out. 'Is this about Izzy?'

'I guess.'

His second lie of the night to his brother.

'Yeah. Well,' Malachi bit out at length. 'No need to get soppy about it.'

'Right.'

Downing the last of the cold coffee and grimacing, Sol crushed the plastic cup and lobbed it into the bin across the hallway. The perfect drop shot. Malachi grunted his approval.

'You ever wondered what might have happened if we'd had a different life?' The question was out before he could stop himself. 'Not had a drug addict for a mother, or had to take care of her and keep her away from her dealer every spare minute?'

'No,' Malachi shut him down instantly. 'I don't. I don't ever think about it. It's in our past. Done. Gone.'

'What the hell kind of childhood was that for us?' Sol continued regardless. 'Our biggest concern should have been whether we wanted an Action Man or Starship Lego for Christmas, not keeping her junkie dealer away from her.'

'Well, it wasn't. I wouldn't have asked if I'd known you were going to get maudlin on me.'

'You were eight, Mal. I was five.'

'I know how old we were,' Malachi growled. 'What's got into you, Sol? It's history. Just leave it alone.'

'Right.'

Sol pressed his lips into a grim line as the brothers lapsed back into silence. Malachi could claim their odious childhood was in the rear-view mirror as much as he liked, but they both knew that if they'd really locked the door on their past then they wouldn't have founded Care to Play, their centre where young carers from the age of merely five up to sixteen could just unwind and be kids instead of responsible for a parent or a sibling.

If there had been anything like that around when he and Malachi had been kids, he liked to think it could have made a difference. Then again, he and Mal had somehow defied the odds, hadn't they?

Would the strait-laced Anouk think him less of an arrogant playboy if she knew *that* about him?

Geez, why did he even care?

Shooting to his feet abruptly, Sol shoved his hands in his pockets.

'I'm going to check on some of my patients upstairs, then I'll be back to see Izzy.'

He didn't wait for his brother to respond, but he could

picture Malachi's head dip even as he strode down the corridor and through the fire door onto the stairwell.

He wasn't ready for Anouk to come bounding up the steps and, by the way she stopped dead when she saw him, she was equally startled.

'You're still here?' she faltered.

'Indeed.'

'I'd have thought you'd have gone home by now. I heard Izzy's mum arrived.'

She glanced nervously over his shoulder, as if checking no one could see them talking. He could well imagine she didn't want to be seen as the next notch on his bedpost. He almost wanted to ask her how much free time she imagined a young neurosurgeon to have that he could possibly have made time for so many women.

He bit his tongue.

What did it matter to him if she believed he was as bad as all those stories? Besides, hadn't he played up to every one of them over the years? Better people thought him a commitment-phobe than realise the truth about him.

Whatever the truth even was.

'Mal and I stayed to help.'

'Mal?'

'Malachi.'

'That's right.' She clicked her fingers. 'Your brother. You did say he was collecting the girls' mother.'

'He's through there now.' A thought occurred to him. 'With Saskia.'

'Okay.' She nodded, but her eyes stayed neutral.

Interesting. She clearly didn't know that Saskia and Malachi had had a…*thing*. He wondered what, if anything, Anouk remembered from that night. The club? The drink? The fact that he'd been the one to escort her safely home? Did she not remember him at all from that night?

'Anyway, I have to go.'

'Women waiting for you?'

That prim note in her voice had no business tingling through him like that.

'Always.'

She shot him a deprecating look and he couldn't help grinning, even as he moved to the flight of stairs, heading down two at a time.

'See you around, Anouk.'

He was briefly aware of her grunt before she yanked open the door and shot through it. Waiting a few seconds to be sure the door closed behind her, Sol turned around and headed back upstairs to the neurology department to check on his patients.

He felt somehow oddly…*deflated*.

Anouk tapped her fingers agitatedly on her electronic pad as she waited for the lift.

Why did she keep letting Solomon Gunn get under her skin? It was ignominious enough that her body was clearly attracted to him but it was so much worse that she kept wanting him to be different from the playboy cliché— *imagining* that she saw glimpses of something deeper within him, for pity's sake.

She who, of all people, should surely have known better?

She'd spent her entire childhood managing her mother. Playing the grown-up opposite her childlike mother—a woman who had perfected all the drama and diva-like tendencies of the worst kind of Hollywood star stereotypes.

She had watched the stunning Annalise Hartwood chase playboy after playboy, fellow stars and movie directors alike, convinced that she would be the one to tame them. It was the same story every time. Of course each finale was as trite as the last. Her biological father had been the worst, by all accounts, but ultimately they'd all ended up using her, hurting her, dumping her.

And Anouk had been the one who'd had to pick up the pieces and put her mother's fragile ego back together.

Not that Annalise had ever thanked her for it.

Quite the opposite.

Anouk had never quite matched up to her mother's mental image of how she should be as the daughter of a famous movie star. She'd been too gawky, too lanky; too introverted and too geeky; too book-smart and too gauche.

It had taken decades—and Saskia—for Anouk to finally realise that the problem hadn't really been her. It had been her mother.

That deathbed confession had been the most desolating moment of all. The betrayal had been inconceivable. It had laid her to waste right where she'd stood.

That was the moment she'd realised she had to get away from her old life.

She'd changed her name, her backstory, and she'd come to the UK. And Saskia, loyal and protective, had dropped everything to come with her.

In over a decade in the UK no one had come close to getting under her skin and poking away at old wounds the way Sol had somehow seemed able to do.

The lift doors *pinged* and she stepped forward in readiness. The last person she expected to see inside was the cause of her current unease. This was the very reason she'd waited for the lift instead of returning via the staircase. For a moment, she almost thought he looked as unsettled as she felt.

But that was ridiculous. Nothing ever unsettled Sol.

'Have you decided against getting in after all?' he asked

dryly when she'd hovered at the doors so long that he'd been compelled to step forward and press the button to hold them. 'Anyone would think you were avoiding me.'

No, they wouldn't. Not unless he'd equally been avoiding her, surely?

Her mind began to tick over furiously. Her school teachers had called her an over-thinker as a kid. They'd made it sound like a bad thing.

'I thought you were leaving? Women to meet.'

'I am.' He shrugged casually, leaning back against the lift wall and stretching impossibly long, muscled legs in front of him.

'Up in Neurology?' she challenged.

'I forgot something.'

She eyed him thoughtfully. No coat, no bag, no laptop.

'What?'

'Sorry?'

'What did you forget?' she pushed.

'What is this?'

He laughed convincingly and anyone else might have believed him. She probably *should* believe him.

'The Inquisition?'

'You were checking on your patients,' she realised, with a start.

Who was that patient he'd mentioned earlier? Ah, yes.

'Mrs Bowman, by any chance?'

He swiftly covered his surprise.

'My patient, my responsibility,' he commented briskly.

Anouk ignored him.

'And now you're going back to support Izzy and her family.'

'Is that so?'

Her heart thundered in Anouk's chest and she didn't

know if it was at the realisation of what he was doing, or the fact that she was confronting him about it.

'You play the tough guy, the playboy, but you've actually got a bit of a softer side, haven't you?'

'Vicious rumour,' he dismissed.

'I don't think so.'

The lift bumped gently as they reached the ground floor and when she swayed slightly, Sol instinctively reached out to steady her. The unexpected contact was a jolt as though she'd grabbed hold of an electrical power cable with no Faraday suit to protect her.

It coursed through her, zinging from the top of her head to the tips of her toes.

His darkening eyes and flared nostrils confirmed that she wasn't the only one who felt it.

A little unsteadily, she made her way out of the lift with no choice but to walk together across the lobby or risk making things look all the more awkward.

The doors slid open and the cool night air hit her hard. In a matter of seconds he'd be gone, across the car park and into that low, muscled vehicle of his.

Any opportunity would have evaporated. For good.

She stopped abruptly at the kerbside.

'Can I ask you something?'

'Shoot,' he invited.

She opened her mouth but her courage deserted her abruptly.

'Those mince pies the other day…were you also the one who decorated the desk with tinsel?'

He grinned.

'Sometimes in a place like this—' he bobbed his head back to the hospital '—it can be easy to forget Christmas should be a celebration. Don't underestimate how much a bit of tinsel and a few mince pies can lift the spirits.'

'Blue and white tinsel hung like an ECG tracing,' she clarified.

'Festive and atmospheric all at once.' He grinned again, and another moment of awareness rippled over her skin.

'Right.'

'Indeed.'

They watched each other a moment longer. Neither speaking. Finally, Sol took a step forward.

'Well, goodnight, Anouk.'

'Can I ask you something else?'

He stopped and turned back to her as she drew in a deep breath.

'How is it you know this family so well? Well enough that you've saddled yourself with four of the worst shifts of the year just to get the night off to sit with those girls in there whilst your brother is helping their mum?'

A hundred witty comebacks danced on his tongue. She could practically feel them buzzing in the air around the two of them. But then he looked at her and seemed to bite them back.

'Malachi and I work with a young carers' group in town,' he heard himself saying. 'Katie and Isobel are two of about thirty kids who come to the centre.'

'So many?'

It was the bleak look in his eyes that gouged her the most.

'That's not even the half of it.' He shook his head. 'You've read the reports, probably around a quarter of a million kids are carers for a parent or other family member. All under sixteen, some as young as four or five. We want to reach them all but we've only just got the council on board. Sometimes the hardest bit is getting people to even acknowledge there's an issue.'

'*You're* raising awareness?' Her eyebrows shot up.

This really meant something to him? He truly cared?

He watched her carefully, wordless for a moment. As if he was waging some internal battle. She waited, holding her breath, although she didn't understand why.

'We're having a fundraiser on Saturday night, to throw a spotlight on the centre.'

'Solomon Gunn is throwing a charity gala?'

Something flitted across his eyes but then he grinned and offered a nonchalant shrug, and it was gone.

'What can I say? Lots of attractive, willing women to choose from, so I guess I get to kill the two proverbial birds with one stone.'

The silence pulled tighter, tauter.

A few hours ago she would have believed that. Now she knew it was an act. And that was what terrified her the most.

Was she being open-minded and non-judgemental? Or was she simply being gullible, seeing what she wished she could see?

'Come with me.'

She had a feeling the invitation had slipped out before he could stop himself.

She frowned.

'Sorry?'

For a moment she thought he was going to laugh it off.

'Be my guest at the gala.'

Something rocked her from the inside. Like thousands of butterflies all waking up from their hibernation, and beating their wings all at once.

She had never experienced anything like it.

'Like…a date?'

'Why not?' he asked cheerfully.

As though it was no big deal to him.

It probably wasn't.

'With you?'

'Your eagerness is a real ego boost for a man, you know that?'

She aimed a sceptical look in his direction.

'I hardly think a man like you needs any more ego massages. You have women practically throwing themselves at you at every turn.'

'I'm not asking them, though, am I?' he pointed out. 'I'm asking you.'

She schooled herself not to be sucked in. Not to fall into that age-old trap. But it wasn't as easy as it had been for all those other men who had flirted with her over the years.

Because those other guys hadn't been Sol, a small voice needled her.

Anouk gritted her teeth.

'Is that why you're inviting me? Because you don't like the fact that I'm not falling over myself to flirt with you?'

'That's exactly it,' he replied, deadpan. 'I find my ego can't take the knockback.'

'Sarcastic much?' she muttered, but a small smile tugged at her mouth despite herself.

'I'll pick you up at half-past seven.'

'I might be on duty.'

'You aren't.' He shrugged.

'I beg your pardon?'

'Relax. I was just checking the rotas before and I don't remember seeing your name.'

She told herself that it meant nothing. It was pure co-incidence.

'What makes you think I want to go?'

'What else are you doing that night? It's fun, and, hey, you can do something for charity at the same time.'

He was impressively convincing.

'People will think I'm just the next notch on your bed-post.'

'Some women are happy to have that accolade.'

'I am not *some* women.'

'No,' he agreed. 'You are not.'

The compliment rolled through her, making long-dormant parts of her body unfurl and stretch languidly. Her head was rapidly losing this battle with her body.

'How about this?' he suggested. 'I'll give you my ticket and you can take Saskia, or whoever you want, as your plus one.'

'You would give me your ticket?'

'Sure. That way you won't feel like I'm trying to obli-gate you in any way.'

'And I could take anyone?'

'Of course.'

She narrowed her eyes.

'Even a date of my own?'

'Oof!' He clutched his stomach as though she'd deliv-ered a punch to his gut, making her laugh exactly as he'd clearly intended. 'You know where to strike a man, don't you? Yes, even a date of your own.'

'And you would miss out? On something as important to you as you've suggested these young carers are?'

'Oh, I won't miss out,' he said airily. 'I'll just go as someone else's plus one.'

It shouldn't hurt to hear. Yet it did. Anouk arranged her features into what she hoped was a neutral expression.

'Of course. You must have a whole host of potential dates just waiting for you to call.'

'So many it can become exhausting at times,' he concurred blithely.

'I'll leave the tickets behind the Resus desk for you before your shift ends tomorrow.'

And then, before she could answer, or say anything uncharacteristically stupid, Sol walked away. The way they probably both should have done ten minutes earlier.

CHAPTER THREE

'THIS PLACE IS STUNNING,' Anouk breathed as she gazed up at the huge sandstone arches that lined either side of the gala venue, and then up again to the breathtaking vaulted ceiling.

'Isn't it?' Saskia demurred.

'I feel positively shabby by comparison.'

'Well, you don't look it.' Saskia laughed and Anouk wondered if she'd imagined the tension she'd noted in her friend over the past few months. 'You look like you're sparkling, and it isn't just the new dress. Although I'm glad I let you talk me into buying it.'

'I'm glad I let you talk me into buying it, too,' admitted Anouk, smoothing her hands over the glorious fabric.

It was amazing how much confidence the dress was giving her, from its fitted body and plunging sweetheart neckline to its mermaid hemline. Three strings of jewelled, off-the-shoulder straps swished over her upper arms whilst the royal-blue colour seemed to complement her blonde hair perfectly.

'You look totally Hollywood.'

'Don't.' Anouk shuddered, knowing Saskia was the one person she could be honest with. 'I think I've had enough of Hollywood to last me a lifetime.'

'Me, too. But still, the look is good.'

'Maybe I should have been in more festive colours.' She glanced at Saskia's own, stunning emerald dress, which had looked gorgeous on the rack, but on her friend's voluptuously feminine body seemed entirely bespoke, complementing Saskia's dark skin tone to perfection.

'I look like a Christmas tree.' Her friend laughed, before waving towards the glorious eighteen-foot work of art, complete with elegant decorations, that dominated the entrance. 'Although if I looked *that* amazing I'd be happy.'

'You look even better, and you know it.' Anouk laughed. 'You've only just walked in and you've turned a dozen heads.'

'They're probably looking at you, and, either way, I don't care. Tonight, Anouk, we're going to relax and enjoy ourselves.'

'We are?'

'We are.' Saskia was firm, taking a champagne flute from the tray of a passing waiter, her beam of thanks making the poor guy fall for her instantly. 'Starting with this.'

She passed the drink to Anouk.

'You still feeling sick?' Anouk frowned.

'Yeah.' Saskia pulled a rueful face but Anouk didn't miss the flush of colour staining her cheeks.

If she hadn't known better she might have suspected that Saskia was pregnant. But that surely wasn't possible? Up until ten months ago Saskia had been engaged and, for all Saskia's confidence and effervescent personality, Anouk knew her ex-fiancé had been only the second man her friend had ever slept with.

But he hadn't been as loyal, and Anouk had never really taken to him. Whenever she'd looked at him she'd seen yet another playboy—just like her mother's lovers.

Just like Sol, a voice whispered in her head.

'Relax.' Saskia nudged her gently. 'Enjoy your drink.'

'I don't really like…' Anouk began, but her friend shushed her.

'You do tonight.'

Anouk balked.

She still wasn't sure what had happened at that night-club. She had the vaguest memory of starting to relax and trying to have a little fun, and then a sense of panic. After that it wasn't clear, but she'd ended up back home, in her own bed, alone.

Safe.

The popping bubbles looked innocuous enough—fun, even—but all Anouk could see was her mother, downing glasses and popping pills. Had anything else passed her lips in those final few years?

'One glass doesn't make you your mother.' Saskia linked her arm through Anouk's, reading her mind.

Anouk offered a rueful smile.

'That obvious, huh?'

'Only to me. Now go on, forget about your mother and enjoy this evening. You and I both deserve a bit of time off, and, anyway, we're supporting a good cause.'

'We are, aren't we?' Anouk nodded, dipping her head and taking a tentative sip.

It wasn't as bad as she'd feared. In fact, it was actually quite pleasant. Not the cheap plonk, at least, with no bitter aftertaste. Including that of her mother.

Sighing quietly, Anouk finally felt some of the tension begin to uncoil within her.

This was going to be a good evening. She was determined to enjoy it.

'I was beginning to think you weren't coming after all.'

His voice was like a lightning bolt moving through her, pinning her to the spot. Her mouth felt suddenly dry, and even her legs gave a traitorous tremor beneath the gorgeous blue fabric.

Gathering up all her will, Anouk made herself turn around, even as Saskia was sliding her arm from Anouk's and greeting Sol as if they were good friends.

Then again, they were. Saskia had been at Moorlands General for years. Admittedly a much nicer hospital than Moorlands Royal Infirmary, where she herself had trained. Why hadn't she made the transfer sooner?

She was so wrapped up in her thoughts that she only just caught Saskia murmuring something about going to check the seating plan, too late to stop her friend from slipping away into the faceless crowd.

And just like that she was alone with Sol.

As if the couple of hundred other people in the place didn't even exist.

It should have worried Anouk more that she felt that way.

'You look…breathtaking.'

Ridiculously, the fact that he had to reach for the word, as though it was genuine and not some well-trotted-out line, sent another bolt of brilliant light through her.

And heat.

So much heat.

Which was why he had a reputation for being fatal. He was the Smoking Gun, after all.

She would do well to remember that.

'You thought I wasn't coming?' she made herself ask, tipping her head to one side in some semblance of casualness.

'I did wonder.'

Some golden liquid swirled about an expensive-looking, crystal brandy glass in his hand. But it was the bespoke suit that really snagged her attention. Expensively tailored, it showcased Sol to perfection with his broad shoulders and strong chest, tapering to an athletic waist. The crisp white shirt with the bow tie that was already just a fraction too loose suggested a hint of debauchery, as though he was already on the brink of indulging where he shouldn't.

With her?

She went hot, then cold, then hot again at the thought. It was shameful that the idea should appeal so much. The simmering heat seemed to make her insides expand until she feared her flesh and bones wouldn't be able to contain her. He was simply too...*much*.

He isn't your type, she told herself forcefully. Only it didn't seem as though her body wanted to listen.

'I thought perhaps I could introduce you to some people.'

'Oh.' That surprised her. 'Is that why you came over, then?'

He hesitated, and then offered a grin that she supposed was meant to look rueful but just looked deliciously wicked instead.

'Not really.' He made it sound like a confession yet he deliberately didn't elaborate and Anouk wasn't about to play into his hands by asking him.

'I see,' she lied.

'Do you indeed?' he murmured. 'Then perhaps you might explain to me why I couldn't resist coming over here the instant I saw you walk in.'

Her chest kicked. Hard. It didn't matter how many times she silently chanted that he couldn't affect her, Anouk realised all too quickly that she was fighting a losing battle. She had no idea how she managed to inject a disparaging note into her voice.

'Does that line usually work?'

'I don't know, I've never used it before. I'll tell you next time I try.'

She bit her tongue to stop herself from asking when that next time would be. He was clearly baiting her, but what bothered her was that it was working.

'Besides…' his eyes skimmed her in frank, male appreciation, and everywhere his eyes moved she was sure she nearly scorched in response '…if I hadn't come over then some other bloke would have. You're much too alluring in that gown.'

'But not out of it?' she quipped.

His eyes gleamed black, his smile all the more wolfish. Too late, Anouk realised what she'd said.

'Is that an invitation? I have a feeling I would be breaking quite a few harassment in the workplace rules if I admitted to imagining you out of that dress.'

'I mean… I didn't mean… That isn't what I intended.'

'Then be careful what you say, *zolotse*, you can build a man up too quickly otherwise.'

'*Zolotse?*' she echoed. It sounded…Russian, maybe?

'*Zolotse,*' he confirmed.

It was the way his voice softened on that word—as if he hardly knew what he was saying himself as he moved closer, his body so tantalisingly close to hers and his breath brushing her neck—that sent a fresh awareness singing through her veins. It made her forget even to draw breath.

Her mind struggled to stay in control.

'You don't intend to elucidate?' She barely recognised her own voice, it was so laced with desire.

'I do not,' he muttered.

Now that she thought about it, Sol and Malachi both had a bit of a Russian look about them. But if they were Russian then it was something Sol didn't share with many other people. Certainly it wasn't common knowledge around the hospital.

Which only made her feel that much more unique.
Dammit, but the man was positively lethal.

Three hours had passed since she'd arrived.
Three hours!
It felt like a mere five minutes, and all because she'd
been in Sol's company.

The man had turned out to be a revelation. She'd known
he was intelligent, witty, devastatingly attractive, of course.
The whole hospital talked about him often enough. But
knowing it and *experiencing* it turned out to be two entirely different things.

He had a way of making her feel…special. And it didn't
matter how many times she cautioned herself that this was
his trick, every time he stared at her as though she were the
only person in the entire room, an incredible thrill skew-
ered her like a javelin hurtling through her body.

Even as he'd introduced her around the room—to con-
tacts to whom many of the top consultants would have
amputated their own limbs to be introduced—she'd had
to fight to concentrate on what he was saying. The feel of
his hand at the small of her back kept sending her brain
into a tailspin.

She felt like a reed, bending and turning, twisting wherever the breeze took her, and right now that breeze took the
form of Solomon Gunn. He was swaying her at will and
yet all he was really doing was moving smoothly through
the throng, his hand barely touching her searing flesh.

Still, she smiled and greeted and charmed, just as she'd
learned to do at the knee of her Hollywood mother. And
she made no objection to what Sol was doing.

*Perhaps because a portion of her longed to wallow
shamelessly in the glances cast their way?*
Some admiringly. Others enviously. She'd been on the

receiving end of enough sugar-coated scowls and under-handed digs to know that she wasn't the only one to have noticed Sol's attention to her. Or realise that this was more than just his usual behaviour towards a woman on his arm.

He was giving her his undivided attention and present-ing her as though she were a proper date. Half of the room seemed to be more than conscious of his body standing so close to hers. As though she were more than just a col-league.

As though there were something intimate between them.

And yet she couldn't bring herself to care the way she suspected she might have cared a few days ago.

His gentleness and compassion with the young family the other night still played on her mind.

Sol might be renowned for caring about his patients, but she'd seen the way he'd stayed with that family even when he was off duty, helping the girls' mother even when he should have been getting much-needed rest.

Too natural, too easy. A world away from the playboy Lothario she'd once thought him to be. It fired her curios-ity until she couldn't ignore it any longer.

'I must say that, whilst I don't know your brother all that well, I wouldn't have thought a gala ball to raise money for kids was something you'd be interested in. Let alone quite so heavily involved with. It begs the question of *why*.'

'If there is something you want to know, then ask. I am an open book, *zolotse*.' He shrugged breezily, and yet it tugged at Anouk.

Was there more going on behind his words than Sol was willing to reveal?

It was all she could do to stay brisk.

'Next you'll be telling me that you're misunderstood. That your playboy reputation is a terrible exaggeration.'

Was she really teasing him now?

'On the contrary.' He shook his head, his stunning smile cracking her chest and making her heart skip a beat or ten. 'My reputation is something for which I've never made any apologies.'

'You're proud of it,' she realised abruptly.

And there was no reason for the sharp stab of disappointment that lanced through her at that moment. No reason at all.

'I wouldn't say I was proud of it, but then I'm not ashamed of it either.'

His nonchalance was clear. She had only imagined there was another side to him because that was what she'd wanted to see. What her mother had always done with her own lovers.

It galled Anouk to realise that she was more like her mother than she'd ever wanted to admit.

'Perhaps you should be ashamed of it,' she challenged pointedly, but Sol simply flashed an even wider, heart-thumping grin.

'Perhaps. But you could argue that I'm better than many people because I'm above board. I don't pretend to be emotionally available and looking for a relationship to get a woman into bed, only to turn around and ghost her, or whatever.'

'No, but women practically throw themselves at your feet and you sleep with them anyway.'

'They're grown women, Anouk, it's *their* choice.'

Anouk snorted rather indelicately.

'You must know they're secretly hoping for more.'

'Some, maybe. But I make no false pretences. Why does this rile you so much, Anouk?' His voice softened suddenly. 'Is this about what happened with Saskia? Or did some bloke treat you that badly in the past?'

He might as well have doused her with a bucket of icy water.

What was she doing arguing with him about this? Letting him see how much it bothered her just as clearly as if she'd slid her heart onto her sleeve.

She fought to regroup. To plaster a smile on her face as though she weren't in the least bothered by the turn of conversation. But she feared it looked more like a grimace.

'No, I'm fortunate that I've never been treated that way.'

She didn't add that she'd watched her mother repeat the same mistake over and over enough times never to be caught out like that.

'Never?'

'Never,' she confirmed adamantly.

As though that would rewind the clock. Back to the start of the conversation when she hadn't been quite so revealing about herself. Or the start of the night before she'd let Saskia walk away and leave her alone with him. Or three days ago when they'd worked together on little Isobel and she'd arrogantly imagined she saw something in the man that no one else appeared to have noticed.

The worst of it was that there was some component of her that didn't want to rewind anything. Which, despite every grey cell in her brain screaming at her not to be such an idiot, was enjoying tonight. With Sol.

'In that case, there's something else you should bear in mind.' He leaned into her ear, his breath tickling her skin, and it was like a huge hand stealing into her chest and closing around her heart. 'There are plenty of women who enjoy no-strings sex just as much as I do.'

Don't imagine him in bed. Don't.

But it was too late.

Anouk wrinkled her nose in self-disgust.

'I get that in your twenties, but you're—what? Mid-thirties? Don't you think you might want to grow up some time? Settle down. Be an adult.' She cocked an eyebrow. 'You aren't Peter Pan.'

'That's a shame, because you'd make the perfect Tinker Bell.'

'I'm not a ruddy fairy,' she huffed crossly.

'See?' he teased, oblivious to the eddies now churning within her. 'You even have the Tinker Bell temper down flawlessly. Clearly we're perfectly matched.'

'We most certainly are not,' she gasped.

And he laughed whilst she pretended to be irritated, even though she still didn't try to pull away. So when Sol's hand didn't leave her, when his body remained so close to hers without actually invading her space or making her feel crowded in, and when he deftly steered her out of the path of a couple of rather glassy-eyed, lustful-looking men, she found it all such an intoxicating experience.

As though Sol wanted to keep her to himself.

No, she was being fanciful, not to mention ridiculous.

And still that knot sat there, in the pit of her stomach. Not *apprehension* so much as…anticipation. She was waiting for Sol to do something. More than that, she *wanted* him to.

Perhaps that was why, when reality cut harshly into the dream that the night had become, Anouk was caught completely off guard.

'Now, these are the Hintons,' he leaned in to whisper in her ear as a rather glamorous older-looking couple approached. 'She was a human rights lawyer whilst he was a top cardiothoracic surgeon. They're nice, too.'

'How lovely to meet you.' The older woman smiled at her, but her old eyes burned brightly as they looked her over thoughtfully. 'Anouk Hart…Hartwood… Hmm. You seem familiar, my dear?'

'No, I don't think so.' Anouk forced herself to smile back but her cheeks felt too frozen, her smile too false.

The woman peered closer and Anouk could feel the blood starting to drag through her veins even as her heart kicked with the effort of getting it moving again.

'Yes, definitely familiar.' She nudged her husband, who was still beaming at Anouk. 'Don't you think so, Jonathon?'

He pondered the question for a moment.

Anouk tried not to tense, not to react, but she could feel herself sway slightly. Not so much that a casual observer might notice, but enough that a man standing with his hand on her back might. Certainly enough that Sol did.

His head turned to look at her but she kept staring straight ahead, a tight smile straining her lips.

'Around the hospital, no doubt.' She had no idea how she injected that note of buoyancy into her voice. 'Or maybe I just have one of those faces.'

'Oh, no, my dear, you do not have *one of those faces.*' The woman chuckled.

'More like a screen icon,' her husband agreed, then his face cleared and Anouk's stomach plummeted. 'Like Annalise Hartwood.'

'Annalise Hartwood,' the woman echoed delightedly. 'And she had a daughter…what was her name, Jonathon? Was it Noukie?'

How she'd always hated that nickname. She was sure her mother had known it, too. It was why Annalise had used it all the more.

'Noukie…' He nodded slowly. 'Yes, I think it might have been. You're Noukie Hartwood.'

As if she didn't already know! They said it as if it were a nugget of gold, a little bit of information that they were giving her.

Anouk wanted to shout and bellow. Instead, she stood exactly where she was, her smile not slipping, muscles not twitching.

'Anouk Hart.' She tried to smile. 'Yes.'

'My goodness, I can hardly believe it. Annalise was such a screen icon in my day. But, my dear, you don't have any American accent at all, do you? How long have you been over here?'

How it hurt to keep smiling.

'My friend and I came to university over here...' she paused as if she were searching for the memory, when the truth was she knew practically to the week, the day '...so a little over ten years ago.'

The moment her mother had died and Anouk had finally felt free of her. What kind of person did that make her?

But then, after her mother's deathbed revelation, who could blame her? To realise that her mother, her grandmother, had been lying to her about her father for eighteen years.

What kind of people did that make *them*?

'It was awful what happened to your mother, dear. God rest her soul.'

Their sympathy was apparent, but all Anouk could feel was how relieved she'd been. It had been awful, but it had also been liberating.

What had felt awful had been getting to the UK, tracking down her father from an address on a fragment of paper, only to discover that he had died a few years earlier. Her eyes pricked, hot and painful, at the memory. It had been the moment she'd realised the truth had been buried from her, quite literally if she thought about it, for ever.

She hastily blinked away the inconvenient tears. This was no time for sentimental nonsense. Sol's eyes were boring into her. Seeing her in a new way. Or maybe seeing her in the old way, the way she hadn't wanted anyone to look at her ever again.

'Yes, well…' The smile was as rigid as ever but suddenly she felt like a sad, lonely, frightened kid all over again.

You are a successful doctor, she chanted silently to herself. *Successful*. That wasn't her life any more.

'I know it wasn't public knowledge, my dear. But we knew of the rumours. The things you did for her.'

'No… I…' The practised denial was on her lips but it had been so long. So many years.

'What a marvellous ambassador for the young carers you will be.' The woman brightened up, and it took Anouk a moment to realise what she was implying.

She opened her mouth to interject but the woman was already turning to her husband.

'Noukie, here, will make a wonderful role model. Don't you think, Jonathon?'

'Oh, quite, quite,' he agreed solemnly, completely oblivious of the turmoil their observations were churning within Anouk. 'Letting them know it doesn't matter what your background—even the glitz of Hollywood—being responsible for someone else, like a parent, can happen to anyone.'

She couldn't focus. They were still talking but the words were becoming more and more distant and muffled. Her brain was shutting down despite her attempts to fight it. She tried to tell them that they had it all wrong, that she wasn't anyone's role model, but they were caught up in their excitement and weren't listening.

She wasn't really aware of Sol taking charge, winding the conversation up in a natural, easy way, but she knew he must have done, because the next thing she knew he was guiding her gently but firmly through the crowds without commotion. Or, certainly, no one seemed to be paying her any more or less attention than they had been before.

It was only when she found herself in a quiet anteroom that she felt herself starting to come to.

CHAPTER FOUR

'SORRY.' SHE BARED her teeth in what she desperately hoped would pass for a wide smile. Her stiff cheeks screamed in protest. 'Don't know what happened there.'

'I think you do.'

It was soft, compassionate even. Something pulled, like a painful band, in her chest. She could deny it, but what would be the point?

'So, Noukie Hartwood? I never knew.'

She really didn't want to answer and yet she found herself speaking. Why was it so much easier to talk to Sol?

'I always hated Noukie,' she managed.

'And the surname?'

She lifted her shoulders.

'I shortened it to Hart when I came to the UK.'

'Why?'

'I don't know.' That was a lie. 'To put some distance between myself and my mother, I guess.'

'Because she'd died?'

'She took an overdose,' Anouk clarified brusquely as she shot him a sharp look. 'I thought everyone knew that.'

'I'm aware of the story,' he acknowledged after a moment.

There was no need for her to say anything else, and yet she found herself speaking, her voice high and harsh.

'Of course, she probably didn't mean to. She had a new movie coming out and I think it was her attempt at a publicity stunt gone wrong. That's who she was.'

She could practically feel the emotions dancing inside her. Or stomping inside her. Not that it made much difference; either way, they were having a field day.

What was she doing, bleating on?

'Anyway.' She shook her head back, straightening her shoulders. As if that could somehow make her feel stronger. 'I don't want to talk about this any longer.'

Whatever she'd expected him to say, it wasn't the quiet observation that he came out with.

'No one ever does, which is part of the problem. Why do you think we're here tonight, Anouk? At this obscenely lavish ball, which costs so much per head that we could probably fund a young carers' centre for a year?'

'Maybe because people have cared enough to come out?' she bit back.

'No, because too many people as rich as most of the guests here tonight would rather throw money at an issue and get back to enjoying themselves guilt-free, than actually look at a problem and talk about it.'

She couldn't say what it was about his tone that made her ears prick up.

'That sounds remarkably like someone who has come from nothing and been on the wrong side of those issues.' She eyed him curiously, glad of the opportunity to set her own personal problems aside for a moment. 'I thought you and Malachi were millionaires? Family money or something?'

'You're changing the subject.'

'And you're evading my question,' she countered.

He contemplated her for a long minute. The band was pulling tighter around her chest with each passing second. So tight that she could barely breathe. Anouk swung around, forcing one leg in front of the other, until she found herself by an exquisitely carved writing desk with a stunning leather inlay.

She reached out to pick up an unusual-looking paperweight as if it could distract her mind, and pretended to herself that her hands weren't shaking.

'I'm not changing the subject, I just don't want to discuss it. I put that chunk of my life behind me a long time ago.'

'If that were true then you wouldn't have gone so white in that ballroom that I feared you were about to keel over. Besides, you don't just lock it away and pretend it doesn't exist. It informs what you do in later life. It's why you're a doctor now.'

She hated that he sounded so logical.

'You think you know me so well,' she threw at him caustically.

'So tell me I'm wrong.'

The worst of it was that they both knew she couldn't do that. So, instead, she spluttered a little.

'Because of course, of all people, you'd understand.'

'More than you'd think.' His voice was still impossibly even whilst she felt scraped raw.

'Then *you* talk.'

'I'm not the one who is struggling right now.'

It was odd, but the more empathetic he sounded, the more she wanted to throw the damn paperweight at his head. Carefully, she used her free hand to prise it out of her clamped fingers and set it back down before turning around. Her teeth hurt from clenching them so she struggled to loosen her jaw, too.

'You think you can help me?' she managed testily.

'Maybe…' he shrugged '…but more likely just talking about it will allow you to help yourself.'

'It was a lifetime ago. It's dead and buried.' She jutted her chin out stubbornly, hoping her whole body wasn't shaking as much as she feared it was.

'I told you, it doesn't work that way. Don't underestimate the monsters inside, Anouk. They exist. They're real. They know where your vulnerable spots are and they know just when to hit you for maximum effect. If you can't even admit they are there, how will you ever defeat them?'

'That's the sort of thing I imagine you say to your patients. Do you really believe that? Have you ever actually practised what you preach, Sol?'

'I've never needed to.' His voice raked over her skin. 'I'm fortunate that my life has been…uneventful.'

She narrowed her eyes, trying to decide whether he was telling the truth. Something in her whispered that he wasn't but he looked so easy, so calm, that she thought she might be wrong. So if he *was* deceiving her then he had to be one of the most convincing liars in the world.

She wasn't sure which truth disappointed her the most.

She stared at him, not trusting herself. She hadn't talked about this in over a decade. The only person who knew the truth—or at least, the sanitised, abridged version—was Saskia.

Solomon Gunn should be the last person in the world she would *ever* talk to about her past. And yet there was a crazy part of her that wanted to open up and spill out every last truth. Right here, right now.

'The term is *confront to get closure*,' he added nonchalantly.

She wanted to gouge that part of her out with the letter opener lying on the desk behind her. And she hated that she felt this way. So out of control.

'The term—' she narrowed her eyes '—is *sod off*.'

He watched her for a moment, his eyes so intense that she had to drop her gaze to his mouth to protect herself from plunging right into them.

'You know it's funny, everyone says you're this gentle, sweet-natured, conservative person. They obviously don't see this other side of you, but I do. Why is that?'

She felt as if she'd been caught with her hand in the proverbial cookie jar. Her heart pounded loudly in her chest and all she could do was be thankful that he couldn't hear it.

'You don't know what you're talking about.' She was impressed at quite how haughty she managed to sound.

Sol, it seemed, was more amused than intimidated.

'Oh, trust me, I do. I know women well enough. I seem to push all your buttons, Anouk Hart.'

'You wouldn't know my buttons if I waved them in your face,' she retorted, congratulating herself on her quick wit.

It was only when he laughed—a deliciously rude and decidedly dirty sound—that she realised quite what she'd said.

Again.

'I do admire a good double entendre. First the invitation to get you out of that dress, and now this. I would say that I believe your subconscious is trying to tell you something, Anouk. But I see you've cleverly managed to manipulate the subject after all.'

'There is a silver lining, then,' she managed, perching on the edge of the desk, her legs stretched in front of her, her arms extended either side of her with her hands resting on the polished wood, too.

It had been a move intended to show she wasn't as cornered as she felt, but she hadn't been prepared for Sol's reaction.

His eyes dropped down her body, as though taking in every new curve she had inadvertently revealed, from the deep plunge of her dress to the way the fabric clung to her thighs. Even the skyscraper heels that she had borrowed from Saskia.

She folded her arms over her chest, realising too late how it made her cleavage appear to swell and threaten to spill over the glorious blue fabric. But then she saw the effect it was having on Sol and her entire body burned.

It was thrilling, the way his eyes raked over her as though he couldn't tear his gaze from her. As though he ached to do so much more than simply look.

It was empowering, too.

Anouk didn't think—she couldn't afford to talk herself out of testing her theory—she just acted. And so what if she didn't believe it when she told herself that all she was trying to do was prevent him from asking any more questions?

Pushing herself up from the desk, she stood and faced him, and Sol didn't miss a moment. His eyes turned molten, his body—all six-foot-three of broad-shouldered, sculpted, wholly masculine beauty—looked suddenly taut and the room started practically humming with sexual tension.

The silence in the room was almost deafening.

Had she ever felt so desired? So confident? So reckless?

'Are you seducing me?' he demanded, the hoarseness of his tone making her blood actually tingle in her veins. 'Because if you are, I can tell you that you're going to need to be a little more persuasive.'

He was lying and they both knew it.

'That can be arranged,' she murmured before her brain even seemed to have kicked into gear.

It was as though someone completely separate to her

had taken control of her body, a confident, sexually assertive persona that she herself had never felt in her life before.

It was exhilarating.

With exaggerated care, she reached around and unzipped the low back of the dress.

'What are you doing, Anouk? This isn't you.'

Another hit of triumph punched through her at the slightly raspy tone to his usually rich timbre.

'I'm shutting down any more of your conversations about my past, in the only way I know you'll respond to,' she replied, shocked at how controlled her voice sounded when inside it felt as if a thousand fizzing fireworks were all going off at once.

'I thought you told me you were only coming tonight on the premise that it wasn't a date, and that you wouldn't be sleeping with me?' he bit out, but she could see him clenching his fists at his sides.

As if he was trying so desperately to keep himself in place and maintain that distance between them. Her heart hammered in her chest, every fibre of her body on edge.

'Oh, believe me, I have no intention of either of us doing any *sleeping*.'

She could see him, coiled and ready. Just about holding himself in place.

'This isn't who you are, or what you do, Anouk,' he growled. 'I'm trying to be a good man here, but there's a limit to how far you can push me.'

'So this isn't what you wanted tonight?' She flicked a tongue out over her dry lips.

She had expected him to break by now and seduction wasn't really one of her skills. How did she convince him that she wanted this, too?

'I'm sick of playing the good girl,' she bit out. 'The responsible girl.'

Noukie Hartwood, the reliable, responsible, *boring* child of the amazing Annalise. Tedious, joyless, a killjoy. And all the other words her mother had flung at her throughout her childhood that had suggested that she didn't have a fun, daring, spontaneous bone in her body.

'Maybe I've decided it's time I had a bit of fun.' She shrugged, almost starting when her dress slipped and threatened to expose her completely, but just about catching herself in time. 'With you.'

'Consider this your last warning, Anouk,' he growled, his gaze riveted on her gaping bodice.

With a final grasp of that confidence she seemed to have acquired for one night only, Anouk shimmied and let her dress slide gracefully down her body to puddle at her feet. She had no idea how she managed to make her legs move enough to step elegantly out of the pool of blue fabric, her eyes locked with Sol's.

'Duly considered,' she murmured.

He moved so fast she was barely aware of it, crossing the space between them to haul her to him.

'Don't say I didn't warn you, *zolotse*,' he growled.

And then suddenly his lips were on hers, only for a fraction of a second, brushing them softly, almost as if he was testing her. It was startling, and it was dangerous, not least because it didn't unsettle her so much as thrill her. Yet still she didn't pull away, not even when he laced his fingers through her hair, met her unblinking gaze again and held it as he slowly—torturously slowly—lowered his mouth to hers and everything…*shifted*.

It wasn't just a kiss. Or, at least, it wasn't like any kiss Anouk had ever known before. It was the most powerful, intense, head-rush kiss that she had ever believed possible.

He was claiming her, teasing her, torturing her. There was something so primal, so raw in his tone that every thought melted out of Anouk's head and it seemed to go on for ever. Dipping and tasting, scraping and teasing. Electrifying her like nothing Anouk had ever experienced before.

But then, *Sol* was like no one she had ever kissed before. With every slide of his lips, hunger seared through her, white-hot, torrid. With every sweep of his tongue she was rent apart. With every graze of his teeth she struggled to control a slew of fracturing sensations, too many to contain. *Too much.*

With each drugging drag of his mouth, and every divinely wicked slide of his tongue, he detonated something inside her. Over and over. Until he angled his head for a better, deeper fit, his hands dropping down her back, skimming the skin, tracing her sides, spanning her lower chest, just under her breasts.

It was how she imagined an initial bump of ketamine would feel, giving her a sudden head rush, making her feel giddy and fluffy. And yet, inconsistently, she was also entirely too aware of herself.

Too hot. Too jumpy. Too *everything.*

He drew whorls on her bare skin, leaving the rest of her body resenting the material that barred him from drawing them everywhere else. And when he returned to cup her face, her entire body ached for him.

Sol was *too much.* And yet she simultaneously couldn't get enough. She placed her hands on his chest as if to anchor herself, realising too late her mistake. The solid wall of warm steel beneath her palms only served to detonate even more fireworks within her. It was impossible to stop her fingers from inching across, exploring and acquainting herself with all the care that her old grandmother used to take reading her braille books. Anouk's imagination filled in all the blanks of the utterly masculine body that lay beneath the slick, tailored suit. Every ridge, dip, and contour. In stunningly vivid technicolour.

How she longed to see it for herself. She felt helpless, and aching, and desperate. Her body entirely spring-loaded with a kind of wanton desire.

When had sex ever been quite like this? So charged, so full of expectation and need? She didn't have an abundance of experience, it was true; but she wasn't exactly an untried virgin, either.

Without quite knowing what she was doing, Anouk flattened her body to his, crushing her suddenly heavy breasts to his chest as though it might afford them some relief. And then Sol let one hand glide down her collarbone, over her chest, and all he did was gently graze one thumb pad over a straining peak and pleasure jolted through her as if he'd just shocked her.

She arched into him, a silent plea for more. She couldn't seem to get close enough. Perhaps she couldn't.

'If you carry on like that, we're not going to stop,' he warned, his mouth barely breaking from hers and yet she felt the loss acutely.

Looping her arms around his neck, Anouk pressed herself closer to him. If she was going to do something so outrageously out of character, then she was going to enjoy every single second of it.

'Promises, promises,' she muttered.

'Not a promise,' rasped Sol. 'Fair warning.'

'Warning taken,' she muttered, her lips tingling as his mouth continued to brush her. 'Now you just need to prove it.'

It was insanity.

Not the fact that he was in a side room at a party with

a beautiful, practically naked woman in his arms—he shamefully had to admit this had happened many times in the past—but rather, the insanity was that he was here with Anouk and she was making him feel more out of control than he'd ever felt with anyone else.

As though he couldn't have resisted her inexperienced seduction even if he'd wanted to. As if she had that kind of power over him. Which, of course, was sheer nonsense.

But he wasn't about to put it to the test and try to pull away from her now. Not when his whole body was igniting at the feel of her smooth, silky skin and scraps of lace beneath his palms; the taste of her skin on his lips and tongue; the way she shivered so deliciously when he grazed his teeth down that long line of her neck.

Not to mention that sinful garter belt, which he really hadn't been expecting from prim Dr Hart. Did he take it off her, or leave it on?

His head couldn't keep track of all the ways he wanted this woman. He wanted her with an intensity, a fierceness that almost floored him. He thought it might kill him and he couldn't even bring himself to care. As long as he had her.

Lowering his head, he claimed her mouth again and again, tasting her with his lips and his tongue, whilst she met him stroke for stroke. He captured each one of her soft sighs in his mouth, emitted as though she was as driven by desire as he was.

He let his hands trail over her body, revelling in the way her body quivered beneath his touch, and every time she pressed herself against him. He relished the way she lifted her hands to fumble with his shirt buttons and then slid them inside to trace the ridges of his chest as if she was trying to commit them to memory merely by touch.

He didn't even remember when he'd lost his jacket or

bowtie. When he'd begun to cup that peachy backside to lift her up to sit on the desk, her hard nipples raking over his chest, his hips locked within the tight embrace of her incredible long, slender legs.

He was so hard, so ready he could barely think straight. *Barely.* But he could think enough to register that if she rocked against him much longer then he was going to be beyond help.

'Are you on the pill?' he muttered.

'Hmm?' She lifted her head to meet his gaze, her eyes glazed and overflowing with naked desire so that it was almost his undoing.

'I don't have any protection on me.' Every word felt as though it was being torn from Sol's throat, especially when he wouldn't have slept with any other woman without protection yet all he could think about with Anouk was burying himself deep inside her and driving them both to oblivion.

It made no sense.

'Oh.'

She flushed, and he couldn't help himself lowering his head and following the pretty flush with his lips.

She moaned softly and it went straight to his sex as surely as if she'd gripped him with her hands.

What the hell had he been saying?

'Protection,' he remembered hoarsely.

Another brief pause and then she shook her head.

'Oh, Lord…no. No pill.'

She loosened her legs from around his hips as though it was the hardest thing she'd ever had to do. But he wasn't about to give her up that easily.

He couldn't.

He might not be able to slide inside her but he had to

do *something* to sate this storm that raged and howled inside him, demanding more of her. *Needing* more of her.

Dropping to his knees, he hooked the shred of lace to one side.

'Wait.' She struggled to sit up, breathless and flustered. 'What are you…?'

But he didn't give her time to finish, he wanted to taste her too badly. Sliding one of her legs over his shoulder, he lowered his head and licked his way straight into her. Her shaky cry, as her hands tangled into his hair, was all the validation he needed.

She tasted of slick, sweet honey, and Sol couldn't get enough. He played with her, toyed with her, drawing lazy whorls with his tongue all around her swollen, molten core, before sliding over her, sliding into her, sucking on her, making her hips meet his mouth with each thrust.

And then she was moving faster, her breathing more ragged than ever, and he gripped hold of her and held her fast, prolonging her agony and ecstasy.

'Sol…please…' she rasped out.

As if she was all his for the taking.

The thought lanced through him with more appeal than it had any right to do.

With one finger sliding inside her, he licked faster and sucked harder. Anouk cried out, bucked against him, and shattered on his tongue. Fragmenting all around him. But he wasn't finished. Over and over he pushed her past the edge until he knew she could fall no more and, reluctantly, he sat back.

He re-buttoned his shirt, locating his jacket and bow tie with surprisingly shaky hands. At least it gave him time to recover, lest he lose all sense of self and pull her onto him to sate them both, there and then.

He watched her as she finally began to come back to

herself. God, but she was beautiful. The need to have her still pounded through him, leaving him edgy and restless in a way he'd never experienced before.

Her eyes flickered to him, seeming to focus.

'You're dressed?'

The distraught shadow in those blue pools caught at him, pulling into a tight band around his chest. Around his sex.

'I have to go back out to the gala,' he gritted out. 'It's my role to raise money. For the charity.'

'Of course.' She pulled her mouth into a semblance of a smile although he wondered what it cost her. 'This was sex. Just sex.'

And there was no reason for that to grate on him as it did.

'And tonight, I intend there to be much more of it,' he growled. 'Properly. When we can take our time.'

'More?' Her hand fluttered to her chest and he found he rather liked it.

'Much more,' he echoed firmly. 'Trust me, Anouk. That was just for starters.'

And then, before she could answer he spun around and left the room, not trusting himself. He had a duty to the charity, and the kids. But if he stayed another moment with Anouk, he wasn't sure he could trust himself not to give in to temptation in the form of this bright, focussed, driven doctor with the blonde hair that sparkled like a glorious beach, and the blue eyes that made him sink fathoms deep.

And, goodness, he could still taste her sweetness on his tongue; still smell her on his fingers. And it was driving him to distraction.

She was driving him to distraction.

Who would have thought that the demure, strait-laced Anouk Hart would have ended up being his kryptonite?

CHAPTER FIVE

SOL SLAMMED HIS car door shut with a vicious whack of his arm and made his way across the hospital car park.

He'd been in a foul mood since the Gala.

Leaving Anouk in that room after such a teaser of her luscious body had been nearly impossible. Promising them both a night full of more carnal discoveries had been the only way he'd managed to get back out to the gala to carry out the role that had brought him there in the first place: to raise money and awareness for the young carers, the kids who already had enough responsibility for people in their lives, and he refused to let them down.

Even for Anouk.

But he couldn't have anticipated that things would become so chaotic with Malachi, who had had to leave. It hadn't occurred to him that the night with Anouk might not happen. But his body had been protesting it ever since.

Even this morning he'd woken in the early hours, his head full of images of Anouk, his body hard and ready. He would swear he could still taste her on his tongue; still close his eyes and feel the heat from her body against his chest. And decidedly lower.

As if he were an overeager adolescent.

When had any woman invaded his every thought like

this? When had any woman made him...*pine* for her? It simply wasn't his usual style.

Yet worse than any of that had been the fact that he'd wanted to tell her that he wasn't as bad as his reputation painted him. Perhaps ten years ago he'd been a playboy, even eight years ago. But recently, between his career and the charity, he didn't have time to seduce the sheer volume of women the rumours would have Anouk believe.

But, to what end?

What would it change?

He might no longer have the time, or the same inclination, for one-night stands with an endless procession of pretty, eager partners—but that hardly meant he was suddenly going to turn into the kind of commitment-ready man that a woman like Anouk would demand.

She might still be haunting his brain, and his body, in a way that no other woman ever had, but that was surely just because that all too brief encounter in the office hadn't quite been enough to slake their desire for one another. He still couldn't offer her any more than no-strings sex.

So then why care whether his reputation was entirely accurate? It was close enough, wasn't it? What did it matter *what* Anouk Hart thought of him?

Disgusted with himself, he had thrown the bedsheets back and stomped down to his home gym, running, rowing and carrying out a brutal training routine designed to really push his body. As if it could drive out the gnawing hunger he felt inside.

He shouldn't want her with such hunger.

Attraction was one thing, but this desire he felt for Anouk was something infinitely more dangerous. It made him wonder, just for a moment, what a normal relationship would be like. And that was much too treacherous a path because he wasn't like most normal people. He didn't have that capacity for love that they had. Hadn't his childhood taught him that? When his mother had been at her most vulnerable, when she'd most needed his care, he'd resented her. Hated her, even.

He had never gone to visit her in that centre Malachi had managed to get her into when he'd been fifteen. He'd only gone to her funeral a year later because Malachi had practically dragged him there by his ear. And he had resented every single second of it. Hadn't he given that woman enough of his precious time and attention? Hadn't he sacrificed his childhood for her? And hadn't Malachi sacrificed even more?

All of which meant he wasn't the kind of man for a woman like Anouk. He didn't love a person, flaws and all. No, he honed in on any imperfections and magnified them until he couldn't see past them to the person beneath. He used those flaws against them and Anouk deserved better than that.

She deserved better than him. If he thought anything of her at all then he would stay away from her.

At least the punishing training regime of the last couple of days seemed to have distracted his body. Hopefully, the demands of a shift in Neurology would occupy his head, as well.

What he hadn't expected was to be called straight down to Resus only to find he was once again needed on Anouk's team.

As if fate were personally throwing them together, he griped, striding through the doors only to come face to face with the woman who occupied too much of his brain. She stared at him in shock for several long seconds before dropping her eyes and switching back into professional mode.

Just like Anouk. Sol couldn't help grinning to himself. He would have been disappointed if she hadn't done so but at least she seemed as disquieted about his appearance as he felt. That was perhaps some consolation.

She cleared her throat and he knew he didn't imagine that overly bossy tone was meant for him.

'Okay, team, can you gather round a moment, please? We have a twenty-month-old girl who fell frontwards down a flight of concrete steps. ETA five minutes. Blood loss, but breathing and conscious. Helipad response team have gone up to the roof now to meet the HEMS. We're just waiting for now.'

The team moved quickly, getting equipment, a fresh mattress, the right materials—a flurry of activity as they prepared for the new patient to arrive. And when it all stilled, he wasn't prepared for Anouk to be standing right in front of him, a startled look on her face as though she hadn't expected to turn around and find him there.

He tried reminding himself of all the reasons he should keep his distance, but suddenly he couldn't think of a single one of them.

'I see I'm not the only one to have been brightening up this place.'

Sol jerked his head to the two-foot counter-top Christmas tree, prettily decorated, on the centre computer tables. He had no idea where they came from, yet the words tripped off his tongue, low and teasing.

'I didn't do it,' she retorted quickly.

Perhaps a little too quickly. And the way she flushed a deep scarlet made him unexpectedly curious. Was there something more to the story? Something that made her blush like a schoolgirl in front of him? Sol discovered he rather liked that idea.

'Ah, but do you know who did?' He took a stab in the dark, delighted when it seemed to pay off as her blush didn't fade, but she did manage to look simultaneously murderous.

As well as ridiculously cute.

'No.'

'Isn't that odd? I don't think I believe you,' he offered soberly, earning him a long-suffering eye-roll.

It delighted him beyond all measure.

'Fine. Saskia did it,' she bit out. 'Now will you leave it alone?'

'And you let her?' he heard himself asking. Laughing.

'I let her?' Anouk folded her arms across her chest.

'You let her decorate Resus? After the go you had at me for the bit of tinsel? Or did my words make you reconsider your rather military stance?'

Anouk scowled. He was obviously baiting her, so the last thing she should do was rise to it.

'You think a lot of yourself, don't you? And for the record, I don't control Saskia.'

'I never suggested you did.' He grinned, beginning to enjoy himself now. 'But she's your best friend. I dare say she wouldn't have done it if you'd asked her not to.'

She glowered, continuing to eye him silently, for several beats too long.

'Fine,' she conceded eventually, grudgingly. Rolling her eyes at him and sending a lick of heat straight through to his sex. 'I thought it might be nice.'

'Nice, huh?'

'For the patients,' she huffed. 'You really do need to stop being so arrogant. I didn't do it because *you* suggested it.'

'Heaven forbid.'

He didn't even attempt to conceal his chuckles.

'In fact, like I said, I didn't even do it at all.'

'No, of course not. It was your friend. And I'm guessing you didn't help her one bit.'

Her bristly demeanour gave her away, and Sol grinned broadly. It was nonsensical how much lighter and happier,

Anouk made things—even when she was irritated with him she managed to flip some unseen switch to turn his day from aggravating to enjoyable.

Even when she was dealing with a casualty, he found his eyes lingered a fraction longer on Anouk. Something about her seeming to shine that little bit brighter than everyone else around her.

She was fascinating.

Which made her so much worse than simply *hot*.

Anouk had taken up residence in his head and was apparently claiming squatter's rights. He couldn't seem to eject her and the harder he tried, the deeper she seemed to insinuate herself.

Which left only one solution. A solution that he would never in his right mind have expected himself to consider, and that he couldn't imagine any other woman in the world bringing him to.

The only way to stop himself from thinking about Anouk Hart was to convince her that they hadn't finished what she'd started the other night. That they both wanted more. Which shouldn't be too hard, given the sexual chemistry still crackling between them right now.

But he refused to lead her on. Just because he would be breaking his rule about second dates—not that it had been a proper first date, given that she hadn't even let him take her to that ball—it didn't mean he was offering her anything more. He wasn't putting a relationship on the table.

Who are you trying to convince? The question popped, unbidden, into his head. *Anouk or yourself?*

He shoved it away for the nonsense it was, but its echo lingered, nonetheless.

He needed more of Anouk. He *craved* her. But it was clear that whatever madness—he flattered himself to think it was their intense attraction—had overcome her the night of the gala, she wasn't going to let it get to her a second time. Not without a fight.

She'd pulled down the *strait-laced* shutters and set up the blockades of *disapproval*. But she didn't quite manage to pull off *forbidding* with the same aplomb as before. There was a flash of memory in her expression, a spike of hunger in her glance.

He had no doubt that Anouk craved him every bit as much as he craved her. But her mind was trying to shut off all that her lush, rather wanton body was telling it.

Which meant that he was going to have to seduce her. *Court her*, as old Mrs Bowman would have said.

Old-fashioned, and prim.

But dammit all if a perverse portion of him didn't relish the thought a little bit too much.

Did she really have to let Solomon Gunn affect her like this? Anouk thought shakily, her eyes locked on the doors at the end of Resus, waiting for the HEMS team to walk in.

She had veered from horror at her lustful display the night of the gala, to regret that they had only enjoyed one single, fiery, sensational act that night and she yearned for more. For the past two days it had been impossible to empty her head of the most vivid, thrilling, X-rated dreams that had kept her entire body smouldering.

No wonder she could barely bring herself to look him in the eye now, for fear that her every last wanton thought was etched right across her face for him to read.

Even now her body pricked with awareness, and she folded her arms over her chest as though she could dull the ache in her heavy nipples, as she relived the feel of his thumb skimming over them.

Mercifully, the doors chose that moment to swing open and the HEMS team hurried in.

'This is Rosie, twenty months old,' the HEMS doctor began handover. 'Normally fit and well. Approximately one hour ago she was in the park with her mum when she tumbled a metre and a half down a flight of concrete steps. She has a laceration above her right eye and has had altered GCS. GCS is eleven. Primary diagnosis is that she has had concussion and a period of observation will determine whether there are any inter-cranial injuries. She's had two hundred of paracetamol and one milligram ondansetron.'

'Pupils?' Anouk checked.

'She won't open her eyes.' The HEMS doctor shook his head gently.

'Right.' She nodded. 'Sol…'

There was little need to say anything. As the neurology specialist, he was already beginning his obs, his low, calm pitch already reassuring the little girl who was beginning to respond to his gentle instruction.

She nodded to her team to begin a fresh set of obs, as they were already preparing to do, and turned back to the HEMS doctor.

'Mum came with her?'

'This is Mum.' He turned to locate the young girl's mother, who was looking ashen but keeping herself together well.

'Okay, Mum.' Anouk smiled reassuringly. 'We're just going to check Rosie over for now, perhaps give her some medication to make her more comfortable, and then we'll be taking her for a scan to see what's going on with her head and neck. You're absolutely fine to stay here with her, let her see you, talk to her.'

'My husband is on his way…?' The mum trailed off uncertainly.

'That's fine. If he goes to the desk someone will bring him straight through to Resus.

'Thank you.' She smiled weakly, her eyes darting straight back to her daughter and her smile becoming deliberately brighter, her voice more upbeat as she tried to reassure the baby girl looking so small on the dark blue mattress.

As soon as they had completed their initial assessment they could wrap her in a blanket, which would stop her from looking quite so tiny and helpless. But Anouk didn't need the neurosurgeon beside her to tell her that, given Rosie's age, her little bones were still quite soft and the concern was that there could be an internal bleed, which might cause pressure and push the child's brain down.

Her team worked quickly and methodically, focussed on their task, feeding the information back to Anouk as she mentally constructed a picture for herself of what was going on with Rosie before preparing to take her little patient to CT.

'You're happy for the mother to accompany the child?' Sol's voice suddenly rumbled, low and rich in her ear, spreading through her body like luxuriously sticky caramel.

Anouk told herself not to be so stupid.

'Yes, I asked her if she was happy to join us before, so they'll be getting her leaded up.'

'Good,' he confirmed simply.

And there was no reason for her body to goosebump at the way they apparently worked so harmoniously together. No reason at all.

She thanked the HEMS team and wrapped up handover before getting straight back to her little patient and preparing her for CT.

'Do you fancy some lunch?' Sol asked quietly a couple of hours later, making her turn her head so fast that her neck cracked painfully. She pretended that it hadn't. 'It's a surprisingly quiet day today. I think we might actually be able to give it a try eating a meal for once.'

'Lunch?'

'Yes, the thing normal people eat around midday.'

'As opposed to the packet of biscuits I usually just about get time to grab?' She tried laughing to conceal her shock.

If she hadn't known Sol better, it might have sounded like an actual date.

'Hence why I want to buy you lunch.'

The temptation to accept was shockingly strong.

'Why?' she demanded instead.

He didn't even blink.

'I thought that, perhaps after the other night, it might be nice to get to know each other a little better. That is to say, *with* our clothes on.'

'Shush,' Anouk hissed, spinning wildly around before bustling him into an empty side room. 'Someone might hear you.'

'They didn't. So, lunchtime?'

'Like…a date?' she demanded stiffly. 'I don't think that's a good idea.'

His mouth crooked upwards.

'Don't panic, it's just lunch. No date.'

'It isn't *just* anything. It's about the optics.'

'No one cares.'

She rolled her eyes at him.

'Lots of people care. And even if they didn't, *I* care.'

'That you're seen on a lunch date at work? Or that you're seen with me?'

'Both. And I thought you said it wouldn't be a date?'

His grin ramped up until it made her stomach tighten. And other things tighten, too.

'I lied.' He winked at her, making her tingle now, too.

She was pretty sure he knew exactly what he was doing. That he could read every embarrassing effect on her hot face.

'You're irredeemable,' she snapped.

'Thanks.'

'It wasn't a compliment.'

'Too late. I took it as one.' He rocked back and leant on the doorjamb, folding his arms over his chest in a way that he must surely know made him look all the more hewn and powerful. All male.

She cursed her faithless heart and the tattoo it was currently beating throughout every vein and nerve-ending in her body. His dark eyes—as glossy and mesmerising as a master chocolatier's darkest mirror glaze—rippled with something she couldn't read but traitorously wished she could.

She ought to back up and put a little distance between the two of them. Or, better yet, leave. Instead, she stayed exactly where she was. Within arm's reach of Sol. A silent invitation even as she pretended it wasn't.

The lazy, insouciant way he watched her warned her that he knew it was pretence. His eyes raked over her body and left it as tingling and *aware* as she'd been that night. Craving more. She couldn't tear her gaze from that mouth, wicked and expert all at once. The things it had done to her should be illegal.

She was glad they weren't.

Everything inside was still. Calm. Expectant.

'Is something wrong?' he demanded suddenly.

And Anouk was aware of an edge to his tone. A hint that he was teasing her, playing with her, but she didn't know what the joke was.

'Wrong?'

'You appear to be rather fixated.'

'Fixated?'

She was beginning to sound a little like the old neighbour's parrot that had had a habit of waking her and Saskia at ridiculous hours in the morning, despite the fact that it was a decent apartment and the walls weren't exactly thin.

'With my mouth?'

She snapped her eyes up.

'I'm not fixated with your mouth.'

'Indeed? Only, I was going to ask if there was something there. A mark perhaps. An ink stain. A crumb.'

God help her, but all she could think of now was that if it had been a crumb, she would have gladly licked it off.

'No crumb,' she managed briskly. 'Or anything else.'

'Shame.'

As though he could read her illicit thoughts.

'I should go.'

'You should,' he agreed.

It took a great effort to galvanise her legs, moving one in front of the other in a great imitation of a newborn foal. Was it any wonder then that as she reached Sol and he refused to budge to let her pass easily, she faltered slightly?

He caught her in an instant, not that she had been about to fall, and suddenly she was being hauled into his arms, and he was holding her there, and she couldn't breathe. All she could do was stare again at his fascinating mouth, silently begging it to come crashing down on hers as it had that night.

When it didn't, Anouk didn't see any other choice but to lean up and press her lips to his.

It was instant combustion. His arms encircled her, pulling her to him. Her soft, pliant body against his deliciously hard one. He dipped his head and tasted her, sampling as though she were some precious vintage wine, leaving Anouk feeling revered and rare.

He dipped in and out, making her arch to him for more, soft moans escaping her lips in spite of herself.

He let his fingers tangle in her hair, mumbling words like *glorious* and *spun-silk gold*.

'It's just hair,' she muttered against his mouth, half afraid that she would fall for his charms when she knew better, probably better than anyone.

'No,' he argued, drawing back from her and tangling his hands deep within the abundance. 'It's like running my fingers through the softest gallium.'

'I don't need the hollow compliments...' she began, but when he raked his thumb over her lower lip, apparently revelling in the feel of her shaky breath on his skin, she found she couldn't even remember what she'd been about to say.

All the while she wanted the moment to last an eternity, maybe two, and yet also wanted the journey to be over, so that he could finally take her to his apartment and release the madness that had been building ever since he'd pressed his head between her legs that night and showed her exactly what she'd been missing all these years. With her two perfectly nice, perfectly dull boyfriends.

He kissed her some more. Slowly, reverently, as though they had all the time in the world and as though they weren't in the middle of a busy hospital.

The hospital, the voice sounded dully through the fog of her brain.

Her shift.

She had no idea from where she found the strength to break his kiss. And then some more, to break his hold.

'This is what you do, isn't it?' she managed in a strangled voice.

'Does it matter? If we're both enjoying it?'

She couldn't tell him that *yes, it mattered*. Especially

when he made her feel as though she were special, only to remember that she wasn't.

That a hundred girls had probably travelled this same road before.

Idiot that she was.

'I have work to do,' she bit out, whirling around and snatching open the door before she could do something as stupid as change her mind.

The last thing she expected was to hear his voice carry, deep and smooth, down the hall.

'Come with me to the centre.'

She shouldn't let him worm his way under her skin. She *shouldn't*.

'Say that again?' she demanded, stopping and turning slowly.

'Come with me to see the Care to Play centre. See what it's all about.'

He was offering to show her into his private world? His private life? She could hardly believe he would be that open with her. Or anyone, for that matter.

By the expression that fleetingly clouded Sol's face, he could hardly believe it either. If she didn't accept quickly, she feared he might rescind the invitation. And, despite all her promises to herself to steer clear of him after the gala, she desperately didn't want him to rescind anything.

Solomon Gunn.

He'd been worming his way under her skin ever since she'd met him. She'd staved him off initially by fixing on his playboy reputation. It hadn't been too difficult, not after watching her self-destructive mother make one poor choice after the next where bad boys were concerned.

Yet, she'd also seen flashes of another side of Sol. A compassionate side lacked by other top-flight surgeons she knew. The incident with young Izzy and her family, if she was going to be honest now, hadn't been the first. Nor the care for his old patient—Mrs Bowman.

But that didn't mean she had to be attracted to him, did it? She was supposed to be immune, for pity's sake.

Anouk was still giving herself a halfway decent talking-to when she heard her own voice replying.

'Okay.' No, not really *okay*, her brain screamed at her to take it back. 'I'd like to see the centre.'

'Then I'll bring you some forms to sign.'

'Forms?'

'Standard security. For being with the kids. As a doctor you'll be fine, but it protects the centre.'

'Right.'

By the book, Sol? Anouk said nothing but filed it away. It was yet another sign of how much this centre, and these kids, meant to him.

Reckless playboy? Or caring protector? Every time she thought she knew him, he morphed into something else. She couldn't pin him down.

It mattered to her more than it had any right to.

CHAPTER SIX

'WELL,' ANOUK MUTTERED to herself as she slapped her steering wheel lightly. 'You've been sitting out here for nearly half an hour. Here goes nothing.'

Yanking open her door, she jackknifed out of her car, clicked the lock button, and marched to the centre before she could talk herself out of anything.

She was barely through the doors before an older woman stopped her.

'Can I help you?'

'I'm Anouk,' she began. 'Anouk Hart. I...'

She trailed off. Should she say she was here to meet Sol? Or just that he'd given her forms to fill out the other day? Or perhaps she shouldn't mention him at all; she didn't want people to think she was just using the centre to somehow wheedle her way in with him.

'Oh, yes, Anouk.' The woman smiled. 'I'm Barbara. Sol has been telling us all about you. So have Izzy and Katie.'

'The girls are here?'

'Yes, Katie particularly, of course. Izzy only got out of hospital yesterday but the first thing she did was ask when you would be coming in.' Barbara laughed.

'It always amazes me how resilient kids are.' Anouk shook her head. 'Only a week ago she was in my Resus department.'

'Now she's home and already back to helping her mum,' the woman agreed. 'Inspirational. Just like so many of the kids I see come through those doors.'

'I can see why Sol cares so much about this place. I guess not everyone with a privileged childhood wants to see what other people have to go through.'

'I know. I like to think that's why Sol—and Malachi, for that matter—set up this place. They might be rich, influential men now, but neither of them has ever forgotten how appalling their own childhoods were.'

Anouk blinked. She fought to keep her expression neutral.

'Right.'

'I mean, not just as young carers themselves but how they had to drag themselves out of the gutter,' Barbara continued, clearly under the impression that this wasn't news to Anouk. 'Without them getting the message out, people with clout wouldn't even know about us. This centre, and the new one they are building, simply wouldn't exist.'

Anouk made a sound of acknowledgement, but her head was spinning.

Sol had been a young carer? He had dragged himself out of the gutter?

It didn't make any sense. But what confused her most was that Barbara didn't seem worried about discussing it. As though it was common knowledge.

As though she was talking about a completely different Solomon Gunn from the playboy neurosurgeon who relished his Smoking Gun nickname.

Was it possible that his colleagues didn't know the man at all?

Even she herself sometimes forgot how other people envied her childhood when they knew she was the daughter of a late Hollywood actress. They couldn't see the darker, uglier side of that life. Was it the same for Sol? People said he was a wealthy neurosurgeon, coming from money, and they made judgements. *She* had made judgements.

Would the real Solomon Gunn please step forward?

'So, anyway, we thought you might like to spend the afternoon with Libby. She's a friendly little girl, six, sole carer for her mother, although…' Barbara paused, half stating, half questioning '…you'll know that we don't discuss that side of things here?'

'Yes, I know. This is a place she can come and just be a child.'

The woman nodded her approval.

'At the moment Libby is making Father Christmas faces for the Christmas Fayre. Are you any good at crafting?'

'I'm not known for it.' Her laugh betrayed a hint of nerves, but that couldn't be helped. 'But I'm keen to learn. Sol isn't here?'

'There was a problem at the construction site. Besides, I think he thought you might find it easier getting to know the children in your own time.'

Without him looking over her shoulder, did he mean? Either way, it was odd but, taking the complication of having to interact with Sol out of the equation, she could practically *feel* some of her tension slipping from her shoulders, through her body to the floor, and away from her.

She exhaled quietly with relief.

'That probably would be better.'

Was it her imagination, or did Barbara's smile suddenly seem brighter? Wider?

'That will do just fine,' Barbara approved, leading her over to where a young girl sat, with a unicorn T-shirt and pink jeans, her hair plaited exceptionally neatly either side of her head.

'Libby, I've got another set of helping hands. This is Anouk. You remember Izzy and Katie mentioned her.'

A six-year-old girl glanced up with a wide, toothy smile.

'And Sol talked about her, too,' she added. 'You're just in time to help me decorate the next lot of faces to stick on the goodie bags. Can you bring those cotton-wool balls over there for the beard? I've got the googly eyes but we'll cut little red hats out of the felt and use a mini pom-pom for the bobble.'

Before she knew it, Barbara had gone, leaving Libby and Anouk alone. Not that it seemed to matter since Libby was quite happy to take charge.

'What if you cut the felt hats and I'll stick them on?' Libby suggested. 'Wait, no, not like that. Like this. Let me show you.'

Quickly, efficiently, Libby demonstrated what she wanted, talking Anouk through each step, not that it seemed particularly complicated. Yet the way the girl approached the crafting task with such meticulousness and attention to detail, in a way that was common in six-year-olds, reminded her of Libby's experience as a young carer.

Her chest kicked. It was an unexpected reminder of her own childhood, when she had organised her mother with care and discipline as though she were Annalise Hartwood's personal assistant rather than her daughter.

And verbal punching bag, of course.

Her brain skittered away from the unwanted memories.

'Are you looking forward to Christmas?' Anouk asked milliseconds before it occurred to her that it might not be the most appropriate question for someone like Libby.

For a moment, the little girl looked thoughtful and then, to Anouk's relief, she managed a slow bob of her head. Anouk hadn't realised she'd been holding her breath until that moment.

'Yes, I think so. It's a lot better now that I have this place to come to.'

'Right,' Anouk agreed, swallowing quickly. 'And these are for the Christmas Fayre?'

'Yep, it's a lot of fun. There are stalls and fairground games, and Sol and Malachi usually arrange something special. Like, one year it was an ice rink, and another it was fairground rides. It can be a chance for the centre to get out into the community and show them that we're good kids.'

'I understand.' Anouk bobbed her head, carefully concealing her surprise.

The maturity with which Libby spoke belied her six years. But then, that was likely a result of being a child carer for her parent. It was testament to her resilience how this little girl could talk so eloquently one moment, and be excited about making Father Christmas faces to stick on paper bags of stocking fillers.

'Plus, we raise money to help keep the centre running,' she added proudly. 'And to buy new pieces for our Christmas village scene.'

Anouk wasn't quite sure what that was, but before she could ask Libby was reaching for a small box beside her to lift up a handful of faces from Santa to Rudolph, and from elves to gingerbread men.

'I made these already.'

'They're amazing.'

Libby beamed, dropping her voice to a conspiratorial whisper.

'And, don't tell the younger girls, but I know that Father Christmas isn't real.'

'What makes you think that?' Anouk asked carefully. Most six-year-olds she knew still believed.

Libby shot her a cynical smile.

'Please. I know he isn't. Last year, when I was five, we

went shopping together and Mummy bought me presents without me knowing. But over Christmas she got unwell again and couldn't get out of bed without my help so she couldn't put them out overnight. She tried to pretend that Father Christmas had got lost and left them under her bed by mistake.'

'That's entirely possible,' Anouk replied steadily, her eyes deliberately focussed on her task.

'You don't have to protect me. I'm not your average six-year-old,' Libby remonstrated softly, echoing words she must have heard people use time and again about her.

The matter-of-fact tone only tugged at Anouk's heart all the harder.

'The point is that Mummy was ill so I'd had to do the hoovering over Christmas. I knew the presents had been there for weeks. I tried to tell Mummy but she got upset and cross with herself so I pretended that I believed her.'

'It's still possible—'

Libby cut her off as though she hadn't spoken.

'But I wanted to tell someone and I like you. I think I can trust you.' She tipped her head on one side and eyed Anouk shrewdly. 'I can, can't I?'

The lump in her throat meant she might as well have been trying to swallow a golf ball.

'You can,' she choked out, and Libby just eyed her a little longer before bending her head back to her Father Christmas crafting and working diligently again. A companionable silence settled over them once more—as long as the little girl couldn't hear how hard and how fast Anouk's heart was beating for her, that was.

A good half-hour had to have passed before Libby spoke again.

'You know there's going to be an entertainer at the Christmas Fayre, maybe a magician or a puppet show?'

As if their previous conversation had never happened.

'Wow.' Anouk hoped she managed to inject just the right amount of sounding impressed but not condescending. 'That sounds like it will be fun.'

'It will.' The girl nodded enthusiastically. 'Especially when it's a real entertainer and not just Sol and Malachi dressed up in costumes. Although they're pretty funny, too. And so cool.'

'You think so?' She tried to sound chatty but her throat felt dry. Scratchy.

Libby's unbridled adoration didn't help Anouk in her fight not to let Sol get under her skin any more than he had already appeared to.

'Of course—' Libby snorted in a little-girl sort of way '—you could normally see it for yourself. They're usually always here. Or at least, they used to be before they started to build our new centre.'

Picking up another face to glue, Anouk tried to sound utterly casual.

'What makes them so cool, then?'

'Well, *everything*, I guess.' Libby looked up, her expression thoughtful. 'They were carers, too, just like all of us, only my mummy loves me and their mummy didn't. But they've still become rich and famous. When I grow up, I'm going to be just like them.'

'A surgeon like Sol?'

It was all she could do to sound normal. Another revelation about Sol. Another description that made him seem like a world away from the commitment-phobic playboy of the hospital gossip mill.

'Sol's a *neurosurgeon*,' Libby corrected. 'He saves lives. Or maybe I'll be an investor and become a millionaire like Malachi. I haven't decided yet, but they're both always saying that if you want something enough, and work hard enough for it, there's a good chance that you can achieve it.'

'Right.' Anouk grappled for something to say.

She wasn't sure if it was Libby's maturity or the fact that Sol was such an inspiration to the little girl that stole her breath away the most.

'Did you know they like to help to actually build the new centre?'

'Sorry?' Anouk snapped back to the present.

'Sol and Malachi?' Libby prompted. 'They are actually helping to build the new Care to Play. We saw them a lot in the summer when the centre organised rounders and football matches in the park. They were carrying bags off a builder's truck and cutting wood.'

'They did?' The image certainly didn't do anything to dampen the ache that constantly rolled inside her these days.

No wonder Sol always looked so healthy. Every time she had failed to push away memories of that mouth-watering physique, slick and hot under her hands, she'd consoled herself with the knowledge that he must spend countless hours in the gym. Her mother had enjoyed enough gym-junkie boyfriends for her to know that they loved themselves more than they would ever be able to love someone else.

She'd almost convinced herself that this fact therefore detracted from how good-looking Sol might otherwise seem. So discovering now that he had achieved that honed, utterly masculine body from genuine physical labour—and not just any labour, but building a centre for young carers—only made it that much harder to pretend there wasn't some empyreal fire to the man.

'Some of the older girls said they were hot.' Libby looked sceptical, all of her six years suddenly showing. 'But I think they were probably okay because they'd taken their tops off to cool down. They put them back on when we passed, though.'

'Right,' Anouk managed. Just about.

She imagined that the temperature of the brothers wasn't the kind of *hot* the older girls had meant. But the image of Sol shirtless wasn't one she was ready to deal with right at this moment.

'Sometimes we take them bottles of water to help cool them down.'

Despite herself, Anouk suppressed a grin.

'Very thoughtful of you.'

Libby, her eyes on her Santa face, didn't notice.

'Sol and Malachi look after us, it's only fair that we do a little for them. They're who we buy the Christmas village scenes for. It's special to them.'

'I'm pretty sure they're looking after you because you already take care of people,' Anouk said softly.

'Well…maybe, but they know exactly what we're going through, and that makes it easier to talk about.'

Another titbit of information. Anouk felt like a tiny bird, starving for every morsel dropped about Sol. She bit her lip.

'How did they come to be carers?'

She'd tried to sound casual, but the little girl glanced up sharply.

'That's their story to tell.' Libby shut down immediately, sounding for all the world like a young woman and not a six-year-old kid. 'Don't you think?'

It was all Anouk could do not to let it show how flustered she felt. She plastered a smile on her face. She wouldn't think about Sol Gunn a second longer.

'Okay, Libby, I've finished that batch of Father Christmas faces. What should I make now?'

And she wouldn't be going anywhere near the new building site, either.

* * *

Sol knew she was there even before he turned around. It was as though the entire air seemed to change and shift around him and where it had been peaceful before, now a kind of energy was pulsating through it.

He took a breath and took his time, turning slowly. She looked delicious standing there, all bundled up in a big coat, a Christmas pudding hat and a very green, Christmas-tree-patterned scarf.

'Anouk.' Even her name tasted absurdly good as it rolled off his tongue. 'Just passing?'

'Don't be fatuous,' she replied evenly. 'Libby said I could find you here. As I imagine you knew she would.'

He wanted to deny it but couldn't.

Libby was confident and talkative, a good kid who would have been able to show Anouk around without becoming tongue-tied. But he supposed there was a tiny piece of him that had also known the six-year-old would have told Anouk about the new centre.

He just hadn't known, until now, whether Anouk would have taken the bait and come to see him for herself. He tried to ignore the sense of satisfaction that punctured him.

'Ah, but you didn't have to come.'

'Of course that's what your response would be.' She drew her lips into a thin line.

Yet Sol couldn't help but notice that it wasn't a denial either. He was barely even aware of dropping his tools and making his way to her, feeling the heat start to come back to his frozen limbs as he stamped his way over the stony ground.

'So why *are* you here?'

'Libby mentioned that you and Malachi are helping to build the place. I had to come and see for myself, and here you are, hauling bags of...' she cocked her head to read the packaging that he still had hoisted on his shoulder '…plaster off a truck. Surely you have guys to do that for you?'

'Every bit Mal and I do means more money saved for the centre itself.'

Plus, the physical labour of it somehow…fulfilled him.

'I thought you were a millionaire playboy? You and your brother come from money. Isn't that what the hospital grapevine says?'

He opened his mouth to make one of his typical, non-committal responses, but found he couldn't. There was a new edge in her tone, almost as if she was testing him. But she couldn't possibly know the truth, could she?

Something dark and unfamiliar loomed in the shadows of his mind. A lesser man might have mistaken it for shame at his past. But he refused to be that lesser man. Malachi was right: it was done. It was history. No need to rake up the humiliation of their childhood for anyone, especially the daughter of a Hollywood starlet who had no doubt enjoyed a charmed upbringing.

Except that wasn't what the Hintons had said, was it?

He stuffed it down and forced himself to be upbeat.

'Mal and I can donate all we want, but these centres need to exist for themselves, support themselves—that way they can keep going long after we're gone. And if the model works then it can be replicated up and down the country.'

'You want more Care to Play centres,' she realised.

'Right. One centre is good, two centres is even better, but what we want is a business model which can be extended nationally.'

'I…didn't think of that.'

'Why would you?' he asked. 'Want a tour?'

Anouk looked surprised, before bouncing her Christmas pudding hat slowly and looking even more ridicu-lously cute.

'Sure. Why not?'

'So, what happened with that toddler who fell down the concrete steps?' he asked as he turned and headed into the building as if it made no difference to him whether she had followed or not. It was only as he lowered the plas-ter bag and heard her boots clicking on the concrete floor that he knew she had.

Why did it give him another jolt of victory?

How had this woman managed to insinuate her way under his skin? It was sheer insanity and he should walk away now.

Sol had the oddest sensation that if he didn't walk now, it would be too late.

And still he unlocked the padlock and unwound the heavy-link chain from around the temporary plywood doors.

'The twenty-month-old?' Anouk looked surprised.

'Yeah. Rosie, right?'

'Yes, Rosie. Believe it or not she was okay.' Anouk grinned, the miraculous recovery of kids never failing to amaze her. 'You knew there were no obvious signs of any breaks or fractures?'

'I did, but there was that inter-cranial bleed that needed to be monitored.'

'Yep, that's it. She stayed in for two nights before being cleared. She was discharged yesterday.'

'Lucky.' He smiled.

'Very.'

'Anyway, welcome to our new Care to Play centre.' He slid the chain through one door handle and pulled the other open to usher her inside. 'We should be in by the new year.'

Anouk walked through what would soon be the reception area, stopping dead practically in the doorway of the new hall. Then she glanced around, silently taking it all in. From the expansive, hi-tech-looking space with its spaghetti junction of wires, evidently in preparation for any number of new gadgets for the kids, and the large heaters to dry the plaster.

It was inexplicable how buoyed up he felt, showing her around and watching her reaction—this unique, complicated woman who pulled at something deep inside him—and he didn't know what name to put to it.

He didn't really want to try.

There was an attraction, certainly, but he'd been attracted to plenty of women in his time. A primal, sexual attraction.

This wasn't that.

He grappled for the word but the only thing he could come up with was…*connection*. And he knew better than to believe that.

Didn't he?

'What's going over there?' she asked, pointing to an area of the room where there was still a fair amount of work to do.

'A stage.' Sol smiled. 'You want to see the talent some of these kids have. They're just bursting for a forum in which they can showcase what they can do. Behind the wall there are a couple of soundproofed music rooms, too. We'll be putting instruments in them and the kids can set up their own bands if they want to. Or just sing, whatever they want.'

'Goodness, this place really is so much bigger than where they are now.'

'By a couple of hundred square metres,' Sol agreed. 'But it isn't just that, it's the way we've teched the place up.'

'I get that.' She smiled, with the kind of radiance that

heated up a person's very bones. Heated up *his* very bones, anyway. 'It's incredible. The kids are going to be bowled over.'

'That's the hope. Come on, I'll show you the rest.'

He continued the tour to the new kitchens, the offices, the music rooms, and finally the small quiet rooms.

'Although the centre is built on the idea that kids can come in and talk about normal things, and just be a kid crafting, or playing, or singing, there are nonetheless times when kids *will* need to talk. Maybe a little group of them will get together.'

'And support each other,' Anouk offered.

'Exactly. Or sometimes someone might just need a quiet room for a one-on-one chat with an adult. We do get kids who have been self-harming and need something more to help them cope. They might have been struggling without any support and things have just got on top of them and they haven't known where to turn.'

He didn't miss the way Anouk dropped her eyes from his, that familiar stain creeping over her skin whenever she was embarrassed.

'Everything okay?'

'So Care to Play can be there for them and make sure they know that they're no longer alone?' she trotted out stiffly. 'That's great.'

Spinning around, she lunged for the door to leave and practically bumped into him.

Instinct made him reach out and grab her upper arms to steady her, before he could stop himself. There was clearly something more going on here and he felt oddly driven to find out what it was.

But the instant he made physical contact with her, electricity charged through him, practically fusing his hands in place. He was wholly unable to pull away. The need to learn more about this woman who had infiltrated his whole being in a matter of a week was almost visceral.

'What's going on, Anouk?' Urgency laced through his voice. 'What is it?'

These rooms were designed to feel closed off. A place where kids could talk about the things they might not even want to admit to themselves. *Safe.*

Right now, with Anouk up against his chest and his nostrils suddenly full of that fresh, faintly floral scent that he associated with her alone, Sol felt about as far from safe as it was possible to get.

He glanced down to see the pulse in her slender neck jolt then quicken, which didn't exactly help matters. The need to bend his head to hers and taste her lips again was almost overpowering.

Almost.

It was only the need to wait for her answer, to understand her better, that held him back. It made no sense and yet he ached to hear her talk to him as though he was someone other than a morally bankrupt tomcat willing to jump on anything in a skirt.

And yet, if she did, was he ready to answer her?

CHAPTER SEVEN

SHE GLANCED UP at him, though he got the impression that it cost her dearly to do so. She watched him for what seemed like an eternity and, for a moment, he believed she was actually going to talk. To tell him…something that counted.

And then the shutters slammed down with a clang.

'I don't know what you're talking about.' She forced a smile, trying to inch discreetly back a fraction. Not that there was anywhere to go in this tiny space.

'I don't believe that.'

She glowered at him, but he didn't miss the way she swallowed. Hard.

He could push her. He wanted to. But something told Sol that would be counterproductive.

The moments ticked by.

'Why would I?' she demanded suddenly.

'Why would you what?'

'Why would I talk to you? Open up to you?' Her voice sounded angry and pained, and raw all at once. It spoke to him in a way he recognised only too well. 'When you wouldn't dream of talking to me.'

'I have talked to you,' he lied. 'I've invited you here. You've spent time with the kids only today.'

He made himself step back, pretending that her soft, plump lips weren't still imprinted in his mind's eye. And that the feel of her arms didn't still sear through his palms. He reminded himself that it was purely physical, sexual attraction, even if it felt alien.

Because what else *could* it be?

'You've told me lots about the kids, and the centre. Between the gala, and my visit, you've given me plenty of information. You've explained how there are lots of charities out there for young carers, and lots of volunteers, really good people, and how your charity is different. You've shown how it still isn't enough. These kids need more.'

'They do.'

'I agree.' She lifted her eyes to his, her gaze almost too intense to bear. 'My point is, Sol, that, in all the talking you've done, the one subject you steer clear of is why you care so much.'

He hadn't seen it coming, but he should have. He should have been ready for the question. In a way, he was. And yet it still had the power to wind him.

His hands dropped from her arms and he swung away—the moment lost.

'Does it matter?' he managed, amazed at how calm, how cool, he sounded when inside his heart was pumping blood around his body as though he was a gold medal winning sprinter.

Behind him, she seemed to ponder for a moment. Though whether about how to phrase her questions, or how she had come to ask them in the first instance, Sol couldn't quite be certain.

'I don't know,' she admitted. 'I suppose that's what I'm asking. If it matters.'

'I don't think I follow.'

'No,' she conceded, pulling her lips together as if she wasn't even sure what she was saying. 'It's just that *this* you isn't the image you tend to put forward of yourself.

Solomon Gunn the playboy is well known, but it doesn't fit with all of...*this*.'

She waved her hand around the construction site that was the centre.

'I suppose I want to know which version of the man is really you. And if it's this one, then wouldn't you rather be Solomon Gunn, tireless advocate for young carers?'

'No.'

She blinked.

'Why not?'

Because it invited too many questions, too much scrutiny, his own childhood would inevitably come out and that wasn't a side of his life he wanted people to see when they looked at him.

As it was threatening to do now.

It was odd the way he wanted her to know he was more than just that playboy—as inexplicable as that was—but when it came to telling her, showing her, the truth, he found he couldn't contend with that either.

Because the truth made him feel ashamed. Lacking. It was a chunk of his life he would readily burn down, if only he could.

'Because I like my playboy lifestyle,' he lied with an aplomb that had been perfected over more than a decade.

And, possibly for the first time, he hated himself for it.

'Do you really?' she asked softly. 'Only, I'm beginning to wonder, from all the things I've been hearing about you today, how you have much time at all for quite the number of amorous conquests your reputation suggests.'

'I'm a skilled multitasker.' He feigned a laugh.

Anyone else would have bought into it. Anouk stared at him, unfazed.

'You'd have to be in two places at once. No one is that good at multitasking.'

It was as though she could see down to his soul.

He reminded himself that even if she did know some scraps of truth about him, that was all she knew. Scraps. Not the whole picture, and it would stay that way. However much he might loathe what he was about to do.

'Trust me, Anouk, you're not the first woman I've slept with who has mistaken sexual intimacy for a more profound connection, and thought it meant they *understood* me. But it's just sex, nothing more.'

She blanched, making him feel the cad he knew he was.

Better that than this irrational ache he had to buy into her better opinion of him.

As the silence tightened around him, seemingly weighed down with anticipation, the last thing he expected was for Anouk to rally.

'I suspect you care about these kids because you understand them better than you'd have your moneyed gala guests believe.'

'Not really,' he denied.

'Of course you do.' She held his gaze, refusing to cow to him. 'Because you were a young carer, too, Sol.'

Of all the things he'd expected Anouk might say, that certainly wasn't one of them. For one brief, heart-stopping moment, he wondered if he could bluff her.

He had the oddest sensation that he wouldn't be able to. She would see right through his façade. The realisation needled him.

Or was he more galled at the idea that some traitorous element of himself wanted her to see through it?

He had no idea how he kept his tone neutral.

'You've been talking to Barbara.'

She shook her head but he didn't believe her and determined to make no bones about it.

'I've warned her about sharing personal information before,' he growled. 'No matter who it's about, or who to.'

'It wasn't Barbara.' Anouk raised her eyebrows.

'Of course it was. It had to be.'

'Actually, Libby told me,' Anouk bit out finally. 'She also told me that you and your brother were young carers. For your mother.'

He couldn't answer. Couldn't even speak.

'What else did she say?' he gritted out when he felt as if he'd finally managed to work his tongue loose.

'That it was your story to tell, not hers,' Anouk admitted.

His short, sharp laugh—if that was what it could be called—bounced off the freshly plastered walls.

'That sounds like Libby.'

There was another beat of silence, which Anouk only broke after it had become more than awkward.

'So, it's true?'

He didn't answer. If he denied it he would feel as though he was betraying a six-year-old girl. At the same time, he had no idea what else to say.

'How young?' Anouk added at last.

He'd answered this question a thousand times to different kids over the years, or considered it not to be the business of any of his hospital colleagues. But somehow it was different with Anouk. He couldn't bring himself to send her home, yet he had no intention of sharing something so personal with her.

Even if a component of him wanted to.

All of a sudden he had to get out of there. This conversation—or perhaps the last few—with Anouk had left him feeling battered and bruised, as though he couldn't work out what he wanted from her.

It was an unfamiliar, unwelcome sensation.

Mostly.

He should leave, but he found that he wanted to spend more time with her and therein lay the issue. The more Sol thought about it, the more he came to the conclusion that he only wanted her because he hadn't had her yet.

As distasteful as it was, there was no other explanation. No other reason why she should have him tied up in such knots.

The solution was to remedy that situation. To convince Anouk that it was in both their interests to finish what they'd started the night of the gala. Once they had indulged their mutual desire, the sweeping need would at last abate.

Surely it was inevitable?

'There's no electricity in this place yet,' he stated abruptly. 'Except for the temporary generator powering the heaters. But there's a decent coffee house on the high street.'

She stood still as they watched each other for a beat too long. He waited for her to make her excuses and leave, and he told himself that he didn't care either way.

And then, abruptly, she grabbed her bag and threw it onto her shoulder.

'Let's go, then.'

'I swear I've heard this Christmas song in the shops since November,' Anouk muttered as they opened the doors to the coffee house only to be blasted by the heat, the gorgeous smells, and the music.

She wasn't even sure what she was doing here. Only that her chest was tight with some nonsensical notion that Solomon Gunn might actually…open up to her. As much as she knew it was ridiculous, she couldn't eject it from her head.

'Or October.' Sol laughed, his earlier unease having apparently melted away as soon as they'd left the centre and she'd dropped her questions. 'Okay, you get the table, I'll get the drinks. Just tell me what you want.'

Anouk tried not to feel deflated. It shouldn't matter that he didn't want to trust her. She shouldn't let it bother her. Just as she hadn't let that moment back in the new centre get to her. When he'd held her so close that she'd been convinced he was going to kiss her again.

When she'd *ached* for him to kiss her again.

But he hadn't. He'd just dropped her as though the moment hadn't crept under his skin even a fraction of the way it had slunk under hers.

And then she'd badgered him about his life, his childhood, being a young carer. As if that could reveal a side of him that she could understand, relate to, trust. But to what end? It wasn't as if she wanted a relationship with him. She wasn't naïve enough to think any woman could tame a perennial playboy, and yet…there was something about him that simply didn't seem to fit with the reputation.

Or perhaps that was what she was telling herself to justify her incongruously wanton forwardness the night of the gala. The night she *still* couldn't bring herself to regret. Even though she knew she ought to.

Maybe wanting to trust him was more about herself than Sol. Perhaps it was her wanting to vindicate that uncharacteristic one-night stand—if you could even call it that—to explain her sudden foray into seductress territory.

And still, it ate away at her that the Sol whom the kids at the centre loved so much was so very different from the bad boy the hospital knew.

She coveted knowing that man, too.

Yet she couldn't push him. The harder she tried, the more she could see the shutters coming down and still she couldn't seem to make herself walk away.

'I'm going for the Christmas cinnamon roast coffee,' he concluded after perusing the board for a moment. 'What would you like?'

'Tea. Nothing fancy, just a plain one, please.'

He raised his eyebrows at her.

'This can't be a manifestation of your aversion to Christmas?'

'It isn't an aversion,' she denied awkwardly.

'You really hate this time of year that much?'

He was turning the tables so casually that she couldn't be sure if it was deliberate or if he really couldn't help it. Nevertheless, she opened her mouth to tell him that *of course she didn't*.

'Pretty much.' She shrugged, the words popping out of their own volition. 'I know you don't feel the same. With your home-baked mince pies, and your gorgeous tree, and the Christmas village scene.'

Instantly his face changed and she sucked in a breath, not sure what she'd said.

'What about the Christmas village scene?'

His tone was too careful.

'I'm not sure,' she admitted cautiously. 'I don't actually know what Libby meant, she just told me that the kids from the centre do all they can to get together enough money to buy you and Malachi a new piece every year.'

She waited for him to push her on the subject, but instead his expression cleared and he dipped his head before striding to the counter, leaving her to find an available table. And remind herself to stop reading too much into everything that concerned Solomon Gunn.

'What are we doing here, Sol?' Curiosity made her drop the question even before he'd finished sliding the tray onto their table. 'I can't imagine you bring *dates* here. At least, not *after* you've already stripped them bare on the desk in an opulent study. Though perhaps before, when you're still trying to seduce them.'

He didn't answer straight away, sliding his coat off and dropping into the seat opposite her to stir his drink thoughtfully.

'I find myself as mystified as you are by this continuing... draw,' he answered enigmatically, sending her mind into a whirl analysing what he might mean by it.

So much for not reading too much into everything he said or did, she snorted quietly to herself.

'Which means what, exactly?'

'I'm debating that,' he told her. 'And I'm rapidly coming to the conclusion that these drawn-out, skirting-the-issue games don't appear to be getting us anywhere.'

'I'm not playing games.' Her indignation wasn't as sharp as she might have expected it to be.

'Therefore, I would like to propose something else,' he continued, as though she hadn't spoken. 'I contend that allowing it to play out seems to be the most logical conclusion.'

She couldn't quite dislodge the pocket of air blocking her throat.

'Play out?' she asked faintly. 'As in...?'

His smile was lethal enough to make her fear for her sanity.

'Sex.'

The statement sliced through the air between them, its simplicity robbing her of all thought for a moment; sending delicious shivers all the way down her spine.

'One night of pure, unrestrained pleasure,' he repeated, as though she might not have understood his meaning the first time—but for the wicked smile carved into his handsome face. 'A conclusion of that night at the gala.'

It was useless to pretend that a restlessness didn't roll

right through her at the audacity of the man. Along with the rudest images of the hot, devilish expression on his face moments before he'd dipped his head between her legs and greedily drunk her in.

It was why, although every grey cell in her head was screaming at her to decline, she could only sit there, her body tense and...*needy*, as she stared at him in silence.

'But if we do, Anouk. Then there will have to be ground rules.'

'Ground rules?' she echoed faintly.

'To avoid confusion at a later date.'

'Avoiding confusion is good,' she conceded, her voice sounding thick and slow.

She felt as though she were outside her own body.

She ought to be telling him *no*. Instead, she just wanted to get the so-called ground rules agreed so they could get onto the meatier portion of the conversation.

Who was this strange woman inhabiting her body? And what had Sol done to the real her that night? She should be disgusted with herself; at how easily she seemed to be falling in with what Sol was suggesting.

Her weak acquiescence was all too reminiscent of her desperate mother.

And yet something niggled at Anouk, even if she couldn't quite place her finger on it.

Something in the way Sol sat, slightly more upright than usual. Or the way he appeared to be choosing his words deliberately. Or the intent look in his eyes. It all gave the impression that he wasn't nearly as blasé about it as he wanted her to believe.

Or possibly it was just in her imagination.

Either way, Anouk made the decision there and then to accept it at face value. When would she ever get the chance to act so daringly with someone who thrilled her the way that Sol did?

'Let me guess, the ground rules are that it's just sex?' she managed hoarsely. 'That it's just for the one night? That there are no troublesome, wild emotions complicating things afterwards?'

'Yes, to all three,' he growled. 'Except for the wild part.'

'Oh?' she managed.

'I intend it to get very wild,' he promised, his voice low and practically pulsing through her. 'And very hot. And very lustful.'

She thought she might have swallowed her tongue for a moment.

'I'd be disappointed if it was anything less,' she managed, at last.

She didn't quite recall moving, but suddenly they were both standing and Sol was helping her into her coat before enveloping her hand in his and leading her outside. They didn't stop, or debate it any longer, but he pulled Anouk close to him and began threading his way through the streets spilling over with Christmas shoppers.

Streets that were still slick and wet from the rain that had fallen whilst they'd been inside but that had now stopped. As if just for them. The darkness enclosed them, the coldness not able to bite into her.

She didn't know when it occurred to her that something wasn't right. Possibly around the same time that Sol slowed down, scanning all around them with a grim expression on his face.

'Something is going on,' he ruminated. 'The roads are too busy, even for this time of year.'

'And the traffic is going the wrong way,' Anouk concurred, twisting around to look. 'A road traffic accident, maybe? A main road closed? Diversions?'

It was one of the side-effects of being an A & E doctor: she could perceive a potential major accident like a sixth sense. Things just didn't…sit right.

'More than one road, I'd say, given the volume of traffic.'

'So a multiple-car RTA?'

'Something.' He nodded, sliding his phone out of his back pocket as they exchanged a glance.

'I don't have to make the call. If they need me, they'll call.'

'It's work,' she raised her eyebrows. 'We both know you're itching to make that call. Anyway, call it a sign.'

'I don't believe in signs,' he scoffed. 'You and I getting together is inevitable, Anouk. We both know it. We can't out run it, and however hard we try it will catch up with us. That need will wrap itself around us and topple us to the ground.'

'Then I'll just have to run faster.'

He laughed. An oddly sensuous sound.

'The faster you run, the further you get, the harder the fall will ultimately be.'

He hadn't even begun to make the call when it rang.

'Here goes.' Raising his eyebrows, Sol took the call.

When he let go of her hand, it felt too much like a loss. All Anouk could do was try to glean all she could from his terse responses. When he started moving, she hurried to keep up.

'It's a major incident,' he bit out, snapping his phone shut a few moments later. 'Some kind of gas explosion on Beechmoor Street. Multiple casualties; they're splitting them between us and the Royal.'

Saskia.

'That's around the corner from where I live,' Anouk cried. 'I have to get back there.'

He stopped momentarily, swinging back to her.

'It isn't safe. The area has apparently been evacuated.'

'I have to get home.' She stepped onto the kerb with the intention of hailing a taxi.

'You won't get a taxi,' Sol told her. 'They said it's gridlock towards the hospital. If we head around the north side on foot, we should make it to the hospital.'

Should she go? For a moment, Anouk wondered whether following Sol was sensible or not. But if people were injured…?

'Okay.' She dipped her head, hurrying after him as he raced ahead.

She hadn't been called, but if things were that serious then extra hands could only be welcome.

And then, her phone began ringing, too.

CHAPTER EIGHT

'BLOOD GAS IS BACK,' Anouk announced to her team. 'She's got a pH of seven point zero four with a lactate of nine.'

'Bicarb?' her colleague asked.

She checked the screen.

'Eight. Basics are minus twenty. Okay, guys, let's go back to the beginning. Airway?'

She waited for her team to communicate that it was unobstructed before moving on.

'Breathing?'

The pause felt like a lifetime, and Anouk knew even before her colleague spoke that the breathing that had been weak before was now absent. Instantly she began CPR.

The casualty had arrived in a bad way. How the crew had even got her from the scene of the explosion to the hospital without losing her was a testament to them, but she could tell this wasn't likely to go the way she would want. And she hated that. She hated losing a patient.

Any patient. Every *patient*.

She knew in this case she was fighting the inevitable, but did it matter? As long as she fought for the young woman lying in front of her?

She completed several rounds of CPR before her head finally reined in her heart.

'Pulse check?'

Even as her colleagues were checking one source, she was checking another.

'No pulse.'

No, not for her either. Anger and frustration coursed through Anouk as she lifted her head to the clock and announced the time of death.

'We didn't stand a chance,' one of her colleagues muttered, tapping her lightly on the shoulder as she passed.

Anouk dipped her head. Much as she knew that, it didn't always help. She reached for the curtains. There wasn't time to stop and grieve; the casualties were coming in thick and fast. No sooner would she step out than there would be another emergency to deal with.

Normally this was what she thrived on—not the losses, of course, but the challenge, the wins, the lives saved. But tonight there were too many other fears racing around her brain, and not all to do with Sol.

In some ways she was almost grateful for the distraction. Perhaps she'd been impulsive thinking that she could have a one-night stand with Sol. With anyone. Maybe it was a good thing they hadn't ended up back at his apartment. At least now she had time to think and realise what a bad decision that would have been.

Wouldn't it?

So why could she only think about surrendering to the temptation that had been haunting her ever since their intimate encounter?

Her head was reeling.

She told herself it was the fear of knowing that the explosion was so close to her and Saskia's apartment block. She'd tried calling her friend on the way to the hospital, but it had gone straight to voicemail. She had no way of knowing if Saskia was all right. Or even where she was.

So that was definitely a concern. But it wasn't what filled her mind with such a confusion of thoughts.

No, she suspected that tangle was more to do with the man who she would have been with, *right now*, if that accident hadn't happened.

It was why she needed a good save more than anything. She needed Saskia and she needed the high of saving lives to push the unwelcome thoughts of Sol from her brain. Given the emergencies flooding in, and not enough staff yet able to get to the hospital, there was plenty for her to do.

As the porters dealt with the deceased patient in the bay, Anouk pushed the loss out of her head and moved on to the next bay, only for Sol to catch her before she went in.

For an instant her heart jolted madly and everything seemed to come into sharper focus.

'What are you doing here?'

'Someone paged Neuro,' he replied evenly. 'A thirty-two-year-old cyclist with T12 and L1 fractures?'

'That's one of my cases.' Whatever her body might be feeling, her brain flipped immediately, locking back into professional mode. 'In here.'

He followed her quickly into a bay, nodding a brief greeting to the girl who was sitting, terrified, at the bedside of her injured boyfriend.

'This is Jared,' Anouk told Sol. 'He came in earlier and we've already had him up to CT.'

'He was caught in the blast?'

'Yes, we understood from witnesses who spoke to the air ambulance team that Jared went over the handlebars and was thrown into another vehicle. He was wearing a crash helmet. The head to pelvis CT scan showed fractured third and fourth ribs with a right-sided pneumothorax. Fractured T12 and L1 with possible evidence of neuro-compromise. He had a deep gash on his right thigh, which we have dealt with. He's had a total of around fourteen mils morphine.'

'Understood,' Sol agreed. 'I need to look at the imaging and decide what to do about the spine.'

'Agreed. I was working on the basis that if he has broken vertebrae at T12 and L1 there are likely to be depressional fractures through the endplates.'

It shouldn't have surprised her how well, how slickly, the two of them were working together. Almost as if the gala evening had never happened.

'Get it to me,' confirmed Sol, already jogging to his next call.

Little wonder the demand on the neuro team would be ridiculously high tonight.

For several hours Anouk worked steadily, hurrying between patients. She struggled to find beds for the unending stream of casualties injured in the blast. Still, she hadn't realised how much time had passed until she dashed from her current patient in order to call Neuro again, only for Sol to appear as she lifted the receiver.

'I've just been looking for you.'

'Thank goodness.' Dropping down the receiver, Anouk pulled a grimace as she turned to him. 'I thought no one was going to be able to get here.'

'About Jared? The cyclist with the T12 and L1 fractures?'

'Sorry?'

'I'm satisfied that the fractures are stable and that no intervention by us is necessary. I'm also confident that there is no neuro deficit so you can admit him to trauma team care, but he doesn't need to be transferred to Neuro.'

'Right.' Anouk hailed one of the nurses to relay the message and ensure the transfer happened quickly to free up a precious resus bed, simultaneously grabbing Sol's lapels as he made to move away.

'Anouk?' he growled as he swung back to her, his dark gaze taking in her hands still gripping his clothing.

She didn't even have time to feel abashed.

'I need you to look at this patient. It's urgent.'

'I came down to give you the results. I have another patient to see. You're probably on Ali's list—she'll be on her way as soon as she's finished with her patient upstairs.'

'There isn't time to wait for Ali.' Anouk shook her head, ushering him to the screen and calling up a new set of images.

Vaguely, it occurred to her that he could have objected. He could have focussed on his next assigned patient, but he was trusting her that this was critical.

'Her name is Jocelyn,' Anouk explained, still bringing up the images. 'She was right outside the building when the explosion occurred and the blast wave knocked her across the road and into a wall. She had a loss of consciousness for approximately ten minutes. On arrival of paramedics she had a GCS of three, which transitioned to a GCS of eleven. Very aggressive and we have confirmed with her husband that it's out of character. The patient was put into a medically induced coma and taken to CT.'

She flashed the images up on the screen.

'A large extradural haematoma.' Sol pursed his lips. 'Very large, in fact.'

'Yes,' Anouk agreed. 'Midline shift.'

'And it has shifted more?' he confirmed.

'Yes.'

They both knew that immediate surgery was imperative. Best case would be that the neurosurgeons could drain the blood and that the brain could move back into place and heal over. Most likely it would never be the same, but the faster they moved, the more chance there was.

Worst case, Jocelyn would die.

'I'll take her,' Sol confirmed after verifying the images for himself. 'I'll push my patient to Ali—he isn't as critical.'

'Thanks.'

With a nod, Sol straightened and moved away quickly, and Anouk couldn't help feeling warm.

She could pretend it was because she knew that her patient was in the very best hands. But she knew that wasn't all it was.

The night flew by, exhausting and chaotic, but with enough saves to bolster Anouk and her team as twelve hours went by, then eighteen, then twenty-four and the casualties had finally thinned out, the wail of ambulances subsiding.

And Anouk could finally go home. She tried not to think of where she might have been now if the gas explosion had never happened. Would she still be at Sol's, or would he have found a way to subtly eject her from his apartment rather than have her stay the night? Somehow, she couldn't imagine it. Playboy or not, it just didn't seem…*Sol-like*.

Then again, what was she doing imagining *anything*?

She rounded the corner, straight into Saskia. They had seen each other in Resus, passing as they darted into different bays but, incredibly, their cases hadn't coincided all evening. But now, without even uttering a word, her friend hugged her tightly.

'I was so relieved when I heard you were safe.'

'Why wouldn't I be?' Anouk laughed. 'And never mind me, the hospital is practically buzzing with some gossip that you arrived by helicopter?'

Saskia thrust her away, her eyes searching Anouk.

'You haven't heard, then?' Saskia demanded, ignoring the comment.

A sense of unease began to creep through Anouk.

'Heard what?'

'That the explosion affected Kings Boulevard?'

'That's us.' Anouk frowned.

'Yes. The whole area has been cordoned off until they can determine which buildings are structurally intact and which aren't. We can't go home.' Anouk couldn't answer as Saskia hugged her again. 'At least we're both safe.'

'We should…book a hotel, then.' Anouk fought off the daze that had settled over her. 'I'll call now.'

'Not for me.' Her friend placed her hand over Anouk's as she reached into her locker for her mobile. 'I'm… I have somewhere to be.'

'Where?'

'I… I'm staying with Malachi,' Saskia apologised.

'With Malachi?'

Sol's brother?

It didn't make much sense but Saskia was already changing her shoes and closing her bag.

'Saskia? Are you in here?' Sol's voice only seemed to ramp up the tension in the room.

Or perhaps it was just her, Anouk thought, flustered.

'Oh, Anouk.' Was it her imagination or did he pause for a fraction of a second when he spotted her, before addressing Saskia again? 'Mal says you need to get going. His heli is on the roof and they want it cleared in case an emergency has to come in.'

'I should go,' Saskia muttered.

Sol looked at her.

'If you're calling for a hotel, Anouk, you're too late. I heard a couple of guys complaining an hour ago that every hotel in the city was booked out. The cordon is quite extensive—lots of apartment blocks have been evacuated.'

'Great.' She gritted her teeth as Saskia hovered, still not leaving. Worry etched in her face.

'You could find an on-call room.'

'I'm guessing they'll be taken, too,' Sol told them. 'They're setting up temporary beds in community centres around the place.'

'Oh,' Anouk bit out as Saskia grabbed her hand.

'I could speak to Malachi? See if you could come with us?'

'Or you could just stay with me,' Sol cut in, quietly, firmly.

He didn't finish the sentence. He didn't need to. It hung there, in the silence between them.

She could stay with Sol...*as she had been going to do before the explosion had happened.*

Only it wasn't twenty-odd hours ago and things had shifted since that reckless moment in the coffee shop. That moment had gone. They could pretend it was just exhaustion from the chaotic shift; she would be happy with that.

'Thanks, but I don't think it's a good idea.'

They both knew what she meant by it. But her objection was drowned out by her friend who, Anouk was sure, cast Sol a grateful look.

'That's a great idea.'

What was going on here?

'I'm sorry, I do have to go,' Saskia muttered, squeezing her hand again.

'I don't understand, Sask?'

'It's complicated. I'll explain everything when I can.'

Then Saskia hurried out of the room, leaving Anouk staring as the door closed behind her friend. The flash-back to her teenage years was as sudden as it was unexpected. The moment she'd first realised that people were moving on whilst she was standing still. Too caught up in her mother's dramas to have time for a life of her own.

Was it possible she'd been standing still ever since?

'Do you know what that was about?' she asked Sol before she could stop herself.

He shoved his hands into his pockets and leaned back against the wall. He looked ridiculously model-like. And dammit if a thrilling shiver didn't dance down her spine.

'Possibly.'

'But you aren't going to tell me?'

'I don't know anything for sure.' He shrugged. 'When they want us to know, they'll tell us.'

'There's a *they*?'

She wasn't surprised when he didn't elaborate.

'I don't believe it's my business,' he said calmly. 'Now, do you want a place to stay or not?'

He just waited calmly, as though offering her a place to stay when there was nowhere else was no big deal. Yet she wouldn't take it, not because she was afraid of what might happen between them, but because she was afraid that she *wanted* it too much.

And if it did, what was the worst that could happen? They'd enjoy a night, maybe a few nights, of intimacy. Even the memory of that night at the gala was enough to have her…*aching.* Just as she'd been ever since.

And hadn't she already considered that maybe it was a good thing she hadn't ended up at his house twenty-four hours ago? That maybe it was *fate*?

Maybe that argument had worked when her mind had been preoccupied by her patients. Her job. Only now the ready-made excuse was gone, it seemed that she wasn't as eager to head somewhere alone, after all. Not when Sol was standing, in all his six-three, honed glory in front of her.

Not when he'd acted as a dashing knight in blue scrubs on several occasions for her patients tonight.

'What happened to Jocelyn?' she demanded abruptly.

'Two hours in surgery. We'll keep her in an induced coma for the next few days and see what happens when she wakes up.'

'And then you take it from there?'

He lifted a shoulder in acknowledgement.

Nothing was certain in this life. But if it had been a test as to whether he cared enough about his patients to know their names, he had passed. With flying colours.

She was going home with him. It was inexorable.

'I'm not one of your conquests.' The words spilled out before she could stop them. 'That is, I'm only agreeing to this if you promise me that no one will find out.'

'Agreeing to *this*?' he challenged, his face a picture of innocence.

She sucked in a deep breath and quelled her irritation.

'You know what I'm saying.'

'I don't believe that I do.' He raised his eyebrows but amusement tugged at that sinful mouth. 'Elucidate.'

Anouk huffed.

But if she couldn't even say the word then how was she going to manage to do it?

'Casual sex,' she clarified stiffly.

'Indeed?' He grinned wolfishly and she felt it like teeth against her soul. 'Forgive me if I'm wrong, but I seem to recall simply offering you a place to stay since there was nowhere else. I don't recall sex ever being a detail of the discussion.'

Heat flooded her body.

'I… You…' She faltered, hardly able to believe her own *faux pas*.

What was it about Sol that had her acting so out of character? So recklessly? First at the gala, and now *this*. Shame chased through her, and then something else.

It took her a moment to realise that it was anger. She grabbed hold of it. At least it gave her a sense of courage, even if it was a false sensation.

'You're right, you didn't. I assumed,' she ground out. 'But then, we both know that's where we will end up. Look where we were headed before we got called in last night.'

'I seem to remember you muttering something about it being a sign.' He smirked. 'Though personally, I've never believed in that nonsense.'

'No, you told me as much,' she reminded him crossly. 'You also told me that it was inevitable. That however much I tried to outrun it, it would catch up with me sooner or later and topple me to the ground. That the faster and further I ran, the fall would be all the harder as a result.'

'I didn't realise you were paying such close attention to every word I was saying.' Sol stretched his legs out languorously. 'Not that I am complaining, you understand.'

'You're playing games aren't you?' she realised, disappointment plummeting through her.

The air around them turned cooler in an instant, as Sol pushed himself off the wall.

'Contrary to the low opinion you hold about me, Anouk, I don't play games every moment of every conversation.'

'Common consensus is that you do,' she rallied.

She wasn't sure what else to do, his reaction was so unexpected. As though she'd hit a nerve, even though she'd never known him to have a nerve when it came to the way he revelled in his reputation. So obviously that couldn't be right.

'You're right,' he managed flatly, moving past her and heading for the door. 'But let's just say that it has been a long, exhausting twenty-four hours, and frankly I'm too weary for game-playing.'

'I see.' Not seeing at all, Anouk grabbed her bag and hurried after him.

Actually, he did look rather...out of character.

'So, for tonight at least, you're safe. All I'm offering you is a place to sleep and nothing more. We'll have to walk; the car is still by the new carers' centre. Does that suit you?'

'Perfectly,' she confirmed. Lying through her teeth.

CHAPTER NINE

'DID SOMETHING HAPPEN with one of your patients?' she ventured after they'd been walking for a while.

'Why?'

'Because you're acting…differently. And I think I get that way, every now and again, when one particular patient gets under my skin.'

He slowed, but didn't stop.

'It was, wasn't it?' she pressed him gently.

They continued walking in silence. Everywhere oddly quiet after weathering that storm in the hospital.

'A baby boy. Nineteen months,' was all Sol said, after what seemed like an age.

She didn't answer. Instead she simply fell into step with him, and hoped that it was enough. She understood only too well.

It was another age before he spoke again.

'It's odd, the way it gets to you sometimes, don't you think?' he said, his head down and his hands thrust into his pockets.

The question was more rhetorical than anything, Anouk knew that, but she answered anyway.

'You mean loss? Death?'

'We deal with it every day. It's so easy to become

desensitised to it.' He shrugged. 'But after an incident like that…'

'Yes,' she whispered. 'I think it's the sheer volume of it. All at once. It makes it feel too much.'

Again, they walked in companionable silence for minutes—though it felt like a lifetime, lost as she was in her thoughts. It was only when he stopped at a shop window that she realised they had made it to the lower part of the town. Slowing down, she backed up, but she wasn't prepared.

'What is this, Sol?'

'You asked me about the Christmas village scene.'

'This is it?'

'This is it.'

She turned to take in the scene. Even through her loathing of this time of year, she could at least admit it was spectacular. Little trains ran in circles around the quaintest village set-up; a snow-covered village green with tiny figures walking, ice-skating, or simply strolling the wintry streets in the warm glow of the orange/yellow lights.

Little old-fashioned shops lined the painstakingly constructed hillside road, which, if she looked closely, Anouk thought might be polystyrene blocks, but they looked for all the world like snowy inclines. Meanwhile, a miniature cable car ran up and down another polystyrene hill scene.

'This is what the kids work so hard to raise the money to buy,' Anouk murmured. 'For you, and for Malachi. Why?'

There was a beat of silence.

'Why, Sol?' She pressed her fingers to the glass, as if proximity could solve the riddle she was sure existed.

'It's become a tradition,' he offered simply.

'What makes it so traditional?' she repeated.

There was no logical explanation for why it should matter to her to know.

Yet it did.

The still night began to hum with anticipation. She turned her head to watch him but his gaze was fixed on the scene, not on her.

'Please, Sol?'

He scowled, drawing in a deep breath before answering.

'Malachi and I were kids when we first saw a village like this,' he began, falteringly at first. He hadn't told this story in…well, ever. 'There was a toyshop in town which had one every Christmas—not that we were ever allowed in, of course. The owner would chase us down the road if we even peered into the window, for steaming it up with our snotty noses.'

'He really said that?'

'He said a sight worse than that. Even clipped our legs with the back of a broom handle on more than one occasion.' Sol shrugged. 'Anyway, sometimes we would wait until it was dark and sneak out of the house if we could leave Mum for long enough. There was a guy with a sugared doughnut stall and if he was still there cleaning up, he used to give us any leftovers, which would otherwise get thrown away.'

'That's nice.' Anouk smiled as though her chest was tight and painful at the thought of Sol's childhood.

She'd had no idea. But then, no one did. Clearly that was the way Sol liked it.

'He was a decent guy. Years later, when Mal had made his first real money as a boxer, he bought the business from the guy for about five times its worth, just to repay him.'

'Did he know?'

'Yeah, he was so damned grateful, it was really nice to do. Mal then gave the business to a couple of kids he knew would appreciate it, from the first centre we built.

They ended up getting four stalls between them and they're still going strong.'

'Wow.'

She thought Sol was going to say more but suddenly he caught himself. As if he didn't know why he'd told her that. Possibly it had all been stuffed down in the same box for so many years that now she'd sprung the lid, random snippets were springing out left and right, completely out of his control and in no logical order.

Or maybe he was just playing her.

'Anyway. Mal and I used to sneak down to watch the little trains going around, and the carousel, and the people going in and out of buildings on that turntable. And we vowed that we would make it through to the other side and we'd buy every damned piece of that village in existence. We swore we'd become the kind of people who idiots like that toyshop owner would fawn over. Never again would we get chased from a shop doorway or window.'

'You guys must have had the kind of money to buy a village *world* years ago. Several times over. But you didn't?' Anouk eyed him thoughtfully. The deep blue pools were fathoms deep.

'We did, as it happens.' He smiled a genuine smile. 'We bought the lot. Just to know what it felt like.'

'And?'

'And it felt good.' He laughed suddenly. 'A bit surreal, that first time we set it up. Young adults reliving a childhood moment that had once been denied them. But after that we felt like we'd made our point, if only to ourselves. So we split it out and sent a bundle to each of about five or six kids' community centres.'

'And one of them was Care to Play?' Anouk guessed.

'Yeah. Once the kids there found out, they decided that was what they wanted to do for us, buy a new piece every year. It's a matter of pride to them, to do something to raise money for a new toyshop, or ride, or ice-skating rink.'

'That's really nice.' She glanced around ruefully. 'Even I bought into the idea. I thought you'd love this, but you just do it for the kids.'

'Why not? They get pleasure from it, too.'

'That's another thing which confused me,' she admitted. 'At the centre you're an inspiration for making good from nothing. At the hospital, the rumour is that you both came from money?'

'At the hospital it's just that,' he growled. 'A rumour. Malachi has become a multimillionaire thanks to his boxing, but I'm not.'

'You must earn a decent salary as a neurosurgeon?'

He raised an eyebrow at her.

'Did I say I was complaining?'

'Well, no,' she conceded. 'So why not just tell people that?'

'Why bother? It isn't any of their business and because it would invite questions, more interest, delving into my past—and Malachi's.'

'Surely that's a good thing? Two boys, with humble beginnings, have done incredibly well for themselves. It's the fairy tale, people would have lapped it up. You'd have had even more women falling at your feet.'

She hadn't intended to sound so cross when she'd made that latter observation.

'I told you,' he cut across her, 'it would have been an invitation for people to rifle through our lives like they're some kind of public property.'

Surprisingly, Anouk was beginning to realise just how protective both Sol, and particularly Malachi, were about their private lives.

Who would have thought it?

But she couldn't ask anything more, she didn't dare. Not after he'd effectively shut down that line of conversation. And still, his gaze held hers and she couldn't move. He might not have told her a lot, but, given his driving need for privacy, she felt as though he'd told her more than she could have hoped he would.

As though she was significant.

'Did you know that ridiculous pudding hat of yours was on inside out?' he told her, lifting it gently and turning it right side out before lowering it back on her head. Infinitely tender, infinitely thrilling.

She waited, pinned to the spot, as he released her hat and cupped her face instead, like a blast of heat in the cold winter air.

'Sol?' she breathed, when neither of them had moved and it was clear that neither of them was going to move.

Still, they both remained motionless. And then, just when Anouk had finished telling herself that she had to be the one to step back, to break the contact, however much she railed against it, he bent his head and brushed her lips with his.

It ignited a fire in an instant, sending the surrounding people, the coffee shop, the entire street, reeling into the background.

With a low moan, she stepped towards him, her arms raised to grab his jacket with her hands. Whether she deepened the kiss or Sol did, it hardly mattered.

His mouth was hot and demanding, his taste every bit as exhilarating as she remembered. It confirmed the one truth she'd suspected since the gala ball—one night with him hadn't been enough. She wanted more. She *needed* more.

He kissed her with ruinous skill, turning her inside out and upside down. He plundered and claimed, teasing her with his lips, his tongue, his teeth; he pulled her body to him until she was sure she could feel every last muscled ridge of that washboard body that had stamped itself so indelibly in her mind, and he made a low sound as he kissed her as if, like her, he needed more.

And she was lost. As enchanted by the man as every other woman before her had been.

She who should know better.

'My place?' he broke contact long enough to mutter.

Anouk didn't even try to speak, she just nodded.

They barely even made it through the door of his apartment before they were undressing each other.

Sol's touch was fire over every millimetre of her skin, smouldering over her wherever he trailed those expert fingers of his. Setting her ablaze every time he lowered his head, and that skilful mouth, to brand her somewhere new.

Her neck, her shoulder, the rise of her breast. One hand laced itself through her hair, cupping the nape of her neck and making her feel cherished and precious, whilst the other hand played a wicked concerto on her body as if it were the most exquisite instrument.

And with every accomplished stroke the fire inside her grew hotter and brighter, until it was too painful to look at. And so Anouk closed her eyes and gave herself over to the sheer beauty of it. She was singing in her head, arias she had never known before. Certainly not like this.

Again and again Sol moved his fingers, his hand, his mouth, over her body, testing her and tasting her. Paying homage to every inch of her, he supported her neck with one hand while the other skimmed over her back and then spanned the hollow at the base of her spine with enviably long, strong fingers, making her feel infinitely delicate.

He took his time, as though they were in no rush. As

though there was no end goal, trailing his fingers up one side and down again, leaving shivers of delight in his wake.

Up and down.

Up again, and down again.

Pleasing and punishing her, until every molecule of her pulsed with burning, intense need. All she could do was respond to him. As if she'd been waiting for this moment for ever. As if she were his to command.

As if she were *his*.

Time stood still for Anouk. She stayed there in his arms, letting all this desire swirl around, and move through her as Sol branded her with every touch, leaving her feeling as though she would never be the same again.

This is his skill, a tiny voice urged silently in her head. *He makes you feel special, unique, and as long as you don't fall for him, it will be fine.*

But the voice was too hazy, too muffled, too deliberately easy for the sensations tearing through her to drown out. Or perhaps it was more that she wanted to drown *in* the sensations. To drown in Sol.

It was only when she heard the loud, delectably rude sound of a zip sliding that she realised he had unfastened her jeans and was sliding his fingers under the material.

They hadn't even made it to the bedroom.

'Do you want to… I mean…here?' she began weakly, the words catching in her throat as, without warning, he brushed one finger tantalisingly over the front of her underwear.

Then the damned man lifted his head and shot her the most devilish grin.

'Sorry, what were you saying?'

But it was the dark, oddly intent look in his eyes that snagged at her the most. As though he wasn't quite as in control as he wanted to appear. As if she was affecting him that little bit more than he wanted to reveal.

It was a heady thought. And then, before she could find her voice, he hooked the material back and repeated the action, this time with no barrier between them.

'Did you want me to stop?'

There was no mistaking the rawness in his voice just then, but before she could answer he let his fingers move over her, stroking her once, twice, before dipping into her heat.

Everything in her clenched in delicious anticipation. But then her eyes flew open as he drew his hand back up, and she was powerless to prevent a small sound of objection from escaping her lips.

'Relax,' he commanded, his tone purely hedonistic. 'I'm not going anywhere. Except here.'

And before she could say a word he lifted his finger to his mouth and licked it. Very deliberately.

'What…' she managed to find her voice, as jagged as it sounded '…are you doing?'

He fixed her with a lazy, hooded look.

'Tasting you.' His voice was thick, loaded. 'And you are as intoxicating as I remember.'

She had no idea how she managed to speak; her whole body was jolting with need.

'You've been remembering this?'

'Yes,' he growled, sliding his hand back into her trousers and his cool, wet finger straight over where she needed him most. 'And I've been imagining a hell of a lot more. So, let me ask you again, shall I continue or did you want me to stop?'

Her eyes fluttered slightly and it was all Anouk could do to bite her lip and shake her head. He'd stolen her voice again with a flick of his fingers, as if he were some wicked sorcerer using his clever fingers to wind the most magical of spells around her.

'Say it,' he growled.

It was an effort to open her heavy eyelids. Even more of one to speak. So instead she lifted her bottom, just a fraction, to brush his hand.

Yet it seemed he was one step ahead of her, and as she moved his hand shifted out of reach. Barely. She could still feel the heat from him rolling over her, but she couldn't make contact.

'I find I want to hear the words from you,' Sol ground out.

The man was a fiend!

She swallowed. Hard.

'Continue,' she managed hoarsely. 'Definitely, continue.'

Sol seemed only too happy to oblige.

'So wet,' he growled in a voice so carnal that it sent another ache slicing through her right to her core.

Anouk tried to answer, but speech was impossible. Even before he slid those expert fingers around to caress her.

It took her a moment to realise that the low moans she heard were her own. This—what Sol was doing to her right now—was like nothing she'd ever known before.

So adrift, so out of her own body, and yet so wholly at its mercy all at the same time. She was vaguely aware of moving her head so that she could fit her mouth back to Sol's, every slip and slide of his tongue mirroring what his fingers were doing, stoking that fire higher with each passing moment.

He moved his other hand from the nape of her neck to cup her cheek, cradling it almost tenderly, if she hadn't known that to be ridiculous. Still, when he angled his head for a deeper fit, she poured more into that kiss than she'd ever known possible.

It was incredible, the sensations rushing through her body from her mouth to her core and back again, everywhere that Sol was; the devastating rhythm he was building inside her. She would be ruined for any other man. She was sure of it. Solomon Gunn would make sure that no other man would ever be able to satisfy her again.

She didn't think she cared—just as long as he never stopped doing what he was doing now.

She sighed, a sound of deep longing, causing Sol to wrench his mouth from hers, his eyes seeking her out and staring at her as though trying to see something in them. Either that, or conveying some silent message that she couldn't understand. She wanted to ask him, but it wasn't in her to speak, his dexterous fingers leaving her only just able to breathe; tracing her shape, holding her, cradling her and then, finally, slipping inside her slick heat. She felt the shudder roll through her even before she heard her needy moan.

His eyes went almost black with desire.

'You respond so perfectly, *zoloste*,' he murmured, his gravelly voice the perfect telltale.

She bit her lip and nodded, unable to speak. Not that it mattered, she wouldn't know what to say even if she could. His fingers were still moving over her, around her, inside her. And she couldn't get enough. Especially when he lowered his head, placing his wicked mouth on her neck and driving her wild with his clever tongue and devilish teeth.

She didn't know when she began moving against his palm, urging him to quicken the pace when he seemed to want to take it at his own leisurely pace—to stretch out the blissful agony in her that much longer—she only knew she could feel herself hurtling along, and the abyss coming up on her so quickly she thought she might hurtle down for ever and ever and ever.

And she wanted Sol inside her. Properly. She reached down his body to his belt buckle, her fingers fumbling in her haste. She could feel him. Steel straining behind the denim, as though he wanted her just as badly. It was a thrilling thought. If only she could work the damned belt.

The driving rhythm didn't stop or even slow for an instant, but with his free hand Sol caught her wrists and moved her away.

'There's time enough for that,' he muttered, every word dancing across her skin as his fingers continued their devastating concerto. 'Right now, this is about you.'

She'd never felt so worshipped, so powerful, or so confident in her own body.

Finally it broke over her, as if every nerve ending in her entire body were fizzing and popping, from the top of her head right down to her very toes, and then he twisted his wrist skilfully, in a way she'd never known before, and she felt herself catapult into the air. Higher and higher, further and longer, soaring spectacularly on a wave of shimmering, magical sensation that she thought might never end.

She certainly never wanted it to. And still Sol touched her, held her. So that as the wave finally began to slow, and drop, she found herself tumbling straight onto another, which took her soaring back up again.

Time after time.

Finally, sated and spent, she felt herself tumbling, her body sagging into Sol's, her breathing rapid and harsh.

And all she could do was hope that he broke her fall when she finally hit the ground.

Anouk was in his bed by the time she started coming back to herself. Right where he'd been imagining her for too long now. As nonsensical as that notion was. He watched her, half amused, half ravenous, as she blinked and tried to focus on her new surroundings.

'Oh.' The small sound escaped her lips and he was powerless to do anything but lower his head and try to catch the sound in his own mouth.

'I took the liberty of bringing you to my bed,' he managed. Then, as her eyes wandered down to his naked form, he added, 'I also took the liberty of stripping. Is that a problem?'

'On the contrary.' Her voice was thick, hoarse, and he liked that she couldn't conceal her need for him. 'I find I rather like that.'

And then, as if to prove her point, she stretched beneath him, parting her legs to settle him against her wet heat, and Sol almost lost it there and then.

'There's no rush, *zolotse*,' he chided gently, as though he himself weren't so perilously close to the edge.

But then Anouk looped her arms around his neck and her legs around his body and shot him a daring, cheeky grin.

'Are you quite sure about that?'

Before he could answer, she lifted her hips and drew him inside her, as taut, scorching need knotted in his belly.

It stole his breath from his very lungs.

With a low moan, he thrust inside her, revelling in her answering shudder. The way she locked her legs tighter around him, and lifted her hips to meet him. He made himself slide out of her slowly, then back in again, setting a deliberate pace and fighting the driving urge to take her there and then.

He had no idea how he kept it going. Whether he even managed it for long at all. But then he found he was moving faster, harder, deeper, and Anouk was matching him stroke for stroke. And he could feel it building inside her, just as it was inside him.

When her breath came in shallower gasps, he hooked his hand under her and angled her perfectly, reaching between them to find the very centre of her need, and then he sent her over the edge, the sound of her crying his name far more potent than it should have been.

And Sol, unable to bear it any longer, followed her.

CHAPTER TEN

HE KNEW SHE was gone even before his eyes had adjusted to the pitch-black of the room. He could sense it. The bed felt…empty without her. And an irrational sense of anger rolled through him that she should have snuck out, like some kind of thief, whilst he slept. He who never slept soundly.

Throwing back the sheet and stabbing his legs into a pair of night-time joggers, he stomped out of the bedroom and down the hallway. And stopped abruptly.

The light to the living area was on and he could hear the sound of cutlery on porcelain. It was insane how glad that sound made him.

Wandering through, he leaned on the doorjamb and watched her, perched on the granite worktop, one of his T-shirts swamping her delectable body, eating his cereal.

'Hungry?'

She jumped instantly.

'It was a long shift and…an energetic night.' She offered him a sheepish grin. 'I didn't mean to wake you.'

'You didn't.'

Stepping in, he opened the cupboards and retrieved his own cereal bowl, filling it up and pouring on the milk she had left on the counter, before putting the bottle away.

'I didn't realise you were a neat freak,' she teased.

'I didn't consider that you were a slob.' He laughed.

She straightened up indignantly.

'I am not, I was going to clean up as soon as I'd finished, so you can take that back.'

'Fair enough.' He took a spoonful of the cereal, watching her wriggle off the counter-top and potter around his kitchen.

He had no idea what rippled through him at the sight but he didn't care to analyse it too deeply.

'So...do I come back to...your bed? Or do I...go to the guest room?'

Ah, so the new, bold Anouk had taken cover again and the old, reserved Anouk was back.

'Come back to bed.' He didn't even bother to keep the amusement from his tone.

'It's all very well for you to laugh.' She bristled. 'But I'm not used to...*this*.'

'I know I have a reputation as a playboy, Anouk. But I'm not a complete bastard. Just because I'm not cut out for relationships, or love, or any of that mumbo jumbo, doesn't mean I throw women out in the middle of the night as soon as the sex is over.'

'About that,' Anouk announced, loudly if a little shakily. 'I think that's utter tosh, as it happens.'

'Say that again?'

To say he was incredulous didn't cut it. Anouk moistened her lips nervously and he had to force himself not to let his eyes linger.

'I think you use sex as a distraction,' she declared.

'Is that so?'

'Yes.' Clearly warming to her subject, she drew herself a little taller and eyed him determinedly. 'I think you use sex as a distraction to stop you from getting too close to anyone.'

Anger and something else—something someone who didn't know him might have categorised as fear—spread through his mind.

'This idea that you're not cut out for relationships, or love is nonsense.'

'Careful, *zoloste*, you're wandering into precarious territory.'

A lesser woman would have backed away at the dangerous edge in his voice.

But then, Anouk wasn't a lesser anything.

'Someone has to,' defiance laced her tone.

'Why? Because you want me to tell you that I love you?'

'No!' she actually looked horrified. 'Not me. Of course not. That's…insane.'

'Of course it's insane,' Sol couldn't pinpoint what charged through him in that millisecond. He didn't want to. 'Because I'm not a man who believes in 'love'. I certainly can't offer it.'

'I think you *are* capable of love.' The panic was gone and her defiance was back again. 'The way you are with your patients, and those young carers, and even your relationship with your brother Malachi. You care, in everything that you do.'

He hated the way she thought he was a better man than he was. It only made it more apparent to him that he wasn't that man.

'You're trying to make me into something I'm not to suit your own agenda, *zolotse*,' he gritted out, suddenly angry. Because anger was easier than these other emotions that threatened to churn inside him. 'Because you hate yourself for a one-night stand with me and you want to make yourself feel better by claiming I can be more than that. But that isn't me. I'm not built that way, Anouk. I don't want to be. I warned you about that.'

She hated hearing those words; he could see it in her stiff stance, and the belligerent tilt of her head.

'That isn't what I'm doing, Sol,' she snapped. 'I'm telling you that I think you're a different man from the image of yourself you put out there, and I don't know if it's because you want others to believe that's all there is to you, or if you actually really do believe it's the truth. But, whatever the truth is, that's for you to know. It has no bearing on me, either way.'

'Your eagerness to change me suggests otherwise.'

If his cereal had contained broken glass, it couldn't have shredded him inside any worse. But Anouk didn't reply straight away. She just watched him, a solemn expression in those arresting blue eyes.

He couldn't help wishing he knew what she was thinking.

'Did I ever tell you that the reason I came to the UK was to find my father?' she asked, just as he was about to give up thinking she was going to speak again.

They both knew the answer to that. Her eyes were too bright, too flitting. He doubted she'd ever told anyone, expect maybe Saskia. Still, he could play the game for her, if that was what she needed.

He realised his previous anger had begun to dissipate.

'No.' He feigned a casualness. 'I don't think you did.'

'Just before my mother…died…' she faltered '…she told me that she had once received a letter from my father.'

'You hadn't known him?'

'Not at all. Only the story she'd told me about him not wanting to be around for us.' Her strained tone suggested that wasn't all there was to it, but Sol didn't press her on it. It was shocking enough that she was telling him this much. 'I didn't know he'd ever contacted us. Her. Me.'

'What did he say?'

'I don't know.' She looked angry for a moment, but then smoothed it away quickly, efficiently. 'Apparently she'd thrown it on the fire in a pique of temper. By the time she'd changed her mind, most of it was gone. She just about managed to retrieve part of an address.'

'To his home in the UK?'

Anouk eyed him speculatively for several long moments. There was patently more to the story than she was willing to reveal to him. And he shouldn't be so desperate to know the truth. To understand it more.

He shouldn't be so wrapped up in the abridged version she was feeding him now. It shouldn't matter to him.

'You came all the way from America because he lives in the UK.'

'Not just the UK. Moorlands itself,' she bit out, at length.

That was why she'd come here?

'Did you track him down?' He couldn't help himself.

What the hell was it about this woman that slid, so devilishly slickly, under his skin?

An internal war waged within Sol and for seconds, minutes, maybe hours, he couldn't breathe. He had no idea what would win.

There was another pause, before she nodded.

'Eight years ago. With Saskia.'

'And?'

'He'd died about five years before that. There was a young family living in the house, but the neighbours confirmed it.'

'You're sure it was him.'

'There's no doubt about it, Sol.' She offered a wan smile. 'I even visited his grave.'

'I'm so sorry,' he told her sincerely.

What more was there to say?

She leaned on the counter, her arms folded defensively across her chest.

'I'm not after pity, Sol. I just wanted you to know that I wasn't telling you that I think you're capable of love because I want you to love *me*. I know our deal was just sex. It's the only reason I agreed to it, so I'm not about to change the rules now. I don't want love in my life either. I don't trust it. I never have.'

Some seething thing slunk around inside him. But the anger wasn't directed *at* Anouk any more. Or himself. It was directed at those people who had never deserved her care in the first place. Who had hurt her. Who had destroyed something as fragile and precious as her trust in anyone who could love her.

'You trusted the wrong people,' he gritted out, realising that he wanted to reach out and pull her to him.

To tell her that she was beautiful, and caring, and lovable. Especially because it was only now occurring to him that she didn't know that for herself. How had he not seen that before? He was usually skilled at reading others.

'Of course, I trusted the wrong people,' she agreed flatly. 'But who would have thought that my mother and my grandmother were those wrong people? They lied to me my whole life. In the end I think my mother only told me the truth to get one final dig at me. To prove to me that she'd had the upper hand right up until her moment of death.'

'That doesn't mean you should still let her get to you now. You can trust people. You can trust me.'

Her eyebrows shot up.

'Said the spider to the fly.'

It was a fair point. Maybe that was why it grated on him. Maybe that was why, instead of shutting her question down as he would have done had any other woman asked, he found himself answering the question she'd once put to him.

'I was five when Malachi started to become a carer.'

She blinked.

'You don't have to do this, Sol. I wasn't telling you about me just to make you feel obliged to do the same.'

'He became a carer for me, and for our mum, when she needed it,' he continued, as if she hadn't spoken.

She only hesitated for a moment.

'She was ill?'

If you could call being a drug addict ill. Some people called it an illness. Having lived through it, borne the brunt of it, he and Malachi had always been considerably less charitable. Not that Sol was about to say any of that aloud.

'Something like that.' He tried not to spit it out in distaste.

Clearly he didn't do a very good job; the expression on her face said enough. Less shock, more a tired understanding. As though she hadn't expected it from him, but, now that he'd said it, she wasn't entirely surprised.

Or maybe he was just projecting. This woman made him rethink things of which he'd long since stopped taking notice. He blinked as he realised she was still talking to him.

'Sol? I asked about your dad.'

'Dead. That's why she became…ill.'

'So he cared for you before that?' She was trying to put it together, like one of the jigsaws at the carers' centre, only it was a jigsaw of his life and he hadn't given her all the pieces.

With anyone else, he wouldn't have wanted to.

'*Cared* is a bit too generous a description,' Sol ground out. 'He was a former Russian soldier.'

'Your parents were Russian?'

'Not my mother,' he clarified. 'My father was medically

discharged due to injury; he had street smarts but no education so he earned a living taking work on the docks when it was available, or as a pub fighter otherwise.'

'Did he hit you and Malachi?'

'No. He wasn't exactly the best father but he didn't hit us, except the odd clip around the ear as many kids got back them, not bad for a man who had been systematically used as a punching bag by his own father. Though he did teach us to fight, from toddlers really, but particularly Mal because he was older. It was his way of bonding with us, I guess.'

'So that's how Malachi became the skilled fighter he is now.'

'I doubt he'd ever have believed it would make Mal a millionaire.' Sol shook his head. 'Love wasn't something our father was good at. Even his relationship with our mother was more passionate and volatile than loving. She showed us some love as kids, and he put food on the table and a roof over our heads.'

'How did he die?'

'Bad fight.' Sol laughed but it was a hollow, scraping sound. 'Brain bleed. And yes, I know all the psychology arguments about that being the reason why I became a neurosurgeon. The point is that my mother fell apart. Started doing drugs to numb the pain. It wasn't a far reach from the world in which we lived back then. The love went pretty fast, then.'

'How old was Malachi?'

'Eight.' He shrugged as Anouk drew her lips into a thin line. 'By the time he was ten, she was a full-on addict and Mal was full-time carer for us both, whilst he also earned money for us to eat and live.'

'He was earning money at ten?' Anouk blew out a breath. 'Doing what? Surely no one would employ him.'

'Local gangs.'

'Gangs?' She looked momentarily stunned. 'So…what did he do?'

Sol crossed his arms over his chest. Even now, over two decades on, it still rattled him that he didn't know exactly what his brother had been compelled to do just to keep the two—three—of them together.

Like holding their lives together with sticking plaster. No, not even something so expensive. His ten-year-old brother had been holding their lives together with a bit of discarded string he'd found blowing about in the filthy street outside their tiny terraced house.

He didn't even understand why he was telling Anouk any of this, and yet he couldn't seem to stop. She drew it out of him, with all the patience and compassion that he had used on the young carers in his centre.

It was odd, the tables being turned on him. And, strangely, not entirely unpleasant.

'Errands like drugs?' she pressed gently.

He emitted another harsh laugh. Given the state of their mother, drug gangs were people Malachi had never, ever worked for.

'No, never drugs. I don't know everything he did, you'd have to ask Mal, but things like being a runner for bookies. They trusted him because of our dad. Maybe he did things which were a bit dodgy but not outright illegal. Even as a kid Mal was always unshakeable on that.'

'He seems so quiet.' Anouk shook her head, evidently trying to absorb it all.

No judgement. No false sympathy or drama. Just…*her*. Listening. Caring. It should have concerned him more that he was letting her get so close, but he couldn't bring himself to back away. Even emotionally.

He told himself that he knew what he was doing.

'Mal isn't as quiet as people think. He has this inner core of steel, I'm telling you. Even as a kid he handled himself with those guys. Enough to make sure that I kept going to school. Believe it or not, I was always better with the discipline than he was.'

'Sol, the playboy, a good schoolboy?'

She offered him a soft smile and he realised she was teasing him. It was like a lick of heat.

'Amazing, isn't it?'

'So how did he get away with not going?'

'Mal has a true eidetic memory. He didn't really need to be in lessons to keep up with school. I used to…persuade some lads in his year to get copies of the work.'

'Persuade as in employ some of the fighting techniques your father had taught you?' she guessed.

'Only in the beginning.' Sol made no apologies. Not even to this woman. 'With those ten- or eleven-year-old lads who had trouble accepting a polite request from an eight-year-old. They rarely had trouble the next time.'

'I never realised.'

'Why would you?' Sol pointed out evenly. 'The point is that we got by, and if he hadn't done all of that I wouldn't have stayed in school, and without him I wouldn't be in medicine, let alone a neurosurgeon.'

Neither of them could have imagined even a half of what they had today. Or just how far the two of them would pull themselves out of the gutter. Together. The way it had always been.

'What happened with your mum?'

He tensed; it was impossible not to.

'He got her the help she needed, but it turned out it still wasn't enough. She died when I was seventeen.'

'I'm sorry.'

'Don't be.' He shrugged, ignoring the odd scraping sensation deep inside his stomach. One that he was sure had more to do with the soft way that Anouk was looking at him than anything else. 'In some ways her death set Mal and me free.'

She stared at him for another long moment and he had to fight the urge to turn away lest she see right down to his soul. Down to where he still felt like that socially awkward, ashamed, inadequate kid.

'Is that where the playboy image came from? Not wanting to commit to someone, or settle down, or have kids because of your experience with your mum?'

Sol didn't answer.

He couldn't. Or wouldn't. Either way, the net result was the same.

He swung away to stare at the tiled wall, his hands resting on either side of him on the counter top. Behind him, he heard her slide off the granite surface. He could sense her approaching him and he turned, unable to help himself.

Suddenly they were facing each other, everything rending apart as Anouk placed her hands on either side of his face as if to make him look at her. He definitely didn't want to talk any more.

He forgot that he'd been doing all this to make her trust him. That he'd been waiting for her to need him so badly that she begged him, as she had the night of the gala.

'Confession time is over, *zolotse*,' he growled, snaking his arms to her waist and hauling her to him.

She didn't object. Especially not when he snagged her mouth with his.

Sol's whole body combusted in that one second. The woman was mouth-watering. Every slide of her tempting mouth, every shift of her delectable body, every tiny groan as he swept his finger over her sinfully hard nipples.

He'd never *ached* so much before to bury himself inside a woman. Not aside from the primal, physical urge, that was.

Anouk was dynamite where before he'd only known black powder.

CHAPTER ELEVEN

'WHAT IS THE matter with you, *bratik*?' Malachi challenged from across the expansive, luxury office just as Sol was filling his mug with hot, rich coffee from his brother's coffee maker.

'What?' Sol cocked an eyebrow, selecting a couple of Danish pastries to put onto a napkin and striding over to flop in a comfortable chair.

The last week had been unparalleled. So much for a one-night stand. He hadn't wanted to let Anouk go and she had been more than happy to stay. There hadn't been a room in his penthouse they hadn't used as their personal playground.

'You're full of the joys of spring,' sniped Malachi.

'And you're grouchy and on edge.' Sol eyed him shrewdly. 'More so than usual, that is. Though I wouldn't have thought that was possible.'

'Funny,' Malachi bit out.

'Thanks.'

'Idiot.'

Sol shrugged, wholly unconcerned, and wolfed down the second pastry before speaking again.

'Hungry by any chance?'

'Always.' Sol grinned, glancing around the room.

'*Vkusno!* So, what's the Christmas tree all about?'

He didn't think he'd ever seen so much as a bauble in his brother's offices before. Only Anouk had been more resistant to festive decorations than his brother always had been. Sol didn't know why, but he found himself staring at it a little harder. It looked remarkably similar to the one in Resus. The one that Anouk had said her friend Saskia had decorated.

He practically heard the clang as the penny hit the floor of his brain.

'I realised it's good for morale,' Malachi sidestepped. 'I'm not the only one who works here, you know. Listen, I've got a board meeting to prepare for, so do you want to tell me why you really schlepped across town to see me?'

Sol stared at his brother wordlessly. That tree had nothing to do with morale; it was about Saskia, plain and simple. Suddenly, he wondered if she was doing for Malachi anything like what Anouk was doing for him. Making him feel whole when he hadn't before recognised how broken he'd been? And, if so, didn't they all deserve this chance?

'You and I have always said that we weren't built for commitment, or love. That everything *she* put us through destroyed that in us. But what if we're wrong, Mal? What if you and I have always been capable of love?'

'This discussion is over,' Malachi ground out. But still, he didn't move.

'There's always been a love between you and me.' What had Anouk said? 'It may be a different kind of love, but it's love nonetheless.'

'Where did those pearls of wisdom come from?' Malachi snorted, but Sol noted that it lacked the level of scorn he might have expected from his big brother. He also noticed that Malachi wasn't outright dismissing him.

Or was he just reading too much into it because of the way Anouk had made him re-evaluate his own priorities?

'I don't know,' he answered honestly.

'A woman?'

'No,' he denied. Then, 'Maybe.'

'Anouk?'

Reality bit hard, and for a moment Sol thought about denying it. What if talking about her with Malachi spoiled what he and Anouk had? *Might* have. Not that he even knew what they were—these...*feelings* that sloshed around inside him like sand and cement and water in a mixer.

'Are you going to take the proverbial?' He glowered at Malachi.

Their brotherly banter was inevitable, joshing each other, but for a moment, Malachi didn't say anything.

'Maybe next time.'

That was unexpected.

'Yeah, then,' Sol admitted. 'Anouk.'

'Something is going on between you both?'

Malachi didn't need to spell out that 'something going on' meant more than just him and Anouk having sex. His brother had mocked him for his playboy reputation plenty of times in the past.

'I don't know. Maybe.'

'Serious?'

Was it? If it wasn't, would he even be here? Doing this for her? He didn't care to examine that too deeply.

'Maybe. She's the reason I came here today, at least.'

His brother studied him, cool and perceptive.

'What do you need?' Malachi asked at length.

'You have people who can track stuff down for you, right?'

Malachi inclined his head.

'I want you to track down all you can on this man.' Sol flicked through his phone and found the notepad where he'd copied down the details from the scrap of paper in

Anouk's picture frame, leaning forward to spin it across the desk to his brother. 'He died thirteen years ago, but he used to live there.'

Wordlessly, Malachi read the screen and made a note of the information. He didn't even question it and, not for the first time, Sol wondered how different his life would have been if he hadn't had his brother.

Anouk was right. Their relationship with their mother might have been destructive and damaging, but the two brothers had always believed in each other, loved each other. In their own fierce way.

How was it that she—a relative stranger—had understood even when he hadn't really been able to see it? He doubted Malachi had either.

What was that saying about not seeing the wood for the trees?

'Do you think you can do this without hurting her, Sol?' Malachi demanded suddenly.

'Sorry?' Sol was instantly on alert.

'Settling down with Anouk. Do you think you, the perennial playboy, can do that?'

'I'm not settling down,' Sol denied.

'Then why care? I mean, I get that you care about your patients, and the kids at the centre. But I've never known you to care about a woman enough to ask for my help.'

'She's…different.' He chose his words circumspectly. 'But that doesn't mean there's anything serious between us.'

'Right.'

Malachi pushed his chair back abruptly and stood up, moving to the window to look out, and it struck Sol that they were so alike, he and his brother.

Perhaps that was why, when he felt the disapproval radiating from Malachi's stiff back, Sol knew it wasn't actually directed at him. Rather, his brother was censuring himself. Which was why he took the plunge into the dangerous waters of asking personal questions.

'Who is she, Mal?'

Malachi swung around but said nothing. The silence seemed to arc between them, dangerous and electric, so many emotions charging over his brother's usually closed face that Sol could barely keep up. But he recognised anger, and he recognised fear.

What the hell could ever make his big, tough brother afraid?

'I think I prefer the Sol who just beds women and moves on,' Malachi said at length. 'You're acting like a lost puppy. Anouk's lost puppy, to be exact.'

But despite the way he bit out the words Sol knew his brother well enough to read that there was no malice behind them, and so he didn't take offence.

'Sod off.' He stood slowly and deliberately, then sauntered over to the sideboard and selected another pastry. A show of nonchalance. 'I'm no one's puppy.'

'Not usually, no.' Malachi shrugged. 'You're usually fending them off with a stick.'

'What? Puppies?' Sol quipped.

'Puppies, women, little old ladies.' Malachi folded his arms over his chest and shrugged. 'But I've never seen you look at anyone the way I saw you look at that one the night of the gala.'

'Her name's Anouk,' Sol corrected instinctively, before realising that Malachi was baiting him. His brother knew her name perfectly well. He'd already used it several times. 'And I didn't look at her any particularly special way.'

Malachi twitched one eyebrow upwards, but said nothing.

'No clever quip?' Sol demanded when he couldn't stand the heavy silence any longer.

'I told you, not this time.'

Sol sized up his big brother. There was something odd about Malachi, and it came back to the fact that the guy was more on edge than usual.

'What's going on, Mal?'

'Nothing.'

'You're being cagey.'

'Not really.' Mal dismissed it casually. Arguably a little too casually. 'No more so than you, anyway.'

'You're kidding, right?' Sol shook his head in disbelief.

'Not particularly.'

'Fine.' Leaning back on the sideboard, Sol eyed his brother. 'Time to tell me something I don't know, Mal. If you've got the balls for it.'

And just like that, they were two kids again, and Sol was pressing his brother on where he'd been that first time he'd done a job for the Mullen brothers.

Just as he began to think it wasn't going to work, Malachi opened his mouth.

'I always thought a wife, a family, wasn't for us. Not after everything with *her*.' Sol didn't answer; they both knew he meant their mother. 'I always thought I'd done that bit. I'd endured that responsibility. I never wanted to do it again.'

'But now?' Sol prompted.

'Lately...I don't know.' Malachi swung around from the window almost angrily. 'Forget it. I'm just... Forget I said anything.'

In all these years, they hadn't talked about what had happened. Or about feelings. They were the Gunn brothers. That wasn't the way they handled their issues. But suddenly, something was different. Not Anouk, of course.

He told himself that would be taking it too far. But... *something*. Maybe a delayed reaction to hitting his thirties. The incident with Izzy and her family. The responsibility of the centre.

'Are we capable of it, do you think, Mal?'

His brother frowned. 'Of what?'

'Of…love.'

'You love Anouk?'

'Don't be stupid,' Sol scoffed. 'I'm not saying that. It's just hypothetical.'

He hated himself for not sounding more convincing. It ought to—it was the truth after all. There was no way he could be *in love* with anyone. Let alone Anouk. Whatever they shared between the two of them, it wasn't love. Was it?

Sol waited for the harmless jeering but it didn't come. Instead, Malachi eyed him morosely.

'Hypothetically, I don't even know if we have that capacity,' Malachi gritted out unexpectedly. 'But maybe the question should be, do we deserve it?'

Sol didn't know how to answer, but it didn't matter because his brother was speaking again.

'More pertinently, does any woman deserve to be subjected to our love, *bratik*? Such as we know what that is.'

If his brother had punched him in the gut Sol couldn't have felt any more winded. As if the air had been sucked from his very lungs.

Was Mal right? Would his love be more of a curse than any sort of a gift?

His mind was so full of conflicting thoughts that he simply let them jostle, his eyes scanning the room almost as a distraction. Which was when they alighted again on the Christmas tree.

'So, you and Saskia?'

'I don't wish to discuss it.' Malachi cut him off harshly.

'But you need to,' Sol answered. He rarely stood up

to his brother, he rarely needed to. This, he felt, was different. This mattered. To both of them. 'Right here, right now. Our mother ruined both of our childhoods. It's time we both decided whether we're going to let her ruin our futures, too.'

'What have we got?' Sol asked, rounding the corner to the bay. It had been a hectic shift so far, but he thrived on that.

The young doctor running the case looked relieved.

'Darren, nineteen, he suffers from epilepsy and this morning he had two back-to-back seizures, which is out of the norm for him. Full tonic-clonic seizures usually months apart and often only if there's already something going on in the body, like an infection.'

'Has he got an infection?' Sol checked.

'I think an ear infection.'

'And you've started a course of antibiotics?'

'Yes.'

'So, possibly not neuro at this point. But keep me in the loop,' Sol confirmed. 'Okay, let me go and check in the next bay. I had a call for them, as well.'

He slipped around the curtain just as Anouk glanced up. Surprise swept over her face for a moment but she regrouped quickly.

'This is Jack, twenty-five. He was drinking and playing football in the park with a group of mates when he collided with a tree. Loss of consciousness for about five minutes. Pupils are unequal and reactive and he's agitated. We're taking him up to CT now.'

'I'll come with you,' Sol confirmed.

Unequal pupils suggested a bleed on the brain, which might be pushing against the brain itself.

'Great.' Anouk nodded, turning back to her team and issuing her final instructions. 'Let's go.'

'He isn't responding to us verbally, although he does react physically if we ask him to do something. I don't know if the verbal is about the alcohol or a possible injury.'

'Are you going to the centre tonight?' she asked quietly as they strode along the corridors behind the patient.

'Yes, why?'

'I was thinking of going.'

'Do you need a lift?' He frowned, not liking her caginess.

It felt like a huge step backwards, but he couldn't pinpoint why.

'No, I just thought that…maybe you'd prefer it if we weren't there together.'

'Why not?'

It shouldn't gnaw at him the way it did. He understood why she might think it should bother him.

'If that was going to be an issue then I wouldn't have invited you to visit in the first instance,' he told her.

Except he still didn't know what had motivated him to ask her. He refused to accept that it was some uncharacteristic need to have her see a different side to him. That didn't make sense.

Although it seemed the most logical conclusion.

'I just wasn't sure.' She lowered her voice even further as the team reached the CT department and people began to congregate. 'After our…one-night stand.'

Her sudden whisper almost made him laugh. Any other time it probably would have done. But Sol was too busy thinking how dismal the term sounded on Anouk's lips. It felt inadequate to describe either of their encounters that way.

One-night stand—admittedly lasting longer than just the one 'night' sounded, frankly, a little pitiful.

What was happening to him? Why was he reading so much into everything? They'd had a good time together. Twice. Surely he should be more than happy to accept it for what it was?

'I'm heading down there after work,' he informed her. 'I'll drive you, too.'

'Oh, it's okay, I can walk.'

'I'll come down to the department when I'm done. If I'm caught up with a case, wait for me, we'll go together.'

It wasn't a request and they both knew it.

Still, when she flashed him a shy smile it twisted inside him, like a ribbon on a maypole. Delicate and pretty.

Sol snorted to himself as he stepped into the room. He was going to have to watch himself. If he wasn't careful then he risked Anouk wrapping herself around him in more ways than either of them could ever have anticipated.

CHAPTER TWELVE

THE CENTRE MIGHT as well have been Santa's grotto itself, Sol thought, surveying the scene in front of him—a hive of excitement and activity, it felt like the very epicentre of Christmas for the whole of Moorlands Wood.

And there, sitting on the floor, with Libby firmly wedged on one side of her and Katie on the other, pressing against her as though each claiming her as their own, was Anouk. It struck him that the girls' easy acceptance of her said more about Anouk than anything a person could say. These kids dealt with so much at such a young age that they often seemed to develop sixth senses about people.

This had to explain why he had let her slip under his skin without realising it. As he'd told Malachi, it wasn't anything as nonsensical as *love*.

Nevertheless, there was a draw there, a magnetism that pulled him in despite his vows to keep his distance. Which meant that, even now, he couldn't tear his gaze away.

Anouk looked totally engrossed in what she was doing. And what she was doing, he realised after a few moments' scrutiny, was measuring chocolate balls into a jar, before gluing reindeer antlers, funny eyes, and a big red nose onto the glass.

By the look of the full box in front of them, the trio had been working together for some time and were so focussed on the task in hand that none of them noticed him. And so he was free to stand and admire this fascinating woman who appeared, bizarrely, to have so captured his attention.

Without warning, Anouk looked up and her eyes—wide with surprise—locked with his. He didn't think, he didn't consider, he just reacted, flashing her a wide grin; something bursting inside him as she responded instinctively with a hint of a smile, her cheeks taking on a delicately pink hue.

Before he realised where he was, he had crossed the room and was standing in front of the trio. Still, it took him a supreme effort to tear his gaze from Anouk and greet the two young girls still nestled so lovingly on either side of her, as though seeking protection from her metaphorical wings.

'So we're making reindeer chocolate jars, are we?' he managed brightly.

'We've just finished.' Katie cast her arm over the full box solemnly. 'Now we're going to make beaded friendship bracelets for each other.'

'*Kruto!* Wow, they look amazing. Can I join in?' He felt Anouk's sharp gaze but he kept his eyes fixed on the girls, gratified when they nodded excitedly and got to their feet.

'We'll go and get the beads and the thread.' Libby grabbed Katie's arm. 'Why don't we use all green and red, like a Christmas theme?'

'Okay, but we should still have silver thread—that will make it brighter,' Katie advised as the two of them hurried off, lost in the carefree happiness of the moment and oblivious to the undertones that swirled around Sol and Anouk.

He settled himself on the floor next to her leaving a decent foot between them, but he still noticed her pulse leap at her throat as she deliberately avoided eye contact with him, inching another fraction away, as though she couldn't trust them to be so close to each other. It offered him a perverse kind of exultation.

At least he wasn't the only one feeling undercut by the intensity of the last week.

'Did you know this thing between Saskia and my brother is serious?'

He hadn't intended to say anything, but Malachi's revelations were still bubbling in his head and he couldn't help but wonder how much Anouk knew.

'Saskia and Malachi? No, how could I know?' Anouk frowned. 'I've been with you, and when I did return home she wasn't there.'

There was no reason for his body to tauten at the mere memory, surely?

'I hope he doesn't hurt her,' continued Anouk, obliviously. 'Saskia isn't as airy and tough as she might appear.'

'Funny, I was going to say the same thing about Malachi.'

She arched her eyebrows at him, waiting for some punchline. But he didn't have one. He was worried about his brother for the first time in for ever.

They weren't prepared for this…thing. Whatever it was. He might not have a name for it yet but he knew it was powerful. It assailed him at the most inopportune moments. Punching through him like a fist through wet paper. Like when he'd seen the naked sadness in her eyes when Anouk had told him about her father, or yesterday when he'd caught sight of her caring for her patient from across the ward, or today when she'd been so caught up with the girls that she hadn't even noticed anyone else in the room.

It wasn't love, but Sol imagined it was something in that family. He certainly *cared* for Anouk. So if whatever Mal felt for Saskia was anything like it, then he pitied his brother.

'Malachi won't hurt her. He isn't like me.'

The words came out automatically. Because he might once have believed them, although now he wasn't so sure.

'Because he isn't a playboy like you are, you mean?'

Why was it that it sounded so...hollow, coming off her tongue? Especially after the conversation they'd had in his apartment that night. It occurred to him that she might be testing him, but he had no idea how he was supposed to answer.

'You could say that,' he conceded, shocked at how much it cost him to sound so nonchalant.

'The Smoking Gun,' she added, and she didn't need to add a roll of her eyes. Her words spoke loud and clear all on their own. As if she was reminding herself of his reputation. Cautioning herself.

And it bothered him. Especially after their time together.

For years he had revelled in his reputation as a playboy, had been proud of the fact that he'd come out of his childhood with such a strong sense of self. He had never pretended to be something he wasn't. He loved being with women, but he had always hated the idea of a relationship with them—how much more honest could a man be?

Yet now, something had shifted and the names sounded toneless, even uncomfortable. Like a familiar old jacket that no longer suited—or fitted—him, but that he'd been trying to hold onto nonetheless.

His head was unusually hazy. As if some of its connections had been unexpectedly broken and it was trying to rewire itself using different paths.

He still wasn't quite sure what it meant.

'Great nickname, wasn't it?' he challenged, but the

words seemed to leave an unpleasant, metallic taste in his mouth.

This was absurd.

The...*thing* he felt for Anouk was absurd.

With her sweet smile and gentle demeanour she had succeeded in hooking him in a way he would not have believed possible a mere week ago. If he wasn't careful, she was the kind of woman who could easily tame him long enough to put him on a leash. But what had Malachi warned him? That a leopard didn't change its spots? That he was under some kind of spell now, but that when he came around again, all hell would break loose and the person he would most likely end up hurting would be Anouk herself?

And the idea of hurting her made him feel physically sick.

He needed to get up and move away. Now. Before it was too late.

Instead, he sat, perfectly still, not making even a sound. And still something swirled around them. He could feel it and he knew she could, too.

'We got loads of beads,' Libby's excited voice reached his ears from across the room.

Just one more night, he promised himself. Just one last time with Anouk, and then he'd find a way to end it without anyone getting hurt.

And when his eyes caught hers, widening a fraction, the pulse leaping at her throat, he knew she was thinking the same thing.

'Come home with me.' His voice was low and urgent, more a command than a request.

Anouk nodded, seconds before the girls raced back across the gallery floor to rejoin them, and he'd never wished for two hours to pass so expediently.

* * *

Last time they had barely got through the door before Sol had pulled her to him. This time, they barely made it to the lift.

Sol claimed her with such reverent kisses it was as though he was committing every detail of her touch to memory. Inscribing himself on her soul and she couldn't seem to get enough of him.

She could never seem to get enough. And that was the essential problem.

Even now, as he peeled off her clothing to kiss every last millimetre of her body, laying waste to her resolve and tearing down every last barrier between them, she couldn't do anything but let him.

A slave to him. Or a slave to her desire for him. Either way, it amounted to the same thing. He was making her forget their arrangement. He was making her want more.

And more again.

Worse, Anouk couldn't bring herself to care. So when he scooped her up to carry her through to the bedroom, muttering hoarsely about *not making it past the hallway otherwise*, all she could do was cling to him, pressing her body to his and meeting his possessive mouth with her own, greedy demands.

It was all she could do to ignore the tight emotions that tumbled through her when he laid her down so very reverently on the bed, removing the last of her clothes until she was naked before him, and rolling back to gaze at her, spread out before him as if she was his own personal feast.

'I've waited for this all day, *zolotse*,' he muttered, before lowering his mouth to her neck, kissing and licking the column of her throat, and fitting his palms to her breasts as if he couldn't bear not to touch her a moment longer.

He trailed scorching little kisses down her neck and to

the sensitive hollow at the base, taking his time, until she was urging him on with little moans. He moved across her shoulder and over the swell of her chest, inch by exquisite inch, as if he didn't want to skip over a single millimetre of her body until finally—*finally*—his mouth took over from his hands.

First he sucked one hard, aching nipple into his mouth, grazing his teeth over it gently but not too gently, flicking over it with his tongue, lavishing attention on her. And only when he seemed truly satisfied did he turn his attention to the other side, to repeat the same, adoring process.

And Anouk arched up to him as though to offer up more of herself, her whole body feeling heavy and restless and wanting more. So much more. But he held her in place, deliberately trapping her legs so she couldn't part them around him, couldn't draw him against her, couldn't nestle him where she burned for him most.

Like some kind of exquisite torture.

But if he didn't slide inside her soon, filling her up where all these wild sensations jousted in her, she didn't know if she could survive it.

Anouk didn't know when it occurred to her that if he could torment her so wantonly, then surely she, too, could tease him?

Slowly, carefully, she ran her hands over his back, indulging, just for a moment or two, in reacquainting herself with those hewn muscles that not even his bespoke suit and waistcoat could conceal.

And when he murmured his approval, he answered her long and low, reverberating through her breasts and into her already molten core.

With deliberate care she slid one hand around his waist and wrapped her fingers delicately around his sex. The effect was instantaneous, making her feel womanly and powerful all at once.

'If you do that, you'll find this won't last anywhere as long as it could,' he growled, and she loved the rawness in his tone.

'That's the idea,' she whispered. 'Because I don't think I can hold out much longer.'

A primal sound slipped from his throat as he shifted from her, easing down her body and using his hand to move her legs apart.

'At last,' she sighed, waiting for him to settle between them.

But instead of his body, he edged down with his shoulders, lifting his head only long enough for her to see the wicked gleam in his eyes.

'You can last,' he rasped. 'I insist on it.'

And then he buried his mouth, his tongue, into her heat, before she could answer, and she heard herself cry out.

Anouk had no idea how long he stayed there, paying homage to her as she could only clutch at his hair, his head, his shoulders, her raspy breath and abandoned cry the only sounds to break the silence. His murmurs of approval echoed through her, against her, as he feasted all the more making her shatter once, twice against his tongue then his fingers.

You are ruined, a voice whispered. *You will never, ever meet another man like Sol. There* is *no other man like Solomon Gunn.*

But she couldn't allow herself such thoughts. That path only led to misery. And so she ejected the unwelcome voice from her head and wriggled out from under Sol, pushing him onto his back, her eyes locking with his as she knelt over him and drew him deep into her mouth.

He was big and hot, like silky steel, and she forgot that

she was meant to be distracting herself from the intimacy of his mouth on her body and instead lost herself in the intimacy of her tongue swirling over and around him. She was tormenting him and pleasuring him with every second. The way she'd learned to do this past week. The way she never seemed to tire of doing. She probably never would.

She shut the errant thought down once again, concentrating on the moment. Reminding herself that this was just about sex. Only ever about sex.

There could be nothing more.

Lifting her eyes, she made herself focus on Sol. The intensity of his gaze and the unmistakeable shudder of need that took over his body made her feel powerful, and wicked. And all woman. She sucked him in deeper, wanting to lose herself inside that power, in a way she'd never enjoyed with any man before Sol.

Only Sol.

But apparently he wasn't prepared to let things end on her terms. With a low, primal groan, he pulled himself from her mouth and flipped her onto her back as he moved his body to cover hers. His hands traced every inch of her as though she was a revelation to him. It was incredible how precious, how *special*, she always felt when she was in his arms. Yet she was too hot, too needy, for any more play.

As though reading her mind, Sol shifted, nestling between her legs until she could feel his blunt end dipping into her.

'Please, Sol,' she breathed, desperate to lose herself in the primitive sensations that might drown out the other, more dangerous emotions that tumbled in her chest.

Emotions she told herself she had no name for.

Even as she was altogether too afraid that she could name them. Every last one.

And when Sol finally thrust inside her, deep and slow

and sure, his gaze holding hers, she refused to let her eyes slide from him. She held her breath, for fear the words she refused to face might fall from them.

Sol moved, pulling out of her before driving home again. Deeper, tighter, hungrier. Driving her faster and faster towards the top. When she finally catapulted over the edge, and heard herself cry out his name, his eyes still holding hers as he followed her, she knew the truth in her heart but she still wasn't prepared to hear Sol say it out loud.

Clear and raw, as though the words had been ripped from the very depths of his soul.

'I love you, *zolotse*.'

'No,' she choked out. Then, louder, *'No!'*

'I'm in love with you, Anouk.' He tried the words again, rolling them around on his tongue, still in shock.

He was in shock. He hadn't intended to say them, much less repeat them, and yet the inexplicable thing was that the more he said them out loud, the easier it felt. The more he liked the way they tasted in his mouth, the way they sounded to his ears.

Like a melody he'd thought he would never want to hear.

'You can't say that.' She was furious. 'I won't hear it. Take it back.'

'Not possible,' he managed. 'It's out there and it can't be taken back.'

She stared at him as though he had physically wounded her.

'Why are you doing this?'

Her evident confusion clawed at his heart. It wasn't as if he understood completely himself. And yet, each time he said it, it made more sense.

Everything made more sense.

'I swore I would never fall in love with any woman.

Ever. But here I am. And I know you feel the same way about me.'

'I don't,' she choked, scrambling to get off him.

Away from him.

He let her, even as he emitted a laugh at the irony of it.

He, who had spent over a decade steering clear of relationships with women who would inevitably declare themselves in love with him, was now in love.

It seemed only fitting that *he* should be the one saying it whilst the woman he loved didn't want to accept it. As if it was a test of his own making. He'd never failed a damned test in his entire career, he wasn't about to start now.

'Our deal was sex. Pure and simple,' she cried, spinning around searching for her clothes. 'You're the king of one-night stands.'

'I was. Until you came along.'

He watched her locate her T-shirt and pull it on, then flail around for her jeans. He didn't try to stop her, he didn't want her to feel trapped or cornered, but he didn't share her fluster. He just felt calm. At peace.

It was odd, the way the minute he'd admitted that he loved her, everything had seemed to start slotting into place, piece by piece. He felt somehow...*whole*.

'You said it yourself—I used sex as a distraction.' He shrugged. 'That I just needed to meet the right person. Turns out you were right.'

'No. No, I wasn't.' She shoved her feet into her jeans, first one and then the other, before yanking them up those slender legs that had spent so much of the night wrapped around him. 'You told me that I didn't know the first thing about you. That I was reading too much into it because I wanted you to be a better man than you really are.'

'Turns out I was wrong.'

'*No!*' Her voice sounded mangled, wretched, and his heart actually ached for her.

'You can deny it as many times as you like, Anouk. It won't change it, believe me. I've been pretending to myself that there was nothing more than sex between us—just like you are now—but I can't pretend any longer.'

'Then try,' she half choked, half bit out.

She looked wounded, and fragile, and even more beautiful than ever. As if finally acknowledging the truth had infused his whole world with a more vivid colour.

How had he ever thought that love was destructive? How had he failed to realise just how glorious it could be?

'More to the point,' he told her quietly, 'I don't want to pretend that it's just sex any more.'

'This is about the chase. You only think you love me because I'm the first woman who made you work for it. Because you had to give a little of yourself, telling me about your childhood and your hardships, in order to get closer to me.'

'You're wrong, Anouk.' At one time her words would have got under his skin, clawing at him, leaving scars. All he felt now was calm acceptance. It was enough to steal his breath away.

'You've confused lust for love.'

'I've never confused lust for anything.' He smiled. 'I always welcomed it, indulged in it. I don't love you because you are the first woman who made me work for you. I love you because you're the only woman who has ever made me *want* to work for it.'

'I don't want this.' She shook her head, sounding as if she was trying to swallow a sob. 'You can't do this to me.'

He stood with deliberate care, so as not to startle her. And despite all her protestations she froze, her eyes fixed on his body, the naked longing in them belying every word she was trying to tell him.

'I think you *do* want this, Anouk.' He reached for his own jeans, pulling them on slowly. Controlled. 'And I think that's what you're most afraid of. That, and the fact that it means trusting another person for the first time in your life.'

'I trust Saskia,' she shot back.

'This is different. *Love* is different. We both know that.'

'I can't offer you that.' Stumbling to the door, she gripped the handle so tightly that her knuckles went white. 'I can't offer you anything. I don't have the capacity for it.'

'Did I ask for anything? I told you I love you; I never demanded that you say it back. But, for what it's worth, you *do* have the capacity for it and one day you will realise it. Trust me. But until that day comes, I have enough love for both of us.'

He watched her stop, sucking in one deep breath after another and straightening her shoulders.

When she turned to him, he could see the forged steel in her eyes. But, behind the steel, stuffed as far back as she could manage, he could also see a desperate yearning to believe.

'You don't know what love is, Sol. Any more than I do. You don't care. Right now, it's thrilling because I've made you feel something you've never felt before. But whatever it is, it isn't love.'

'It's love, Anouk,' he assured her, calmly and quietly, because he'd never been so sure of anything in his life. 'I thought I wasn't capable of it. It turns out I just wasn't capable of it with anybody but you.'

'They're just hollow words,' she gasped, and even as she tried to argue he knew she was struggling to stay standing. 'I know that even if you don't, which is why I'm leaving now. And one day, in the not too distant future, no doubt, you'll thank me for it.'

'I want you to do whatever it is that you need to do, Anouk. I won't thank you for leaving, but neither will I blame you for it. Just as long as you remember you can come back.'

'You're so sure of yourself, aren't you? So arrogant.' She blinked, apparently not realising she'd raised her voice until she heard it echoing back at her.

'I've never apologised for who I am.' He kept his voice even. 'So yes, I'm willing to bet on myself. You'll come back to me. It's inevitable.'

'I'll never come back,' she gritted out.

Then she opened the door and lurched out, leaving him where he stood.

Sol had no idea how long he stood there, not moving, barely even daring to breathe. Waiting for Anouk to walk back through the doorway.

But she didn't. The truth was that he didn't know if she ever would. Yet he regretted nothing. He loved her.

He had never loved any other woman. He knew he never would.

All he could do was hope that she was as strong as he thought she was. That she would be able to trust herself and admit what he already knew to be true.

Anouk loved him, too.

And he could hope that, one day, he would have the chance to *prove* to her that he cared. That his actions would tell her he loved her in a way that she could believe, even if she couldn't accept his words.

Maybe it would take days, perhaps weeks. It could even take years. But he had to believe it would happen.

And when it did, he wouldn't miss his chance.

CHAPTER THIRTEEN

'This is Adam. He's eight years old and he fell approximately eight feet over the retaining wall at the bottom of his garden and onto grass below. He is normally fit and well with no allergies. He's not on any meds and he's up to date with all his jabs. He was playing at the bottom of the garden with his sister when the fence gave way and he fell down to the grass below, landing on his face and knocking out two teeth and there are a couple more loose in his mouth. He suffered a loss of consciousness of approximately one minute. Mum travelled in the helicopter with us, and Dad is on his way by car.'

'You have the teeth?'

'In some milk in there.' The HEMS doctor indicated a plastic fruit box his colleague was carrying.

'Okay, thank you.' Anouk bobbed her head. 'Okay, guys, let's get started.'

As her colleagues worked to set up the drips and take the bloods for testing, Anouk concentrated on the young boy.

'Adam? Can you hear me, sweetie? My name is Anouk and I'm the doctor who will be making you better. Can you tell me what happened, at all?' She turned to her team. 'Let's give him two point five mil of morphine, try to make him more comfortable.'

'Sure.' Her colleague nodded. 'Do you want me to get Maxillofacial?'

'Good idea,' she agreed. 'Give them a shout. Okay, let's get this little boy comfortable so that we can get him for a CT scan and check what's going on in his head.'

Even as she spoke, the monitors began to bleep, and her colleagues around the boy simultaneously declared the patient was becoming breathless.

'He's going tachycardic,' Anouk warned. 'Let's bag him.'

'Do you want to intubate?'

Anouk frowned. Adam's airway was at risk because if one of those loose teeth dislodged and he inhaled it, it could potentially block off his airway.

'He hasn't stopped breathing,' she confirmed. 'Let's see if we can't give OMS a chance to see him first.'

And the sooner she could get the little boy to the scanner to check his brain, the better.

'You've been avoiding me.'

Anouk jumped at the quiet voice by her shoulder. She didn't look up from the screen but she could no longer see a single word or image that was now swimming in front of her eyes.

'No,' she tried to deny it. 'I've just been...busy.'

It was partially true. She had been busy. Mostly she'd been busy trying not to relive his declaration to her, because she honestly didn't know how she felt about it.

She was supposed to not believe in love. She had spent years telling herself what love looked like and it had been an ugly, selfish, cruel image that she'd painted in her own head.

But the minute those very same words had come out of Sol's mouth, they had erased all of it, leaving something so beautiful, and precious, almost ethereal in their stead. Almost too perfect to be real.

So how could she trust it?

'I don't regret saying it,' he announced softly, as though he could read her thoughts.

The worst thing about it was that she so wanted to believe him.

'I'm sorry… I can't.' She shook her head, her words almost lost between her voice box and her ears. 'They're just words. They don't prove anything.'

'You need to come with me.'

'I'm working.'

'The place is quiet. In an hour it probably won't be, but, for now, you have half an hour. Come with me.'

She didn't need to hear him move to sense that he was leaving without her. She ought to let him.

Rising from her stool, with just another quick glance around to check that all was okay, Anouk followed him out of Resus.

'Where are we going?'

The winding nature of the old part of the hospital seemed to conspire with Sol to add to the sense of suspense today.

It had been a good day. Even her young patient, Adam, had defied the odds to avoid any serious injuries.

'You'll see.' Sol didn't slow his pace.

She tried not to dwell on the fact that he sounded so serious and intent. It was just her second-guessing herself. Not wanting to give away the fact that she'd realised she was doing something as wholly and utterly stupid as falling for the man.

She'd have to be an idiot to forget who she was dealing with.

And the worst thing about it was that she seemed to be exactly that idiot.

Where *was* Sol leading?

'We're going to the cafeteria?' she guessed, as she stretched out her stride trying to keep up with him.

He seemed sharper, edgier than usual.

'Yes.'

'Sol, it's been a long shift. I don't want to eat here. I'd rather just finish my shift and go home.'

'You're not eating here.' He stopped, taking her chin in his hands and tilting her head up to his.

The look he shot her was altogether too hot, and she shivered at the naughty thoughts that he could stir up with just a glance.

Her breath caught in her chest. Almost painful as it lodged there.

'What's going on, Sol?'

He turned her so that she was looking in through the internal cafeteria window.

'Can you see that woman sitting at the table over there? Sixties to seventies? Red coat on the back of the chair?'

Anouk scanned the room, focussing on the area where he was pointing. There was no reason in the world for her heart to thump. But it did.

'Why? Who is she?'

'That's your grandmother, Anouk. Your father's mother. Mal found her.'

Something dark, and angry, and...*panicky* rolled through her.

'Malachi did?' She could hear things crashing around her. It took a moment to realise it was in her head. 'You had your brother *track her down*?'

How could Sol have contacted her grandmother behind

her back? How could he have brought her here? How could he have ambushed her like this?

Anouk didn't know how long she stood there. Probably only a few seconds but it felt like days. Her hands were clenched so tightly that her fingernails scored marks deep into her palms. And then she was spinning around, plunging back across the room, knocking chairs flying outside a consultation room, but wholly unable to stop, or turn, or pick them back up.

Sol caught up with her as she tore along the corridor away from the dining area.

'Anouk, stop. *Stop.* Don't run away.'

'Don't run away?' she snapped, her voice just about managing to work again. 'Don't *run away*?'

This time it was louder. She felt Sol's hands on her shoulders and she shrugged them off with a violence she would never have thought she possessed.

'Anouk—'

'How *dare* you do that to me?' she roared, because it was either that or give into this thing spiralling inside her that would make her crumple and fold.

She was dimly aware of Sol checking up and down the corridor as staff moved curiously through, before he tested a few doors and then pulled her into a consultation room. She didn't know whose. She didn't care.

Fear and anger duelled inside her, and she couldn't risk letting the former win.

'You just need to hear her out, Anouk.' Even the black look on his face couldn't deter her.

'Why, because *you* think I should? I'm not ready to do that yet. And you don't get to be the one to order me otherwise.'

'I'm trying to help you,' he growled.

The worst of it was that a part of her believed him. She

barked out a hollow, unpleasant laugh, all the better to drown out the pounding of her blood through her veins.

'By dictating to me? My, how lucky am I?'

'You're twisting what's happening here.' Sol reached out as though he was going to take hold of her shoulders again, then thought better of it and rammed his hands in his pockets.

Half of her gave herself a satisfied air-punch whilst the other half lamented the loss. She felt twisted inside out, as if she didn't know who or where she was. Everything was wrong. Unsettled.

'And here, of all places?'

'It's neutral territory. You're a skilled doctor. This is where you feel safe and confident. It will translate into the conversation.'

'No, it won't,' she gritted out. 'Because there isn't going to be a conversation.'

'Anouk, don't be scared…'

'I'm not scared,' she cried, the lie mocking her even as it hung in the air. 'I'm an idiot but I'm not scared.'

'You are and you're lashing out. And that's fine. But you don't need to be frightened. I'm here to support you.'

'Support me? You?' She laughed, a brittle, harsh sound. 'You can't support me, or anyone. I was wrong when I said that you knew how to care for someone, how to love them. You don't have it in you to think of anyone but yourself. Deciding you know what's best for me without thinking to discuss it with me for one single second. My God, you even said the words to me. But you don't know what they mean. You don't know what it is to love someone. You're every bit as selfish and arrogant as you said you were.'

And before she could fall apart completely in front of him, Anouk whirled herself around and ran—as fast as she possibly could.

* * *

Sol watched her go, her words stinging him as if every one had been a knife going into his heart.

He'd hoped that bringing her here would resolve the impasse between them. He'd hoped it would show her that he was sincere. That he wanted to be worthy of her.

He loved her.

It had been almost a week since he'd told her. Since he'd heard himself say the words out loud. And oddly, it was getting easier and easier to accept, with each passing day. He'd always thought love was something to fear but Anouk made it seem like something special. Something new. Something to *aspire* to, rather than dread.

Unlike any other woman he had dated, he knew, he just knew, that Anouk understood why he had to be a part of centres like Care to Play. She would never pout, or complain, or moan that the kids got more of his time than she did. Or that she would rather be going to a fancy, high-society gala than another football-and-barbecue-in-the-park event. In fact, Anouk would most likely be right there beside him. Organising every single event.

She made everything shift and change when she was around. People, places, situations. They all sparkled that little brighter under her touch. And Sol wanted, more desperately than he could remember wanting anything for such a long time, to be a part of her life.

It made no sense, yet here he was fighting every instinct to go after her and *make* her listen to him.

He had to let her go—for now. The best thing he could do would be to take a leaf out of the book of the woman sitting in that cafeteria back there. The woman who was so utterly desperate to meet her granddaughter for the first time, and who had longed for this moment for over three decades yet still had the patience to wait that little bit longer.

Turning around, Sol strode back down the corridor. For one thing, he owed the older woman an apology and, for a second, she was the closest thing to a source he had on Anouk.

He could give Anouk her space, but still, the more he understood this complex and enigmatic woman who had somehow crept inside the heart he'd thought locked down for good, the better.

At least he knew one thing. Tracking down Anouk's grandmother had been the right thing to do. Whether Anouk wanted to accept the truth or not, it was clear that she needed to meet her other grandmother and learn what had really happened between her father and her mother.

Until Anouk had closure, for better or for worse, she was never going to be able to move past it and into a relationship with anyone.

With *him*.

Anouk had no idea how long she stood at the bright green front door, her eyes locked balefully onto the Christmas wreath and her hand poised to knock but her heart clattering much too wildly against her ribs to let her. So when the door opened, almost cautiously, she almost stumbled back down the steps.

'Hello, Anouk.'

It took a moment for Anouk to realise that she was still standing with her arm raised. She lowered it—it felt like in slow motion—but still couldn't work her mouth enough to answer.

'You've been standing there for the better part of ten minutes. Would you like to come in?'

Would she? Her mind felt split in two.

Stiffly, she bobbed her head, trying not to allow the

older woman's soft smile to work its way inside her, and let herself be ushered carefully into the house.

A string of Christmas cards adorned the hallway, testament to how popular this new grandmother of hers appeared to be, and a decent, prettily decorated tree stood proudly in one corner of the living room.

'Your father decorated it every year. For me,' she was told by this older woman whom Anouk supposed was her grandmother. 'I don't think he ever had one at his own home. He always said Christmas was for the children, and he'd enjoy it when he had you to share it with.'

Anouk didn't know how to respond.

A couple of minutes later they were sitting in silence at a small, glossy, yew dining table with quaint coasters in front of them and a teapot, cups and saucers, and a quintessential plate of biscuits. It was so utterly English that Anouk had to swallow a faintly hysterical gurgle.

'I got the bag,' she managed awkwardly after what felt like an age. Maybe two.

Someone—presumably Sol—had left it in Resus for her the next day. But he hadn't been to see her.

She told herself it was for the best.

Her companion nodded and offered an encouraging smile. It occurred to Anouk that the older woman—it was hard to think of her as her paternal grandmother—was as nervous as she was, if not more so.

Somehow, the knowledge bolstered her.

'It meant a lot. I never…knew…'

'There are more bags like that,' her grandmother said sadly. 'Full up. Every Christmas, every birthday, without fail. We gave up sending them to you—they always got returned. But we never gave up on you.'

'I didn't even know you wrote to me,' she managed,

her voice thick. 'I only knew about one letter, but I didn't know what it said, or when it had been sent.'

'We wrote to you all the time. Letters at first, as you saw in that bag. But diaries after a while.'

'Oh.' Anouk took a sip of tea by way of distracting herself, but suddenly it was impossible to swallow.

'Do you want to see them?'

Her grandmother pushed her chair back and Anouk almost fell over herself to stop her.

No.' She hadn't meant to make the older woman jump. 'No. Sorry. It's just…'

'Too much to take at once,' her grandmother guessed. 'Another time, perhaps.'

'Another time,' Anouk agreed, surprised to realise that she really meant it.

She still hadn't processed the emotions that had crashed over her, threatening to overwhelm her, when she'd looked into that bag and found a selection of gifts from when she was a baby, to this very year.

The letters that had accompanied them—the first few marked *Return to Sender* in her mother's unmistakeable loopy handwriting—had been like a sledgehammer to her heart. Every word thumping painfully into her. Words she'd longed to hear as a kid but which her self-obsessed mother had never once uttered to her.

Her father and her grandmother had each penned letters that had been so heartfelt, so pained, that Anouk couldn't have denied their veracity even if she'd wanted to. Which she didn't.

They spoke about how much they loved her, how the dimples on her baby cheeks, or the gurgle of her laugh, had filled them with such pride, such joy, and such a feeling of completeness. And the only thing that had undercut it all had been the fact that the two of them had been compelled to snatch every snippet they could from the magazine articles, or the news items, or the TV interviews, in which her mother had trotted her out with the sole reason of making herself look like a good and doting mother.

It had taken Anouk almost two days to track down a VHS player so that she could see the recordings her father had made on the two occasions he'd travelled to the States to try to speak to Annalise Hartwood, only for her security team to practically manhandle him away.

So much for her mother's claims that her father had wanted nothing to do with them.

'He wanted to be with you from the moment he knew Annalise was pregnant.' Her grandmother shook her head when Anouk voiced her thoughts out loud. 'He even proposed.'

'My father proposed?' Anouk felt her stomach twist. All the stories her mother had told her seemed more and more like lies. The worst of it was that she knew, instantly, that the version of events this relative stranger was recounting made more sense than anything Annalise had ever said.

'But your mother didn't want to know. She was rich and famous and he was nobody. Even when you came along there was nothing he could do. She refused to acknowledge him as the father, let alone allow him to have contact. But he did try, you must know that.'

'I do now,' Anouk murmured.

At least Annalise had never tried to pretend her father was someone else. The one consolation she had was that the identity of her father had remained constant throughout the years, even if only to her.

'He was so proud of the way you were growing up. He would have been over the moon to know you'd become a doctor. And that you'd come over to the UK.'

'I wish I had tried to make contact sooner. I just… I always thought… I was led to believe…'

'That he didn't want to know you,' her grandmother supplied.

Incredibly there was no bitterness or rancour to the older woman's tone, just a deep kind of grief, even as they both silently knew that Annalise had been the one to pour all that poison.

'It couldn't have been further from the truth.' Her eyes shimmered and Anouk ducked her head for a moment, pretending she didn't notice.

She didn't want to succumb, as well. There seemed little point in telling the woman—her grandmother—that she'd gone to his house years ago. That could be a discussion for another time.

'You have a good one there, you know.'

'A good one?' Anouk frowned as her grandmother smiled warmly.

'Solomon. The young man you're courting…or I should say dating, shouldn't I?'

'Oh. No. We're just friends.' She could feel the blush creeping up her neck and she knew her grandmother's surprisingly sharp eyes hadn't missed it.

Even the older woman's smile was suddenly faintly delighted.

'You don't go to the lengths your young man went to, or talk about a young lady the way he talked about you, if you're just friends. Take my word for it.'

'You're wrong.' Anouk flushed, but she could feel the tiny smile playing at the corners of her mouth, the spearhead of hope working its way around her heart like a sharp screwdriver prying the lid off an old tin of paint.

For the rest of the conversation, Anouk listened as her grandmother recounted some stories about her father, revelling in their obviously close relationship and trying not to resent her mother for keeping her from such a loving home.

She learned how her father had never married, his heart always belonging to her mother and herself, as cruelly as Annalise had treated him. Anouk didn't know if that made him single-minded or, frankly, a bit of a wet lettuce, but she liked to think of him as loyal and loving. And for now, that would work.

Her grandmother had an unexpectedly naughty sense of humour, which began to shine through once their initial nervousness had been overcome. And, Anouk discovered to her shock, the older woman had been very happily married three times. Widowed all three times.

'I was a bit of a saucy young lady,' her grandmother told her, 'but I loved each one of them very dearly. And I was always a good and faithful wife.'

And then the older woman twinkled in a way that Anouk suddenly realised was all too familiar. She had caught a glimpse of it in herself every now and then over the years, usually when Saskia had convinced her to relax on those rare nights out, but especially recently when Sol had been a part of her life.

Was it possible that Sol, like this woman with the twinkling eyes, had been a *bit saucy* until he'd found his soul mate? Could it be that she was Sol's? That Sol really did love her?

Anouk filed that little nugget in a box to dissect later. When she was alone. When she had the courage.

Still, the afternoon was emotionally exhausting. No doubt even more so for her grandmother.

'Maybe I should go,' Anouk hazarded after a while. 'I think I need to…absorb some of this.'

Her grandmother's eyes raked over her. The evident

need for time to regroup obviously warring with the fear
of never seeing her new granddaughter again.

'I'll come back,' Anouk added quickly. 'If you're happy
for that, of course.'

A slender hand covered hers instantly, its grasp surprisingly strong.

'Do you promise me?'

It was so small a gesture, yet so strong, making something kick hard in her chest.

'I do,' she choked out.

'And you'll thank that young man of yours?'

Despite herself, Anouk couldn't help but smile.

'I told you, he isn't my young man.'

'He is if you want him to be,' came the surprising response.

For a moment, Anouk turned the idea over in her head.
Was he?

She wrinkled her nose and tried not to reveal her emotions. Everything seemed to be running so close to the
surface these days, it was so unlike her usual self.

'No. I don't know if it really was once the case,' she
heard herself confessing. 'But, if it was, it isn't any more.'

'That's up to you, my flower. I know enough about men
to know that one is yours for the taking. If you want him,
go and get him.'

Anouk wasn't sure if it was the grandmotherly advice
or the term of endearment that tugged at her the most, but
all of a sudden she had to fight the urge to break down.
Right there and then.

But on the way home, her mind couldn't stop spinning.
The events of the past hour, and the past few weeks, all
whirling around her head. She was a mess.

She was never a mess.

But was it because of her father? Her grandmother? Or

just Sol? And, more significantly, how was she going to sort it—and herself—out? Whatever this thing was inside her, this gnawing, empty, hollow thing, it needed Sol to assuage it. She wasn't prepared to go back to the life she'd had before him. She needed him. And whatever the hell that meant—they would work it out together.

If Sol really was hers for the taking, how on earth was she to even set about doing such a thing?

And then it came to her. What had Libby once said about Christmas Eve being the most magical time? First, she was going to need to take a detour to the Care to Play centre.

CHAPTER FOURTEEN

SOMETHING WAS DIFFERENT.

His home was...*changed*.

He had spent the entire day looking for Anouk. Checking her apartment, the hospital, the centre, even phoning Saskia so many times that an irritated Malachi had told him to give it up and go home for the night.

He hadn't wanted to.

The moment he'd heard that Anouk had approached Malachi for her grandmother's address, the need to find Anouk and ensure that she was okay had been overwhelming. He had no idea what her grandmother had ultimately told her and the fear that she was somewhere, alone and hurting, tore him up in a way he would never have believed possible.

If she was traumatised, then it would be his fault. He'd never intended for her to be ambushed by the knowledge of a grandmother she'd never met. He'd expected to be with her when they first met. And now he couldn't find Anouk anywhere. She had to be somewhere.

All he could do was head home and try again tomorrow. She couldn't hide out from him for ever. He wouldn't let her. He couldn't.

Sol stood, the front door still open behind him, as he tried to work out what it was. Slowly, as if his mind couldn't believe what his body already sensed, he kicked the door to and moved carefully to the archway.

The scene beyond was like something out of his childhood.

The main lights were low, and the place was illuminated with pretty, twinkling Christmas lights whilst a miniature winter, Christmas village covered the entire room, from little shops and houses to ice-skating rinks, Ferris wheels and small-gauge trains.

Beyond it all, Anouk stood, her hands twisted together and her face set in an anxious expression.

'What *is* this?' he demanded, his voice thick through his constricted throat.

He told himself not to believe, not to hope. He needed to wait, and hear the words.

'An apology.' Her voice was ragged, no better than his, and he allowed himself a moment to take that in.

To some degree it made him feel better. Still, he jammed his fists into his pockets as if that might stop him from striding across the room and reaching out for her the way he wanted to.

He moved further inside, wanting to kiss her. Claim her.

But by the way her arms were in front of her chest, her fingers knotting together, he had a feeling she needed to explain herself. Though perhaps not before babbling nervously a little first.

He could let her have that, too. After all, he wasn't entirely sure he knew what to say, himself.

'I went to see my grandmother today,' she breathed, a note of awe in her voice. 'She told me that I had to thank you.'

'I shouldn't have ambushed you at the hospital that day.' He exhaled sharply. 'I just thought that maybe the location would be the best place for you to feel in control. Strong.'

'It's okay.' She jerked forward, as though she was going to step up to him, before stopping awkwardly. 'I owe you an apology, for all those awful things I said. They were horrible, unkind. I'm so, so sorry.'

'Forget about them.' Closing the gap he caught her hands, trying to make her look at him. If she did, then he might be able to convince her that it really didn't matter.

She'd been frightened and cornered and she'd lashed out. Hell, he knew that feeling only too well.

'I can't. I didn't mean them…'

'I know. Anouk, look at me.' He crooked his finger under her chin. 'Forget it. Really.'

'I can hardly believe you did that for me.' Anouk smiled wanly, and, to Sol, even that was like the sunshine cracking through the heaviest sky after a thunderstorm. 'I can hardly believe you *cared* enough to do it.'

'It wasn't a big deal.'

'It was to me,' she said earnestly. 'No one has ever bothered to do anything like that for me before. Not unless they thought they could get something out of it. Usually access to my mother.'

'She did quite a number on you, didn't she?' Sol frowned as Anouk pulled away from him abruptly.

'My mother was…manipulative,' she confessed unexpectedly, her frankness taking him by surprise. 'She treated me like a precious daughter in public, but in private I was an inconvenient burden she couldn't stand to look at. And I was so desperate for her affection that I spent my whole life, whilst she was alive, turning myself inside out trying to win it. I even made myself sick trying to do everything I could for her. For her love.'

'The fault was never yours,' Sol said, shoving his clenched fists into his pockets just so that he wouldn't haul her into his arms.

He mustn't crowd her. She would come to him fully when she was ready.

'I know that. Logically.' She pulled a wry face. 'But I grew up in Hollywood, where there are altogether too many sycophants willing to excuse my mother's behaviour and agree that she was a saint and I was a problem child. And I was too young, too needy, too naïve to argue.'

'So you ended up believing them?'

'I saw a twisted kind of relationship where people used each other, all the while bandying about the word *love*. So I learned it can be a flawed, cruel concept more effective as a weapon than any kind of gift.'

Anger barrelled through him that someone as sweet, intelligent, and kind as Anouk could have allowed people who were *nothing* to drag her down and think less of herself. She seemed so strong, so sure, it was hard to believe it was just an act.

And yet…not hard at all. Because he saw her. Her virtues and her flaws. And he loved her despite them, or maybe *for* them.

'I know you don't believe me when I tell you that I love you, but it's true, Anouk. I love you with every fibre of who I am and, if you'll let me, I'll spend the rest of our lives trying to make you believe that.'

It felt like an eternity that she stood, watching him, immobile. And then suddenly she took his hand in her smaller ones.

'That's the point, Sol.' She smiled. 'I already believe you.'

It was like a thousand victories all spiralling through him at once.

'What changed?' He couldn't help but ask.

'You, contacting my grandmother. It showed you listened to me, you cared, and you understood.'

'I'll always listen to you, Anouk.'

'I think I really believe that,' she agreed. 'It's why I came back, and why I did this,'

He followed her head as it scanned the room, encompassing the entire Christmas scene, not realising that he was pulling her back, closer to him, as he did so.

And, what was more, she was letting him.

'I love it,' he murmured, not entirely sure which bit he was talking about.

'It was the one thing I could think of to show you I had listened, too,' Anouk babbled. 'Even if you and Malachi aren't into it any more, except for the kids.'

'Shh. I love that you wanted to do something for me. I love that you thought about this, especially when I know how much you hate Christmas. It makes it all the more special that you did this for me.'

'It wasn't as bad as I'd feared,' she admitted.

'That's good.'

'It is?'

'Sure.' He grinned suddenly. 'It bodes well for any kids we might have.'

'You want children with me?' Anouk breathed in wonder.

'If you'd like that.' He slid his fingers to her chin, tilting her head up until they were eye to eye.

Deep down, she'd always wondered if she would ever want to be a mother. She'd doubted she had it in her. Her life had been about her career as a doctor and nothing else had ever pulled at her.

And then Sol had slammed into her life and everything had changed. She might not have considered babies with him before, but the moment he had mentioned it there had been no doubt in Anouk's mind that she wanted nothing more than to start a life—and a family—with him.

'I want children with you,' she managed, then seemed to draw in a deep breath. 'And, as for Christmas, it turns out my father always wanted to celebrate the holiday with me. He might not be here, but maybe I can do it in memory of him? Maybe you can help me?'

He felt his mouth crook, a sense of triumph punching its way through him. Who would have thought it would feel this good to be wanted by a woman like Anouk? To want her back?

Before he could answer, she was speaking again. Suddenly serious. 'And you were right, of course. I was running away.'

'Understandable,' he growled. 'Given the circumstances.'

She shook her head.

'You misunderstand me.' She ran her tongue over her teeth, her nerves clearly threatening to get the better of her in a way that touched him deeply. 'I wasn't just running away from my grandmother. Or my fear that whatever she or my late father had to say, it wouldn't match up to the fantasy in my head. I was also running away from you. Or, more to the point, my growing feelings for you.'

It was more than he'd thought she would say. More than he could have hoped she would say. He couldn't bite his tongue any longer.

'Whatever you were worried about, don't be. I love you, Anouk Hart, with all that I am.'

It was the look of wonder in her eyes that made his heart swell so wildly that he feared his chest couldn't contain it.

'You still love me?' she whispered, her eyes scanning his, almost in disbelief.

'I will *always* love you. You had to know that, otherwise why come here?' He arced his arm around the room. 'Why do all of this?'

'Because *I* love *you*, you idiot.' She snorted, half laughing, half sobbing.

The words spun around him, lifting him and making him feel somehow complete.

'I can't believe you did all this yourself,' he told her at length when the breath in his chest finally felt like his again.

'Not all myself.' Anouk offered a wry smile. 'I had a little help. Quite a bit, in fact.'

'Is that so?'

'Libby, Katie and Isobel.'

He groaned loudly, but only half-heartedly.

'You realise those girls will for ever be able to say that I was wrong and they were right?'

'I do.' Her eyes twinkled mischievously, sending a streak of desire straight through him. 'Just as I know you won't begrudge them a moment of it.'

'I won't,' he murmured, revelling in the way Anouk's body was finally moulding to him.

As if she'd always been meant to be there.

'I love you,' he repeated, just because it felt incredible to say it. Because he couldn't get enough of hearing it. Because he didn't think he'd ever tire of basking in the tender glow of her sapphire gaze when he told her how he felt about her.

Now that her barriers had finally dropped.

'I love you, too, Solomon Gunn,' she whispered fiercely, all her tentativeness put aside in that moment. 'And I will continue loving you for the rest of my life.'

'I intend to hold you to that,' he managed gruffly, 'because I think it will take a lifetime to prove to you how much I love you, too.'

'Just the one?' she teased.

'Trust me, that's all we'll need, you and I. Together.'

He couldn't hold back a moment longer. Lowering his head, he claimed her mouth with his, letting her wind her arms around his neck, and lifting her up so that she could wrap her legs around his hips, as her heat poured through him.

And then he laid her down within their twinkling, magical Christmas village scene, and they welcomed in the first perfect Christmas of the rest of their lives together.

* * * * *

MILLS & BOON

Coming next month

THEIR ONE-NIGHT CHRISTMAS GIFT
Karin Baine

'We keep a few rooms made up just in case of emergencies.' Charles led her up the stairs to one of the bedrooms. She couldn't help but wonder which door led to his.

'Do you get many late-night, uninvited women calling in on you?' she teased, when he was such a stark contrast to the man who'd literally sent her packing in a previous lifetime.

'No, I don't, but sometimes we get patients arriving too late to be admitted to the clinic, so we put them up here for the night.' Her teasing fell flat with him, but she supposed his defence from her insinuations was understandable when she was accusing him of having loose morals. She knew nothing about him any more.

'I'm sure it's most appreciated. As it is by me.' She had to remember he was doing her a favour by letting her stay when she had no right to be here. Their risky behaviour in London had been her idea and as such she was fully prepared to take on the consequences single-handedly.

'Bed, bathroom, wardrobe. All the essentials.' He did a quick tour of the room before turning back to her. 'Do you need help bringing in your luggage?'

'I just have an overnight bag in the car, but I can

manage that myself. As I said, this was a spur-of-the-moment visit.'

'Ah, yes. The talk. Is this about what happened in London? I must admit it's been harder to put out of my mind than I'd imagined too.' He was moving towards her and Harriet's heart leapt into her throat at the thought of him kissing her again. She wanted it so much but that's not what had brought her here.

'I'm pregnant, Charles.'

His outstretched arms immediately fell limply to his sides. 'Pardon me?'

She sat down on the edge of the bed, wishing it would swallow her up. 'That night in London…I'm pregnant.'

Continue reading
THEIR ONE-NIGHT CHRISTMAS GIFT
Karin Baine

Available next month
www.millsandboon.co.uk

COMING SOON!

LET'S TALK

Romance

For exclusive extracts, competitions
and special offers, find us online:

 facebook.com/millsandboon

🐦 @MillsandBoon

📷 @MillsandBoonUK

Get in touch on 01413 063232

For all the latest titles coming soon, visit
millsandboon.co.uk/nextmonth

MILLS & BOON

THE HEART OF ROMANCE

A ROMANCE FOR EVERY KIND OF READER

MODERN

Prepare to be swept off your feet by sophisticated, sexy and seductive heroes, in some of the world's most glamorous a romantic locations, where power and passion collide.
8 stories per month.

HISTORICAL

Escape with historical heroes from time gone by. Whether y passion is for wicked Regency Rakes, muscled Vikings or ru Highlanders, awaken the romance of the past.
6 stories per month.

MEDICAL

Set your pulse racing with dedicated, delectable doctors in high-pressure world of medicine, where emotions run high passion, comfort and love are the best medicine.
6 stories per month.

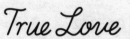

Celebrate true love with tender stories of heartfelt romance the rush of falling in love to the joy a new baby can bring, a focus on the emotional heart of a relationship.
8 stories per month.

Desire

Indulge in secrets and scandal, intense drama and plenty of hot action with powerful and passionate heroes who have it wealth, status, good looks…everything but the right woman
6 stories per month.

HEROES

Experience all the excitement of a gripping thriller, with an romance at its heart. Resourceful, true-to-life women and st fearless men face danger and desire - a killer combination!
8 stories per month.

DARE

Sensual love stories featuring smart, sassy heroines you'd wa best friend, and compelling intense heroes who are worthy
4 stories per month.

To see which titles are coming soon, please visit
millsandboon.co.uk/nextmonth